MAKE ME
Yours

THE BELLAMY CREEK SERIES

Melanie Harlow

For Melissa Gaston

My name might be on the side of this ship,
but you are undoubtedly its captain.
Thank you for all you do to get me where I want to go.

I wanna eat pancakes for dinner
I wanna get stuck in your head
I wanna watch a T.V. show together and when we're under the
weather we can watch it in bed

So please save all your questions for the end and maybe I'll be
brave enough by then
Well, maybe I won't ever say what's in my head
No, I won't have to say anything
You'll say it instead

—*Lizzie McAlpine*

MAKE ME
Yours

One

Cole

"**I**S THAT WHAT YOU'RE GOING TO WEAR?" MY NINE-year-old daughter, Mariah, assessed me from my bedroom doorway, her nose wrinkled.

I studied my reflection in the mirror above my dresser. "Yeah. What's wrong with it?"

"It's boring. I thought you were going to a party."

"It's just my friends at the pub." I frowned at the hunter green polo shirt I'd chosen because it was on the top of the pile in my drawer. Was that the problem? Or was it the khaki pants?

Mariah entered the room and flopped onto my bed, chin propped in her hands. "But it's a *party*, right? A bachelor party for Uncle Griffin?"

"Yes." Bachelor parties were not my favorite thing, but Griffin Dempsey and I had grown up next door to each other, and we'd been best friends since we were younger than Mariah. He was getting married in two weeks, and I was the best man—in other words, tonight was a must-show.

"What's a bachelor, anyway?" Mariah wondered.

"It's a guy who isn't married." I scratched my jaw. Maybe the belt was wrong. I unbuckled it, deciding to swap it for a darker brown leather.

"Are *you* a bachelor?"

"No."

"But you're not married."

"I *was*."

"But you're not divorced. Is there a name for what you are?"

"A widower," I told her, slipping a new belt through the loops.

"That sounds like an old man."

"I am an old man."

"Daddy! You're thirty-three. That's not *that* old," she said, letting me know with her tone that it was *somewhat* old.

"Thanks. Is this any better?" Turning around, I held out my arms, showing off the new version of my party outfit.

Mariah shook her head. "No. You're still boring."

I gave her a dirty look.

"What? You asked. I'm just being honest." A cheeky grin appeared. "You look like the guy who came to measure for the new windows yesterday."

I groaned. "Come on, that guy had a huge pot belly."

"Or maybe the guy who sold Grandma her new car."

"Fred Yaldoo? He's got a pot belly *and* he's bald! That's it." I dove for her.

She squealed and tried to scramble off the bed, but I managed to get her in my grip and tickle the spot behind her left ear that always made her giggle and squirm. "No! No! I'm sorry!" she shrieked. "I take it back! You're the handsomest daddy in the world!"

"Too late!"

My mother appeared in my bedroom doorway, arms crossed. "What on earth is going on in here?"

I gave Mariah a quick noogie before releasing her. "My daughter says I look like Fred Yaldoo."

Just to make sure she wasn't on to something, I jumped up and checked my hairline in the mirror. Thankfully, it looked fine. I probably could have used a closer shave, but whatever. Griffin and the guys weren't going to give a shit about my scruff.

Mariah scooted off the bed and put five feet between us. "I did not say that! I just said that his outfit was boring."

My mother studied me critically from the doorway, one hand on her hip. "Is that what you're wearing to the party?"

I rolled my eyes, then leaned down and yanked my brown dress shoes from the closet. "Yes. And I'm leaving now, before my self-esteem gets any worse."

"Well, it wouldn't kill you to dress up a little more," my mother went on, taking it upon herself to enter my room and start straightening up the items on the top of my dresser.

I sat on the bed and put the shoes on. "Mom, stop. You don't have to clean my room. I'm not ten."

"You live in my house, you deal with my cleaning." She gathered up stray coins and dropped them into a little painted clay bowl Mariah had made in art class last year. "You want to live in a mess, you get your own house."

Mariah and I exchanged a *here we go again* glance. My mother's definition of a mess was not the same as a normal person's. Crumbs, dust, and clutter were the enemy. Growing up, I rarely saw her without a broom, the vacuum, a rag and a spray bottle in hand. My older brother Greg and I had learned early on that you take your shoes off at the door, you wipe up your spills immediately, and you make your bed in the morning *or else*. We used to joke that she wore hand sanitizer like perfume. We'd wrap it up for her at Christmas.

"Actually, I've been thinking about that," I said, tying my shoes.

"About getting our own house?" asked Mariah, surprise evident in her voice.

"Yes." I straightened up and looked at her, trying to gauge her reaction. "What do *you* think about that?"

Mariah bit the tip of her thumb. "Where would it be?"

"I don't know. We'd have to look. Take your thumb out of your mouth."

She did as I asked. "Would we move far away?"

"Not necessarily."

"Could I think about it?"

"Of course." I understood her hesitation—this was the only home she'd ever known. We'd moved in with my mother right after she was born, which was also the day we lost Trisha.

"Don't worry, Mariah, I'll come over and clean it," my mother said, using her apron to wipe off a framed photo of Trisha and me on our wedding day before replacing it at a slightly different angle on my dresser.

"That won't be necessary, Mom."

"Really?" She spun around to face me, arms folded. "Are you planning to hire a housekeeper? And while you're at it, a personal chef and a babysitter?"

"No."

"Who's going to make your meals?"

"I will."

"You can't cook! And with your work schedule? You don't even get home until seven o'clock. What's Mariah going to do after school?"

"I'll figure it out, Mom."

"Would I have to stay alone?" Mariah's voice trembled.

"Of course not," I assured her.

"I can come over after school and make dinner for you, Mariah," my mother said. "Or you can come here. Although it does seem sort of silly to move out if that's going to be the case. I mean, really, Cole, if you're not going to get remarried, what's the point of—"

"That's enough, Mom." Anxious to avoid the same old fight, especially in front of Mariah, I went over to my daughter and tugged one of her braids. "And what are *you* up to tonight?"

Mariah beamed. "Miss Cheyenne said I could come over to her house for a mani-pedi and a movie."

"Oh yeah?"

Cheyenne was Griffin's younger sister. She was a kindergarten teacher at Mariah's elementary school and had moved back home with her mother next door about a year and a half ago. She was wonderful to Mariah—a sort of surrogate aunt and big sister combined.

She was also gorgeous, with a body that wouldn't quit, and lately she was on my mind all the time—and my thoughts weren't always clean. I felt like an asshole about it, and I'd never *act* on the attraction, but frankly, a quiet evening in on the couch watching a movie with Cheyenne sounded a hell of a lot better than a loud night out at the pub.

"Aunt Blair is coming too." Mariah tilted her head. "You think it's okay to call her that even though she hasn't married Uncle Griffin yet?"

"I think it's fine. In fact, I bet she likes it." I leaned a little closer to examine Mariah's heart-shaped face, which resembled her mother's more every year, although she had my blue eyes and light brown hair. "Did you have something chocolate for dessert tonight?"

She licked her lips. "Moose Tracks ice cream."

"Well, you've got a Moose-stache, just like in that book you used to make me read every night. Go wash your face."

Giggling, she put her hands over her mouth. "Okay."

When she'd gone, I turned to my mom. "Listen, don't scare her out of the idea of us moving out. I've been thinking about it for a while, and I feel like now's the time. I don't have all the details worked out yet, but I'm asking for your support."

She held up her hands. "Of course you have my support, darling. You're always welcome here, but I understand wanting your own space. I think it's a good thing. A healthy step in the right direction."

"Thank you."

She smiled, tucking her silvery bob behind her ears. "Now about that outfit . . ."

"My clothes are not up for discussion," I said, switching off the light and heading out of my room.

"But it's a party," she said, hot on my heels. "How about a nice shirt and tie?"

I started down the stairs. "I'm just meeting my friends at the pub, Mom. The same guys I've been hanging out with since grade school. They won't care what I have on."

"But there will be other people there too. Maybe you could meet someone new."

And there it is, I thought. The real reason she cares what I'm wearing—the "right direction" she'd been referring to.

My mother, like nearly everyone else in my life, seemed to be on some kind of endless quest to convince me to find a replacement wife. No matter how many times I told them I wasn't interested in getting remarried, they never gave up.

"I'm good being single, Mom," I said, heading into the kitchen.

"You say that, but—"

"I say that because it's true." Double-checking for my wallet and phone in my pockets, I grabbed my keys off the counter. "I don't know why everyone thinks I'm so unhappy on my own. I'm not."

"It's not that we think you're unhappy, sweetheart. We just think you're, you know . . ." She groped for the right words.

"Go ahead and say it."

"Stuck," she blurted, twisting her hands together.

I widened my stance, folding my arms across my chest. "That's ridiculous," I said.

"Is it? You haven't dated anyone seriously in nine years, Cole."

"Because I'm not interested in serious dating. That doesn't mean I'm stuck."

"But you're *choosing* to be lonely."

"I'm *choosing* to be a good, present father to my daughter."

"Plenty of single dads get remarried! Don't you think Trisha would have wanted that for you?"

I lowered my voice. "What matters is what Mariah wants—and doesn't want. My getting remarried is something that scares her. She's been very honest about that in the past."

"Mariah is a child. Yes, she worries about losing you, but she'd come around. You need to move on, Cole."

I took a deep breath, the way I always did whenever my mother or anyone else tried to tell me what Trisha would have wanted, what was best for our daughter, or what I *needed* to do. I didn't have a bad temper, but I didn't like being told how to run my life. I was a grown man, and I knew what I wanted.

"Look," I said. "I appreciate your concern, but you're wrong—I have moved on, Mom. I've accepted that I'm single, I've accepted that I'm going to raise my daughter alone, and I've accepted that life doesn't always go the way we plan. Now you need to accept it too."

She shook her head. "You're not even giving yourself the *chance* to fall in love again."

"The truth is, Mom, that's never going to happen."

"How can you be so sure?"

"Because lightning never strikes the same place twice."

A knock at the back door made us both jump. Through the glass panes, I saw Cheyenne smile and wave.

"Come on in, honey," my mother called.

Cheyenne pulled the door open and stepped inside the kitchen. A chilly breeze came with her, bringing with it the scent of dead leaves and burning wood, as if someone in the neighborhood had their fireplace going. Her cheeks were pink from the cold, and her blond hair was pulled back into a ponytail, but it seemed like half of it had escaped in the wind and blown around her face.

"Hey," she said brightly. "I just came to see if Mariah wanted to run to the store with me and pick out some snacks for our girls' night."

"Oh, she'd love that," my mother said. "I'll go get her."

When we were alone, Cheyenne turned to me and smiled. "How's it going, Cole?"

"Fine."

"What's wrong?"

I shook my head and muttered, "My mother."

"Oh." She held up her hands. "Believe me, I get it. Living with your mother when you're over thirty is a special kind of torture."

"I'm moving out," I announced, making the final decision right then and there.

Her eyebrows rose. "Are you?"

"Yeah. I've been thinking about it for a while, but I feel like now's the time." I paused. "As long as Mariah is okay with it."

She nodded slowly, chewing on her full lower lip. "You think you'll stay local?"

"Yeah. Unless I put in for a transfer to a different police department or something, I have to. And I doubt Mariah would enjoy being yanked out of her school, taken away from the only friends she's ever known, or away from family."

"Right." She sighed. "I can't wait to move out. But I promised myself I wouldn't until I paid off all my student loans and credit card debt."

"That's smart. How long will it take you?"

She shrugged, her fuzzy, peach-colored cardigan slipping off one shoulder. Beneath it she wore a white lacy thing that looked like a bra and a shirt combined. It sent a tiny jolt of electricity to my crotch, and I immediately averted my eyes. "Originally I thought it would take me two years," she went on, "but I'm *super* motivated, so maybe just a few more months." Then she laughed. "I love my mother, but she drives me crazy."

"Same."

"If she would just mind her own business, I'd be fine."

"*Exactly*."

"Like, I get it, she had life all figured out by the time she was my age—the husband, the house, the kids—but some of us are still working on it. Anyway." She shook her head and smiled at me. "So, you heading over to the Bulldog for Griff's party?"

"Yes." I looked down at my clothes. "Although both my mother and my daughter have made it clear that I'm not dressed for the occasion. You think I look okay?"

"Definitely." She hesitated. "If the occasion was a PGA tournament."

I groaned. "Mariah said I looked like Fred Yaldoo."

Cheyenne laughed, her eyes lighting up. "From the car dealership?"

"Yeah. Is she right?"

Rather than answer, she put her fingers over her mouth and tried unsuccessfully to stop giggling. "I better not answer that."

"Goddammit, *fine*. I'll change. But what am I supposed to put on?"

"A different shirt? Like a dress shirt or something? And maybe not the khakis."

"Dress pants?"

"Maybe. Or dark jeans. Depends on the shirt you pick."

"This makes me glad I wear a uniform every day." I checked the time on my phone. "Shit. I'm running late already. Can you just come up and pick something out of my closet?"

She laughed again. "Sure. If you trust me."

"I trust you." Setting my keys on the counter again, I led the way out of the kitchen and up the stairs, wondering belatedly if this was wise, bringing Cheyenne up to my bedroom. I'd had a hard enough time keeping my thoughts appropriate in the kitchen.

Moving down the upstairs hall, we passed Mariah's

room—which had been my brother Greg's back in the day—where my mother was trying to convince her to put on a different shirt, one without an ice cream stain on it.

Pushing my door all the way open, I snapped on the overhead light and gestured toward the closet. "Dress shirts hanging in there, along with good pants. Jeans in the dresser, second drawer down." Then I dropped onto the bed, leaning back on my hands. "Good luck. Fashion is really not my thing."

She stood at the door for a moment, almost like she was afraid to come in. Her eyes darted around—from the closet to the dresser to the walls to the bed. "I've never been up here before. It's so clean."

"House rules."

Entering the room with a few tentative steps, she sniffed. "It even smells good. Griffin's room always smelled horrible."

I laughed. "Mine probably smelled just as bad as a teenager. My mother was always in here fumigating it."

Grinning, she went over to the closet and riffled through my shirts, the plastic hangers making noise as she slid them along the wooden bar. "How about this one?"

I glanced over and saw her holding up a button-up dress shirt in a navy and royal blue checkered pattern. "Okay."

"The colors will match your eyes." She shut the closet door and handed me the shirt, still on the hanger. "You have such great eyes."

I looked up at her, and a compliment stuck in my throat—*I like your eyes too.* They were big and brown, with little flecks of gold in them, framed by thick black lashes. And she had a way of looking at you that made you feel like you were the only person in the room. But all I said as I took the shirt was, "Thanks."

"You're welcome." She gave me a tiny smile before she turned toward my dresser and pulled open the second drawer. "Jeans would be best with that. Your darkest denim."

"I think I have some dark denim in there."

Bending over, she sorted through a stack of jeans. I watched her, letting my eyes wander over her curves. As I had in the kitchen, I felt a rush of arousal. But this time, I didn't look away. Instead I found myself wondering what she'd do if I reached out and put my hands on her hips. Pulled her onto my lap. Buried my face in her neck. Put my hands beneath her sweater. Cheyenne had the kind of body you could spend hours exploring—you could get lost and never want to be found.

Before I could stop it, the thickening surge in my pants grew into a full-blown erection, and I knew I wouldn't be able to stand up without an obvious bulge in my khakis. Sometimes—but only sometimes—being well-endowed was *not* an asset.

"Here we go. These are perfect." Cheyenne straightened up and tossed a folded pair of jeans on the bed.

"Thanks," I said, leaning forward so my elbows rested on my knees, shielding my crotch.

She eyed my feet. "The shoes are good. Do you have a dark brown leather belt?"

"I'm wearing it."

"Can I see it?"

"No."

Slightly taken aback, she tried again. "I'm sure it's fine. I just want to see it and make sure."

"Well, you can't."

She rolled her eyes. "Cole, come on."

"No."

"You're being silly. Why can't I see the belt?" Laughing, she grabbed my arm and tried to pull me onto my feet, but I yanked it back so hard, I jerked her right off her feet.

"Oh!" she cried as her body crashed into mine, the force of it sending me over backward. She wound up sprawled on top of me, and instinct took over—I flipped her onto her back and pinned her wrists to the mattress, my cock bulging against her thigh. There was *no way* to hide what she was doing to me.

Our eyes met. "Oh," she said again, softer this time.

I almost lost my mind and fucking kissed her.

Instead, I jumped off the bed and backed up against my dresser. "So. How's the belt?"

She sat up, and her eyes went wide. "Um, it's big."

I nearly grinned. "It's what?"

Then she panicked, her cheeks turning scarlet. "I mean, it's perfect. The belt. The *belt* is perfect. For your outfit." She scrambled off the bed and bolted for the first door she saw, yanking it open. "I'll just get Mariah and head out."

But it was the *closet* door she'd gone for, which she realized when she tried to exit through a row of hanging shirts.

"Other way," I said, pointing her toward the hallway.

"Right," she said, making a beeline out of the room without looking at me. "Okay, have a good night. Bye."

When she was gone, I shut the door behind her and leaned back against it, running a hand over my jaw and trying not to laugh.

Fuck. No more inviting Cheyenne Dempsey up to my room.

Years ago, clear back in high school, Griffin had made his three best friends—me, Enzo Moretti, and Beckett Weaver—promise we'd keep our hands off his little sister. He'd probably forgotten all about it, but I hadn't. And I'd always been a man of my word, but damn.

Damn.

As I changed my clothes with the irresistible scent of Cheyenne's perfume lingering in the air, and the memory of what her body had felt like beneath mine, I couldn't help wondering if there was a statute of limitations on a promise like that.

I mean . . . those eyes. Those curves. Those lips.

Just . . . *damn.*

Two

Cheyenne

"I'm positive," I whispered frantically to Blair in the kitchen. "I *felt* it. Then I looked right at it. I said, 'Um, it's big.' Then I tried to escape through his *closet*." Cringing, I shook my head. "It was so embarrassing!"

"I'm sure he was more embarrassed than you were." Blair giggled as she dumped a big bag of barbecue chips into a bowl. "What did he say?"

"Nothing!" I poured two glasses of Pinot Grigio and plunked a few ice cubes into a tumbler for Mariah, who was waiting for us in the den. "What on earth could he say?"

"What did you do to turn him on?"

"I have no idea." I pulled a pitcher of lemonade from the fridge and poured some into the tumbler. "Chose his outfit? Complimented his eyes? Bent over in front of him?"

Blair munched on a chip. "Those jeans do look amazing on you."

"You think?" I glanced at my behind, which was where I felt like I carried every single one of the ten pounds I was always trying to lose.

Okay, fifteen.

"Definitely," she said.

I took out a second bowl and dumped a bag of Skinny Pop in it. "I was still getting over my shock that he invited me up to his room in the first place. It was like my greatest fantasy coming to life. Except that there was a wedding picture of him and Trisha on the dresser."

Blair looked surprised. "Still?"

I ate some popcorn. "Did I ever tell you, the night they got married, I cried myself to sleep?"

"Aww, really?"

"Yep. I'd been away at college for a year already. I'd finally lost my virginity to some dormitory asshole who vaguely resembled Cole but—it turned out—had none of his kindness or integrity. But anyway, I was nineteen and thought I was over Cole Mitchell once and for all. Then I saw him standing at the front of the church in a black suit, tears in his eyes, watching Trisha walk toward him, and it hit me—I'd *never* be over him. And he'd never be mine. I stayed as long as I could at the reception, then I came home and bawled my eyes out."

"You're killing me." Blair ate another chip. "How many guys have you dated because they reminded you of Cole?"

"Ugh. Too many." I shoved more popcorn in my mouth. "And they always turned out to be jerks."

"Maybe you should date, like, the *opposite* of him."

"I've done that too," I said. "Believe me, I've put myself out there. I've dated plenty of guys. A couple times I even thought I was in love. But deep down, my heart was always secretly, stubbornly loyal to Cole. I keep waiting to feel *that way* about someone else. Because . . . shouldn't I? Shouldn't the guy I'm with be the one who gives me butterflies and makes my heart pound? If not, what's the point?"

She sighed. "I guess you're right. I wish he'd open his eyes and see how great you guys could be together."

"Ha. Do you know how many times I've made that wish? On every first star in the sky, every birthday candle I've ever blown out, every coin I've ever thrown in a fountain." I ate another handful of popcorn. "But it's no use. I feel like there's this . . . Trisha-shaped hole in his life, and I'll never fit into it." I glanced at my behind again. "I think my butt's too big."

"Oh, Jesus." She rolled her eyes. "It's not that."

"Then what is it?"

"I don't know for sure." She sipped her wine. "It's been eight years since Trisha died, right?"

"Nine. She had severe hemorrhaging after a placental abruption while delivering Mariah." I spoke quietly so the little girl wouldn't hear me.

"God, that's so sad." Blair picked up her wine glass and took a sip. "But nine years is a pretty long time. Think he's been celibate all those years?"

"No idea. But this is such a small town, and he's so well-known, being a police officer and all, I feel like there would be rumors if he was sleeping around. I've never heard a thing. I think he's too gentlemanly."

"Well, we know he's still capable," Blair said with a grin. "At least judging by the bulge in his khakis."

Groaning, I squeezed my eyes shut. "Stop. You know, for a moment, I actually thought he was going to kiss me."

"Maybe he was. He's obviously attracted to you, Cheyenne."

"I don't know," I said dubiously. "I mean, why would he want me? He could have anyone."

Blair crunched loudly on a chip. "Not even going to dignify that with a response."

We took the snacks and drinks into the den, where we'd already set up the facial mask and mani-pedi stations, and cued up *Grease*, which I'd gotten permission to show Mariah. While the opening credits played, we covered our faces with a DIY mask made from banana, orange juice and honey. While singing along to "Summer

Loving," I painted Mariah's toes. While she returned the favor by polishing the fingernails on my right hand, I sipped wine and commiserated with Sandy as she crooned "Hopelessly Devoted to You." When "Hand Jive" came on, Blair and I both jumped up and danced along.

"Jeez, how many times have you guys *seen* this?" asked Mariah incredulously.

"A lot," I said, laughing and out of breath. "It's addictive. You'll see."

By the end of the movie, the snacks were gone, the wine bottle was empty, and Mariah was yawning.

"I'll walk you home in a minute, okay?" I told her. "See if you can find your flip-flops. They might be under the couch."

"Okay."

Blair gave her a hug. "See you soon, sweetie."

I walked Blair to the front door. "Thanks for coming over."

"Of course! Thank you for hosting my wild and crazy bache-lorette night." Laughing, she dug her keys from her purse. "Think the guys are still at the pub?"

"Probably. It's only eleven."

Blair rolled her eyes. "I know, but those four are like a bunch of old ladies. They talk a big game, but their guys' nights usually wrap up long before midnight."

I laughed. "Are Moretti and Beckett bringing dates to the wed-ding?" In addition to Cole, those were Griffin's other two closest friends and groomsmen.

"Not that I know of. And if they are, they better tell me, be-cause the wedding is only two weeks away and I have to finalize the seating chart." She shrugged. "But it's kind of hard, you know? Unless you're already dating someone, you can't really bring them to an out-of-town wedding, especially if you're in the wedding party."

"Right." Griffin and Blair were getting married up at Cloverleigh Farms, which was about three hours north of Bellamy Creek.

"But there will be some single girls there. Maybe one of them will find their soul mate." She poked my shoulder. "Or maybe you will."

I sighed. "I'd settle for someone to dance with."

"Someone with broad shoulders, piercing blue eyes, and a nice big dick?"

"Shhhh!" I glanced behind me, worried Mariah might have wandered out of the den.

"You'll get that dance, because you're the maid of honor and he's the best man. Wedding party dance."

"That's not the same as being *asked* to dance, Blair."

"So ask him."

"I can't do that!"

She rolled her eyes. "Yes, you can, Chey. One of these days you're just going to have to be brave and tell him how you feel. Either that or pine for him the rest of your life."

"At least I'd keep my dignity."

"Maybe, but your dignity isn't going to keep you warm at night, is it?" Rising up on her toes, she gave me a hug. "I'll see you Thursday, but I'm sure we'll talk before then."

"Okay." Thursday was Thanksgiving, and my mom and I were hosting dinner at our house. It would be small—just Griffin and Blair, Cole and Mariah and Mrs. Mitchell, my mom and me—but I was looking forward to the long weekend and cooking a big, traditional meal. I loved to cook. "'Night. Drive safe."

"'Night."

I watched Blair hurry through the chilly dark and jump behind the wheel of her car, then gave her a wave as she pulled away from the curb and headed down the street. She and Griffin were so lucky they'd found each other. They had such a great story—stubbornly single mechanic falls for beautiful woman stranded in his small town. It was straight out of a movie.

And I felt lucky too, that she and I got along so well. Neither of us had a sister—I only had one brother and Blair was an only child—so it was fun to finally experience that kind of close relationship. I'd been moved to tears when she'd asked me to be her maid of honor.

After her taillights disappeared, I returned to the den, where Mariah had found her flip-flops and was zipping up her hoodie. "Ready to go?" I asked.

"Yes. That was so fun," she said, looking at her bright blue toenails. "Can we do it again sometime?"

"Absolutely."

"And watch *Grease* again too?"

I grinned, pulling my cardigan tighter around me. "You know it. *Grease* and I go together like *rama-lama-lama, ka-dinga-da-dinga-dong.*"

She laughed as we went out the front door. "Who's your favorite character?"

"Hmm. I'll say Sandy. I identify with her." I looked at her as we cut across the lawn in the dark. "How about you?"

"I liked Frenchy. Think my dad would let me dye my hair pink?"

"Um, no."

Mrs. Mitchell had said she would leave the back door open, so Mariah and I were walking up the driveway when headlights flashed at us from behind. We quickly scooted out of the way and up onto the back porch.

"Your dad's home," I said, watching him pull into the garage at the back of the yard. "Want to wait for him?"

"Sure." She turned around and caught me breathing into my palm to check my breath. "What are you doing?"

"Nothing," I said quickly, smiling as Cole approached, the garage door closing behind him.

"Hey," he said.

"Hey." Butterflies took flight inside my belly, remembering the way he'd flipped me beneath him and pinned me down. "You're home early."

He nodded, slowly climbing the porch steps. "Did you guys have fun?"

"Yes," Mariah said. "Look at my toes, aren't they cute?" She held up one foot.

"Blue, huh?" He chuckled and shook his head, as if girls were a mystery to him.

"Can I dye my hair pink?"

"*No*. What do you say to Miss Cheyenne?"

Mariah wrapped her arms around me and squeezed. "Thank you, Miss Cheyenne."

I embraced her. "You're welcome, honey. We'll do it again soon, okay?"

"Okay."

Cole pushed the door open, nudging Mariah inside. "Go on up and brush your teeth. I'll be up in a minute to tuck you in."

"Can Miss Cheyenne tuck me in tonight, Dad?" Mariah asked.

"Not tonight, peanut. It's late."

"Please?" she wheedled, clasping her hands beneath her chin.

"I don't mind," I said.

Cole looked at me. "Are you sure?"

"Of course."

"Okay." He looked at his daughter. "But no wasting time. Get up there, get your pajamas on and teeth brushed, and get in bed. And be extra quiet, so you don't wake Grandma."

"Okay," she said, hurrying into the house.

Cole held the door open for me, and I stepped inside the kitchen, my heart beating overtime. Only the light over the stove was on, leaving the room shadowy and intimate. The hum of the refrigerator seemed loud.

"How was the party?" I asked quietly.

He closed the door behind us. "It was okay. Mostly I played darts with Beckett while Moretti flirted with a waitress and Griffin kept telling people to stop buying him shots."

"I hope he wasn't driving himself home." I followed Cole to the front of the house, where he took off his coat and hung it in the hall closet.

"Nah. Beckett was driving him." He shut the closet door and turned to face me. "Thanks again for having Mariah over tonight."

"My pleasure."

"I'm really grateful for the time you spend with her." He glanced up the stairs. "She needs it, I think. Especially as she's getting older. I'll just say it right now—I'm dreading puberty."

"Don't worry. I'll always be there for her. No matter where you live."

"Thanks," he said, his voice deep and soft. He moved a little closer to me in the dark. "I appreciate you, Cheyenne. I hope you know that."

My lips fell open.

"And listen," he went on. "About earlier, in my room."

"Okay, I'm ready," whispered Mariah from the top of the stairs, breaking the spell.

Cole cleared his throat and stepped back.

With my heart pounding like ocean waves in my chest, I went up the steps, gripping the banister for balance. What had he been about to say?

At the top of the stairs, I followed Mariah to her room and watched her slip beneath a yellow comforter covered with daisies. Then I went and sat on the edge of the bed. Her bedside lamp was on, and I noticed the photo of Trisha next to her clock on the nightstand. It was a close-up of her smiling face, and she absolutely radiated happiness, the kind of glow you couldn't get from mashed bananas.

Mariah saw me looking at it. "That's my mom," she said.

I smiled at the little girl. "I know."

"Were you friends with her?"

I tilted my head this way and that. "Not really. She was three years ahead of me in school and had her own group of friends. But she was around a lot, because she hung out with your dad and Griffin. And she was always nice to me."

"Do you think I look like her?" she asked, glancing at the photo.

"Yes. I do. And that's a good thing because she was very beautiful. Even though looks are not the most important thing about a girl," I added quickly, trying to navigate this rocky terrain on the fly. Every girl wanted to feel beautiful, right? So how did you assure her she was without making it seem too important? "Kindness is more important. And your mom had lots of that."

"I never got to meet her."

My heart ached. "Well, if you ever want to talk about her, I'm here. I miss my dad a lot, and sometimes it helps me to talk about him."

"Thanks." She tucked a stuffed dog under her arm. It was raggedy, the fur all matted.

I reached over to switch off the lamp, then brushed a hand over her forehead. "Sweet dreams, kiddo."

"Sweet dreams," she echoed.

I stood up and turned around, surprised to see Cole's tall, broad silhouette in the doorway. "Oh. I didn't realize you were there," I whispered.

"Just for a minute," he said quietly, slipping past me. "Wait for me downstairs. I'll walk you home."

"You don't have to do that," I said. "I live right next door."

"I want to." He touched my forearm. "Wait for me, okay?"

"Okay." My pulse raced a little as I went down the stairs, even though I knew his insistence on walking me home was probably more about his innate police officer protective streak than any romantic feelings for me.

Even so, I went down the stairs and ducked into the first-floor lavatory. I checked my hair and teeth in the mirror, redid my ponytail, and frowned at my complexion, which did not seem any more glowy than it had yesterday. *What a waste of three perfectly good bananas*, I thought. *I could have made banana bread in the morning.*

When I came out of the bathroom, Cole was descending the stairs, which creaked beneath his feet.

"Ready?" He pulled the front door open.

"Yes."

We descended the porch steps and walked side by side down the front path, and I made sure to stroll a little slower than necessary, wishing I lived several houses down and not right next door. Our breath made puffy clouds in the cold night air.

"Listen, I'm sorry about earlier," he said. "In my room. I shouldn't have"—he glanced at me—"grabbed you like that."

"It's okay." I wanted to keep things light. "I suppose I was taking my role as your personal stylist a *bit* seriously."

He chuckled. "Maybe a bit."

"So did you have any fun tonight?"

He shrugged as we turned onto the sidewalk between our houses. "Sure, I guess."

"That's not very convincing."

"Bachelor parties aren't really my thing."

"Did you have one when you got married?"

"Probably. Is it bad that I don't remember it?"

I laughed. "It's fine. Guys like you and Griffin, who actually *want* to be married, probably don't even need bachelor parties. It seems like kind of an outdated tradition."

"I agree." He glanced at me as we headed up my mother's front walk. "Do *you* want to get married?"

Oh my God, yes! my inner teenager shrieked. *I thought you'd never ask!*

"Someday," I said. "If I can find the right person. I'd really like to have kids."

"You should. You'd be a great mom."

"Thanks." Even in the icy air, I felt heat in my cheeks. "Griffin and Blair are just so damn *lucky* that they found each other," I said as we reached my mother's porch steps. Then I turned to face him and blurted, "Don't judge me, but sometimes I get really jealous of them."

He tucked his hands in his pockets.

"It's not that I resent them being happy," I said quickly. "I'm thrilled for them. But sometimes it feels like love is just a numbers game, you know? Some people are lucky while other people aren't. And I think I'm just destined to be one of the unlucky ones."

He studied me for a moment, then shook his head. "Nah, I don't think that's true."

"No?" A brisk wind rustled leaves at our feet. "Then how come I'm thirty years old and haven't found it yet?"

He looked toward the street. "I'm not saying it's easy to find. And there are definitely a lot of idiot guys out there who can't see what's right in front of them—although most of them wouldn't deserve you anyway." His eyes met mine again. "But don't give up . . . it's worth waiting for."

A shiver moved through me, and I wrapped my arms around myself.

"You're cold. You should go in."

"I'm fine," I said, thinking I'd stand out here under the stars all night talking to him like this, no matter what the temperature. "I wish you'd come in and say all that to my mother. She thinks I'm still single because I'm too picky or not making enough effort. Like my soul mate is right up there on the high shelf, but I'm not willing to use the ladder."

"Yeah, my mom gets on me about being single too. She thinks the reason I don't want to get remarried is because I don't want to move on from Trisha. But it's not that at all." He rubbed the back of his neck. "And frankly, my friends can be just as bad, calling me a monk or constantly telling me I need to get out there again. But they don't know what it's like to be a single dad, raising a daughter who never even met her mom. Loving her enough for two parents. Making sure she's safe and healthy and happy and doing well in school and has plenty of friends and gets enough attention and makes it to soccer practice on time—or Girl Scouts or ice skating lessons or her therapist—while also holding down a full-time job with twelve-hour shifts. And in addition to all that, constantly reassuring her that she's never going to lose me."

"I'm sorry," I said softly, my heart breaking for him. "That must be—"

"Do they think I don't get lonely sometimes? Of course I do. Do they think I don't miss sex? Of course I do. Do they think it's easy to pretend I don't need it or want it as much as they do? Because it isn't." His eyes were locked on mine, flashing with fire in the dark. "It fucking isn't. But I'm trying to do the right thing."

I opened my mouth, but nothing came out. His words had knocked the wind out of me.

He put both hands over his face. "Fuck. I'm sorry, Cheyenne. You did not need to hear all that. I don't know what's with me tonight."

"Don't apologize." I managed a smile. "You're only human, Officer Mitchell. You might *look* like a superhero—especially in uniform—but underneath it all, you're a mere mortal like the rest of us. You can admit it. And you can always talk to me."

A small, crooked grin appeared, making him look like a teenager again. "Thanks."

"You're welcome."

Cole glanced behind him. "I should get back."

"Okay." Impulsively, I moved forward and gave him a friendly hug, holding my breath as I rose on tiptoe and wrapped my arms around his neck.

He seemed a little stunned at first, but then his arms came around me, and I let myself hold on for a few seconds and just breathe—inhaling the scent of his cologne and maybe just a hint of fabric softener or starch from his shirt underneath. Reluctant to let go, I wondered what was going through his mind as we stood chest to chest.

"I smell banana," he said, answering my question. "Is that your perfume?"

Laughing, I let him go and rewrapped my cardigan around me. "No. There were mashed bananas in the face mask I had on earlier. It was supposed to make my skin glow. Did it work?"

He chuckled. "I don't know. But you look beautiful, just like always."

My cheeks warmed. "Thanks."

"You're welcome."

"And thanks for walking me home." I giggled self-consciously, fussing with my hair. "I feel like I'm thirteen years old, saying that."

He cocked his head. "Did I walk you home when you were thirteen?"

"Only in my dreams." Immediately I clapped both hands over my flaming cheeks. "Oh my God. Forget I said that."

He laughed. "Why?"

"Because it's embarrassing! You're not supposed to know about my hopeless teenage crush on you." *Jiminy Cricket, Cheyenne! Shut up, shut up, shut up!*

"Well, I'm flattered. And I'll keep your secret if you keep mine."

"What secret was that?"

"The one where I'm a mere mortal."

"Oh. Right." I mimed locking up my lips and throwing away the key.

Grinning, he took a few backward steps. "I'd have walked you home back then, if I'd known."

"Liar." But I grinned back, my heart ready to explode.

"'Night, Cheyenne."

"'Night." I watched as he turned and headed across the lawn, then I climbed the porch steps and let myself in the front door.

Upstairs, I put my pajamas on, washed my face, took my pill, and brushed my teeth before climbing beneath the covers in the same bed I'd slept in as a lovesick teenager, dreaming of the day the boy next door would finally look at me differently. Was it possible that day might still arrive?

Yesterday, I'd have said no way.

But tonight . . . tonight was making me wonder.

Three

Cole

AFTER LOCKING UP THE HOUSE, I WENT UPSTAIRS, got ready for bed, and slid beneath the covers. I was tired, but I was restless too.

Okay, hot and bothered.

I couldn't stop thinking about Cheyenne. The way my body kept reacting to her. The things I'd told her. The undeniable temptation I'd felt to kiss her tonight—like three separate times.

I hadn't walked a girl home in fifteen fucking years. I'd almost forgotten how good it felt to be a little protective of someone. To stand there at her door and wish I could mess around with her, but be gentleman enough to keep my hands to myself.

It hadn't been easy.

Cheyenne stirred something up in me, something I hadn't felt in a long time. Before I realized it, my hand had slid down inside my boxer briefs, my hard flesh slipping through my fist. I felt guilty about it, but I couldn't resist. My cock was too hard and my muscles too tense, my blood too hot in my veins. I needed the release or I'd go crazy.

And hadn't I known I would do it tonight? Hadn't I locked

my bedroom door? Hadn't I been sitting there tonight at the pub, thinking about Cheyenne's ass in her tight jeans, that white lace clinging to her perfect round breasts, the way she'd felt beneath me for those few, incredible seconds?

Stifling a groan, I worked myself harder and faster, imagining what it would be like to feel her lips on my mouth, on my chest, on my cock. To hear her murmur in appreciation as her hands swept over my shoulders and arms and abs. To see her skin shimmer in the dark as she writhed and arched beneath me. To hear the sharp gasps as I plunged inside her again and again, until our bodies reached the breaking point, and she cried out my name.

A few seconds later, my hand and stomach were a mess. After I'd mopped myself up with some tissues, I pulled on some sweatpants and went down the hall to the bathroom. Already, the shame was settling in, and I avoided looking at myself in the mirror as I flushed the tissues and washed my hands, scrubbing them as if I could undo what I'd done—or better yet, unthink what I'd thought while I was doing it.

Afterward, I went back to my room and got into bed again, pulling the covers to my waist. My body was more relaxed, but I still wasn't sleepy enough to drift off. Instead, I lay with my hands behind my head, staring into the dark, trying to rationalize what I'd done.

Maybe it wasn't *that* bad. After all, I hadn't really broken the promise. And she wasn't just Griffin's little sister anymore. She was *my* friend too. She was someone I'd known more than half my life, someone I trusted. She loved my daughter, and she went out of her way to show it. She listened to me. She understood me. She didn't try to tell me what I should do.

So no wonder, right? No wonder I was feeling something for her, something strong enough to cause a physical response. But it was over now. Out of my system.

Next time I saw her, it would be like it had never happened at all.

The following day, I woke up early like I usually did. Griffin and I normally ran together on Sunday mornings, but I didn't think he was going to be in any shape for it today, so I got out of bed, pulled on running clothes, laced up my shoes, and set off alone.

The air was bracing—I could see my breath—and it took my muscles longer than usual to warm up. Generally, I was in good shape—I ran a few times a week, lifted weights, played baseball for the county men's league in the summer and pickup hockey in the winter—but there were some mornings I felt my age creeping up on me.

I picked up the pace a little, lengthening my strides.

Maybe it was a mental thing. My mother wasn't totally wrong about my feeling stuck—although she *was* wrong about how to fix it. I didn't need a girlfriend to get out of this rut, I just needed a change of scenery.

As I finished up the second mile, I thought more about moving out of my mother's house. We'd needed my mom's help after losing Trisha so tragically and suddenly, but my plan had never been to stay in my childhood home forever. I'd just sort of grown accustomed to the way things were . . . my mom getting Mariah ready for school because I had to be at work by seven a.m.; meals on the table when I got home twelve hours later; laundry done, folded, and left in a basket at my bedroom door; the house always clean.

Not that I didn't do my share—I did all the outdoor work, and because my mother was so fastidious, it involved constant mowing, edging, weeding, power-washing, bug-spraying, painting, and other repairs. I was also fairly handy inside the house and was usually able to fix anything that broke, and I took care of her car as well, bringing it to Griffin's garage for service whenever it was necessary. Whenever I tried to give her money for rent or groceries, she always refused, telling me to put it toward

Mariah's college education fund instead. Once a month, Mariah and I took her out for dinner someplace nice as a gesture of thanks for taking such good care of us.

But it was time for us to move on.

I needed something to get excited about. A project. A place we could make our own. In the past, Mariah had sometimes struggled with change, but I'd involve her in the process every step of the way. She could have any room in the new house she wanted for her own. She could help me paint it. She could get the bunk beds she'd always wanted. I'd talk to the chief about my work schedule, see if there was any room for flexibility on my shift's start time. We'd have fucking pancakes for dinner if we had to.

And I could jerk off under my own damn roof.

Mind made up, I cut the run short by looping back toward my mom's after only three miles instead of the usual five, did some cursory stretches in the back yard, then headed inside to call Moretti. He was a builder, not a real estate agent, but he owned rental properties and often bought and flipped houses on the side. I figured he would have an inside scoop on the local market.

Maybe we could even find something in the next couple weeks, and Mariah and I could move in before the holidays.

We could start the new year in a new place. Get a new lease on life. A new beginning.

I felt better already.

Moretti was hungry, so we met at the Bellamy Creek Diner for lunch.

"How was the rest of the night?" I asked after we were seated in a booth at the back.

"It was fine. I left not long after you did," said Moretti, shrugging out of his jacket.

"Alone?" I asked, but it was a joke. Enzo Moretti rarely left a bar alone on a Saturday night.

"Actually, yes. I'm kind of into this girl, Reina—she's a server there, but she had to work until two and then get up early for church."

"The dark-haired one?" I unzipped my Carhartt. "I saw you talking to her, but she didn't look familiar. Is she new there?"

"Yeah. I'd never met her until recently either, but apparently her grandmother and my grandmother are friends. They sort of set us up."

I laughed. "She's Italian, I take it?" Moretti's family was like my mother times a *hundred*—constantly on him to find a nice girl, settle down, and have kids. Lately his father had been threatening to retire and leave the family construction business, Moretti & Sons, to his younger brother Pietro, who was already hitched and had two little kids.

"She's at least Catholic, which is what they really care about. And she's cool. But . . ." He cringed. "She's a little young."

"How young?"

"Just turned twenty."

I laughed. "Legal, at least."

"Legal, yes, but have you tried talking to a twenty-year-old recently? Sometimes I feel like I have no idea what she's saying. I never thought I'd say this, but I might be too . . ."

"Old for her?" I supplied.

"*Mature* for her," he stated, sitting up taller in the booth and running a hand over his dark, wavy hair. "Not old."

"Right."

"I mean, her big ambition is to be an Instagram influencer," he said. "What the hell kind of job is that?"

"I don't know."

"She was fucking *born* in the year 2000," he said, shaking his head. "I was thirteen that year, jerking off to pictures of Britney Spears in that little plaid skirt. I had a filthy mouth and an even filthier mind. And she was, like, a *baby*."

"She's not a baby *now*," I said, trying to be helpful.

"No, but . . ." His dark brows furrowed. "It weirds me out. The priest was looking at me during Mass this morning, and I felt like he was judging me." He paused. "Although that could have been because I haven't gone to Mass in months."

"What made you go today?"

"I need to get back on my parents' good side before they ruin my life by giving the business to fucking Pietro. If that means going to Mass and dating an adolescent whatever-a-grammer, I gotta do it."

I laughed. "Have you taken her out on a date?"

"We've had dinner a couple times. You know, you could join us next time. I could see if Reina could bring a friend or something. At least we'd have each other to talk to."

"Are you kidding? She's closer to Mariah's age than mine. No, thanks."

Moretti groaned. "I wish my dad wasn't being such a dick about this whole 'settling down by age thirty-five' bullshit. It's fucking medieval."

"But not a surprise," I pointed out. "You've always known what they expected of you."

He frowned. "I know, but thirty-five used to seem a lot farther away than it does now."

"Tell me about it," I said as the waitress dropped off my coffee and Moretti's beer.

He took a big gulp of it. "What did you want to ask me about?"

"I want to buy a house."

His eyebrows rose. "You're moving out of your mom's?"

"Yes. It's time."

"I agree." He frowned as he picked up his phone from the table. "Let me get some info from you. Do you have a realtor you'd like to work with?"

"You think I need one?"

He shrugged. "Not necessarily. I know the area and the comps around here pretty well. You'll have to hire an appraiser and probably a lawyer to look over the contract, but a realtor isn't a must."

"Good. I'll stick with you."

"Any particular neighborhood?"

I thought for a moment. "I guess it would be convenient to be close enough to my mom's that Mariah could walk or ride her bike there. But if we couldn't find the right house near enough, I'd deal with it."

Moretti nodded. "Three bedrooms?"

"Sounds good."

"Number of full baths?"

"Maybe two?" I liked the idea of Mariah and I each having our own bathrooms.

"Attached garage?"

"Not necessary."

"Square footage?"

I shrugged. "No idea. I'd say maybe like twelve to fifteen hundred?"

"Any preference for particular style, like a ranch or colonial?"

"Nah." I thought for a moment. "I'd like a nice-sized yard though. Maybe a patio or deck. I could build one if there's enough space."

"Got it." We discussed my price range, and he put his phone away. "I'll get back to you in a day or so with some options."

Tuesday afternoon while I was at work, Moretti left me a voice-mail. "Hey, I found some listings you might be interested in. I'll email you the links. If there are any you want to see, maybe we can get appointments this weekend, although with the holiday, I'm not sure. Anyway, let me know your work schedule. I can never remember what days you're on or off."

My work schedule was a little confusing since it varied every week—a rotating series of two or three days on, followed by two or three days off—but I liked it. Shifts were long, but I never worked more than three days in a row, and every other week I got three consecutive days off. I could volunteer at Mariah's school, get household projects done, run errands . . . and if the days fell over a weekend, sometimes Mariah and I went to visit Trisha's parents, who lived in Indiana now.

After dinner that evening, I opened my laptop at the kitchen table and looked at the listings Moretti had sent. There were ten of them, but a few I was able to dismiss right off the bat—too expensive, too far from my mom's, too small. But three or four of them had potential, and I invited Mariah to come sit next to me and look at the photos. Thankfully, my mother was at the usual Tuesday night meeting of the Ladies Benevolent Sewing Circle, where the grandmotherly ladies of Bellamy Creek pieced together quilts for families in need while discussing all the latest rumors. They spread as much gossip as benevolence, if you asked me. I'd show her the listings too, of course, but I wasn't really interested in her opinions just yet.

Mariah seemed excited to see the houses in person—there was one with a little doghouse in the yard, and she hoped the house came with a puppy—so I gave Moretti a call back right away.

"Hey," he said when he picked up. "Have a chance to look at those listings yet?"

"We did."

"See anything you like?"

"Definitely. I'm off Thursday and Friday this week, but I'm assuming since Thursday is Thanksgiving, that day is out. Would it be possible to get appointments on Friday?"

"Maybe. Reply with the addresses you want to see and I'll make a couple calls tomorrow."

"You sure? I don't want this to take up your workday or anything."

"I'm sure. I'm not that busy this week."

"Okay," I said. "Thanks a lot. I owe you."

I'd just hit send on the email with the addresses to Moretti when I heard a knock at the back door. Mariah jumped up from the table to go answer it. "It's Miss Cheyenne," she said excitedly, pulling the door open. "Hi, Miss Cheyenne. Come on in."

My pulse kicked up, and I quickly ran a hand through my hair before turning around in my chair.

"Hi, Mariah." Cheyenne smiled as she stepped into the kitchen and shut the door behind her. "Brrr, it's just getting colder and colder, isn't it? Think we'll have snow for Thanksgiving this year?"

"I hope so," Mariah said.

"Me too. Snowy days just make me want to curl up in a window seat with a mug of tea and a good book." Cheyenne laughed. "Not that I have a window seat." Then she noticed me sitting at the table, and her smile changed. "Oh. Hey, Cole."

"Hey," I said, rising to my feet and trying hard not to think about how I'd fantasized about her Saturday night. Had I really thought that would get her out of my system? I wanted her even more now. "What's going on?"

"I'm hoping you can help me. I had this last-minute idea for a Thanksgiving project for my kindergartners, and I need to make an example to show them, but I don't have any construction paper. I was hoping maybe you had some, Mariah?"

"I think so." Mariah hurried over to what my mother referred to as the craft cupboard. "Do you need fall colors?"

"Sure, if you've got them. This is what I want to make." She tapped her phone screen and held it up. "And I already cut the turkey bodies out from cardboard delivery boxes before realizing I didn't have anything to make the feathers with. I could probably go in early tomorrow morning and get the example done, but I'll already have to go in early and cut out five feathers for each kid—which will be a hundred and thirty feathers."

I moved closer, checking out the picture on her phone of cardboard turkeys with multicolored feathers that had words written on them like MOM, DAD, MY HAMSTER, SCHOOL, and COOKIES. "Cute. Are those things kids are thankful for?"

Cheyenne laughed. "Yes. I'll have their fifth grade reading buddies help them with the writing. We're hosting the buddies for a project, story, and snack right after the Thanksgiving Sing assembly."

"Sounds like a busy day," I said. I could smell her perfume— not bananas this time, but something floral, feminine and sweet. She was dressed in what looked like her work clothes, fitted navy pants, a navy blouse with flowers all over it, a soft pink cardigan sweater, and beige flats. The front of her hair was neatly pulled back, and her skin seemed luminous, her cheeks pink from the chilly night air. It made me want to warm her up.

"I found some!" Mariah came rushing over to the table with a stack of colored construction paper. "Will this work?"

"Absolutely," Cheyenne said. "Thank you so much. See what we're making?" She flashed the phone screen at Mariah, who gasped.

"I want to make one! I wish I was in fifth grade so I could have a kindergarten reading buddy."

"Next year," Cheyenne promised.

"Can I still make one with you tonight?" she asked hopefully.

"Sure." Cheyenne looked at me. "Unless it's bedtime?"

I checked the clock on the wall. "She's got about half an hour—an hour if I'm nice."

Laughing, Cheyenne glanced at the kitchen table. "Want to work here or at my house, Mariah?"

"Here," Mariah said. "That way Daddy can make one too."

"I don't know about *that*," I said, ruffling her hair, "but I'll sit with you guys."

"Yay!" Mariah ran over to the table for four and pulled out the chair between mine and hers. "Miss Cheyenne, you can sit here."

"Okay. But first I need to run back to my house and grab a couple things. I'll be right back."

While she was gone, I quickly snuck up to my room and checked my reflection in the mirror above my dresser. Shit—there was a faint yellow stain on the white T-shirt I'd thrown on after taking off my uniform. After swapping it for a nicer blue one—I remembered how she'd liked me in blue—I ran a brush over my hair and gave myself one squirt of cologne. At the last second, I decided to duck into the bathroom and brush my teeth, so by the time I got back downstairs, Cheyenne and Mariah were already seated at the table, tracing feather shapes onto the construction paper.

They both looked up at me as I walked into the kitchen.

"Did you change your clothes?" Mariah asked.

"Just my shirt," I said, cursing my daughter for being so observant. "I spilled something on it."

"When?"

"Earlier." I went directly to the fridge and grabbed a Heineken. "Cheyenne, would you like a beer?"

"No, thanks."

"How about a glass of wine?" I asked.

"Okay."

"You like merlot?"

"I like it all," she said with a laugh.

I opened a bottle and poured her a glass, bringing it to the table along with my beer. When I sat down, Mariah studied me carefully.

"Did you comb your hair?" she asked.

Self-conscious, I ran a hand over it. "No," I lied.

"Oh." She went back to tracing. A moment later, she picked up her head again and sniffed. "What's that smell? Dad, are you wearing cologne?"

Stifling the urge to throttle my kid, I took a long swig from the Heineken bottle and changed the subject. "Maybe I will make one of those things. Got an extra turkey for me?"

"Of course." Cheyenne picked up a cardboard turkey cutout and handed it to me.

I could have taken it from her without any skin-to-skin contact at all simply by grabbing the other end of it.

But I didn't.

Instead, I reached over and covered her hand with mine—and I didn't let go. Mariah's head was bent over her work, so she didn't notice, but Cheyenne stared at our hands, a blush creeping into her cheeks. Not from the cold this time, but from the warmth of the touch.

Then I loosened my grip and slid the cardboard from her grasp, setting it in front of me. Immediately I reached for my beer bottle, and Cheyenne did the same with her wine glass.

My heart was beating hard and fast. I felt ridiculous, like a fifth grader who'd just held hands with a girl for the first time. For fuck's sake, I'd tackled her on my bed the other night. This was nothing.

Except, it felt like *something*.

Four

Cheyenne

COLE MITCHELL HELD MY HAND.
Cole Mitchell held my hand.
Cole Mitchell held my hand.

I took another sip of wine, traced the same damn feather I'd already traced five times, and reviewed the moment again.

Had I imagined it?

I'd picked the cardboard turkey up off the table, held it out to him, and instead of just taking it from me, he'd sort of enclosed my hand inside his and paused for several seconds.

Could I call that handholding? Did it count? Did it mean anything that he'd changed his shirt, combed his hair and put on cologne? Because Mariah was right—he'd definitely spruced himself up a bit before coming back to the table. Was I flattering myself that it could be for me? But what other reason was there?

I took another swallow of wine. At this rate, I was going to finish the entire glass inside five minutes.

"Okay, I'm ready to cut out my feathers," Mariah announced, reaching for the scissors.

I snuck a peek at Cole, who was tracing a feather on red

construction paper. His profile gave nothing away. He looked the same as he always did—and by that, I mean *perfect*. I'd always loved the color of his hair, not quite blond, not exactly brown, which he'd worn short as long as I'd known him. His jaw was slightly stubbly, somewhere between a five o'clock shadow and next-morning scruff. His nose was long and straight, his lips and lashes full. But it had always been his eyes that made me melt into a puddle of *take me now*. They were just so blue. So clear and bright, like they could see into your soul.

I may have sighed.

He glanced over at me, and I realized too late that I was staring at him like you'd stare at a double rainbow or a really spectacular pair of Louboutins. Embarrassed, I straightened up in my chair and focused on my work. "I'm about ready to cut out my feathers too."

"I'm done cutting out," said Mariah, setting her scissors aside. "Now I need a glue stick."

I handed her a glue stick and forced myself to concentrate on cutting out feathers, but in the silence I discovered I could smell his cologne, which took me down a sexy rabbit hole of imagining his naked body moving over me in the dark, the scent of him filling my head. I thought of that bulge in his pants the other night—the way it felt against my thigh—and how it might feel slowly easing inside my body, inch by hard, thick inch.

Suddenly I realized I was panting. And both Cole and Mariah were staring at me.

"Are you okay, Miss Cheyenne?" Mariah blinked at me. "You're, like, breathing really hard."

"Um. I'm fine. I was just . . . thinking about something." Before I could stop myself, I fucking glanced at Cole's crotch.

And he saw me do it.

I could tell, because he followed my gaze directly into his lap, and shifted uncomfortably in his chair.

Shit!

Setting down the scissors, I grabbed my empty wine glass and held it upside down above my lips until two tiny drops fell into my mouth. Then I shook it, hoping for more.

"Can I get you another glass?" Cole asked, rising from his chair and adjusting his jeans.

"Sure," I said, even though the last thing I needed was to have a headache in the morning. All-school assemblies were enough to make my temples pound on their own.

But when Cole returned with a second beer for himself and my glass refilled, I gave him a grateful smile. "Thank you."

"You're welcome." He took his seat next to me, and I concentrated *very hard* on keeping my eyes on my work and not breathing too loudly.

While we finished our turkeys, Mariah chattered a little about some of the houses Cole had shown her online. She was excited about getting to paint her room any color she chose— she was leaning toward yellow—and hoped her dad would let her get a puppy if they bought the one with the doghouse in the yard.

"Ooh, you should go down to the shelter and pick one out," I said. During the summer, when I wasn't teaching, I volunteered at a local shelter. Once I had my own place, I couldn't wait to rescue a couple animals.

"Can we, Daddy?"

"We'll see," said Cole, setting down a glue stick. "Okay, I think I'm done."

"No, you're not, you have to write things you're thankful for on the feathers," insisted Mariah. "Like this." She held up her turkey so we could read the words she'd carefully printed. Her feathers read, FAMILY, HOME, SCHOOL, NEIGHBORS, SHELTER DOG.

"You don't have a dog yet," Cole pointed out. "Shelter or otherwise."

"I know." Mariah closed her eyes. "I'm trying to manifest it by positive thinking."

I laughed. "Those are good choices, Mariah. And there's nothing wrong with positive thinking." Maybe I could manifest *sex with Cole* if I wrote it on my turkey.

Cole quickly scribbled words on his feathers and held it up. "Okay, here are mine."

I leaned forward so I could see them better and grinned. They read, FAMILY, FRIENDS, BASEBALL, TAX REFUNDS, BEER.

"Dad," Mariah scoffed. "You can't say beer."

"Why not?" He picked up his beer and took a sip. "It's one of my favorite things."

"Because this is supposed to be for *kids*."

"Oh." Cole picked up a marker, crossed out BEER with an X, and wrote MILK. Then he wrote NOT FOR KIDS with a little arrow pointing to the crossed-out word.

"Now it looks even worse," Mariah said, giggling.

"That's okay, Mariah," I said. "I'll use yours for the example. And mine." I finished labeling my feathers and held my turkey up. "What do you think?"

"Family, friends, students, holidays, love," Mariah recited. Then she smiled in approval. "Those are good. Better than my dad's."

Cole crumpled up a piece of construction paper and threw it at his daughter like a snowball. "Enough, you. It's time for bed. Let's get this table cleaned up."

"I'll clean it up," I said, rising to my feet and reaching to gather up all the scraps. "You can put Mariah to bed."

"She can help," Cole insisted, taking his maligned turkey over to the fridge and sticking it onto the front with a magnet. "Mariah, return Grandma's scissors to her junk drawer and put the glue sticks and extra paper back in the craft cupboard."

"Okay."

A couple minutes later, the table had been cleared except for my wine glass and Cole's beer bottle. "Say goodnight to Miss Cheyenne, and get upstairs," Cole told his daughter.

"Can't she come up and say goodnight like she did before?" Mariah asked.

Exhaling, Cole looked at me. "Do you mind?"

"Not at all," I said. "That gives me a chance to finish my wine. I'll come up in five minutes?"

"Great!" Mariah grinned and scooted out of the kitchen, and I sat down again.

Cole lowered himself into the seat next to me. "Thanks for staying."

"No problem." I picked up my wine and took a sip. "I didn't realize how much I needed this."

He laughed. "Stressful day?"

I shrugged. "My mom is a little extra these days, with Thanksgiving this week, and my brother's wedding in two weeks, and then Christmas not long after that. But with Griffin well on his way to giving her the grandchildren she's always wanted, you'd think she'd let up on me a little, but no."

"No?"

I shook my head. "Yesterday she left this pamphlet on the kitchen table called 'Beating the Biological Clock.'"

Cole winced. "Ouch."

"Tell me about it. I was so furious, I crumpled it up and threw it away right in front of her. And then late last night, of course, I got out of bed, dug it out of the trash, and read the whole damn thing front to back. And it turns out she's sort of right! Women lose, like, a *thousand* eggs a month, and peak fertility occurs when girls are between the ages of eighteen and thirty." I tossed back the rest of my wine—so much for taking it slow—then set the glass on the table with a *plunk*. "And you know what else? Men continue to make sperm and testosterone at virtually the same rates throughout their entire lives. So not only is the asshole biological clock a real thing, it's a real thing *only women* have to deal with."

"Sorry," he said.

I looked at him, and his expression was so contrite I had to laugh. "It's not your fault. And I don't think my body is shriveling up and wasting away *that* quickly. I have at least a few good years left."

"Your body is fucking perfect, Cheyenne."

I swear to God, those words came out of his mouth.

My jaw fell open.

His face went red. "Fuck. Sorry."

"For what? It was a compliment."

"Men shouldn't comment on women's bodies."

"But did you mean it—what you said?"

"Yes."

"Then say it again," I demanded, my pulse racing.

He looked me in the eye. "Your body is fucking perfect, Cheyenne."

"Okay, I'm ready!" called Mariah from the top of the stairs.

With my face flushed with pleasure, I pushed back my chair and hurried out of the kitchen. *He likes my body! He likes my body! He likes my body!* I kept repeating the words in my head, even though it made me feel like the world's shittiest feminist. But it was the first time Cole had ever given me any indication he saw me like that.

Up in Mariah's room, I watched her scramble beneath the covers and lowered myself to the edge of her bed. Once she was tucked in, her stuffed dog beneath her arm, I switched off the lamp on the bedside table. I was afraid if I left it on, she'd notice how pink my cheeks were and ask why.

Oh, no reason. I've just been waiting for your dad to notice me for twenty years, and he just sort of admitted he thinks I'm hot, but I'd like you to please remember when I said looks aren't the most important and not how happy I am right now, okay? Thanks.

But she had something else on her mind. "Miss Cheyenne, are you in love?"

The question startled me. "Why do you ask?"

"On your turkey, you put love as one of the things you were grateful for."

"Oh." Somewhat relieved, I thought for a moment. "Well, there are all different kinds of love. Love between family members, love between friends, love for our co-workers and neighbors, love for our country, love for our pets."

"And for our stuffed animals," Mariah added, kissing her dog on the head.

I smiled. "Definitely for our stuffed animals."

"But have you ever been *in love*? Like a mom and a dad?"

"I thought I was, a couple times," I answered truthfully. "But sometimes that kind of love is really just other things dressed up in a fancy costume."

Mariah nodded. "And when the fancy costume is off, you see that it wasn't really love?"

"Sort of. Yes," I said, deciding that it wasn't a perfect metaphor, but it was good enough for a Tuesday night after a couple glasses of merlot. "I think real love will keep feeling like real love, even after the costume is off and the novelty wears thin."

"What's novelty?"

"Newness," I told her. "Real love should last, you know? It should grow even stronger over time, not fade away."

"I didn't know love could fade away." Mariah's voice trembled a little.

"It can't," I promised her. "Real love doesn't fade. It only gets stronger."

"I love my dad the most out of anybody."

Girl, same, I wanted to say. Instead I leaned down and kissed her forehead. "I know."

"Sometimes I wish he wasn't a police officer," she

whispered, as if she felt guilty about it. "I saw a movie once where a police officer died."

My heart ached for her. "Listen to me. Your dad is a *very* careful and smart police officer. And Bellamy Creek is a *very* safe town. You don't have to be worried about him, okay?"

"That's what he says too."

"Because it's true," I said. "I've known your dad a very long time, and he always tells the truth. Guess what else I know about your dad."

"What?"

"He loves *you* the most out of anybody. And he always will. So that makes him extra careful and safe on the job."

She smiled. "Okay. Can you send him up?"

"Of course. Goodnight, honey."

"'Night."

Downstairs, Cole was rinsing my wine glass at the sink. "She's all ready for you," I said, taking my book bag off the back of my chair and slinging it over my shoulder.

"Okay." He set the glass upside down on a towel to dry and turned to face me. "Thanks for staying."

"Thanks for the help with the project." I glanced at his turkey on the fridge and laughed. "You did a great job. A-plus work."

He chuckled, folding his arms over his chest. "Right."

"Well, I should get home. Early morning tomorrow," I said, moving for the door.

"Want me to walk you back?"

Of course I did, but I shook my head. "No, that's okay. Your mom isn't here, and I don't want to leave Mariah alone. She's . . . a little emotional tonight, I think."

His face grew concerned. "She is?"

"She's okay," I said quickly, "but she just told me she sometimes wishes you weren't a cop."

He nodded, his expression grim. "She saw a movie recently, where—"

"She told me. And I think it's only natural for her to be afraid of losing you, given what happened to her mom."

"I know. And I tell her all the time that I'm safe, and she's safe, and that nothing can take me away from her." He took a deep breath, and as he exhaled, he shook his head. "Still, it gets to me."

I smiled. "You're only human, remember?"

"Right." He smiled at me, then put a finger over his lips, reminding me that was our secret. "Anyway, I've kept you here long enough. Let me get the door for you." He crossed in front of me and pulled the back door open. Icy air blew in, and snow-flakes were falling from the darkened sky. "Looks like you guys are going to get your wish for a white Thanksgiving."

"Yay," I cheered softly, coming to stand next to him.

He looked down at me. "Wait a minute. You can't go out without a coat."

"Cole, really, it's such a short walk. I'll be fine. You need to go say goodnight to Mariah."

But he'd already disappeared into the front hall, and a mo-ment later he was back with a dark gray Carhartt I recognized as his. Secretly pleased he was offering his own jacket, I slipped my arms into it.

"Thanks," I said, freeing my hair from the collar. "I'll make sure to get it back to you tomorrow."

"No rush."

I faced him again, wishing I didn't have to go home at all, but instead could stay here and curl up under a blanket with him, watch some television, or even go to bed early. My eyes traveled over his shoulders and chest, imagining what it would be like to rest my head on them, bury my face in his neck, snuggle up be-neath the covers on a cold night like tonight, instead of falling asleep alone. Then I remembered what he'd said earlier—*your body is fucking perfect, Cheyenne*—and I couldn't help but smile as I met his deep blue eyes. "See you Thursday."

"See you Thursday." He pulled the back door open once more. "Hey, shoot me a quick text when you get into your house, okay?"

I laughed, shaking my head. "You're such a dad."

He gave me his crooked grin. "Can't help it."

Glad my mother was already up in bed when I got home, I dropped my school bag by the front door and dashed up the stairs and into my bedroom. Shutting the door silently behind me, I flopped across my bed on my back and hugged the jacket close, bringing it over my face and inhaling deeply.

It smelled like soap and shaving cream and maybe a little like the pub, but it was a hundred percent *him*. I couldn't get enough. Would it be creepy to sleep in it?

I sat up again and grabbed my phone off the charger on my nightstand.

Me: Made it home in the blizzard. Thanks for the coat.

There was no immediate reply, and I figured he was still in Mariah's room.

I waited for a minute or two and then gave up on a reply. Reluctantly removing the coat and tossing it on the bed, I took off my work clothes, put on my pajamas, and chose an outfit for school tomorrow. After checking my phone one more time—still nothing—I went across the hall to the bathroom, washed my face, took my pill, brushed my teeth, and rubbed moisturizer into my skin.

Back in my room, I switched off the light and slipped between the sheets, reaching for my phone again.

He'd written me back!

Cole: Thanks for letting me know. You're welcome for the coat. It looks good on you.

Another compliment!

My entire body hummed with pleasure and I wiggled from side to side. *You'd look good on me*, I typed, wishing I had the guts to send it. I laughed silently as I deleted the words and sent a real reply—flirty, but not dirty.

Me: It kept me nice and warm all the way home. I might never give it back.

Cole: Ha.

Me: Would you arrest me for theft?

Cole: Definitely. You've always been a menace to society.

I grinned and typed another message I'd never send.

Would you cuff me? Throw me in the back of your car? Get rough with me?

It felt good just *pretending* I was the kind of girl who'd actually text him that. But since I wasn't that brave, I deleted the words and typed something else.

Me: Mariah okay?

Cole: Sound asleep. I should get to bed too.

Me: Same here. Goodnight.

Cole: Night.

With a smile lingering on my face, I set my alarm, replaced my phone on the charger, and snuggled beneath the covers. I imagined him doing the same thing, and I liked that I was the last person he'd spoken to—even if it was only via text message—before falling asleep.

Was it as good as being next to him? Hell no. But I was thinking about him, and maybe he was thinking about me, and tonight, there had been something different about the way he'd looked at me.

It was enough for now.

Also . . . Yes. I slept with his coat.

Don't judge.

The following day was a half-day at school, and I spent the rest of the afternoon making pie crust dough and helping my mom prepare for Thanksgiving. We dusted the furniture, put the leaf in the dining table, and dragged the Christmas tree from the attic along with boxes of lights and decorations. While my mother strung the lights, I hung the ornaments, laughing at the ones Griffin and I had made by hand during grade school.

We sliced Brussels sprouts, prepared the mashed potatoes, and made cranberry sauce. Since my mother's house only had one oven, tomorrow I'd get up early and bake two pies—one pumpkin, one lemon meringue—before we had to put the turkey in. The mashed potatoes could be done on the stove, Mrs. Mitchell had offered her oven for the casserole and was also bringing hot appetizers, and Blair was bringing dinner rolls, a cheese plate, and her famous apple pie.

Finally, we set the table for seven with my parents' wedding china and late grandmother's silver, which only made appearances at Christmas and Thanksgiving. We decided to set a place at each end of the table, then have three people on one side, and two on the other.

"Well, I guess that's everything for today," my mother said, hands on her hips as she surveyed the table with a critical eye. "Unless you think we should swap out the ivory tablecloth for the burgundy."

"No, I like the ivory." I smoothed a ripple in the pristine damask as someone knocked loudly on the front door.

My mother and I exchanged quizzical glances. "Are you expecting someone?" she asked as she went to answer it.

"No," I said, wondering if it was Cole coming to ask for his coat back. I'd been planning to return it this evening, but I wanted to change my clothes and clean up a little first. I'd put on sweats after work, and I was covered in dust and silver polish.

"Well, hi there!" I heard my mother exclaim. "Come on in, Mariah. What do you think of all this snow?"

Breathing a sigh of relief, I went to say hello.

"I like it," Mariah said, stomping her boots before stepping into the front hall.

"Hey, Mariah," I called.

"Hi, Miss Cheyenne." She beamed at me and held up a brown paper bag. "I made place cards for tomorrow. Want to see them?"

"Of course I do! Take your boots off and come put them on the table."

"How thoughtful of you," my mother said, shutting the door behind Mariah as the girl tugged off her boots. "Can I take your coat?"

"Yes, thanks." Mariah unzipped her jacket and handed it to my mother, then scooped up the paper bag again.

"The kids *loved* your turkey," I told her, leading the way into the dining room. "Thanks again for making it."

"You're welcome. I used the idea to make these." She stuck her hand in the bag and pulled out seven miniature versions of the turkeys we'd made last night, each of them with three colorful feathers and labeled with a name.

"Oh, they're so cute!" I exclaimed, picking up the one that said *Miss Cheyenne* in a fourth grader's round, swirly cursive. "I love them! Mom, look what Mariah made."

My mother came in and praised Mariah's work. "Adorable! Would you like to set them out?"

"Sure," Mariah said happily. "Mrs. Dempsey, you should sit here, because it's the head of the table," she went on, setting my mother's place card at one end.

"And also the closest to the kitchen, which definitely helps me," my mother said.

"I'll sit here," Mariah said, placing her turkey on the side of the table with the three settings. "Can I sit by you, Miss Cheyenne?"

"Of course." I set my turkey on the plate next to hers.

"And Daddy can sit on the other side of you." She set the card that said *Daddy* at the setting to my right.

"Perfect," I said, because I was no better than a seventh grader who wanted to sit next to her crush in the lunchroom.

"Then Grandma at this end of the table, and Uncle Griffin and Aunt Blair across from us." She finished setting out all the turkeys and looked at us for approval. "Is that okay?"

"It's marvelous," my mother said with a smile. Then she looked wistfully at the table. "Maybe next year we'll have eight places to set."

"*Mom*," I said, shooting her a look. We'd managed to go all day without an argument, and I didn't want one now.

"What?" She held up her hands, all wide-eyed with innocence. "I'm just saying, eight is a nice, round, even number. Don't you think, Mariah?"

"Um, yes." Mariah looked uneasily at me, like she wasn't sure how to answer. "Eight is an even number."

"See?" My mother gestured to Mariah. "Even a nine-year-old knows that you can't sit around waiting for Mr. Right to just appear like a rabbit out of a hat. Relationships aren't magic, Cheyenne. They take some effort."

"I know, Mom," I said through my teeth.

"I'm not sure you do, what with the outfit you're wearing." She gestured with distaste at my clothing. "It does absolutely nothing for your cute figure."

Admittedly, my leggings had a hole in the butt and below one knee, and my vintage Queen sweatshirt had seen better days—probably in 1982. But I'd worn them for cleaning, not a night at the opera. "This isn't an outfit, Mother. It's sweats."

"Mariah, do you like that outfit?"

"It looks comfy," Mariah offered.

"Comfy is for babies and grandmothers," my mother huffed. "You can't go around being *comfy* and expecting to attract the love of your life."

I rolled my eyes. "Don't listen to her, Mariah. A good person looks beyond appearances to what really matters—your heart."

"Not if it's covered by *that* ratty old sweatshirt," my mother muttered under her breath.

"If a man doesn't appreciate Freddie Mercury, he is not the man for me." Shooting her one last evil glare, I turned Mariah by the shoulders and steered her toward the front door. "Come on, honey. I'll walk you back. I have something to return to your dad, and I could use some fresh air."

Of *course* Cole got home from work while I was leaving his house in my frumpy old sweats and snow boots.

"Hey," he said, walking toward the back porch from the garage. He took my breath away in his uniform like he always did. "How did it go with the turkeys today?"

"It went great." I gave him my brightest smile, hoping it would distract him from my raggedy clothes and hair. "The kids had fun."

"Good." He stepped onto the porch and looked me up and down. "*Still* no coat? It's thirty degrees out here, Cheyenne."

I laughed. "Don't scold me, Dad. I just left your jacket inside. Mariah stopped over and I walked her back so I could return it. I needed to cool off anyway."

"Why's that?"

"My mother was singing her favorite tune. It's called All the Reasons You're Still Single. I swear to God, I might strangle her in her sleep one night. Or smother her with a pillow. Is that more humane?"

He laughed. "I'm not sure I can recommend homicide, but would a beer help? Or a glass of wine?"

"It might."

"Why don't you come in? Or better yet, let's avoid both our mothers. Why don't we escape our houses and go out for a drink?"

For a few seconds, I couldn't breathe. Had Cole just *asked me out*?

"That sounds like fun," I said, attempting to sound casual while inside I lost my shit completely.

"Have you eaten yet?"

I shook my head. "No."

"Me neither. Let's grab a bite in town."

I glanced at my clothes. "Do you mind if I clean up a little first?"

"Not at all, but I actually dig the Queen sweatshirt."

I burst out laughing. "Thank you. My mother just insulted it."

"Don't listen to her. But I have to change too. Why don't you text me when you're ready?"

"Okay. I might need like half an hour. Is that okay?"

"Sure. See you in a bit."

"See you in a bit." I hopped off the porch and headed down the driveway, crunching over the inch or two of snow that had accumulated today, although what I really felt like doing was cartwheeling through it. Dancing on it. Scooping up giant armfuls of it and tossing it over my head like glitter.

Cole and I were going out for dinner! Alone! Together! And *he'd* done the asking!

Not that this was an official first date or anything, but it was something.

It was *something*.

Five

Cole

FOR A MOMENT, I STOOD ON THE BACK PORCH watching her walk away. It struck me then what I'd done—I'd asked her on a date.

Part of me wanted to call out to her, tell her to forget it, apologize for suggesting we go out tonight and explain that I couldn't go through with it because I didn't really date. Another part of me thought that was ridiculous. This didn't have to be a *date*. It could be two friends going to grab a bite to eat and a beer. Totally casual.

Not that such a thing was possible in this town. If I so much as chatted with a woman at the deli counter at noon, by five o'clock the rumor would be circulating that I was about to propose. Bellamy Creek was a wonderful place, full of old-fashioned traditions and good-hearted people, but the only thing those people loved more than helping their neighbors was spreading rumors about them.

And one of those people was washing dishes at the kitchen sink as I entered the kitchen.

"How was your day?" asked my mother.

"Good." I took my boots off at the back door as my brother and I had been trained to do our whole lives, so we wouldn't track snow through the kitchen.

"I made beef barley soup for dinner. Can I get you a bowl?"

"No, thanks. I'm going to go grab a bite in town if that's okay."

"Of course, dear. With the boys?" She still referred to my friends as *the boys* even though we were thirty-three years old.

I cleared my throat. "No, with Cheyenne, actually."

"Oh." A pause as she digested this. "She was just here."

"I know. I saw her outside." I made my way across the kitchen quickly, hoping to get out of the room without having to discuss it further.

No such luck.

"So is this a date?" she asked.

"Nope, it's just dinner. She's been so great with Mariah lately," I added. "I thought I'd treat her to say thanks."

"Oh. Well, that's nice of you."

I could hear from her tone of voice that she thought there was more to it, but I left the kitchen before she could prod any further.

Before heading upstairs, I poked my head into the living room, where Mariah was watching television. "Hey, you."

She looked up at me and smiled. "Hi, Daddy."

"How was school?"

"Good. Did you hear back from Uncle Enzo? Can we go see the new houses?"

"Yep. We have three appointments on Friday."

Her face lit up. "Really?"

"Really."

"Are we seeing the one with the doghouse?"

"We sure are."

"Yay! I'm excited," she said.

"Me too." I started up the stairs, then paused. "Hey, is it okay with you if I go out for a little bit tonight?"

"Sure. Where are you going?"

"Just to get something to eat with Miss Cheyenne."

"Can I come too?" she asked hopefully.

"Not this time, kiddo."

"Why not?"

I felt guilty trying to come up with a reason. "We just need a little grown-up time."

"Oh. Okay." Her disappointment was obvious.

"But we still have our movie date Friday night, don't we?"

She brightened again. "Yes. Hey, maybe we can invite Miss Cheyenne to come to the movies with us!"

"Maybe," I said, continuing up the stairs, careful not to commit. People would *really* start to talk if they saw the three of us at the movies.

Upstairs, I shut the door and took off my uniform, deciding at the last minute to quickly shower and shave.

Back in my room, I pulled some jeans from my drawer, put on a clean T-shirt and underwear, and considered the dress shirts hanging in my closet. Deciding it would be too obvious to choose something blue again, I chose a black button-up this time, taking a moment to roll up the sleeves. I traded my work watch for a nicer one, ran a comb through my hair, and gave in to the temptation to wear a little cologne. I was replacing the bottle on my dresser when the framed wedding photo caught my eye.

I picked it up and looked at it closely, which I hadn't done in months. Maybe even years. At this point, it was almost just part of the furniture.

What struck me first was how *young* I looked. No furrow between my brows. No crinkle lines at the corners of my eyes. Nothing but joy and optimism in my expression. We were only twenty-two when we'd gotten married. People had tried to tell us to wait, to break up and date other people, to put off making a lifelong commitment until we were older and wiser. Our marriage wouldn't last, they said. We were too immature.

We'd laughed and insisted we knew better. After all, we'd been together for six years, and we'd never broken up once. We'd never cheated on each other. We'd never been with anybody else. Promising to love, honor, and cherish her forever had been easy for me. Of course, things hadn't gone the way I'd thought, and I'd lost her before forever was even on the horizon.

For just a moment, the old fears kicked in—a gut reaction. Was it because I'd been too complacent? Too confident in my ability to protect people I loved from harm? Was that smile on my face a little too cocky? Had I really believed that bad things didn't happen to good people?

Because they did.

All the time.

I saw it on the job every single day. You could be a good man, the best man you knew how to be, but you were a fool if you believed what you love couldn't be taken from you. It could. In an *instant*.

That's why I was better off alone.

My phone vibrated on the dresser. Grateful, I picked it up and looked at the screen.

Cheyenne: I'm ready.

Me: Me too.

Cheyenne: Should I walk over?

My gut instinct was to go get her, but that would make it seem more like a romantic thing. Best to keep this strictly platonic in every way.

Me: Sure. I'll meet you outside.

I shoved my phone into my pocket, said goodbye to my mother and Mariah, and went outside. When I saw her coming up the driveway in the backyard, my body temperature soared, and I dropped my keys in the snow.

She looked *gorgeous*. Her hair fell in loose, honey-colored waves around her shoulders, and she was wrapped up in a giant gray sweater that looked like a blanket I wanted to crawl under. And her lips—they were a bright scarlet color, which stood out against all the white surrounding us, like a neon sign shouting KISS ME ALREADY YOU FUCKING IDIOT!

As I bent to retrieve my keys, I felt like dunking my head in the snow. Maybe even lying down in it and rolling around.

I ran way too hot around her.

"So tell me about the houses you're going to see on Friday," Cheyenne said, lifting her glass of white wine.

Tearing my eyes from her mouth for what felt like the hundredth time in the last hour, I took a quick drink of my beer and set it down. "One of them is pretty close to my mom's house—maybe too close," I added, making her laugh, "and the other two are south of town, closer to the water. One is right near the creek, although it's a little out of my price range."

"I'm excited for you." She picked up her fork and twirled it in her linguine.

When I'd asked her what she felt like for dinner, she'd suggested Italian, which I was happy about. Not only did I love the food at DiFiore's, but it was small and quiet, with dim lighting and deep leather booths in the back that offered some privacy.

"Thanks. We're excited too." I cut into my osso buco, which was my favorite thing on the menu. "They're all nice houses, but each of them needs some work."

"How does your mom feel about you moving out?"

"I think she's conflicted, to be honest. We've been there so long, and she likes having people to take care of. I remember how lonely she was after my dad died. When Mariah and I moved in, that gave her a purpose."

"That's understandable. I'm a caretaker personality too."

"But it was never supposed to be permanent, our living with her."

"I think you two will love having a place of your own. And your mom is going to be just fine."

"I hope so." I picked up my beer. "She loves to drop these passive aggressive comments about how she doesn't really see the point in buying a house of my own if I'm not going to get married again. She keeps asking if I'm going to hire a house-keeper and a cook, because she cannot imagine how I'm going to be able to keep the place clean or my child fed."

Cheyenne grinned. "*Can* you cook?"

"A little," I said defensively. "I can make pancakes, grilled cheese, and spaghetti."

"Boom." She snapped her fingers. "That's breakfast, lunch, and dinner right there."

"I can also make meatballs," I announced.

"Meatballs!" Cheyenne arched one brow. "I'm impressed."

"Yes. Believe it or not, Mrs. Moretti taught me. But I was made to understand that if I ever gave the recipe to anyone else, she'd have to kill me."

Her head fell back as she laughed, and I was distracted by her throat—its pale skin, the hollow at the base, the curve of her neck to her shoulder. Earlier, in my car on the ride to town, I'd caught the scent of her perfume, and imagined the way it would fill my head if I put my lips beneath her ear, or brushed them against her collarbone, or swept them along her jaw.

"Cole?"

Blinking, I snapped my attention back to her eyes. She was studying me with a curious look on her face. "What?"

"I asked if you were hoping to move before the holidays."

"Oh." I realized how hard I was gripping my beer and set it down. "Um, I'd love to be in a new house by the new year. But there's a lot of things that would need to be in place for that to happen."

She took another bite of her pasta and sighed. "I'm so jealous. I wish I could move out by the new year."

"Your mom gave you a hard time today, huh?"

"And then some. Right in front of your daughter, who's

probably going to end up with a warped sense of self-esteem because if she listens to Darlene Dempsey, she's going to think a woman can't be happy without a man."

"No wonder our moms are such good friends," I said.

She laughed and shook her head. "Maybe they just really miss their husbands, you know? I sometimes have to remind myself that my parents were really happy together and I'm sure she wants the same for her kids. She probably can't conceive of what her life would have been like without my dad."

"I think you're right about that."

"And my mom cannot stop crowing about Griffin and Blair, how she was right about them all along, even when he was adamant that there was nothing going on with them and he was not interested in a relationship."

"Yeah," I said, recalling how stubbornly Griffin had insisted he was *not* going to fall for his soon-to-be wife. "He was a fucking idiot for a while, wasn't he?"

"He was," she agreed. "And I hope you remind everyone of that when you give the toast at their wedding reception."

I groaned, picking up my beer again. It was my second one and just about gone, although I'd been trying to pace myself. "Don't remind me about that. I'm dreading it."

"Why?"

"Because public *service* is my thing, not public speaking."

She waved a hand in a dismissive gesture. "You'll be great. Just tell a cute but embarrassing story about when he was young, remind everyone how he swore up and down he was never going to get married, especially not to a Tennessee debutante who didn't know a carburetor from a camshaft, and wish them well. Then ask us all to raise a glass and do the same." She picked up her wine glass, which was nearly empty. "Cheers."

I tapped my bottle against her glass. "Can *you* please give the toast?"

Smiling, she shook her head and finished her wine. "It's all you, my friend. But you've got this. Just say the thing about love being worth the wait that you said to me the other night."

I squinted at her. "What?"

"The other night when you walked me home, you said love isn't easy to find, but it's worth the wait."

"I said that?"

She laughed. "Yes, you did."

"Huh. That's not bad." I tossed back the rest of my Belgian ale and grinned. "I think I read that in a fortune cookie."

"What?" She wadded up a cocktail napkin and threw it at me. "A fortune cookie! I totally took that to heart. Now you're telling me it was some mass-produced, factory-generated BS?"

We were still laughing when the server appeared at the edge of our table and asked if we'd like another round.

"Not for me, I'm driving," I said, although I *wished* I could have a third beer, or maybe a shot of whiskey—anything to numb her effects on me. "I'll take a cup of coffee though."

"Sounds good. And for you?" the server asked Cheyenne.

Cheyenne bit her lip. "I probably shouldn't. I have to get up early tomorrow."

"Oh, go ahead," I said, nudging her foot beneath the table. "It's my treat."

"Cole, no—you are not paying for all this."

"She'll have one more," I told the server, whose name tag said Lara. She looked vaguely familiar to me, but I couldn't place her.

"Great! And would you like to see the dessert menu?"

I looked across the table. "Would you?"

She sighed. "Of course I would. But considering the amount of pasta I just ate and the number of calories I'm going to consume tomorrow, I'm going to say no."

I looked up at Lara. "We're all set. Just the coffee and wine, and then the bill."

When we were alone again, Cheyenne reached forward and put her hand over mine. "You do *not* have to treat me, Cole."

"Quiet," I told her gruffly. "I asked you to dinner, so I'm paying for it."

"Well, thank you. I appreciate it, even if you did give me made-up advice." She left her hand on mine as she smiled. "This is actually the best night out I've had in a really long time."

"Yeah?" It made me happy to hear it.

She nodded, her gorgeous lips curving into a smile. "When you spend all your days with a bunch of five and six-year-olds, and all your evenings with a meddlesome mother, you forget how nice it can be to spend time alone with someone closer to your own age."

I looked down at our hands. My wedding band peeked through our fingers. "It is nice. I haven't been out like this in a long time either."

"Then we should do it again sometime. And *I'll* treat."

"Sounds like a plan," I heard myself saying, even though making a habit of having dinner out with her sounded suspiciously like dating.

But she was right—it *was* nice to spend time alone with someone your own age. I loved Mariah to the moon and back, and I had the greatest group of guy friends on the fucking planet, but this was different. I'd forgotten how good it could feel to sit across from someone pretty and talk quietly and make her laugh and admire the way the candlelight on the table put those warm, golden flecks in her eyes.

Except that I knew what she was waiting for, and I couldn't give it to her.

The snow had continued to fall while we were at dinner, and a couple more inches had accumulated. Cheyenne was delighted, tossing handfuls of it over our heads as we made our way to my car.

"Are you drunk?" I teased, worried she was going to slip in those high-heeled boots she was wearing.

"Yes. Which is your fault." She tipped her head back and opened her mouth to catch snowflakes on her tongue. A second later, she stumbled over an uneven sidewalk slab, and I instinctively reached for her.

"Jeez, I can't take you anywhere, Miss Dempsey," I scolded, holding her by the elbow as we walked down the street.

She giggled again. "You sound like my students. Did I tell you one of them asked me the other day why I wasn't called *Mrs.* Dempsey?"

"No. What did you say?"

"I said it was because I'm not married. Then the kid asked why I wasn't married, and the girl next to him elbowed him and said, 'You shouldn't ask her that. It will make her feel old.' And the kid goes, 'She *is* old.'"

"Little shit," I said.

"Oh, it gets better. The girl tried to defend me."

"Yeah?" We reached my SUV, and I unlocked the passenger door.

"Yeah." She hiccupped before going on. "She said, 'I know she's old, but she's still pretty . . . for an old lady.'"

I laughed as I opened the door for her. "Get in, Miss Dempsey. Or should I call you Miss *Tip*sy?"

She climbed in, but leaned over and poked my chest. "Jerk."

Grinning, I walked around to the driver's side and got in. "Well, she was right," I said, starting the engine and turning up the heat. "You're very pretty for an old lady."

She batted her lashes at me and hiccupped. "Why, thank you. And you're quite attractive for an old man."

"There are definitely days when I feel like an old man," I admitted as I started the drive home. "And then there are days I feel exactly like I did at eighteen."

"Believe me, I hear you."

I drove in silence for a few minutes, one hand rubbing over the stubble on my jaw, wondering what eighteen-year-old me—or even thirty-three-year-old me—would have done with a tipsy, flirty Cheyenne Dempsey on a night like tonight, if my life had taken a different path.

But immediately I felt guilty for thinking it, so I shut my imagination down. If my life had taken a different path, I wouldn't have Mariah, and that was unthinkable.

Still, the woman next to me with the perfect lips and snow melting in her hair was right here right now, and something told me if I leaned over at this red light and kissed her, she'd let me.

As my SUV came to a stop, I looked over at her and thought about it. She met my eyes and went still.

But the light changed to green before I could make up my mind, and I focused my attention out the windshield again. Put my foot on the accelerator and left the moment behind.

We didn't talk the rest of the way home.

Out of habit, I pulled into my own garage. "Oh shit," I said. "I meant to pull in your driveway and forgot."

"I can walk," she said, unbuckling her seatbelt. "The cold air will be good for me."

"Are you sure?"

"Positive." She got out, and I followed suit, meeting up with her outside on the driveway. The snow still fell in thick, heavy flakes.

Once more, she tipped her face to the sky, although this time she just smiled. "I really love snow."

"I can tell. Come on, I'll walk you home."

She lowered her chin and opened her eyes. "Cole, you don't have to."

"I know," I said, taking her arm again, "but the driveway is slippery and I feel responsible for making sure you get home safe since I made you drink that last glass of wine."

"That's true, you did."

"See? What kind of monster would I be if I left you to stumble home alone through a foot of snow in the dark?"

"The worst kind," she agreed as we turned up the front walk to her house. "An inconsiderate cad."

"Exactly."

"Instead, as always, you are the perfect gentleman, Officer Mitchell," she said as we climbed the porch steps. "And I am very grateful."

"I don't know that I'm the *perfect* gentleman, but—"

"I do," she interrupted, turning to face me. "You've always been one of the good guys, Cole. It's just who you are."

God, she was beautiful. And warm and sweet and close, and I really just wanted to fucking make out with her right here on the porch. Taste her lips once and for all.

That's it. I'm doing it.

But just as I made up my mind, she placed a hand on my chest, rose up on her toes, and kissed my cheek. "Thanks again for dinner. I had a great time."

"No problem." As the scent from her hair—something lush that reminded me of a summer day—filled my head, I shoved my hands in my pockets. "I'll see you tomorrow."

She pulled her keys from her purse and unlocked the door. After stepping inside, she turned and gave me one last smile. "Goodnight."

"'Night." I watched her shut the door, listened to the lock click, and exhaled.

Breathing in gulps of bitter cold air, I walked back home and let myself in the back door. My mother and Mariah had already gone up to bed, but my mom had left a light on for me in the kitchen. I turned it off, made sure the house was locked up, and went upstairs.

Inside my room, I stripped out of my clothes, alternately glad nothing had happened and cursing myself for not making a move when I had the chance.

If only, I thought, stretching out beneath the covers in my boxer briefs. *If only* she wasn't my best friend's little sister. *If only*

I didn't always have to do the right thing. *If only* she didn't think I was such a perfect gentleman. *If only* I knew what was going on in her head. *If only* I could be sure that she wanted me like I wanted her, with no strings attached, no promises required, maybe I could forget everything else and just make her feel good—make us both feel good—without worrying about the past or the future or anything but right here, right now.

And I could make her feel good. I knew I could. With my hands and my mouth and my cock.

My hand was already sliding down my abdomen when I heard my phone pulse with a text, and I realized I must have forgotten to silence it.

Grabbing it off my nightstand, I checked the screen, half expecting to see a message from God warning me to stop being such a perv and get my mind out of the gutter.

Instead, I saw a text from Cheyenne.

Cheyenne: Thank you again for a perfect evening. It was exactly what I needed.

Me: You're welcome.

Cheyenne: Well, I'm already in bed, so goodnight!

Me: Night.

For a few minutes, I lay there with the phone in my hand, picturing her lying in bed, wondering if she ever touched herself and what she thought about when she did. My erection grew even thicker and harder, begging for attention.

Suddenly my phone pulsed again, and I looked at the screen.

It was a long message from Cheyenne—and what I saw made my jaw drop.

Something in me snapped.

Six

Cheyenne

I GOT READY FOR BED AND SLIPPED BENEATH THE SHEETS, feeling like my feet still hadn't touched the ground.

After all this time, he'd finally invited me to dinner, and I'd ridden alone with him in the front seat of his car, and I'd sat across from him at the most romantic restaurant in town, and I'd held his arm as he walked me home in the snow, just like in a movie. Had we kissed passionately on my front porch at the end of the night? No, but I could leave that for my dreams.

Still a little tipsy, or maybe just giddy with excitement, I decided to send him a quick text.

Me: Thank you again for a perfect evening. It was exactly what I needed.

Cole: You're welcome.

Me: Well, I'm already in bed, so goodnight!

Cole: Night.

I set my alarm and put my phone on the charger, giving my pillow a fluff before lying back and pulling the covers to my chin. Closing my eyes for a moment, I pictured Cole's blue eyes and broad shoulders, imagining what it would be like if he were next to me right now. In my head, I heard his deep, sexy voice repeating his words from last night: *Your body is fucking perfect, Cheyenne.*

God, what I wouldn't give to hear it again. This time, I'd say it right back to him.

Without thinking, I picked up my phone again and started to type a fantasy text like I had last night. Even if I never sent it—and I wouldn't, of course I wouldn't, I wasn't *that* tipsy—it would feel good to pretend I was the girl who would. To see the words on the screen. To imagine what he'd say if he ever read them. It would take the fantasy one step further.

My fingers moved frantically over the letters.

I can't sleep, because I can't stop thinking about you. This might come as a surprise, but it happens a lot. And it's been going on for years.

When I was a teenager, I used to dream about kissing you. Touching you. Feeling your body on mine in the dark. I used to lie awake and picture you in your bed next door, and I'd fantasize about sneaking into your house and up to your room. I'd have let you do anything you wanted to me.

I still would.

I could never, ever say these things out loud to you, so I'm hiding behind this text I will never send, but it's the truth.

I lie in bed at night and crave you. Your body. Your mouth. Your hands. I fantasize about them on me.

I fantasize about a lot of things.

You arrest me. Put me in handcuffs. Force me into the back of your car. Take me somewhere no one could find us.

You're angry with me for being bad. You say I need to be punished. You take that baton off your belt and rub it between my legs until I beg you to fuck me.

You'd take off your—

And it happened.

I don't know how it happened, but it happened.

I hit send.

I saw the giant blue block full of white text show up on the screen and gasped. My heart screeched to a halt and then raced ahead. I dropped the phone, covered it with the quilt, and put my hands over my face, screaming internally.

Could I get it back?

Even though I knew it wasn't possible, I frantically dug my phone from the blankets and stared at it, desperately wishing a RETRACT option would appear. Why didn't they make one of those? Imagine how much better the world would be if we had a chance to take back words we never should have said and never meant to send!

Oh God, oh God. This couldn't be happening. A sweat broke out across my neck and back and chest. I kicked my feet under the blankets in a tantrum fueled by regret and humiliation.

What was I supposed to do now?

I should apologize, right? Apologize and then beg him to forget he'd ever read those words and make him promise he'd *never speak of them again.*

Then I'd move to Montana.

No, no, that wasn't far enough.

Mumbai. That should do it.

Choking back tears of shame, I typed **OMG I AM SO SORRY! PLEASE FORGET YOU EVER—**

But before I finished what I wanted to say, my phone buzzed in my hand.

Cole: My belt.

Huh? For a second, I just stared at his text in confusion.

Then he wrote again.

Cole: My gun belt. That's what I'd take off next.

Oh.

My.

God.

Cole: If I'm in uniform and I had the baton, I must be wearing it.

My pulse roared like a freight train. My fingers trembled.

Cole: Keep going.

I took a deep breath and began to type.

Me: OMG. You were not supposed to see that.

Cole: Too late now. Are you going to tell me the rest?

Me: Do you really want to hear it?

Cole: Yes.

Biting my lip, I jumped out of bed, rushed over to my closed bedroom door, and locked it. Climbing back under the covers, I paused, my heart galloping out of control.

Could I really do this? Did he really want me to? He must, I decided. Because Cole did not play games. He didn't really flirt or even make dirty jokes. When he said something, he meant it.

And I might never get this chance again.

I tapped the blank text box, my fingers poised, my breath coming fast. But I was terrified to dive in. I had to sit next to him at the Thanksgiving dinner table tomorrow!

Cole: Did you forget where you left off?

Me: No. I have stage fright.

Cole: You were begging me to fuck you. What happens after that?

Okay. Okay. We were doing this.

I made up my mind right then to just let go.

Me: You take off your belt. Unzip your pants. You take your cock in your hand.

Cole: I'm so fucking hard.

I dropped the phone and fanned my face. Did he mean *right now*? Or in the story? Either way, my entire body flushed with heat. My nipples grew stiff and tingled with pleasure.

I picked up the phone again. I'd never sexted anyone before, but I knew this story front to back. I'd imagined every little detail.

Me: You tease me, stroking yourself and making me watch. I want you inside me.

Cole: I want your clothes off.

Me: I'm only wearing a T-shirt and panties. It's the middle of the night, remember?

Cole: Take them off.

I smiled as I typed.

Me: I can't. You cuffed me, Officer Mitchell.

Cole: Take them off. Right now.

The smile faded from my lips. I'd never heard him be so demanding before. I did what he asked and lay back.

Me: Now what?

Cole: Keep going.

I bit my lip.

Me: First tell me something. Are you really hard?

Cole: Yes.

Me: You've got me so hot, Officer. Hot and wet and desperate for you.

Cole: Spread your legs.

I did, imagining it was him pushing my knees apart.

Me: What are you going to do to me?

Cole: First I'm going to taste you. Then I'm going to fuck you.

My jaw dropped. This wasn't the path my fantasy usually took. Somehow Cole was controlling it like a Choose Your Own Adventure book.

Cole: Put your hand between your legs.

Me: I won't be able to type.

Suddenly, my phone vibrated. He was calling me.

Oh my God, he was *calling me.*

"Hello?" I whispered, pulling the covers over my head.

"Do what I say." His voice was so low I could barely hear it.

"Okay." Licking my fingers first, I reached between my thighs.

"Can you feel my mouth on you?"

I rubbed my wet fingertips over my clit in soft, slow circles, imagining it was his tongue. "Yes."

"I can taste you. I swear, I can fucking taste you." He sounded different, and not just because he had to be so quiet. There was something in his voice I'd never heard before—an urgency, a quiet intensity that had me burning up from the inside out.

"Cole," I whispered, the flames licking higher inside me. "It feels so good."

"I want to make you come."

"Yes," I whimpered, unable to believe what I was hearing, unable to stop my hips from rocking beneath my hand to the soundtrack of his heavy, ragged breath in my ear. In no time at all, I was hovering on the brink. "I'm so close."

"Me too." His voice was raw. "God, I want to fuck you."

"Do it," I breathed. "Right now. Don't stop until you come."

For a moment, I heard nothing but low, hushed sounds that turned me on even more as I imagined him struggling, like I was, to stay silent in the throes of an impending orgasm. I pictured him lying in the bed that I'd seen, his long, athletic legs stretched in front of him, his muscular chest bare, his powerful hand fisting his cock, his eyes closed, his thoughts on me.

I wished he was here. I wished we were alone. I wished I could see him and smell him and hear him and feel him driving into me. Squeezing my eyes shut, I did my best to imagine it, working my fingers expertly over my wet, swollen clit. The blankets above me muffled my strangled sighs.

"Fuck. Do you want it?" he growled with quiet intensity.

"Yes, I want it," I whispered as the tension in me coiled so tight I couldn't breathe. "I want everything."

He exhaled—one final, drawn-out rush right as my own climax hit, and I imagined his cock pulsing inside me as my body tightened rhythmically around him.

Ohmygod, ohmygod, ohmygoddddddd.

I don't know how much time passed before he spoke.

"Jesus. I don't know what to say." It was his regular voice again. As if something had clicked back into place between us.

"Don't say anything," I said quietly, terrified he was going to apologize.

"I need a minute, okay?"

"Okay."

My mind raced as I yanked my panties and T-shirt back on. What were we going to say to each other? Had we just ruined our friendship? How would we get past this?

A moment later, he was back. "Hey."

"Hey."

"So . . . that was a surprise."

"Um. Yes. It was."

Silence stretched out between us.

"I've never done that before," he said.

I relaxed a little. "Me neither."

"I feel like I should apologize, but . . . I'm not sorry."

Relief rushed through me. "I'm not sorry either. Embarrassed, but not sorry."

"Why are you embarrassed?"

"Because you were not supposed to see that text," I whispered as fiercely as I could. "I was never really going to send it."

He laughed gently. "I'm glad you did."

"You are?"

"Yes. I was lying here thinking about you in all sorts of inappropriate ways, and feeling terrible about it, and then I saw your message. It made me feel better."

"You were thinking about me?" I snuggled down beneath the covers again, happy right down to my toes.

"Yes." He paused. "I've been thinking about you a lot lately."

"Well, as you now know, I've been thinking about you a lot since I was thirteen."

He laughed again. "Stop."

"I'm serious. I'm going to take it as a compliment that I hid it so well you never knew."

"I promise you, I never knew. But I wasn't all that observant back then."

"Neither was Griffin, and I think even *he* knew."

"Speaking of your brother . . ."

"What about him?"

"I don't know. I feel weird about—what just happened. Because he's my best friend. And you're his sister."

"Well, don't. It's none of his business."

"But back in high school, he made us all promise we'd never touch you." He must have realized how ridiculous that sounded, because he laughed after he said it.

"Oh my *God.*" Shaking my head, I laughed too. "I'm a big girl, Cole. I don't need Griffin to protect me. And frankly, you were just as protective of me growing up as he was. You were nicer, too."

"I don't know about that," Cole said, loyal to his best friend.

"I do. Don't get me wrong, Griffin is a great guy and I love him to death, but as a kid he used to torment me endlessly. You were always sweet to me."

"I thought Griffin was lucky to have a little sister. All I had was a smelly older brother who used to kick the shit out of me."

"Same," I said. "I can't say Griffin was physically abusive, but he did used to do that thing where he'd pin me down and let drool hang from his mouth over my face and then suck it back in again at the last second. He made armpit noises while I'd practice piano. And he'd leave dead bugs where I'd find them in the bathroom we shared—in the sink, the shower, on the counter by my toothbrush."

"What an asshole."

"I know. It's amazing he turned into a decent human being. And for what it's worth, I don't really think he'd care about . . . what just happened. It's not like he'd think you were taking advantage of me or something. For heaven's sake, *I* started it."

He laughed a little. "You did. But I took it to the next level."

"True. But Cole . . ." I took a deep breath and said what needed to be said. "This doesn't have to change anything. I know we're just friends."

He exhaled. "You have no idea how relieved I am to hear you say that."

"It's the truth. Teenage crush aside, I think what happened tonight was just . . . letting off steam or something." It wasn't *exactly* the truth, but it was close enough. "We just got carried away."

"Yeah."

"Maybe it's the wedding that has us all worked up," I said, even though I'd been worked up over him my entire life.

"Maybe."

"And the holidays," I said. "Nothing makes you feel lonelier than pumpkin spice lattés and sweater weather. And wasn't there a full moon tonight? No wonder we're acting crazy."

There it was again—that low, sexy laugh I wanted to wrap around me like a thick, cozy robe. "It was fun, though."

"It was," I agreed.

"So we're okay?"

"We're okay. I'll see you tomorrow."

We hung up, and I set my phone on the charger. Curling into a ball beneath the blankets, I lay awake wondering if he was still thinking about me, what it would be like to see him tomorrow, and if it would truly be possible to remain *just friends* after what we'd done.

Part of me hoped it would be . . . and part of me hoped it wouldn't.

My alarm went off at seven.

For a moment, I was so groggy and disoriented I forgot what day it was, but then I remembered—Thanksgiving. I had to go downstairs and get the pies in the oven.

I sat up and stretched, my feet hanging off the side of the bed, my arms overhead. And then I remembered something else—Cole. What we'd done. The things we'd said.

My stomach whooshed, and I put both hands over it. Had it all been real? For a moment, I was scared it had been a dream. I grabbed my phone off the charger and checked my texts.

And there it was, right there on the screen. The entire night, from my first *I'm ready* before we'd gone to dinner, to my frantic *I won't be able to type* and all the messages in between.

It *had* been real.

In a pleasant, sleepy haze, I tugged on some sweats, put my hair up, and wandered down to the kitchen. My mother, always an early riser, had already made a pot of coffee.

"Morning," she said from where she sat at the kitchen table, wrapped in her robe, a Bellamy Creek Garage mug in her hand, a newspaper open in front of her.

"Morning." I took a mug from the cupboard that said WAKE UP, TEACH KIDS, BE AWESOME on it and filled it up.

"How was dinner last night?"

"Fine." I took the creamer from the fridge and added a little to my cup.

"Where'd you go?" She was trying to keep her tone casual, but her eyes had lit up like torches yesterday when I'd come home from the Mitchells' house and told her Cole and I were going out for dinner. I'd tried to downplay it, even while my heart had done its best to ram right through my rib cage, but I could tell I'd set her wheels spinning.

"DiFiore's," I answered.

She glanced over at me, her eyes assessing me above the lenses of her reading glasses. "Fancy."

"We were in the mood for Italian, that's all." I sipped my coffee. "It was very casual, just like I said it would be."

"So, not a date?"

"Not a date." *Just dinner, drinks, and phone sex.*

My mother returned her attention to the newspaper, picking up her mug. "See anyone you knew?"

"Nope."

"How was the food?"

"Good."

"Did Cole pay for dinner?" She didn't even look at me, as if she wasn't desperate for my answer. As if it wouldn't, in her mind, tell her absolutely everything she needed to know.

"Yes, he did."

"So it *was* a date, then." Her tone was smug.

I sighed. "No, Mom. It wasn't. I told you last night—Cole doesn't date."

She glanced at the ceiling, and I knew what was coming. She did that when she spoke to my late father. "You hear that, Hank? She says it wasn't a date." Then she looked at me again. "In *our* day, you see, we called it a date when a gentleman took a lady out for dinner." She cocked her head, pretending to be confused. "What does your generation call it?"

I took another sip and set my cup on the counter. "We call it being friends," I said, pulling my pie crusts and a brick of cream cheese from the refrigerator. "The end. I think I'm going to make the carrot cupcakes with brown butter icing too."

My attempt to change the subject failed. "Don't be so closed-minded, Cheyenne." My mother got up from her chair to refill her mug from the pot. "You two could be just right for each other. I don't know why I didn't think of it before. Cole might come with a little bit of baggage, but who doesn't?"

"I'm not worried about his baggage, Mom." I grabbed the bowl from beneath the aqua blue KitchenAid stand mixer, a luxury purchase of mine that pretty much summed up why I struggled to pay off my credit cards every month. The red one had been on sale, but I didn't *want* the red one. I wanted the aqua blue.

"Then what *are* you worried about?"

"I'm not worried about anything," I said, annoyed that she was ruining my good mood. I grabbed the whisk attachment from a drawer and shut it angrily with my hip.

"Then I don't understand why you're not even giving him a chance."

Inhaling and exhaling, I felt my nostrils flare as I turned to face her. Maybe the stark truth would shut her up. "If he wanted a chance with me, Mom, I'd give it to him. He doesn't."

"Nonsense," she said, shooing the idea from the air between us like it was a fly. "Why wouldn't he?"

"Because he's not interested in a relationship."

"Why not?"

"He's a single dad who works twelve-hour days, and every minute of his spare time is for his daughter. She's his number one priority." I went over to the fridge and took out the butter and eggs. "He just wants to be friends, and I'm okay with that, so you'll have to be okay with that too."

She sighed heavily. "I know he's a single father. But he's still a *man*."

"Drop it, Mom." I went to the pantry and took out a can of pumpkin.

"And you're sure you gave him all the right signals?"

"I said drop it."

"Well, I'm just wondering if maybe he doesn't know you're interested. Your romantic history suggests that successful flirtation might not be in your skill set."

I had to laugh as I started unwrapping the dough. "And what would your idea of successful flirtation be? Bat my lashes above my handheld fan? Swoon on my fainting couch? Drop my hanky and see if he picks it up?"

My mother clucked her tongue. "Go on and make fun of my old-fashioned ideas. All I'm saying is that sometimes it takes a little extra effort to get someone to see you differently."

"We see each other just fine, Mom." I gave her a pointed

look over one shoulder. "So I don't want any nonsense today. Are we clear?"

"I have no idea what you're talking about," she sniffed, looking away from me and sipping her coffee.

"Yes, you do. And I am being one hundred percent serious about this. Do not make things uncomfortable for me or for Cole. No meddling allowed."

She faked a hurt expression. "How could you even think it of me?"

"Because meddling is your favorite sport."

"It is not! Perhaps I do occasionally *get involved* when I can see things so much clearer from *my* side of the fence, but that's not the same thing as meddling."

"That is *exactly* the same thing." I pulled a rolling pin from a kitchen drawer.

"Well, I wouldn't have to do it if I could trust my kids to run their lives as well as I can," she huffed, setting her empty mug in the sink and breezing past me. "I'm going up to get dressed. And since you're so busy down here, why don't you let me choose an outfit for you today?"

"No. I am perfectly capable of dressing myself, thank you."

"Fine." She gave me one final harrumph before leaving the room. Five seconds later, she poked her head back in again. "But no jeans."

"Mom!" I brandished the rolling pin like I might whack her with it.

"You say no meddling, I say no jeans!" she yelled, disappearing from view once more.

Alone again, I took a deep breath, set down my rolling pin, and took out my phone.

Me: Is it too early for whiskey in my coffee?

Blair: LOL probably. What's up?

Me: Come over a little early if you can. I have a story for you.

Blair: Does it have a happy ending?
That made me laugh. **Actually, yes,** I typed. **It has two.**

"Wait a minute. You did *what*?" Blair, looking shocked beyond belief, sank onto my bed.

"I accidentally sexted him after we had dinner last night," I said, putting on my second gold earring and checking my reflection in the mirror. In the glass, I saw Blair shake her head.

"I don't understand how that happens."

"I was typing out this fantasy where he arrests me and then things get hot and heavy in the back seat of his cop car, and I hit send by mistake." I turned sideways, checking to see if my black sweater dress was too short. It was a chunky, off-the-shoulder style that didn't cling to my curves or anything, but it did show some thigh.

"Oh my God! Why would you even type it if you weren't going to send it?"

"For kicks. I was *pretending* I was going to send it. It was supposed to be a game."

"So he texted back?"

"Yes. And then he *called* me." I didn't bother swearing her to secrecy—with us, it was understood. Turning to face her, I gestured at my burgundy suede thigh-high boots. "Too sexy for Thanksgiving?"

"Not at all. Now stop getting ready for a minute and tell me everything before he gets here!"

Laughing, I leaned back against my dresser and folded my arms. "Let's just say he was glad I hit send and things ended up getting hot and heavy even though we weren't in the same room."

"Eeeek!" She bounced up and down on my bed. "You and Cole had phone sex!"

"Shhhhhh!" I glanced at my bedroom door, making sure it

was shut. "Be quiet. I don't want my mother to hear you. She's been insufferable since I told her Cole paid for dinner last night. Apparently, that makes it a date in her book."

"It kind of does. I mean, what else do you call it?"

"Dinner with a friend."

"Even after the phone sex?"

"Yes. We talked about it afterward, and we agreed—just friends."

"And you're okay with that?"

I shrugged. "I have to be."

Blair pouted as she crossed her arms over her chest. "I don't love this journey for you."

"It's not really a *journey*, Blair. It was more of a quick and dirty road trip."

"Why's he being so stubborn?"

"Because he doesn't have room in his life for a relationship. His heart belongs to his daughter. He likes being single."

"But . . . forever?"

"I didn't push him on the timeline. But he told me he's not interested in getting remarried and he hates the way his mother and his friends get on him about it, or act like they know what's best for him or for his daughter. I'm not going to be like that."

"No, but maybe you could—"

I cut her off. "Look, don't feel bad for me. Last night was a dream come true. I spent the evening alone with him, we did the thing on the phone, and I feel closer to him than I ever have before. We talk. We understand each other. It's enough."

She eyeballed me the way only a bestie can. "Is it?"

I sighed. "Of course not, but at this point in my life, I'm a realist, Blair. I'm thirty, not thirteen. And there's no point in sitting around mooning over what I can't have. I've been that girl, and it's no fun."

From downstairs, we heard the front doorbell ring.

"He's here!" Heart racing, I turned and checked out my reflection one last time.

Blair laughed as she rose from the foot of my bed. "You sure you're not thirteen?"

I laughed too, pulling open my bedroom door. "When it comes to Cole, sometimes I wonder."

My stomach felt like it was full of bouncing ping-pong balls as I made my way down the steps. Cole's family was standing in the front hall at the base of the staircase, so first I saw his legs, then his torso, then finally, his face.

Our eyes met.

I don't know what I expected—an awkward moment, I guess—but I was pleasantly surprised by the smile he gave me. It was warm and private, like we shared a new secret.

Which we did, of course.

The heat of his gaze and the memory of his voice in my ear rendered me motionless, and I stopped before reaching the bottom.

Blair promptly bumped into me from behind, and I heard her laugh, whispering quietly. "Just friends. Right."

Seven

Cole

MY EYES ABOUT POPPED OUT OF MY HEAD AS SHE came down the stairs.

Her hair was all tucked up into some kind of nest on the top of her head, with loose strands falling around her face. Like a ballerina fresh from a hurricane. Her shoulders were bare, and her eyes captivated mine with the secret we shared. Her full lips were colored scarlet again, and those boots—those boots should have been illegal.

I felt tongue-tied as I greeted her, and I'm pretty sure everyone noticed the way I couldn't stop staring.

Just friends, I reminded myself as she gave me a hug and I inhaled the scent of her perfume.

Just friends, I reminded myself as I sipped bourbon and mentally undressed her in the living room over hors d'oeuvres.

Just friends, I reminded myself as Mariah excitedly showed us to our places at the table and I discovered Cheyenne would be seated right next to me.

Everyone sat down in the dining room, and Cheyenne poured wine for those who wanted it. Griffin carried the platter of turkey to the table, which was already laden with vegetables, rolls, sauces, and condiments. Mrs. Dempsey removed her apron and dimmed the overhead lights. Candles in tall holders flickered on the table.

"This looks incredible, Darlene," said my mother from one end of the table. "Thank you so much for having us."

"Of course," Mrs. Dempsey said, taking her seat at the opposite end. "Thank you so much for coming. There's nothing like a traditional holiday meal with family and friends so dear they *feel* like family."

"Well said." Griffin reached for the turkey. "Let's eat."

"Wait a minute. Shouldn't we *all* say what we're thankful for?" Mariah suggested.

"Sure, honey." Darlene beamed at her. "That's a wonderful idea. Let's hold hands."

Across from me, I heard Griffin grumble, but he put down the serving fork and joined hands with Blair to his right and my mom to his left. I reached for my mother's hand on one side and Cheyenne's on the other, a jolt of electricity flowing up my arm when I felt her palm against mine. It was her right hand. Was that the one she used to—

"You start, dear," said Darlene to Mariah.

"Okay," my daughter said. "I am grateful that I get to be a junior bridesmaid in Uncle Griffin and Aunt Blair's wedding."

"We're grateful for that too," said Blair, smiling across the table.

"Your turn, Miss Cheyenne," Mariah said.

"I'm grateful for . . . good friends." Cheyenne glanced at me, and I wondered if she was thinking about what *good friends* we'd become last night.

It was my turn next. I cleared my throat and frantically tried to think of something other than Cheyenne's hand between her legs.

"I'm grateful for my job," I blurted, even though I knew it was lame. But what could I say? The things I truly felt appreciative of right now—Cheyenne's accidental sext, the rush of her breath in my ear as I imagined her body beneath mine, the fact that somehow this morning I'd woken up a little less lonely than I had the day before—were not things I could announce over roasted Brussels sprouts and sweet potato mash. My job would have to do.

"And we're grateful you keep us all safe," said Darlene warmly.

My mother spoke up next. "Well, I already said how thankful I am to be here, but I'll say it again—it's just so heartwarming to know that our families have been here for each other, through good times and bad, for so many years now."

"I'll second that," Darlene crowed. "It *has* been a long time, hasn't it?"

"Twenty-seven years," my mom said. "We moved right before Cole started kindergarten."

"That's right." Darlene shook her head, her eyes misting over. "I'll never forget that first day. Griffin and Cole were so cute with their crisp new jeans and little superhero lunch boxes. Inseparable from the start. And you're so right—we've all seen each other through many wonderful occasions and some sad ones. But we're still here together, and that's what counts. That's loyalty."

"Are we ever going to eat?" Griffin said, eyeing the turkey again.

Darlene clucked her tongue. "Patience, please. It's your turn."

"I'm grateful only one more person has to speak after me," Griffin announced, "because I'm hungry and the food looks amazing."

"Booooo," Blair scolded, elbowing him in the ribs. "I'll speak for both of us and say that we could not be more thankful for everyone around this table, and we're so happy you'll all be there in two weeks when we tie the knot."

"Cheers to that!" my mother said, letting go of my hand to pick up her wine glass. "There's nothing like a wedding to remind us all of the importance of love, commitment, and family!"

"You're absolutely right, Barb." Darlene lifted her wine glass too. "To love, commitment, and starting a family!"

"That's not exactly what she said, Ma," Cheyenne muttered under her breath, but I was probably the only one who could hear over the chorus of cheers and clinking glasses.

After everyone took a drink and began reaching for serving dishes, she and I exchanged a look and another inside joke of a smile.

Mothers, she mouthed.

Motherfucker, I mouthed back.

She laughed, tipping her head back like she'd done last night, and I wished more than anything that I could take her hand again. Kiss the back of it. Hold it on my lap under the table.

But I couldn't.

Just friends, I told myself again. *You are just friends because you like being single.*

But I was beginning to like her more.

After coffee and dessert, Griffin and I moved into the den with after-dinner drinks to watch football, while Mariah, Blair, and Cheyenne stayed at the table and chattered nonstop about the wedding. My mother and Darlene began clearing the dishes, talking about who'd said what at the sewing circle last week, how my older brother Greg and his family were doing since he'd been transferred to Tokyo for a year, and whether the forecast for a lot more snow this week might deter some wedding guests from driving up to Cloverleigh Farms.

From my seat on the couch, I had a perfect view of Cheyenne's back, and every now and again, she glanced at me over her shoulder.

"I heard you're looking at buying a house," Griffin said during a commercial break.

"From Moretti?"

He nodded. "He came in for an oil change yesterday."

"Yeah. I think it's time Mariah and I got our own place."

"I agree. Good for you, man. I don't know how you've been living back at home for so long. I'm here for an hour and I get hives."

Tearing my eyes off Cheyenne, I took a sip of my bourbon, but when I heard her laugh, I looked again. She was giggling at something Mariah had said, but she must have felt my eyes on her because she glanced back and gave me that flirty little smile, the one that made me feel like she could read my mind.

"Christ, Cole." Griffin laughed as he swirled whiskey around in his glass. "Why don't you ask her out already?"

My pulse tripped. "What do you mean?"

"I mean, it's pretty obvious there's something going on between you and Cheyenne."

"There's nothing going on." My lip twitched, as it always did when I told a lie, and I tried to cover it with my glass.

"I'm totally fine with it, whatever you want to do."

"I don't want to do anything," I said, more irritably than necessary, because I was caught in my own deceit. I wasn't used to hiding things from Griffin, and it felt weird.

"Okay." Griffin held up his palm. "I'm just making sure you know it's cool with me, in case you were worried about how I felt."

"I wasn't." Another lie.

Griffin had known me a long time, which meant he probably knew I was full of shit, but it also meant that he knew not to push it. "No worries either way," he said, turning back to the game.

But the exchange had left a bitter taste in my mouth, and I felt uncomfortable the rest of the night. *This is exactly why you should not mess around with your best friend's sister,* I reminded myself. Even with permission, it made things awkward.

Later, we stood waiting in the living room while Darlene went upstairs to get the coats. When she returned, everyone reached for theirs, myself included. But rather than put it on, I stood motionless, mesmerized as Cheyenne stretched with her arms over her head, which caused the hem of her dress to rise. At least another two inches of her thighs appeared. I might have drooled.

Then she sighed, dropping her arms. "You sure you guys can't stay longer? If you leave, that means it's time for me to do the dishes."

"Now?" Mariah asked as she buttoned up her coat. "Can't you just do them in the morning?"

Cheyenne ruffled her hair. "Nope. Gotta get them done tonight."

"Don't you have a dishwasher?"

"We do, but the good dishes—the wedding china, we call it—all have to be done by hand to be sure they don't break. They're too old and delicate for the dishwasher."

Darlene spoke up. "*My* mother passed them down to me, and I want to make sure they're in good condition so I can leave them to Cheyenne when *she* gets married." Then she crossed herself and closed her eyes, her lips moving in a quick, silent prayer.

Cheyenne ignored her mother and addressed Mariah again. "My brother and I always had to wash and dry the wedding china on holidays before we went to bed. It took forever."

"I'd stay and help you, sis, but I have to get Blair home. Sorry." Griffin gave her a grin that said he wasn't the least bit sorry, and Cheyenne stuck her tongue out at him.

"Cole, why don't you stay and give Cheyenne a hand?" My mother suggested, wrapping her scarf around her neck.

"That's a great idea," Darlene said brightly. Then she sort of bent over and rubbed one hip, her expression agonized. "I'd help her myself but I've been on my feet a lot today and the doctor said that isn't good for my joints."

"You should just get to bed, Darlene," my mother said, shepherding Mariah toward the front door. "Cole will be more than happy to stay and help Cheyenne."

"Oh, that's okay." Cheyenne smiled at me and shook her head. "I can handle them."

But Darlene beamed at me, reaching over and snatching my coat out of my hands. "That's *so* nice of you, Cole. I'll just hang this in the front closet." Before she left the room, she and my mother exchanged a look that had me wondering if the whole helping-with-the-dishes thing had been a setup.

Either way, ten minutes later Cheyenne and I were pushing up our sleeves in the kitchen, the house dark and silent except for the running faucet and the hum of the dishwasher.

"I'll wash, you dry?" she asked, adding dish soap to the side of the sink she'd plugged and lined with a towel.

"Sure."

She took a plate from the stack to her left and placed it in the warm soapy water. "Oh! I almost forgot." Slipping her rings and bracelets off, she set them on the windowsill above the sink. "So I don't scratch anything," she explained.

"Oh." I glanced down at my wedding ring.

"It's okay," she said quickly. "You don't have to take it off."

"It's fine," I said, working it off my finger and placing it on the sill next to her jewelry. For some reason, I felt compelled to explain why I still wore it all the time. "Mariah once told me she likes when I wear it, so . . ."

"I think it's nice," she said. "I like a guy who wears his ring. It says something about him, you know?"

I nodded, my attraction to her growing even stronger. "Still, we'd better be careful with these dishes."

"Damn right, we'd better," she deadpanned. "This is my

fucking wedding china, Cole. If we even *look* at it wrong, I might end up a spinster." She laughed as she gently scrubbed the plate with a cloth. "My God. Is she not totally ridiculous?"

"She's pretty bad," I agreed, taking the plate from her and carefully drying it with the soft clean towel she'd given me. "But mine wasn't much better tonight. Did you have the feeling something was up between them as we were saying goodnight?"

"*Yes*," she said. "And it's probably my fault because I made the mistake of telling my mom you bought me dinner last night. In her mind, I believe we are now betrothed."

I laughed. "That's all it takes, huh?"

"Apparently. Tomorrow I'll be pregnant because we washed dishes together after dark."

"Wow. Guess I should have worn the rubber gloves."

She snort-laughed. "Right."

"Good thing they don't know about the phone call last night."

Her body tensed, and then she giggled shyly. "Um, yes. A very good thing."

We worked in silence for a minute, during which I was entirely too aware of how close she stood.

"I thought it might be weird today," she said, her voice a little quieter. A confession. "Seeing you."

"I worried about that too."

"But . . . it wasn't." She handed me another plate. "I mean, maybe it was a *little* weird sitting next to you at the table with our families right there, because I kept thinking about it, even though I was trying not to—"

"Same," I confessed.

She stopped what she was doing and looked over at me. "Really? You were thinking about it too?"

"Every fucking minute." The tension between us pulled taut, and I knew I had to say something to diffuse it or I'd end up kissing her. I cleared my throat. "But you were right."

"About what?"

I focused on drying the plate in my hand, even though it was already dry. "About staying friends."

"Oh. Of course," she said, starting to wash the same dish again. "Absolutely. Friends."

"Which is why we can't—shouldn't—mess around."

"No. Definitely not." She handed me the plate without looking at me. "It would only confuse things."

"Right," I said, and I should have been glad that she agreed so easily, but somehow I wasn't. Had I been expecting, or hoping, that she would argue?

"I mean, we're going to be seeing a lot of each other, with the wedding and the holidays and all," she went on. "The last thing we need is to create an awkward situation. And our mothers are already driving us crazy. Why throw fuel on that fire, right?"

But the only fire I could feel was the one burning inside me. I set the plate down without drying it. "Cheyenne."

"And like we said last night, what happened was just a momentary lapse in sanity," she said, as if she hadn't heard me. "Letting off steam. A one-time thing." She reached for another plate, but I grabbed her wrist.

"Cheyenne."

Her eyes met mine. Her lower lip trembled. "It won't happen again."

But it was too late—in an instant my mouth was on hers. If there were words of protest on her lips, I didn't want to hear them. If making out with her in the kitchen was the worst idea I'd ever had, I didn't want to know it. If I was going to be sorry on the other side of this kiss, I didn't fucking care. I wanted this. I *needed* this.

I needed *her*.

I let go of her wrist and took her head in my hands as my tongue searched for hers. Her wet hands found their way up my chest, and she clutched my shirt, her fists curling inside the material. I moved my fingers into her hair and kneaded them against her scalp, loosening the bun so that pins clattered to the kitchen's wood floor.

I changed the angle of my head, deepening the kiss, a sound of frustration tearing from somewhere in my chest. I ran my palms down her shoulder blades and lower back, pulling her in tighter against me. She looped her arms around my neck until her chest was crushed to mine, and I couldn't resist sliding my hands lower, grabbing her ass.

Now our lower bodies were pressed together as well, my erection trapped between us, pushing against her pelvic bone. Without thinking, I turned her back to the counter and rocked my hips, grinding against her. My mouth moved down her throat, eliciting a tiny moan from her that ratcheted my blood pressure up even higher. She reached for my belt. I yanked up her dress. She jumped up onto the counter.

At the sound of the splintering crash, we both gasped.

"Oh, fuck." I stared at the shattered plate on the floor and then looked at Cheyenne. "Oh fuck, I'm so sorry."

"Shit!" she shrieked, sliding off the counter and dropping to her knees next to the shards. "Shit, shit, shit."

I went down next to her, but all we could do was gaze mournfully at the broken wedding china. "It was my fault," I said. "I'll take the blame."

"It wasn't your fault, Cole."

"I started it," I argued.

"I wanted it."

"I pushed you against the counter."

"I *jumped* onto the counter."

I shook my head at the mess. "Your mom is going to kill you."

"She'll get over it." But her bottom lip was caught between her teeth as she gathered up the bigger pieces. "It's just a plate."

"I don't think it was just a plate to her."

"Well, it was supposed to be *my* plate eventually," she said, dumping the pieces into the trash beneath the sink. "Although she'll probably be so mad at me, she'll decide Blair and Griffin should have the set."

As if on cue, Darlene Dempsey appeared in the kitchen doorway in her robe, cold cream all over her face. I'd have laughed if the situation hadn't been so serious. She glanced at the remains of the plate on the floor and put a hand over her heart. "Don't tell me."

"I'm sorry, Mom. It just slipped out of my hands," said Cheyenne. "I'll replace it."

"You can't replace it. They don't even make this pattern anymore." She shook her head. "How could you be so careless, Cheyenne?"

"I'm sorry," Cheyenne repeated. "It just . . . slipped."

"It was my fault, Mrs. Dempsey," I said. "I knocked it off the counter."

Darlene folded her arms over her chest and regarded us both with narrowed eyes, as if we'd just gotten caught sneaking in after curfew. She tapped her slippered foot. "Well, which is it? Who broke the plate?"

"I did," we both answered at once. Then we glared at each other and whispered, "*I* did."

"Oh, for heaven's sake." Darlene took a deep breath, gathering herself up. "Well, accidents happen. But when you have something precious in your hands, you need to hold on tight. Understand?"

"Yes," Cheyenne said quietly, while I nodded.

Darlene put a hand to her ear. "I didn't hear you."

"Yes," we both answered loudly.

After a heavy sigh, she looked back and forth between us. "Can I trust you two to finish the rest without breaking anything else?"

"Yes," we answered together again.

"Good." Darlene swept dramatically out of the kitchen doorway and left us alone again.

The moment she was gone, Cheyenne and I looked at each other and started to laugh, trying hard to stay quiet so her mom wouldn't hear us.

"Got a broom?" I asked, feeling much lighter.

Cheyenne nodded, wiping tears. "In the pantry."

I went over to the pantry and pulled out the dustpan and broom. "Let me," I said, when she reached for them.

"Cole, you don't have to—"

"I know," I said, sweeping the bits and dust into a neat pile before bending down to brush it into the dustpan. "But this is good practice for me, right? For when I have my own house."

She watched me dump the mess into the trash, leaning back against the counter. "You think it's bad luck?"

"That the first time I kiss you, we destroy a piece of your mother's wedding china? Yes, that is some bad luck." I replaced the broom and dustpan in the pantry and shut the door.

"Not that. I mean, maybe that too, but do you think it's bad luck that I broke what was supposed to be *my* wedding china? Is it a sign I'm doomed to be single forever?"

I turned to see her biting one thumbnail. "No. I don't think that at all."

"But what if the universe is telling me something?"

"Like what?"

She shrugged helplessly. "I can't have nice things?"

Her face was so despondent, I couldn't resist tugging her hand, pulling her into a hug. "Hey. Come here."

She moved forward into my embrace, wrapping her arms around my waist. Her cheek pressed against my chest, and I kissed her head before resting my chin on top of it. It felt so fucking good to hold someone like that—protectively, a little possessively, almost as if she was mine.

"You deserve all the nice things," I told her. "What the

universe was telling us tonight is that maybe going at each other while we were supposed to be washing your mother's most fragile dishes wasn't the best idea we've ever had."

She laughed a little, the sound muffled against my shirt. "Maybe not."

"And maybe what we should do is just . . . slow down. Make sure we know what we're doing. Mistakes—and accidents—happen when people get careless and move too fast."

She looked up at me. "So the universe was giving us a speeding ticket?"

"More like letting us off with a warning."

She sighed, replacing her cheek against my chest. "You're probably right."

I didn't want to let her go, so I didn't. I kept talking, stroking her back. "I just don't want to do something that . . . can't be undone," I told her. "Something that seems like a good idea in the moment, but turns out to be wrong for everyone."

"I know. I don't want that either."

"I love having you in our lives, Chey. That makes this complicated. If I only had to think about what *I* want right this second, believe me—it would be so easy."

She laughed a little, although it was a sad kind of laugh, tinged with regret for what couldn't be. "Yeah."

I stopped moving my hand and pulled her even closer. Her body was soft and warm, and I'd never wanted anyone so badly. "So fucking easy."

In my arms, her body stilled, and she inhaled, like she needed to breathe in enough of me to last her a while. "Can I ask you something?" Her voice was quiet.

"Anything."

Another deep breath. "Do you ever see things being different for you? I mean, do you ever see a juncture in your life where you might feel differently about . . . about letting someone in?"

I knew what she meant, and I wanted so fucking badly to

be able to offer her something—anything—that would give her hope. But I couldn't, not without sugarcoating the truth at best and lying at worst. And Cheyenne deserved so much better. Why should she hang around waiting for me to change my mind about getting involved in a serious relationship—which might never happen anyway—when she could have everything she wanted if she moved on?

I swallowed hard, and instead of answering her question, I told her a story. "When Mariah was about five, I made her a promise. She asked me if I was ever going to get married again and leave her behind, and I said no. Apparently, someone at school whose parents were divorced had been talking about their dad getting remarried and moving away to have a new family—it scared her."

"Poor thing."

"Anyway, I promised her that was never going to happen to us. That's when she told me she likes that I wear my wedding ring. I think it reassures her."

"Of course."

"I thought she'd forgotten all about that conversation we had back then, but last year—this was when I asked you for a recommendation for a therapist—my mom was cleaning her room and found this letter she'd written to me but never showed me."

Cheyenne tilted her head back and met my eyes. "What was in it?"

"A lot of things—questions about Trisha, about her death, wondering if she was to blame, wondering if somehow there had been a mistake and her mom wasn't *really* gone." I shook my head, my heart breaking all over again. "Again, she expressed her fear that she was going to lose me—either to an accident or another family. She described this nightmare that she has often, in which she wakes up one morning and I'm just gone. She's alone in the house, and she realizes that everything I've said has been a lie—I *did* leave her."

"Oh, Cole." Her eyes grew shiny. "I'm so sorry. Did the therapist help?"

"Yes. Eventually, the therapist got Mariah talking about her fears, even about the letters she wrote but never sent. Apparently it's healthy and normal, functioning sort of like a diary. A safe place to express her feelings."

"That makes sense. Did she ever talk to you about what was in the letters?"

"No. And I didn't want to confront her with what I knew because it felt wrong—like a violation of her privacy. But it also tore me up inside. I want her to know she'll never lose me." My chest grew tight. "When I brought her home from the hospital, I set my feelings aside and made a promise to her and to myself that I'd give her all I had. I'd be the best father I could. I'd go above and beyond to protect her, even if it continued to mean setting my feelings aside."

Cheyenne smiled sadly. "You can't get involved in anything that would hurt or scare your child. I understand."

Knowing I had to let her go, I kissed her forehead and released her. "You're one in a million, Cheyenne. And you deserve the guy who can put you first, give you all the nice things, and never let you down."

She sniffed. "Ha. Does that guy exist?"

"Yes. And someday I will probably kick myself for not saying it's me." I cradled her face in my hands. "But I'll always be here for you."

She looked away, but not before a tear slipped down her cheek. "Thanks."

I dropped my arms, feeling like the biggest dick on the planet. How had I fucked this up? A few minutes ago, we'd been laughing.

"You don't have to stay," she said, adjusting her dress and then her hair. "I can finish up on my own."

"Are you sure?"

"I'm positive. I should probably just get it done without any distractions."

"I understand. I'll let myself out."

"Okay, thanks." She offered me a half-smile and turned toward the sink, and it took every ounce of strength I had not to wrap my arms around her again.

I was walking away from her when she called out to me.

"Cole, wait."

I turned. "Yeah?"

"Your ring. You forgot it." She came toward me, holding my wedding band in soapy fingers.

"Oh." Shocked, I took it from her and slipped it on. "Thanks."

Her smile was forced. "No problem. 'Night." She faced the sink again.

I walked out of the kitchen, wishing I could flip the dining room table on my way to the front door.

Ten minutes later, I got into bed with the scent of her still on my hands and in my head. *Don't do it*, I scolded, as my fingers stole beneath the waistband of my boxer briefs. *She deserves more than starring in your adolescent fantasies*, I thought, gripping my swollen cock. *She deserves someone who can give her what she wants, just like you said*, I told myself, slipping my flesh through my palm. *The more you think about her like this, the more you want her like that. And you can't have her*, I repeated silently as I worked myself into a frenzy, fucking my fist like I wished I could fuck her.

You can't have her.

You can't have her.

You can't have her.

I exploded in a hot rush of fury and desperation and desire, agonizing that there was no way to be two men at once, to keep my promises and have her to myself.

Nothing seemed fair.

Eight

Cole

I HADN'T SLEPT WELL, AND I WAS DRAGGING WHEN MORETTI picked Mariah and me up the next afternoon at one o'clock. We piled into his car—Mariah liked his SUV better than mine because it was a Mercedes, which she insisted was superior to my trusty old Dodge Durango. You only had to push a button to start it, it smelled new, and it had a sunroof.

"It's freezing cold," I told her irritably. "We can't even open it."

"The hell we can't," said Moretti, turning up the heat and opening the sunroof. "It's not even snowing today."

Mariah laughed. "Yay! Dad, can we get a new car with our new house?"

"No. Now buckle your seatbelt back there."

"Jeez, you're cranky today," Mariah muttered. She was aggravated with me because I'd said no to inviting Cheyenne to the movies with us tonight. My reasons—it was a tradition just the two of us shared, I wanted some father-daughter time, Cheyenne probably had plans anyway—were not to her satisfaction, and she'd marched up to her room after the argument and hidden out in there until it was time to go.

My mother had annoyed me too this morning, dropping all kinds of hints about Cheyenne, wanting to know how things had gone last night, remarking again and again on how beautifully she'd grown up, what a sweet daughter she was, how much Mariah loved her. Finally, I'd gotten tired of it and locked myself in my room just like Mariah had. I didn't need anyone to tell me how amazing Cheyenne was. It wasn't that I hadn't noticed she was beautiful and sweet and great to Mariah—and beyond that, I knew she had a dirty mind and she sometimes imagined doing filthy things with me—it was that I couldn't *do* anything about it.

And *that* was driving me fucking insane.

Our first appointment was at the house nearest to my mom's, a stout brick colonial with three bedrooms, two bathrooms, a den off the back, and a kitchen that looked like it had last been remodeled while Reagan was in the White House. It was okay, but I didn't get a *feeling* when I walked through it that told me I'd live there.

We shook hands with the agent, a woman named Florence Billingsly with a towering beehive hairdo whom I recognized as a town council member and Bellamy Creek Historical Society volunteer. She asked after my mother and made sure to emphasize how close we'd be to her house if we lived here. "Why, you wouldn't even have to *call* her to borrow a cup of sugar," Mrs. Billingsly said with a laugh. "You could just walk right over."

I shuddered.

"So what did you think?" Moretti asked as we drove away.

"I don't know," I said, craning my neck to look at the Dempseys' house as we drove past it. Was Cheyenne home? Was she thinking about me? "Some of those kitchen appliances are older than we are."

"They could easily be replaced," he said reasonably. "The bones of that house are good." As a builder, Moretti was used to looking beneath a house's cosmetic appearance to the foundational structure.

"The deck in the back looked a little warped, didn't it?"

"Another easy fix," Moretti replied. "We can replace those boards. Or better yet, tear the whole thing off and build a new one in a weekend."

"It's *really* close to my mom's."

Moretti laughed. "I can't help you there."

The next one was only a few blocks off the lake, almost walking distance and definitely biking distance to the public beach. Mariah liked one of the bedrooms, which was painted a pale blue with an underwater mural scrolling across three walls. "A mermaid room," she gushed. "And it has its own bathroom right there! I wouldn't even have to go down the hall."

The kitchen was definitely an improvement over the previous one, but the house was slightly newer construction—about fifteen years old compared to fifty—and Moretti wasn't as confident in its bones. The central stairway seemed to tilt slightly to one side, and when we checked out the back of the house, he said the gutters had obviously been dumping water right next to the foundation for years, the yard wasn't graded properly, and I was definitely looking at replacing the roof soon. "They went cheap on those shingles," he said, shaking his head. "You might get another couple years out of them, but that's it."

On our way out, we stopped in the kitchen to say goodbye to the agent, who was doing a crossword puzzle at the table. He wore a cardigan sweater and bow tie, and his name was Moe Kravitz. He was an old-timer, retired from the Post Office, and he'd taken up real estate after his wife died a few years back. Confidentially, he whispered behind one hand, he thought this one was overpriced.

"I think you're right," said Moretti, looking over the spec sheet.

Moe looked pleased someone agreed with him. "And what's your name?" he asked Mariah.

"Mariah Mitchell," she recited.

"And how old are you?"

"I'm nine."

"That's a wonderful age," he said. He shuffled over to a brief-case on the counter, opened it up and took out a Dum Dum sucker. "Would you like a lollipop?"

Mariah looked at me dutifully. "Can I have it?"

"Sure," I said, stifling a yawn.

Moe handed it to her, and she thanked him. "You know, there's a beautiful old house that just came on the market over on Rosebud Lane," he went on. "I forget who has the listing, but it's real nice. Needs a little TLC, maybe, but the lot's terrific and it seems to me the price is right."

"We're actually headed there now," Moretti told him, fold-ing the spec sheet. "It's Joy Frankel who has that listing."

Moe nodded enthusiastically. "Yup, yup. That's it. It was Charlie Frankel who told me about it last week at the Rotary Club meeting. That's his daughter-in-law."

"Right." Moretti caught my eye and jerked his head toward the front door, and I got the message—we had to get out of here, or Moe was going to want to talk forever. He held out his hand. "Thanks for showing us the house, Moe."

"Oh, sure." Moe shook Moretti's hand and then mine, but kept right on talking. "Joy's the one who won that beautification award from the Historical Society for the work she did on those flower beds out in front of the general store."

"Is she?" Moretti said absently as he steered Mariah out of the kitchen by the shoulders.

Moe followed us. "Yup. Yup. Fine job she did there. She's married to Chuckie Frankel. Remember when he hit that home run to win the state tournament back in, ohhh, what was it, sev-enty-nine or so?"

"Can't say that I do, but I've heard the story." Moretti pushed the front door open and herded Mariah and me through it. "Well, we should go. I don't want to leave Joy waiting."

"Right. Enjoy your afternoon!" Moe stood on the front stoop of the house, waving at us as we got into the car like a grandpa saying farewell after a Sunday visit.

"What a nice old man," Mariah said from the back seat, tearing the wrapper off her sucker.

"He is, but he'll gab your ear off," Moretti said, starting the car. "And I don't think that's the house you want."

"It's not," I agreed, yawning again. "I don't mind some manual labor, but I really don't want to have to buy a new roof so soon. Or deal with water in the basement. Or a crooked staircase."

"This next one should be better, at least structurally," Moretti said. "It's at the top of your price range because it's got four bedrooms, more square footage, and it's on a huge lot, but we can probably get them to come down a little since it needs some cosmetic work. No deck, but like I said, we can build one in a weekend. And it's definitely far enough away from your mom to avoid unannounced drop-in's."

"Not even the moon is that far," I mumbled.

As we headed west, we passed the elementary school Mariah attended. "That's my school!" she said.

"Oh yeah? What grade are you in now?" Moretti asked.

"Fourth. Miss Cheyenne teaches kindergarten there too."

I pictured her there, sitting with her little students on a colorful rug, reading them a story, teaching them to add and subtract, making construction paper turkeys. She was probably a great teacher. I bet the kids adored her.

She was a great kisser too. I propped an elbow on the door and rubbed my thumb along my lower lip, recalling that bourbon-and-pumpkin-pie-flavored kiss last night—her mouth beneath mine, her hands fisted in my shirt, our bodies pressed together. It seemed unreal, like a dream. My eyes drifted shut, and next thing I knew, my head nodded and I jerked myself awake.

"Hey. Everything okay?"

The SUV was stopped at a red light, and Moretti was looking at me. I straightened up in the passenger seat and ran a hand over my hair. "Yeah."

"You seem kind of out of it today."

"I'm tired. Didn't sleep well last night."

"Why not?"

"A lot on my mind, I guess."

The light turned green, and he focused on the road again. "How about a beer when we're done?"

"I'm taking Mariah to the movies tonight, but we could go for a beer before dinner. Just have to drop Mariah off at home first and check with my mom."

"Cool." Then he squinted, his neck elongating as he pulled up in front of the house for sale and stared out the windshield at a car parked in front of it on the street. "What the . . ." He groaned, long and loud. "No fucking way."

Mariah gasped in the back seat. "Uncle Enzo, you said a bad word."

"Sorry, Mariah. It's just that . . . what the hell is *she* doing here?"

"Who?" I looked at the charcoal gray Audi in front of us. The license plate read BDR.

"Bianca DeRossi." Moretti's tone was venomous.

"Who's Bianca DeRossi?" Mariah wondered. "She has a fancy name."

"She's a real big pain in the"—he stopped himself and reconsidered—"*culo*."

"What's a *culo*?" Mariah asked.

"Never mind," I said. "What's your problem with her?"

Moretti glanced in the back seat. "I'm not sure I can say without using some salty language. Can I swear in Italian?"

"Just give me the highlights. The PG version please."

Moretti grimaced. "Her family and mine are friends, and she was kind of close to my sister Eva, but she and I have never gotten along."

"Did we go to school with her?" I asked, trying to recall a Bianca DeRossi.

"No, she went to St. Mary's," he said, naming a nearby all-girls Catholic school. "So I only saw her at church or when our families got together."

"Why didn't you get along?"

"Because she was an evil little redheaded snot who thought she was too good to talk to me. My parents made me take her to a dance at St. Mary's once, and she didn't speak to me the entire night. She brought a book with her, for God's sake! And she read it the whole time!"

I laughed for the first time all day. "I think I remember that."

"She also insulted my"—again, he glanced toward the back seat, then cleared his throat—"my *man*hood."

"She's familiar with it?"

"No! That's the thing. Maybe we used to run around without clothes on or something when we were babies"—Mariah giggled at that—"but definitely not since. Yet she took it upon herself to disparage me in front of a whole group of friends at St. Mary's—one of whom I later, uh, *familiarized*—and *she* told me what Bianca said." He straightened up in the driver's seat and held up one finger. "I'd also like to mention that the friend said Bianca was wrong."

I rolled my eyes and grabbed the door handle. "Good. So it's all ancient history. Can we go in now?"

"No! It's not ancient history. Because the evil, lying red-headed viper moved home from Chicago last year and has proceeded to outbid me on every house I've wanted to buy and flip since. She's ruthless."

"She's a realtor?"

"She's an interior designer, I think." He smirked. "The only justice is that she's still about the size of a ten-year-old girl. Her nickname was Tiny, although if I remember correctly, she hated it."

"I think it's cute," said Mariah.

Moretti glared at her. "Well, she isn't cute. She's like a killer bee—small and mean. I bet her *culo* has a stinger in it."

I shook my head and opened the door. "Come on."

As we headed up the front walk, I took note of the house's exterior. It was an old brick farmhouse with a wraparound porch on one side, empty of furniture for the winter and in desperate need of a paint job. But I immediately pictured it with a fresh coat of white and two rocking chairs, or maybe a glider swing, and an emerald lawn stretching out in front of it. It lifted my mood.

We climbed the porch steps, but before we could knock, the door was pulled open by a woman who was definitely not tall, fifty-something Joy Frankel. This woman was our age and short—five feet nothing—with wavy auburn hair that barely skimmed her shoulders and bright blue eyes behind glasses with thick black frames.

"Oh, hello," she said, smiling at me and then Mariah. Then her eyes fell on Moretti, and recognition flickered. "Enzo. What a surprise."

"Bianca," he said stiffly. "In the market for a new house?"

"Oh, you know," she said airily, tugging on black leather gloves. "I'm always on the lookout for an investment opportunity. What about you?"

"We're looking for a house."

"How nice." She smiled wider, her eyes moving back and forth between Moretti and me. She held out her gloved hand. "I'm an old family friend, Bianca DeRossi."

"Cole Mitchell," I said, shaking her hand. "And this is my daughter, Mariah."

Bianca smiled at her. "What a beautiful name."

"I like yours too," Mariah said shyly.

"My mother never mentioned that you got married," Bianca said to Moretti. "Congratulations."

Moretti scowled. "We're not married."

She patted his shoulder. "It's okay, Enzo. Love is love. You don't have to be ashamed."

"I'm not ashamed!" he yelled at her back as she headed down off the porch. "And I'm not in love with Cole!"

Bianca turned around and walked backward for a few steps, a huge smile on her face. "Really, you're a *gorgeous* couple. You should come by the house sometime. My parents would love to meet your new family. Best wishes to you both!"

"Go to hell!"

She winked at me. "Nice to meet you, Cole. Congrats on tying the knot—Enzo here is quite a catch. Just ask him."

I couldn't help laughing as she walked to her car, but Moretti was seething. "See what I mean?"

"Oh, relax. She was kidding," I said, wondering if I'd just met the one woman on earth who was immune to Enzo Moretti's smoldering good looks and charismatic charm.

Joy Frankel appeared in the doorway. "Hello," she said. "Have you been waiting long? I'm so sorry—I was on the phone. Chuckie just called asking about lunch. I swear, the man is fifty-seven years old and still doesn't know how to make himself a sandwich. Please come in."

We entered the front hall, and she held out her hand to me. "Cole, right? Or should I call you Officer Mitchell?"

"Cole is fine," I said, shaking her hand.

"Enzo Moretti. We spoke on the phone." Moretti held out his hand. "Cole and I are just friends," he added quickly.

"How nice." Joy shook Moretti's hand and turned to Mariah. "And who's this young lady?"

"This is my daughter, Mariah," I said. "We're the ones looking at the house."

"Wonderful," she said. "Let's have a look around."

Straight ahead was a staircase; to the left, the living room. It was empty of furniture, and the floor was carpeted in a matted, ugly brown. But there was something about the room I liked—maybe it was the high ceilings or the original wood paneling. Maybe it was the fireplace or the arched entryway into the dining room. This house had character. I could feel it.

"Sorry about the carpet," Joy said. "But I promise, beneath it is a gorgeous original wood floor just dying to be polished. You can see it if you pull back the carpet a little. Go on, take a look."

Moretti wandered over to the corner of the room as Joy handed me a spec sheet. "It's four bedrooms, two full baths upstairs," she said. "But there's plenty of room to expand on the first level. You could build a fabulous master suite."

"Cole. Take a look at this."

I walked over to where Moretti had peeled back the musty old carpet to reveal the original wood floor. "Oh. Wow."

"This floor will refinish like a dream," Moretti said with confidence.

"I agree," said Joy. "The same floor is in the dining room, but at some point it was covered with linoleum."

Moretti groaned. "What is *wrong* with people?"

Joy laughed. "Wait 'til you see the wallpaper in the bedrooms."

Joy was right—the wallpaper in the bedrooms was ridiculous, and the upstairs carpeting was in the same sad shape as the downstairs. But the rooms were spacious, with high ceilings, big windows, and fairly big closets for an old house.

The master bedroom had a fireplace and its own bathroom, and there was a second full bath off the second-floor hallway. Both baths had black-and-white tiled floors, white tiles halfway up the walls, pedestal sinks, and clawfoot tubs. It was a bit like stepping into a time machine.

"As you can see, the bathrooms need a bit of updating," Joy said sheepishly.

"No, I like this tub," said Mariah, climbing into it.

Eventually, we made our way back downstairs to look at the kitchen, which had been updated at some point, but would still need a fairly big remodel. I was ready to tell Moretti and Joy that this was just too much of a project, when we went into the backyard.

That's when I got it—the feeling I would live there.

The property, blanketed with snow, seemed magical and endless, stretching all the way back to the woods. It was quiet and peaceful. "The creek runs right through the trees back there," said Joy. "It's frozen now, but I bet in the spring, you could hear it."

There was plenty of room for a beautiful deck or stone patio, maybe even a pool if I could ever afford it. I imagined ball games on the lawn in summer and building a whole family of snowmen in the winter. Maybe we could even put in an ice rink.

It would take a ton of work, lots of money, and all my spare time. But what else did I have to spend it on?

"Daddy, look!" Mariah pointed to the dilapidated doghouse over to one side. She turned to Joy. "Does a dog live in there?"

"Not anymore," Joy said with a smile.

"But it comes with the house, right?"

Joy laughed. "Definitely."

Mariah came over and slipped her hand into mine. "I like this one, Daddy. Can we live here please? Just you and me?"

"Maybe we can, peanut. We'll see."

After saying goodbye to Joy and telling her we'd be in touch, we took Mariah home. My mother said she had no plans to go anywhere, and she didn't mind at all if I went out for a beer with Moretti. I promised to be back in time for dinner and headed back out.

"So what's with you?" he asked, once we were seated at the

bar of the Bulldog Pub, our favorite watering hole and the sponsor of our baseball team in the Allegan County Senior Men's league.

"Nothing, really," I lied, lifting my beer bottle and taking a long drink. "I'm just thinking about buying a house. It's a big, expensive decision."

"It is," Moretti agreed. "And don't worry if nothing you saw today was right. We've got more to see."

"I actually really like that old one on the big lot by the creek. It would take some serious renovation though."

"Nothing structural," reasoned Moretti. "Unless you wanted to take out that dining room wall and have one big open kitchen-dining area. And even that wouldn't be a monster project. The rest of the work would all be cosmetic, and if you need a designer, I know some people."

I couldn't resist. "Like Bianca DeRossi?"

He scowled. "I said people, not she-devils."

"She didn't seem that bad to me. And she's cute." I laughed. "Is she Italian? Maybe you should audition her for the role of Mrs. Enzo Moretti. I bet your parents would be happy."

"Bite your fucking tongue, Mitchell. I wouldn't ask her out if you paid me. Anyway, I'm off the market for now."

"Oh yeah? Things are going well with Reina?"

He tipped up his beer, glancing over to where Reina was standing at the servers' station. She gave him a little wave. "I guess. She's got tomorrow night off, and I'm taking her to dinner. Want to join us?"

"No."

"Why not? You could bring Cheyenne or something."

I looked at him sharply. "Why Cheyenne?"

He shrugged. "I don't know. My cousin Lara told me yesterday that she waited on you guys at DiFiore's a couple nights ago. I said you were just friends, but she thought there was definitely something going on with you two."

My neck felt sweaty. I took another drink.

"*Is* there something going on with you two?"

I meant to say no. Instead I blurted, "I kissed her last night."

Moretti nearly choked on his beer. "What?"

"I kissed her last night. After everyone else left and Mrs. Dempsey went up to bed." Grimacing, I shook my head. "But I shouldn't have."

"Why the fuck not? Cheyenne's hot." He pointed a finger at me. "You can *never* tell Griff I said that, by the way."

"Because I don't want to lead her on. She wants a serious relationship, not a one-night stand."

"Okay, but there's a lot of middle ground between those two things," Enzo argued. "Can't you just date? Hang out and have some fun?"

"No, because dating someone comes with responsibilities. If you're dating someone, you owe them things—time, attention, feelings. Cheyenne wants those things. She deserves those things."

"What do *you* want?"

"Me?"

"Yeah. You told me what Cheyenne wants, but what about you?"

"I want something I can't have," I said. "I want to be the guy that isn't worried about something bad happening before things even get good."

Moretti clapped me on the shoulder. "Listen. You need to get back out there, buddy. All this pent-up frustration is clogging your brain. Want my advice?"

"No."

"Here's my advice." He set his beer on the bar and talked with his hands. "If you want Cheyenne, go for it. From what I can see, she wants you too. As long as you don't tell lies or make promises you can't keep, I don't see the harm in having a little fun. Do you?"

While I considered it, the bartender came over. His name was McIntyre, and he worked for Griffin at the garage in addition to playing for our baseball team. He'd picked up a few bartending shifts to help cover the costs of his wedding, which had just occurred over the summer. "Hey assholes," he said, setting down two shots of whiskey. "These are on a woman at the end of the bar."

"See?" Moretti elbowed me. "You're putting out that hot single dad vibe already. Women can't resist."

McIntyre grinned. "Actually, she seems to think *you two* are a couple. She said to congratulate you on your wedded bliss and she hopes you'll be very happy in the new house."

I looked down at the end of the bar, and there was Bianca DeRossi, grinning sweetly and holding up her own shot.

"Fucking hell," Enzo growled, his dark eyes stormy. "I quote George Clooney as Ulysses Everett McGill: 'Woman is the most fiendish instrument of torture ever devised to bedevil the days of man.'"

"George might be right," I said, thinking about the boots Cheyenne had worn yesterday. Talk about torture.

"If only they weren't so fucking hot. It's maddening, isn't it?" Moretti was still looking at Bianca, his expression nothing if not bedeviled.

"Yep." I picked up my shot and tossed it back.

Nine

Cheyenne

"I DON'T UNDERSTAND IT," BLAIR SAID. "NOTHING from him all week? Not even a text message?"

"Nothing."

We were on the phone, me in my room packing my bags, and Blair already up at Cloverleigh Farms. It was Thursday afternoon, which meant a whole week had gone by since the Thanksgiving night kiss.

A kiss I'd been dreaming about since I was twelve years old. A kiss I'd never forget as long as I lived. A kiss I'd replayed in my head, over and over again, every single night since he'd walked out of the kitchen.

"I don't understand it," she said again.

"I do." I added a stack of bras and underwear to my suitcase. "He told me flat out that we needed to slow down, that he felt like things were moving too fast."

"Yeah, but there's a difference between slowing down and slamming on the brakes. All you did was kiss!"

"Yeah, but that was a huge deal for us," I said. "This isn't like I just met someone random at a bar and he brought me home and kissed me. This is *Cole*." I placed a pair of jeans and two sweaters into the suitcase. "He's not like anyone else. And he's too good a guy to feed me bullshit. He doesn't want to start something he can't finish, and I don't want to be that girl clinging to blind hope for the rest of my life. He was honest with me, and I respect that."

"Maybe he was just really busy this week," Blair said brightly. "I told you he put an offer in on that old house by the creek, right?"

"You did, and I'm excited for him. But he and I have talked about moving out a lot, so I kind of thought he might tell me about it himself." I caught sight of my reflection in the mirror and glared at it. "See? This is the problem with me. I say I'm not going to get my hopes up, and then I do. I say I'm okay with things, and then I'm not. I pick unavailable people, and then I wonder why I get disappointed."

"Grr, it's so maddening," said Blair. "Any idiot could see the way he was staring at you at Thanksgiving."

I went back to packing, purposefully tossing in some pajamas that were not sexy in the least. "Thanksgiving was a good time. But I think it scared him."

She sighed. "Has your mom forgiven you for the plate?"

"Who knows? She says she's not mad, but she's been weird this week."

"Weird like how?"

"I don't know. Just quiet. But I feel like she's looking at me and silently judging. Wondering what I did wrong with Cole. Why he doesn't want me." I squeezed my eyes shut. "Or maybe that's me projecting."

"Has she asked about him?"

"No," I admitted, tucking some socks into my suitcase. "Tell me again how dressy I need to be for the rehearsal dinner."

"I thought you had an outfit planned already."

"I did, but now I don't know if I'm in the right mood for it."

I sank onto my bed and stared at the black dress hanging on the back of my closet door. "Maybe it's too sexy."

"It's not."

"I can't wear a bra with it."

"What are you, my grandma?"

"And it's tight."

"It shows off your fantastic body!"

I sighed. "What if it looks like I'm trying too hard?"

"Cheyenne. Stop. If anything, Cole is going to spend the entire night drooling over you and kicking himself for ignoring you all week."

"I doubt that."

"You didn't see what I saw on Thanksgiving. When he watched you come down those stairs, he lit up like he had fireflies under his skin. I've never seen anything like it. Wear the damn dress."

I smiled, despite everything. "I'll at least bring it."

"What time are you leaving?"

"Soon, I hope. It would be great to get up there before the snow starts."

"Oh God, don't talk about the snow. Do you really think we're going to get as much as they're saying?"

"I hope not." The forecast was dire—we were supposed to get about six inches of snow by tonight and something like another foot and a half by Saturday morning. Blair was terrified the weather was going to prevent people from being able to make it to the wedding. Not only were lots of people driving up from Bellamy Creek, but her family was flying in from Nashville. "When do your parents arrive?"

"Their flight is supposed to leave first thing tomorrow."

"Are you excited to see them?"

"Yes and no." Blair laughed. "I haven't let my mother *near* my wedding plans, so she'll be sure to have plenty to say about all the things I'm doing wrong, but that's okay. The whole reason I left that life behind was because I didn't want to live by anyone else's rules or traditions."

Blair had been brought up a wealthy, blue-blooded debutante, but her family had lost all its money after her father took some bad advice and wound up being convicted of tax evasion. But rather than marry rich just to live in luxury again like her mother wanted her to, she'd chosen a different path. She'd been on her way to her new life when her car broke down in Bellamy Creek.

"Well, I'm excited to meet them," I said, determined to focus on the bright side. "What are you guys up to this afternoon?"

"We're meeting with the wedding planner at four-thirty to go over some final details, and then we've got a dinner reservation at six. I'm just waiting for Griff to get out of the shower, so we can get going."

"Hey, does Griffin . . . *know*? About Cole and me?"

"He definitely thinks something was up between you guys last week, but I didn't tell him any specifics. It's weird, because you're his sister. He's said a hundred times that he wishes Cole would get back out there, but he can't exactly be like, 'dude, Cheyenne's into you, you should hit that.'"

I frowned. "Ew. Gross."

Blair laughed. "But Cole's his best friend. I'm sure he'd be happy to see you together."

"Never going to happen," I said, willing it to sink in once and for all. "I've always known it."

"You never know. Maybe this weekend will change things. Weddings are romantic occasions."

"I know."

"I'll see you later tonight. Drive carefully, okay?"

"I will."

We hung up, and I slipped the black dress and my crimson velvet bridesmaid dress into a garment bag.

For a moment, I stood there, touching the velvet bodice, imagining Cole in his suit, his arms around me on the dance floor.

That was probably as good as it was going to get.

My mother remained uncharacteristically quiet on the drive up to Cloverleigh Farms. I finally asked her about it, even though I was worried the answer was going to be something like, *I'm just so happy for your brother, but I can't help wondering when you're going to find the one.*

"Something on your mind, Mom?"

She sighed. "Not really."

I gritted my teeth. "I can tell there's something. You haven't said a word since we left home. And you've been giving me the silent treatment all week. Are you still mad about the plate?"

"The what?" My mother seemed genuinely confused for a moment. "Oh—no. It's not that."

"What is it?"

She stared out the passenger side window a moment. "I miss your dad. He should be here for this."

Immediately, I felt horrible. Of *course* she was missing my dad. We all were. Griffin and I had talked about it at Thanksgiving, how sad we were that he'd miss all these big moments in our lives—weddings and babies being born and every milestone afterward—as well as just being around for the little moments, like Sunday dinners and telling dad jokes and the occasional beer after work.

I shook my head, ashamed I'd assumed her silence this week had been about me. "You're right. He should be, and I miss him too."

We were both quiet then, reliving our memories of a man who'd worked so hard all his life, loved his family so fiercely, and had deserved the easy retirement surrounded by grandchildren he never got. A heart attack had stolen everything from him—and him from us—six years ago.

"He'd like Blair, don't you think?" I asked, attempting to lighten the mood.

"Oh, definitely." My mother nodded. "But who wouldn't?"

"It's so incredible, the way they found each other, isn't it? I mean, what are the chances that your soul mate is the mechanic who fixes your car after you get stranded in his town?"

"Probably about the same as your soul mate being the boy next door who's been there all along," she said breezily.

"Mom, don't start. I told you. We're—"

"Just friends. I know. Because he doesn't date."

"Exactly."

"Although, I did hear the strangest rumor about Cole at the dry cleaners the other day."

"You did?"

"Yes. Someone said they'd heard he'd recently come out as gay and was in a relationship with Enzo Moretti."

I burst out laughing. "What? That's ridiculous!"

She laughed too. "Apparently they were seen looking for a house together."

"That's because Enzo is helping Cole find a house for him and Mariah to move into."

"Oh. Well, that makes more sense." She paused. "But if he *was* gay, that would explain why he isn't interested in you."

"Mom. He's not gay."

She sighed. "Fine." A minute later, she chuckled. "But they would make a handsome couple, don't you think?"

"Definitely." I laughed again too, then turned my windshield wipers on. "Looks like the snow is starting."

"Oh, dear," my mother fretted. "I wish they'd chosen a venue closer to home."

"Well, Blair had her heart set on Cloverleigh Farms. And maybe they're overestimating how much we'll get. That happens all the time."

My mother crossed herself. "I hope you're right."

But the snow fell steadily for the rest of the drive, thicker and heavier the farther north we got. I white-knuckled the steering wheel of my Honda, ramrod in my seat, glad I'd let Griffin talk me into new tires this year.

We should have arrived at Cloverleigh Farms around seven, but thanks to the weather, it was after nine. We checked into our rooms at the inn—my mother's was down at the far end of the second floor, and mine was closer to the rest of the wedding party's—and planned on meeting down at the restaurant for a quick bite, but I was still hanging things up in the closet when she called and said she was too tired and had decided to just order room service instead.

"Are you sure?" I asked. "Blair just texted and said she and Griffin are down there with some other people."

"Positive. You go ahead. I'm pooped, and tomorrow is going to be a long day."

"Okay, get some rest. I'll see you in the morning."

"Night, honey."

"'Night." I grabbed my purse, tucking my room keycard inside it, and headed down to the bar.

The inn was only two stories, and although there was an elevator at the end of the hall, I chose to use the lobby's grand staircase, which was decorated for the holidays with fragrant evergreen boughs and white lights. As I descended the steps, I looked around and thought it was no wonder Blair wanted to get married here—the whole place radiated elegance, warmth, and romance. At one end of the room was a huge stone fireplace with logs ablaze inside it. In the corner stood a gigantic Christmas tree hung with white lights and colorful ornaments. In the air was the scent of woodsmoke and apples and cinnamon. From the bar came the cheerful sound of clinking glasses, the hum of conversation punctuated by bursts of laughter, and beneath it all, joyful holiday music.

I couldn't help smiling as I entered the cozy, low-lit bar,

which was styled like an English pub, with lots of dark wood paneling, a leather banquette and small tables along one wall, and a crackling fire in the fireplace. Right away I spotted Blair and Griffin at the long wooden bar opposite the banquette and headed their way—then stopped in my tracks when I noticed Cole was with them.

Shit!

I touched the ribbed knit cap on my head, wishing I'd washed my hair today. What was he *doing* here? Hadn't Blair said he wasn't coming up until tomorrow morning?

I looked down in dismay at my traveling outfit, which had clearly been chosen for comfort, not for style. I still had my North Face boots on, for fuck's sake. And giant slouchy socks. My black leggings were okay, but my rust-colored sweater was a giant baggy thing with a turtleneck and sleeves that were too long. Cozy, but not terribly cute, and a far cry from sexy or alluring.

I was considering sneaking back up to my room to change, or maybe even order room service, when Blair caught sight of me. "Cheyenne's here!" she cried out, loudly enough that everyone around her turned to look at me.

No backing out now. Embarrassed, I lifted a hand, which was hidden inside my floppy sleeve. "Hi."

Blair came rushing toward me, grabbing me in a hug. "Sorry," she whispered. "I didn't know he was coming early. He just showed up a little bit ago."

"Why didn't you text me?" I whispered back.

"I was afraid you wouldn't come down."

I let her go and gave her a dirty look. "That was a mean trick. Look at me—I look like I just crawled out of bed. Through a blizzard."

"You look adorable," she said, taking my hand and tugging me toward the bar. "Come on. Frannie's here, and she can't wait to see you."

"Oh, good! I'm excited to see her too."

Frannie was also one of Blair's bridesmaids. She was an old friend of mine from when I'd student taught in this area, and her family owned Cloverleigh Farms. I'd actually introduced Blair to her, and for a while—before Griffin had finally figured out that he was in love with Blair and begged her to come back to Bellamy Creek—she had lived at Cloverleigh and worked as a pastry chef at Frannie's coffee shop. Carefully avoiding Cole's eye, I let Blair pull me over to where Frannie stood with two other women, a blonde I didn't recognize and an auburn-haired beauty who looked vaguely familiar.

"Hey, you!" Frannie said, giving me a huge hug. "Long time, no see!"

"How are you, Frannie?"

"I'm fine. Life is crazy with five girls at home—I'm amazed Mack hasn't lost his mind yet—but everything is good."

I laughed. Mack, her husband, had three daughters from his first marriage, and Frannie had given birth to their twins the year before. "Is he here?" I asked.

"Yes, he's over there with the guys." She nodded in the direction of Griffin and Cole and laughed. "Soaking up the testosterone."

I looked over there too, accidentally locking eyes with Cole. He gave me a half-smile, which I returned before looking away, my heart tripping over its next few beats.

"How was the drive?" Frannie asked. "Did you get caught in the storm?"

"It was a little rough," I said. "That snow is coming down hard."

Blair closed her eyes a second. "Don't talk about it. Let's get you a drink."

"Sounds good," I said. "I could use some food as well. Is the kitchen still open?"

"Yes," answered the redhead, who held out her hand with a

smile. "Hi, I'm Frannie's sister April. I think we've met, but it was a long time ago."

"Oh, you're the wedding planner!"

She nodded, giving Blair a meaningful look. "Yes, and everything is going to be perfect, blizzard or not."

"I agree," said Frannie. "Honestly, I think Cloverleigh is more beautiful and romantic covered with snow in the winter than at any other time of year. It's going to look like a winter wonderland. You'll see."

Blair took a deep breath. "Right."

"Hi, I'm Alexis," said the blond woman I didn't recognize, holding out her hand.

"Oh, Blair's college roommate!" I exclaimed, taking her hand in both of mine. "So nice to meet you. I'm glad you made it in from California before the storm."

She smiled. "Me too. They're already canceling flights."

Blair moaned, her face troubled. "You guys, I have the worst feeling my parents are not going to make it."

"Stop." I put my arm around her. "No matter what happens with the weather, you are marrying the love of your life tomorrow, right?"

She nodded. "Right."

"And you're getting me as a sister!"

That brought a smile. "Right."

"And like Frannie said, it's going to look like a winter wonderland," Alexis added. "Like a fairy tale."

"Absolutely," agreed April.

Blair smiled, her eyes tearing up. "Thanks, you guys. I'm so glad to have you here."

I squeezed her shoulder. "And now I need wine."

April suggested we sit at one of the tables opposite the bar. I ended up seated on the banquette, which gave me a perfect view of the guys as they stood sipping whiskey and beers, occasionally guffawing loudly or clapping Griffin on the back. At one point, my brother came over and said hello, asked how the drive was and how our mom was feeling, but Cole continued to keep his distance.

Several times, I caught him glancing over at me, but I pretended not to notice. It made me sad that things were strange between us now, after feeling as if we'd grown closer in the days leading up to Thanksgiving. For heaven's sake, we'd had phone sex! Good phone sex! I'd *heard* him have an orgasm, even if it had been mostly silent. Had one real kiss ruined everything?

I enjoyed chatting with the girls at the table, and the food and wine I'd ordered was delicious, but I was preoccupied the entire time wondering how I was going to get through the weekend if this is how it was going to be between Cole and me.

Eventually, Frannie and Mack left for home, and April's handsome fiancé came to pick her up—he didn't want her driving alone in the storm—although when Griffin and his friends realized her fiancé was former MLB pitching star Tyler Shaw, they dragged him over to the bar and kept him there another twenty minutes. April had to pry him from the conversation to get him out the door. Alexis excused herself shortly afterward, saying she wanted to FaceTime with her kids before they went to bed, which left just Blair and me at the table.

She tipped her head onto my shoulder. "You okay?"

"I'm fine."

"I can tell you're not. Also, Cole is not. He's been looking over here all night."

"I've been trying not to notice that." I tossed back the wine left in my glass.

Blair picked up her head. "Well, your job's about to get harder, because the guys are headed this way."

I looked up, and sure enough, Griffin and Cole were approaching our table. I fought the urge to fuss with my hair by pulling my hands inside my monster sleeves.

"Hey," Griffin said, yawning. "I've been up since five, and I'm beat. You about ready to call it a night?"

"Yes, but you go ahead. I'll stay with Cheyenne. She's just waiting for the server to bring her check."

"No, go with Griff," I said. "I'll be fine."

"I can wait with her," said Cole. "If that's okay."

Our eyes met. "It's fine."

He dropped into the chair across from me, and Blair stood up. "Okay. Goodnight, you guys. Cheyenne, I'll see you at breakfast at eight-thirty?"

"Sounds good." I watched them walk away, Blair frantically mouthing *text me* over her shoulder while pantomiming exaggerated typing motions with her thumbs.

Cole had some whiskey left, and he swirled it around in the glass. "How was your drive?"

"The first half was okay. Second half a little scary." I forced a smile. "How about yours?"

"About the same. I wasn't going to come up until tomorrow, since I didn't want to pull Mariah from another day of school, but I ended up changing my mind because of the weather. It's only going to get worse tomorrow, so I picked her up at lunchtime."

"I'm sure she was excited. Is she in bed already?"

He nodded. "She was down here with my mom for dinner, but then they went up to bed. They're sharing a room, so I've got my own."

"Oh." Immediately my mind went to all the inappropriate activities that could go on in Cole's hotel room. "That's nice."

An awkward silence descended on us. It was late—almost midnight—and the bar had pretty much emptied out. Cole finished his whiskey.

"So are you—"

"I wanted to—"

After speaking at the same time, we both laughed, and the tension eased up a little. "Go ahead," he said.

"I was just going to ask if you were excited about making the offer on the new house. I heard you fell in love with the one by the creek."

He nodded, his crooked smile appearing. "Yeah. I am excited. We heard today the offer was accepted."

"Congratulations."

"Thanks. It needs a lot of work, but Mariah and I both loved it, and Moretti thinks it's a good buy for the price. He's going to help me with the renovations over the winter."

"Can I see it sometime?"

"Of course," he said, sounding surprised I'd even asked. "The inspection is happening next week, and if all goes well, I'm hoping to close two or three weeks after that and be in by the first of the year."

"That's really exciting, Cole. I'm happy for you."

The server brought my check, and I signed it to my room. When we were alone again, Cole smiled at me across the table. "So is your mom still mad about the plate?"

I laughed. "I think she's forgiven us."

"Good."

Another silence, during which we locked eyes and the air between us crackled with tension. Was he remembering that kiss?

"I should go up to bed," I said, rising to my feet.

"Same." Cole stood too. "What floor are you on?"

"Second."

"Me too. I'll walk up with you."

My legs felt shaky as we left the bar and climbed the lobby stairs. As we neared my room, I pulled my keycard from my purse. "This one's mine," I said, gesturing toward the door.

He nodded. "I'm in two-eighteen."

"Oh." I wasn't sure what to do with that information—other than imagine myself sneaking down to his room.

NO, my inner adult scolded. *No sneaking.*

No sneaking and no sexting and no saying anything but goodnight.

Because the way he was looking at me was making it hard to breathe.

"Well, goodnight," I said, opening the door to my room.

"Goodnight." He stuck his hands in his pockets.

I entered my room and shut the door.

At least, I tried to shut the door—Cole's hand shot out and stopped it. "Cheyenne, wait."

My breath caught. "Yes?"

"I just want to say that I'm really glad to see you made it up here safely. I was worried about you making that drive."

"I'm fine." I glanced down at my outfit. "A little grungy and disheveled, but fine."

"You're always beautiful."

Our eyes met. I wanted to thank him, but I couldn't speak.

"Also . . ." He struggled for words. "I want you to know that I thought about you all week. And I wish . . ." He paused. "I keep wishing things were different."

I smiled and lifted my shoulders. "I wish things were different too, but I appreciate your honesty."

"So we're okay?"

The tightness in my throat made it hard to get the words out. "We're okay."

He nodded. "'Night."

"'Night." I closed the door and leaned back against it, trying not to cry.

We might be okay, but I was not.

Ten

Cheyenne

BLAIR TEXTED ME EARLY, BEFORE MY ALARM EVEN went off.

Flights out of Nashville are grounded.

Reading my screen in the dark, I gasped and sat up. Before I could reply, she called me.

"Hello?"

"I knew it," she said, and I could tell she was crying. "I knew everything was too perfect."

"I'm so sorry," I said in my most soothing voice. "But the wedding is still going to be perfect, Blair. It's going to be okay."

"They say they don't want to drive up because the roads are so bad," she sobbed. "How can they do this to me? My own family."

"Listen to me. Let's focus on the most important thing— you are getting *married* tomorrow. And they're not your only family anymore, okay?"

"What if no one can get here, not even from Bellamy Creek? I'll have a wedding and no guests!"

"Listen, people from Bellamy Creek are used to driving in

the winter. They'll be fine. And next spring, you'll get married again down in Tennessee. I've never been to Nashville, and I'd love for you to show me around!"

She sniffed. "Okay. You're right. I need to focus on the good."

"That's my girl." I got out of bed and went over to the window to pull open the drapes. The brightness nearly blinded me—the entire landscape surrounding Cloverleigh Farms was *covered* in snow, and it was still coming down. "Yikes."

"Yikes, what?" Blair asked, alarmed.

"Nothing." I bit my lip, blinking at the world of white outside my window. "Everything is beautiful."

In a way, Blair's panic about the weather was a good distraction for me—keeping her calm and thinking positively took up all my time and effort. I had no headspace left over to be upset about Cole.

The day passed quickly—champagne breakfast with all the bridesmaids, plus Mariah and my mom; a slow, careful drive into town for our spa appointments; a light lunch in town before we all went to our rooms to get ready for a late afternoon wine tasting at Cloverleigh's winery, which would be followed by the rehearsal and then dinner.

I wasn't sure what the guys did all day, but Blair was on the phone with Griffin constantly, and between my brother and me, we did our best to reassure Blair that the wedding of her dreams was still possible, even if half the guests didn't show.

We were on our way back to Cloverleigh Farms after lunch when she clutched my arm. "Oh my God, who's going to walk me down the aisle? I can't believe I didn't think of that!"

"Don't worry about a thing," I said, patting her hand. "I have an idea."

When we got back to the inn, I sent Blair up to her room to

rest and headed for the lobby desk. It surprised me to see April there at reception.

"Hey," I said. "What are you doing here?"

"Our regular desk manager had to stay home with her kids today—snow day, no school," she explained. "I was already here, so I said I'd fill in this afternoon. How's Blair holding up?"

"Okay. She's disappointed her family won't make it in, but what can you do?"

April nodded in understanding. "Always a risk with a winter wedding in Michigan."

"I wondered if you might be able to help me," I said. "Blair is worried about who will walk her down the aisle since her dad won't be here, and I have an idea. Can you tell me if a certain guest has checked in yet?"

"Sure," she said, moving over to her computer screen. "What's the name?"

I gave her the name, and she shook her head.

"Not yet, but they haven't canceled."

"Okay, good. Can you let me know when they check in or if they cancel?"

She nodded. "Sure thing."

"And don't say anything to Blair, okay? I think it will be a nice surprise for her—something sweet."

She winked at me. "You got it."

The wedding party met up in the lobby at four, and together we all walked over to the winery, laughing as we slogged through the snow in jeans and boots, none of us wearing the dress clothes we'd packed for the occasion.

I walked with Blair and Frannie, but I was keenly aware of Cole's presence behind us with the rest of the guys. Both Enzo and Beckett had made the drive safely, along with Enzo's parents and Beckett's dad, and we'd also seen lots of familiar faces from Bellamy Creek in the lobby checking in. Blair had cheered up immeasurably.

Inside the winery, we tasted wines poured by Frannie's sister Sylvia and her husband Henry, snacked on charcuterie and cheese, and shook our heads at the apocalyptic way the snow continued to fall.

I probably—make that definitely—drank a little more wine than I should have, and I found myself pleasantly buzzed as we walked over to the wedding barn, where the rehearsal was taking place.

"Can you believe this weather?" Cole asked, falling in step beside me. "I haven't seen this much snow in a long time."

"Me neither. Where's Mariah?"

"My mom is bringing her over." He glanced at me. "Having fun?"

"Yes. Although I tasted too much wine."

"Same here."

"My head is spinning. Is my nose red?"

"No. You look perfect, Cheyenne."

"Thanks." I laughed. "This is not the outfit I planned on wearing, but given the blizzard, I decided against the sexy black dress and heels."

"You were wearing that sweater the night we had dinner at DiFiore's," he said.

"Was I?" I slipped in the snow, and he caught me before I went down on my ass.

"Whoa. You okay?" he asked.

"Fine," I said, recovering my balance and laughing a little. "You know how I love getting tipsy when it snows."

He laughed too, keeping his grip on my arm. "Right. I walked you home that night so you wouldn't fall."

I giggled. "I fell *years* ago."

"What?"

"Nothing." *Jiminy Cricket, did I say that out loud?* We

reached the door to the barn, which Griffin was holding open for everyone. "You know what? I just need a minute," I told Cole. "Some fresh air before I go in."

"I'll wait out here with you," he offered.

"No, that's okay. You can go in and find Mariah. I'm sure she's looking for you."

"Mariah will be fine for a minute." Cole nodded at Griffin to go in, and a moment later, we were alone.

Staying a good two feet away from him, I drew in deep breaths of icy air, willing it to defog my brain.

"Blair seems to be holding up okay," he said. "Too bad about her family."

"Yeah, but I have a surprise for her." I smiled. "Charlie Frankel is going to walk her down the aisle. He should be here for rehearsal any minute."

Cole grinned. "She'll love that. Those two have always been close, haven't they?"

I nodded. "He's like her adopted grandpa. She adores him. Right before we went over to the winery, I got the news that he'd checked in, and I went to his room to ask him. He almost cried."

"He made that drive alone?" Cole was surprised. "He's in his eighties, isn't he?"

"He drove up with Beckett and his dad."

"Oh, good. Well, it's a great idea."

"Thank you." I dipped into a little curtsy, making him laugh. Then I shivered. "Ooh, it's chilly. Should we go in?"

"Sure." He pulled the door open for me. "You know, I'd have liked to see you in that black dress."

My jaw dropped. "You would have?"

"Sure. But that's not really news, is it? I mean, I'd like to see you in anything. And nothing."

I cocked my head. "Officer Mitchell, are you drunk?"

He gave me his crooked grin. "Maybe a little. Mostly I

just wanted to know what it would feel like to say what I was thinking."

"I know *exactly* what you mean. So how did it feel?"

He moved closer to me, letting the heavy door swing shut behind us. His mouth was at my ear. "Pretty fucking good."

I gasped.

It was the phone sex voice.

I had a hard time concentrating after that.

The rehearsal went fine, although Blair burst into happy tears when Charlie Frankel showed up offering his arm, and much of the wedding party was kind of drunk, which made April a little concerned that none of us were going to recall where to stand and what to do tomorrow, and every time Cole and I locked eyes I felt my cheeks catch fire. As he escorted me back down the aisle, my hand tucked inside his elbow, I felt like the heat was coming off him in waves. I actually started to sweat.

On the way back to the inn, someone—probably Griffin—started a snowball fight, and pretty soon we were all hurling snow at each other, slip-sliding on the lawn, pumping our fists if we landed a good shot and shrieking in outrage if we got hit. Afterward, I joined Mariah in making snow angels, and by the time we made it inside the inn, every one of us was wet and shivering.

"Okay, you guys," Blair said. "You have thirty minutes to get yourselves cleaned up and respectable. Dry clothes, nice shoes, and no hats."

"You sound like a kindergarten teacher," I teased her.

She pointed in the direction of the stairs. "Go!"

Up in my room, I yanked off my boots, peeled off my damp sweater and popsicle-leg jeans, and considered the items in my closet. One floral blouse, one long velvet gown, and one sexy black dress.

I bit my lip. Should I?

While I was standing there, my phone pinged with a text. I ran over to the bed to check it.

Cole: Wear the dress.

I grinned.

Me: Are you still drunk?

Cole: Nope. I just want to see you in it.

Me: I will take that into consideration.

Unable to wipe the smile off my face, I swapped my boring underwear for something black and lacy, shimmied into the dress, and stepped into my heels. The dress was long and clingy, with a high slit and camisole straps. It didn't reveal a lot of cleavage, but it definitely showed off my curves. I didn't have too much time to fix up my hair and makeup, but I did the best I could—repairing my mascara, fussing with a hair dryer and curling iron, and reapplying my lipstick.

When I was ready, I wrapped an ivory cashmere scarf around my shoulders, blew myself a kiss in the mirror and headed out.

I had no idea if Cole had changed his mind about putting on the brakes. I had no clue what might happen between us tonight. I could not imagine what was behind his sudden flirty behavior.

But I refused to ruin my effervescent mood and rare burst of confidence by overthinking it. Maybe it was the wine, maybe it was the dress, maybe it was just being tired of wanting something so badly and holding it in, but I felt good in my skin tonight. Sexy. Confident.

The moment I walked into the bar, Cole turned around like he knew I was there. His eyes went wide. His jaw dropped. He grabbed the knot on his tie and pulled it loose.

Smiling, I moved closer, slipping in next to him at the bar. "Hi."

"Holy shit." His eyes ran over my skin, head to toe. "You're stunning."

"Thank you. You look good too." Good was an understatement. He looked like a men's fragrance ad, all glittering blue eyes and sharp chiseled jaw. He wore dark dress pants, a white shirt, and a tie that matched the color of his eyes. "I like the tie."

"Mariah chose it."

I laughed. "I've been replaced as your stylist, I see. Is she down yet?"

"She's coming down with my mom in a minute." He shook his head. "I'm beginning to regret telling you to wear the dress. I'm not going to be able to keep my eyes off you tonight."

"Good," I said, perching on the edge of the bar stool and crossing my legs just so.

Again, his eyes did the thing I'd been waiting for them to do since I was twelve years old—see me.

And only me.

Eleven

Cole

I CORNERED MORETTI AT THE BAR AFTER DINNER. "HELP."

"With what?" He looked confused.

"I did what you said to do, and now I need help."

"What did I say to do?"

"You said to have a little fun, and I did. I said things."

"So?"

"So now she's wearing that dress and I'm about to lose my mind!" I tossed back the rest of my bourbon and ordered another, although I knew I should slow down.

Moretti laughed. "Yeah, you're toast, dude. I saw the way you were looking at her during dinner."

Groaning, I glanced over to where she stood talking to Griffin and the wedding planner, and the wedding planner's husband, who happened to be Tyler fucking Shaw. As a pitcher, I should have been over there too—I was a baseball fanatic and I'd followed Tyler's career from the time he was a first-round draft pick right out of high school. But I couldn't think about baseball. I couldn't think about anything except Cheyenne in that dress and how badly I wanted to get my hands on her. At dinner she'd been seated right across from me, and I couldn't even tell you what I'd eaten—in fact, I wasn't even sure I had eaten—because I was so preoccupied with the tilt of her head and the curve of her shoulder and the glow of her skin.

"I'm a mess, Moretti. I fucking told her that we had to slow down, if not stop altogether, and now I'm a mess. I haven't been able to think about anything but her for a week."

"Jesus Christ, Cole. Relax." Moretti sipped his whiskey. "If you get too worked up ahead of time, you're gonna go off like a rocket, especially if it's been a while."

"Oh, it's been a while."

"Like how long?"

I had to think about it. "A few years."

Moretti almost choked. "*Years*? Damn, that's even worse than I thought. How do you live, man?"

"Look, it's not easy for me, okay? I'm a cop in a small town, and everyone knows me or knows my kid or knows my mom. I don't fuck around."

Moretti shook his head. "You must have willpower of steel."

I grabbed my new drink off the bar. "It's never been this difficult to control myself."

"I say go for it. All she can do is say no."

"You think she'll say no?" Panicking, I swallowed some more bourbon.

He shrugged. "Depends. I don't think you should lie to her and tell her you're in love with her just so she'll sleep with you, but if you invite her back to your room and she says yes, I'd say that's a pretty good indication she's up for a good time tonight."

"Is that what you'd do? Invite her to your room?"

"Definitely." He looked around. "But where's Mariah? Is she staying with you?"

I shook my head. "No. She's with my mom, and she already went to bed."

"Okay, good. So here's what you do. Find out what she's

drinking, order her another one, and then say something like, 'It's so crowded in here, maybe we—oh, fuck no.'"

"Huh?" I frowned at him. "You lost me there at the end."

"This cannot be happening."

"What?"

"It's *her*."

I followed his line of sight and saw that Bianca DeRossi had entered the bar and was giving Blair a big hug. "Oh."

"What the hell is she doing, following me?" He tipped up his drink again.

"I don't know. Looks like she's friends with Blair."

He grimaced as Bianca made her way toward us. "Gentlemen," she said smoothly, giving us a smile. "Nice to see you again. You're *quite* the most dashing couple in the room, all due respect to the bride and groom."

"Knock it off, Bianca. You know we're not a couple." Moretti glared at her.

She laughed and held up both hands. "Fair enough, I surrender. Way to ruin a girl's fantasy." Turning to me, she said, "I hear you made an offer on the house by the creek."

"And it was accepted," Moretti said with smug triumph, as if it had been a competition between them.

"Congratulations." She gave me a genuine smile. "It's a great house. You and your daughter will love it, I'm sure. If you need any help with the interior, just let me know."

"Thank you," I said.

"What are you doing here, anyway?" Moretti demanded, like this was his turf and she was trespassing on it.

"I'm a friend of Blair's."

"Since when?"

She gave him an odd look. "Since I moved back and we met at book club and hit it off."

"Book club?" Moretti looked like he wasn't sure he believed her. Either that or he'd never heard of a book club.

"Yes." She put a hand up to her mouth and stage whispered, "We both love teenage vampires, but don't tell anyone." Then she dropped her arm, her voice returning to normal. "Now if you'll excuse me, that drive was harrowing and I could really use a drink. Enjoy your evening." With one final smile—and a glitter of mischief in her eye when she looked at Moretti, she melted into the crowd by the bar.

"That woman," he said through gritted teeth, his eyes still on her. "I don't know what it is about her, but she drives me crazy."

I tossed back some more bourbon. "Okay, but we were talking about me. *My* problem. So you think just go over and say, 'Hey, want to go up to my room?'"

Moretti made a face like he'd sniffed something bad. "Is that how you're going to do it?"

"What was wrong with that?"

"You need more subtlety, more smolder. You can't just proposition her like that."

"Well then, show me how to do it," I said impatiently, eyeing her across the room. She was laughing at some other guy's joke and *touching his arm*. He was alarmingly buff and good-looking too. A stab of jealousy pierced my gut.

"Okay, try it like this." Moretti lowered his chin for a second, and when he raised it again, his eyes were hooded and seductive, and he spoke in a low, sultry voice. "Hey. What do you say we ditch this crowd and go someplace quieter?"

I blinked. "Wow."

Moretti dropped the act. "Okay, now you try it."

I took a deep breath and tried to arrange my face the way he had. I leaned toward him and repeated his words.

He frowned. "It's not quite right. Maybe try it like this." His face went from critical to *come hither*, and he swayed toward me again. "Hey. I don't know about you, but I've had about enough of this crowd. You want to get out of here?"

"Oh, now see? That's more like it." Bianca had snuck up on

us, catching Moretti pretending to seduce me. She sighed and sipped her wine. "I gotta say, real couple or not, you two are sexy as hell. Do you have a YouTube channel? I'd like to subscribe."

Moretti rolled his eyes and looked at me. "Go. You got this. I'll handle the viper."

"Okay." I loosened my tie a little—why was it suddenly so hot in here?—and made my way through the crowd toward where Cheyenne stood chatting with some people I didn't recognize. The room spun a little, and the floor seemed to tilt beneath my feet. I'd definitely drunk too much too fast. It gave me a moment's pause—maybe coming onto her after this much bourbon was a mistake?

But then it was too late. I'd reached her side, and she turned to smile at me. "Hey, Cole. Have you ever met my cousin Liam Dempsey?"

Understanding and relief swept through me. The buff dude was her *cousin.* And if memory served, he was a Navy SEAL who lived somewhere out east. "I think we met once way back when." I offered my hand, and Liam shook it.

"Good to see you, Cole," he said.

"And this is his wife, Natalie." Cheyenne gestured toward a pretty blonde whom I hadn't noticed standing on his other side.

"Nice to meet you." I shook her hand as well. "You're from out of state, right?"

Liam nodded. "Virginia Beach. We were lucky to make it in late last night. So many flights were canceled today."

"Hopefully, you're not stuck here for weeks on end," said Cheyenne. "They've got two kids," she said to me. "Aarabelle and Shane."

"Oh, really? Did you bring them with you?" I asked, thinking Mariah might like having some kids to hang out with at the reception.

"No, they're back home," Natalie said. "Our daughter is in second grade and had school today, and our son is only three.

We decided to take a long weekend just for ourselves. We haven't done that in forever." She wrapped her arms around her husband's waist and he gathered her close, kissing the top of her head.

Another stab of envy—I wished I could touch Cheyenne in front of people like that. Go away with her. Spend the night with her.

But it was impossible.

"Well, enjoy," I said. "I've got a nine-year-old daughter, and I know how hard it is to get away."

"His daughter Mariah is standing up in the wedding tomorrow," Cheyenne added. "She's just the sweetest thing ever."

Natalie beamed. "She must be thrilled. How exciting to stand up in a wedding at that age."

"Yes." I wasn't sure what else to say—and how on earth was I supposed to entice Cheyenne up to my room with an audience looking on?

Thankfully, Cheyenne put things in motion. "Well, it's getting late," she said, looking into her empty wine glass. "And I've probably had enough wine tonight."

"I hear you," Natalie said. "I had to cut myself off already or I'd be a mess tomorrow." She looked up at her husband. "What do you say, babe, should we turn in?"

"Sure." Liam nodded at Cheyenne and me. "See you guys tomorrow. Sleep well."

"Goodnight." Cheyenne faced me as they retreated, giving me a smile. "Hey, you."

"Hey." I knew what I was supposed to say, but somehow my tongue was tied in knots and I couldn't get the words out.

"Having a good time?"

"No. I mean, yes—I was—but now I'm not."

Her expression was confused. "Okayyy."

I exhaled, my shoulders slumping in defeat, my eyes slamming shut. Then I straightened up and looked at her again—and what came tumbling out of my mouth was the bourbon-infused truth. "That did not come out right. What I was supposed to say was some bullshit about the room being crowded. Then I was going to ask you if you wanted to get out of here and go up to my room."

"You were?"

"Yes. But not because the bar is crowded." I took a step closer to her. Reached for her hand. "Because I can't stop thinking about you. Because you're killing me in that dress. Because I don't want to lie awake tonight wishing I'd had the courage to tell you how much I want you."

Her plush bottom lip had fallen open. Her brown eyes were wide. "Cole," she whispered, her hand tightening around mine. "Let's get out of here."

Twelve

Cheyenne

WITHOUT ANOTHER WORD, COLE TURNED AND pulled me out of the bar, stopping only to set his empty glass and mine on a vacant table.

He moved quickly, his long legs striding purposefully into the lobby—then he stopped, looking at the people still milling around.

I knew what he was thinking—they'd all see us racing upstairs together. "Elevator," I said.

Hand in hand, we hurried around the back of the stairs and down the first-floor hall to the inn's single elevator. Cole punched a button, and the doors opened immediately. He tugged me inside, and hit the number two, and as soon as the doors closed, he spun me against the wall and pressed his body against mine.

I couldn't breathe.

He hesitated for a fraction of a second, his breath on my lips, before crushing his mouth to mine. The elevator began to ascend—at least I think it did. Either way, I felt like gravity had failed. Everything was going up, up, up.

All too soon and not soon enough, the doors opened and Cole broke the kiss, taking my hand once more and pulling me down the hall. In front of his door, he paused to pull his keycard from his wallet and inserted it. Once we were inside, he tossed the keycard and his wallet to the floor and slammed the door behind us.

Then his hands were in my hair again, his lips were on my throat, his body was nudging mine backward toward the bed. I went willingly, falling backward across it.

One lamp was on in the corner of the room, illuminating him in soft gold light as he yanked his tie off and unbuttoned his collar. Propped on my elbows, I watched, panting and eager.

A second later he was on me, a fantasy come to life.

Cole, Cole, Cole, I thought blissfully as his mouth slanted over mine. He kissed me hungrily, like he'd been starving for it the way I had, like he'd been holding back for years. His tongue stroked between my lips as he pinned my arms over my head, then slid his palms from wrist to elbow to the sides of my ribs. His cock, thick and hard, pressed against my thigh, sending electric pulses of anticipation throughout my body.

He's going to be inside me, I thought. *He's going to link his body with mine and it's going to feel so good to be that close to him. Finally. Fucking finally.*

I kicked off my heels, and heard his shoes hit the floor too. Slipping his forearm beneath my lower back, he moved me up the mattress, closer to the headboard so our bodies were pressed together from head to heel.

I wrapped both legs around one of his. "God, I want you," I whispered. Even the feel of his muscular thigh between my legs was enough to have me rocking my hips beneath him. I'd dreamed about this night for so long.

"Fuck, I can't wait to taste you." His mouth moved down my neck, and I threaded my fingers into his hair. Every nerve ending in my body was tingling, every inch of my skin on fire. One question echoed inside my head.

"Is this real?" I whispered.

"God, I hope so." He kissed my shoulder, my collarbone, my breast through the clingy black material of my dress, before bringing his lips back up to mine. "You're making me crazy tonight."

Tonight? You've been making me crazy for twenty years.

He moved to one side of me so he could reach inside the slit on my dress. I shivered as his fingers touched my skin and his palm slid up my inner thigh. At the first skim of his fingertips over my black lace panties, a sigh escaped me and I raised my knee toward the ceiling, tilting my hips toward him.

He caressed me gently through the silk before edging one finger beneath it, groaning as he slipped it easily inside me. I moved my hips against his hand, my fingers fumbling with the buttons on his dress shirt. He worked two fingers inside me, and I moaned against his lips. "That feels so good," I panted.

"I want you so fucking badly tonight," he growled, his other hand fisting in my hair.

There it was again. That word—*tonight.*

"Cole, wait." I pushed against his chest slightly, just so I could look up at him. "What about tomorrow?" I asked breathlessly.

"Huh?" His hand went still.

Stop! screamed teenage me in my head. *Don't ruin this! We've waited long enough!*

But I couldn't help it. "What about tomorrow? Will you want me then? And what about yesterday?"

"I . . . I don't understand." He took his hand from my underwear.

"I don't either. And I'm probably going to hate myself for this, but something doesn't feel right."

"It doesn't?"

I took a deep breath, willing myself to have the strength to say what needed to be said. "The first night you walked me home, you told me why you don't date, and I understood. Last week, you explained to me in heart-wrenching detail why you and I should probably just be friends, and I agreed. Last night you said you wished things were different, and I did too . . . so are they?"

"I . . . I don't know." He sounded genuinely confused, and then he rolled onto his back. "I'm sorry. I guess I was just trying to let go and have some fun."

I sat up, pushing my dress down and bringing my legs together. "I was too."

"And I really do want you. Everything I said tonight is true."

I pressed my lips together, knowing a *but* was coming.

"But you're right. Nothing has changed. I'm still the same guy I was last week, with the same issues." He flung his arm over his eyes, and I caught the shine of his wedding ring in the lamplight. "I can't make you any promises. And I can't lie to you."

I nodded, knowing deep down this was wrong for me. While I wanted nothing more than to let him love me for the night, some gut, *adult* instinct told me to protect myself, even while teenage me threw a tantrum in the corner of my mind, my girl parts backing her up.

"I'm sorry," he said again.

"No need for apology, Cole." I took another deep breath. "I came up here willingly, and part of me is still desperately hoping tonight ends with me in your arms, because I can't tell you how badly I've always wanted to be there."

He looked over at me. "I want you there too."

"But not enough," I said, hearing the catch in my voice, even as I smiled. "And it's okay. The truth is, Cole, I don't want it enough either—not enough to invite the heartbreak that would follow. Because I won't be able to just walk away from this and be okay. It will mean too much to me."

He didn't say anything. His chest rose and fell with quick, shallow breaths.

"It's not your fault," I said. "You can't read my mind, and

I've never been entirely honest about my feelings for you. So I'm sorry too, for leading you to believe I could be that girl who's up for anything. It wasn't fair."

"Cheyenne." He reached over and put a hand on my leg.

"I really thought I could be her tonight. I wanted to be her tonight. God knows I've been her every other night of my life." My eyes blurred with tears. "The truth is, Cole, I've loved you hopelessly for so long that I don't know any other way to do it. But being with you like that would give me hope, and that's something I can't afford right now."

"Cheyenne, I—"

"No, don't," I said, sliding off the bed, away from his touch, his scent, his blue eyes looking at me with despair. I couldn't bear to hear him explain why he couldn't love me back. I'd always known. "Don't say anything. Let's just leave it be and do what we said, okay? Let's be friends. My feelings will fade again." Slipping my feet into my shoes, I heard myself laugh nervously. "They always do."

He propped himself up on his elbows. "I don't want you to go."

I turned to him with a tearful smile. "I have to, Cole. I have to go to my room alone, where I will put myself in a timeout, curse myself for blowing my chance to sleep with you, and wallow in the humiliation of everything I've just confessed. But once I get over all that, I'm hoping to feel good about this."

It took him a moment to reply. "I understand."

"Thank you. Goodnight." Aiming for a dignified exit, I headed for the door, but then turned around again. "I don't suppose there's any way you could just *forget* everything I said to you tonight and pretend like this never happened?"

He shook his head slowly. "I'll never forget the things you said to me tonight."

So much for dignity. Cheeks burning, I moved for the door again.

"Cheyenne, wait!" He got out of bed and darted past me, reaching the door first, flattening his back against it.

Yes, Cole. Beg me to stay. Give me hope. Say you want me—not just for tonight.

"Yes?" I held my breath.

"I want you to know . . ." He ran a hand over his jaw. "I want you to know that I understand how you feel. And I hope you know how much I care about you. There hasn't been anyone since Trisha that I—that I want this way."

But not enough, I thought again, the lump rising in my throat. *Not enough.*

"I'm sorry if I messed up our friendship by saying one thing and doing another," he went on. "I won't do it again."

I swallowed the lump in my throat, wondering how the hell I was going to get through tomorrow. "Okay."

He opened the door for me, and I held my head high as I walked through it.

At the sound of it closing behind me, I burst into tears.

After a near sleepless night, I dragged my ass out of bed at eight the next morning and knocked on the door of the bridal suite fifteen minutes later.

Blair took one look at my puffy face and bloodshot eyes the next morning and gasped. "Oh my God. What happened to you?"

"Do you have coffee?" I croaked.

"Yes. Come in, no one else is here yet." She shut the door behind me and hurried over to a table where coffee, tea, and breakfast had been set out for the female wedding party. The entire room was big and bright, with lots of white everywhere—white carpet on the dark wood floor, white sheers on the windows, two white sofas facing each other, three white salon chairs facing three white-framed mirrors on walls painted a soft gray. In a couple hours, a hair and makeup team would arrive—they'd have a hell of a job whipping my sorry self into shape—and we were all due for a photo shoot at three.

Sometime between now and then, I had to prepare myself to face Cole. Walk down the aisle with him. Dance in his arms.

I sank down on a white sofa and gratefully accepted the cup of coffee Blair handed me. "Thanks."

"What's the matter?" she asked, sitting opposite me with her legs tucked beneath her. She wore a white fleece robe that had the Cloverleigh Farms insignia on it, and her hair was loose around her shoulders. Even with her face bare of makeup, she looked radiant—like a bride should.

"I feel like such a shitty friend for doing this to you on your wedding day," I told her. "Part of me wants to lie and tell you everything is fine."

"I wouldn't believe you anyway," she said. "You look like you cried yourself to sleep, if you slept at all."

"Accurate," I admitted, taking a sip.

"So talk. We have at least forty-five minutes before the rest of the gang arrives."

I told her what had happened, watching her expressions run the gamut from surprised to angry to sad to impressed to sympathetic. "Oh, honey," she said, learning forward to hug me.

"Oh God, don't make me spill coffee on this white couch," I said, setting the cup down on the glass coffee table.

"You poor thing." Blair sat back again. "I can't believe you walked away."

"I had to," I said, spying a box of tissues across the room and getting up to retrieve one. "All of a sudden, it hit me that we weren't on the same page. I was doing it because I'm in love with him, and he was doing it because it would be fun. But fun can be had with anyone, you know? I was afraid it wouldn't mean anything to him, and it was going to mean everything to me." I groaned, snatching a couple tissues from the box. "God, that sounds so juvenile and stupid."

"No, it doesn't," Blair said. "It sounds mature and self-aware. Of course jumping into bed with Cole would be fun, but you know that it probably would have made it harder to deal with the fact that you want something he can't give."

"Right," I said, blowing my nose. "But that's nothing new. I just wish I hadn't told him so much, you know? Like why couldn't I have just pretended like I'd changed my mind about sex and walked out? Now he knows how I *feel*."

"Maybe it's better he knows," Blair said hopefully. "Maybe he just needs time to process it."

"No. The more he thinks about it, the more pathetic I'm going to look. I told him I *loved* him, Blair." I tossed the tissues out and studied my blotchy face in one of the white-framed mirrors. "Ugh. Can I wear a paper bag over my face today?"

"No," Blair said, getting off the couch and coming over to where I stood. She wrapped her arms around my shoulders from behind and met my eyes in the mirror. "You are beautiful, and you've got no reason to hide. I'm so proud of you for standing up for your heart. I love Cole and I know he's a good guy, but he doesn't deserve you if he's not willing to give a little."

"I don't even know what to ask him to give," I said, trying so hard not to cry, my nose burned. "He's not lying about how tough it is for him to take on a relationship as a single dad."

"Plenty of single dads have relationships."

"But his situation is different, and Mariah is special, and he's made promises to her and to himself that he can't break, not even for me." I squeezed my eyes shut against the tears. "Why would I even expect him to?"

"Because you're worth it," Blair said softly, giving me a squeeze. "And something tells me he knows that, and it's only a matter of time before he comes to his senses."

I smiled and hugged her arms. "Thank you. Spoken like a true sister. Now what do you say we forget about all my romantic troubles and focus on the fact that you and my brother are getting married today?"

She squealed. "*Yes*, sister!"

I laughed, feeling better. I might not have romance, but I had love in my life.

Today, I'd celebrate that.

Thirteen

Cole

I'D FUCKED UP, AND I KNEW IT.

But it was hard to pinpoint exactly where I'd gone wrong. Was I trying to be someone else? Was it Moretti's advice? Was I trying to have my cake and eat it too, getting Cheyenne in bed while maintaining our *just friends* status?

After staying up half the night thinking about it, I came to the conclusion that the truth was probably all of the above.

I could admit to myself that a lot of it *was* me trying to be someone else—someone more like Moretti, who enjoyed acting on his impulses and always managed to have a good time and keep things light. Take a girl back to her hotel room, have some fun, say goodnight. No lies, no promises, no problems.

But I wasn't Moretti, I thought as I got out of bed and into the shower. And while taking his advice to let go and have fun had made me feel young and alive, pumped full of testosterone and adrenaline, it hadn't turned out the way I'd hoped.

Because with Cheyenne, there was no way to keep things light. We'd known each other too long. I felt too much for her.

And she loved me—at least, she'd said she did. It had

knocked me out the way she'd confessed it. *I've loved you hopelessly for so long . . .* I'd been shocked. She'd hinted at a childhood crush before, but this felt like something different. Something deeper. Something stronger and yet more fragile.

Spending the night with me would give her hope, she'd said, her eyes full of tears, but her smile a little sheepish, as if she were embarrassed that being so close to me would mean so much to her. My chest had felt like it was caving in.

I'd wanted nothing more than to pull her back into bed, put my arms around her, and show her it would mean everything to me too. That I wouldn't take it lightly. That I'd never hurt her. That I'd guard her heart as fiercely as she would.

Stay with me, I wished I could have said. *Kiss me. Touch me. Whisper my name, and I'll whisper yours. Tell me again how you love me. Let me give you hope. Let me give you everything.*

But the words had been stuck in my throat.

Instead, I'd fallen back into the rut. Kept the walls in place. I'd let her go and promised to stay away.

It was all I could offer her.

"So how'd it go last night?" Moretti asked. He, Beckett, and I were seated by the fireplace in the lobby with cardboard cups of coffee, waiting for Griffin to come down. Then we'd all head into town for a proper shave at a barber shop. "I didn't want to say anything in front of Griff, but I saw you and Cheyenne leave together."

"I saw that too," said Beckett from next to me on the couch. "What's up with you guys?"

I sipped my coffee. "Uh, we left together, but it didn't exactly go as planned."

Moretti's smile faded. "Don't tell me. You fucked up the line."

"No, the line was fine the way I delivered it."

"What was the line?" Beckett wanted to know.

"I just asked her if she wanted to go up to my room."

Moretti rolled his eyes. "You fucked up the line."

"So what happened?" Beckett leaned forward, elbows on his knees.

I took another sip of coffee, debating how much to say. "We went to my room, and she changed her mind."

"Why?" Moretti asked.

I shrugged. "She realized it would be a bad idea. And she was right."

"But she wanted to?"

I thought of how wet she'd been when I touched her. The way she'd sucked my tongue into her mouth. How her body had moved against my hand. The thought of it nearly made me groan. "Yeah."

"And *you* wanted to?"

"Yeah."

Moretti shook his head. "I really don't understand this."

I tried to explain it without betraying her feelings. "She was thinking ahead."

"Ahead to what?" Beckett asked.

"Ahead to how she'll feel once it was over," I said, thinking that of all my friends, Beckett would probably understand the situation best. He was the quietest one in our foursome, but definitely the deepest thinker. We joked that he was probably the only cowboy in existence that had an MBA.

From fucking *Yale*.

But Moretti jumped in. "She'd feel fucking *great*, because you'd give her at least two orgasms—you do remember how to do that, right?"

Beckett laughed, and I rolled my eyes. "Yes, asshole."

"So what's the problem? Why is she able to think beyond orgasms in your hotel room?" Moretti shook his head. "Maybe you're not doing it right."

"Will you fuck off? It's not just about that with us. There are other things involved."

"Like what?" Beckett asked.

"Like feelings."

"Oh. Well." Moretti sat back, like he was giving up. "*Feelings.* You didn't mention those before."

"Yes, I did," I said defensively. "I told you she didn't want just a one-night stand."

"I meant *your* feelings. You didn't mention those when you said you wanted to bang Cheyenne."

"I never said it like that," I snapped. "And you guys better not say anything to Griffin about this."

"Griffin isn't an idiot, Cole. He can see the way you look at her—everyone can." Moretti appealed to Beckett. "Am I right?"

"He's right," Beckett confirmed. "My dad saw you guys at dinner last night and asked me when you'd gotten married."

That almost made me smile.

"And Griffin's okay with it," Moretti went on. "The question is, why aren't *you* okay with it?"

I leaned back, grumpy and confused. "I don't know. What if I fuck it up? Or what if things just go wrong, the way they always do, and we'll all end up worse off than we are now?"

"You could definitely fuck it up," Moretti agreed casually, taking another sip of his coffee. "And sure, things can always go wrong."

I looked at him incredulously. "Is this supposed to be a pep talk?"

"Yes. But no sense ignoring the obvious. Relationships are hard. They're risky. There's a reason why I prefer to play it safe."

"I thought you had a girlfriend," said Beckett.

"Still safe," Moretti insisted. "Because it's more of an arranged thing. I don't have the feelings Cole has."

Exhaling, I shook my head. "I don't know what to do. My head says one thing, my gut says another."

"What about your—"

"Don't ask," I said, noticing Griffin walking down the staircase. "You know what my dick says."

Moretti looked offended. "I was going to say your heart." He took a drink of his coffee. "You're such an asshole. I'm glad we're not a couple anymore."

Beckett choked on his coffee. "What?"

"Long story," I told him. Then I turned the tables on Moretti. "So what happened with Bianca last night?"

He frowned. "It was a real struggle, I tell you. I ordered her a holy water martini garnished with garlic on a crucifix, and I *still* couldn't exorcise the demon."

Laughing, I stood up as Griffin reached the bottom of the stairs and headed our way. "Well, keep trying," I said. "And thanks for the advice—I think."

After we finished up at the barber shop, we came back to the inn and grabbed a quick lunch at the restaurant. Afterward, I went back to my room and checked in with my mom, who was chaperoning Mariah in something called the "bridal suite," where all the girls were getting ready. I felt bad that I hadn't spent more time with her over the last couple days, but I also knew she was having the time of her life being included in almost everything the wedding party did.

My text to my mom went unanswered for a few minutes, and then it buzzed.

Mom: Hey, it's Cheyenne. Your mom handed me her phone because she decided to get her makeup done at the last minute. One of the artists had time.

At the sight of her name, my stomach muscles clenched.

Me: No problem, I was just checking on Mariah.

The next text came from Cheyenne's number.

Cheyenne: She's great. Dress is on, and she's perched like a princess on a throne in one of the salon chairs getting her hair curled.

Me: Sounds good. Thanks for including her the last couple days. She's in heaven.

Cheyenne: We love her. You guys doing okay? Griff holding up?

Me: Griffin seems cool and calm.

As opposed to me, who felt so uneasy you'd have thought I was the groom instead of the best man. None of this casual shit was what I really wanted to say to her.

Cheyenne: Blair is surprisingly calm too.

Me: I think all the nerves are mine.

Cheyenne: The toast?

I thought for a moment, then decided it was best to blame all my anxiety on the toast—at least for now.

Me: Yeah. I know what I want to say, I'm just scared it's going to come out wrong.

Cheyenne: Speak from your heart. If you do that, you can never go wrong.

While I was thinking about that, and what I'd say to her if I spoke from the heart, she texted again.

Cheyenne: And if all else fails, think fortune cookie.

I smiled.

Me: Thanks.

Cheyenne: Mariah is done. Want to talk to her?

Me: Sure.

A moment later, my phone vibrated. The screen said *Cheyenne calling*, and it gave me a little kick, even though I knew it would be Mariah's voice on the other end.

"Hello?"

"Hi, Daddy."

"Hi, peanut. Having fun?"

"Yes. I'm so excited!"

I smiled. "I miss you. I feel like I haven't seen you in days."

"That's because the bridesmaids aren't supposed to be with the groomsmaids before the wedding."

"Groomsmen," I corrected with a chuckle.

"Groomsmen. Are you guys ready yet?"

"Not quite. I have to put my suit on, but then I'll be ready."

"We're already dressed. We're going to take pictures in a minute. As soon as Blair is ready." A big sigh. "She looks so beautiful, Daddy. Like a fairy tale princess."

For a fleeting second, I thought of my wedding day—the nerves, the excitement, the hope, the thrill. Would I ever feel that way again, like I had everything to look forward to? Or would I always have to look back in order to experience joy? Why did happiness have to be just a memory? I glanced down at my ring.

"Miss Cheyenne looks beautiful too," Mariah was saying.

I swallowed hard. "I'm sure she does. I can't wait to see you all."

"Okay, I have to go because the photographer is telling us we're leaving."

"Okay. I'll see you soon, peanut. I love you."

"Love you too, Dad."

I waited for a moment in case Cheyenne came back on the line, hoping she would, but there was only silence on the other end.

Disappointed, I tossed my phone on the bed, and started to get undressed.

As I traded my jeans and flannel for a dark blue suit, white dress shirt and burgundy tie, I couldn't help noticing how empty and quiet the room was. I glanced around, wondering what it would be like if there was another suitcase on the floor, a black dress hanging in the closet, makeup and hairspray and earrings on the bathroom sink. It would even smell differently in here—like orange blossoms in the middle of winter.

There would be someone to talk to at the end of the night, someone familiar in a strange bed. Someone to hold, to whisper to in the dark, someone whose skin felt like satin against mine, who put her hands and mouth on me, who was warm and soft and beautiful. Someone who wanted me.

Someone who loved me.

I looked behind me at the bed, where I'd lain with Cheyenne last night, where I'd slept fitfully and alone, missing her, where I'd sleep alone again tonight, unless I was willing to take a risk.

Straightening my tie, I looked at my reflection and made up my mind.

Then I pulled off my ring and headed out.

"You ready, man?" Beckett clapped his hands on Griffin's shoulders. We'd just finished taking groomsmen photos down in the bar, which wasn't open yet, and we were having a quick shot before heading over to the barn.

"I'm ready," Griffin said, and he looked it. No sheen of sweat on his forehead, no nervous laughter, no shaking hands.

"Here you are, gentlemen." The bartender placed four shot glasses of whiskey on the bar with a grin. "For courage."

"Look at him, he doesn't even need it," Moretti said with a grin, handing Griffin a shot.

"No, but I do," I said, grabbing one for myself.

"You're gonna be great." Griffin slung an arm around me.

Moretti held his up. "*Beviamo alla nostra,*" he said. "To us."

"Don't be a dick." Beckett elbowed him. "Make it to Griffin."

"Relax, will you?" Moretti shot him a look. "We've been drinking to Griffin for weeks. And we'll be drinking to him all night. I just wanted to take a moment and appreciate our friendship. It's been a long time, and we've seen each other through a lot of things."

I nodded, thinking about the struggles we'd endured as friends over the last twenty-plus years. It was easy to forget how rare our bond was—these guys were like brothers to me, and I couldn't imagine my life without them.

"A lot of hardships, but a lot of good times too," Moretti went on. "Especially those baseball championships where we beat the pants off the Mason City Mavericks."

I raised my glass. "To the Bellamy Creek Bulldogs."

"To brotherhood," said Beckett.

"To the next twenty years," added Moretti.

Griffin lifted his glass higher. "And fuck the Mavs."

We laughed and tossed back our whiskey.

After one more shot—for warmth, we decided—we set our empty glasses on the bar and made our way through the ice and snow over to the barn, where the ceremony and reception would take place.

"You really as calm as you seem?" I asked Griffin as we walked along the shoveled path.

"Yeah, I really am." Even *he* sounded a little surprised. "Proposing to her was a way bigger deal. I was a fucking wreck that day. This feels like a formality."

"I get that," I said, again recalling my own experience.

Griffin glanced at me—he knew what I was thinking. "How about you? You holding up okay?"

"Yeah. I'm not really thinking about the past today." And I wasn't—not the way he meant.

"Good." He put an arm around me. "Because I happen to think the future could be pretty fucking awesome if you'd let it."

He made it sound so simple, and maybe it was.

I knew what I wanted.

And I knew what I had to do to get it.

Fourteen

Cheyenne

IT WAS TIME.

The guests were all seated. The barn was lit by candles and party lights. The music had started.

Griffin and Blair had wanted a small wedding to begin with, and the weather had also prevented a couple dozen people from being there, so the occasion seemed even more intimate. Half the barn was set up with round tables of ten for the reception, and the other half had rows of chairs on either side of a short aisle. At the head of the aisle, beneath a trellis hung with evergreen boughs and more white lights, my brother waited for his bride. Behind him stood his three best friends—Cole, Enzo, and Beckett, just like always.

From the back of the room, I watched Alexis and then Frannie make their way up the aisle, their long ruby-red dresses a dramatic splash of color amid so much white. When April signaled it was my turn, I turned and gave Mariah and Blair one last smile, tears in my eyes. "Here we go," I whispered.

Mariah beamed. "Here we go."

Blair smiled, radiantly beautiful, in a strapless gown fit for a princess. Her hair was pulled back from her face but loose around her shoulders, and she carried a bouquet of jewel tone roses, emerald greens, and eucalyptus. Beside her, eighty-something Charlie Frankel looked as dapper as I'd ever seen him, and as proud to have Blair on his arm as a father would be. He gave me a wink.

"Okay, Cheyenne," whispered April. "Now."

I walked slowly, clutching my bouquet of greens, breathing deeply, smiling widely, and trying desperately not to cry. Meeting my brother's eyes didn't help, because I saw that his were shining too. Then I looked at Cole—his eyes were dry, but I could see he was emotional too. He touched his heart for a moment. My throat grew tight and I felt a little dizzy. With tears blurring my vision, I walked a little faster, and took my place near Frannie.

Next came Mariah, smiling brightly, her joy and pride evident with every step. Her dress was a deep blue velvet and brought out the color of her sapphire eyes, which she'd inherited from her dad. But I could see her mom in her face too, and I wondered if Cole was struggling at all today, grappling with memories or ghosts.

As Mariah reached the front of the room, everyone rose, and a reverent murmur floated through the air as Blair made her way toward Griffin on the arm of her surrogate grandad. There may have been only forty or so guests, but every single one of them had to feel choked up as they watched Griffin behold his bride for the first time and wipe his eyes, and Charlie Frankel kiss Blair on the cheek before shaking Griffin's hand. Once Charlie was seated, Blair and Griffin stood side by side, and the officiant stepped forward.

I held back sobs all the way through the ceremony, dabbing at my eyes several times during the vows, letting a few tears fall during a moment of silence for my father and all the other loved ones we wished were here, and finally weeping openly when

Griffin kissed the bride and the officiant proudly pronounced them "Mr. and Mrs. Dempsey."

The entire place erupted in applause and whistles and shouts, and as the speakers blasted "Jackson" by Johnny and June Carter Cash, Blair and Griffin began to dance back down the aisle.

Since it was unexpected, I was laughing when Cole took my arm, and we followed behind the jubilant new Mr. and Mrs. Dempsey.

"They did it," I said, my heart pounding.

"They did it."

With his eyes still on me, he stumbled. "Shit—sorry." Recovering his footing, he held my arm a little tighter. "Guess I need to look where I'm going. But it's hard to take my eyes off you."

"Thank you," I said, feeling heat in my cheeks.

"Listen, maybe we can talk later. I know it's kind of chaotic tonight, but there's something I want to—"

"Chey!" Blair squealed, rushing over to hug me. "It's done! We're sisters!"

Cole and I were separated as I embraced Blair, then April herded us all into a room at the back of the barn, and there was a mad scramble to crowd the newlyweds and smother them with love and congratulations. Someone popped several bottles of champagne, and I sought out my brother, who wrapped his arms around me.

"Congratulations," I whispered as he held me tight. "It was perfect. I only wish Dad could have been here."

"I think he was," Griffin said. "At least, Mom said he was."

Laughing, I released him and stepped back. Someone handed us each a glass of champagne and I raised mine to his. "Cheers, big brother. You did good."

He clinked his glass to mine. "Your turn next?"

"Maybe," I said, swallowing some bubbly.

But first, there was the small matter of getting over my feelings for Cole Mitchell. I snuck a glance at him across the room, and saw that he was with Mariah. He took her hands and held them both out so he could admire her, then hugged her close. As she wrapped her arms around him, pressing her cheek to his chest, her eyes closed.

Sadness lumped up in my throat, and I tried to wash it away with champagne. He'd said he wanted to talk later, but I wasn't sure I could handle it. No doubt he was feeling bad about last night and just wanted to apologize again, make sure there were no hard feelings—that's the kind of guy he was—but I was already an emotional grenade.

No reason to pull that pin tonight.

There were pictures and pictures and more pictures after that—indoors by the trellis and outdoors in the dusky winter light, staged and casual, portraits and group shots, wedding party and extended family. By the time we were done, my cheeks hurt from smiling, my feet hurt from standing, and it was dinnertime.

I took my seat next to Blair and saw the name Cole Mitchell at the place setting next to mine. I glanced at her. "Really?"

"Sorry," she whispered. "The seating chart was made weeks ago. Want to switch spots with someone real quick?"

I shook my head—I would not make anything difficult for Blair today. "No. I'm okay."

"So how are things? Have you spoken to him at all?"

I shrugged. "A little. It's not as horrible as I thought it might be, but still kind of awkward." I looked around at our table—Alexis and her husband, Beckett and Moretti, Frannie and Mack. "Where's Mariah sitting?"

"With Mack and Frannie's girls," said Blair. "I figured she'd have more fun with them."

"Good idea."

"He's coming." Blair sat up taller and raised her voice. "Hey, Cole. Ready for the toast? I think you're up next."

"I hope so." He pulled out the chair next to mine. "Is this okay?"

"Of course," I said, my pulse picking up. "Don't worry. You'll be fine."

He gave me a tight-lipped smile. "Thanks. I just want to get this part done so I can have a drink."

"Well, you're in luck, because April is coming this way with a mic."

"Fuck." He wiped his hands on his pants. "Why didn't I write shit down? My head's a mess."

"You'll be fine," I whispered, unable to resist patting his arm.

He stood and took the mic from April. "Good evening, everyone. Can I get your attention for a minute?"

The guests quieted, and all faces turned toward him.

"My name is Cole Mitchell, and on behalf of Griffin and Blair, I want to thank you all for braving the blizzard to be here tonight. I know it means a lot to them." He paused before going on. "As the best man, I'm honored to have the opportunity to say a few words. I've known Griffin almost all my life, and he's like a brother to me. In all those years, I've seen him do a lot of good things. He's a stellar first baseman. He served his country. He runs a successful business. He's been the best friend a guy could ask for—loyal beyond measure. But I've never been prouder of him than I was today, watching him take this leap of faith. We all know marriage isn't easy. It takes patience and understanding. It takes forgiveness and acceptance. It takes courage, sacrifice, and unconditional love. Finding someone willing to give you all that—well, it takes time. And luck." He glanced at Griffin and Blair. "And sometimes, a blown tire."

The guests laughed, and Cole's face relaxed into a smile. "I couldn't be happier for Griffin and Blair, and I couldn't have chosen a more perfect person for my friend. It's rare when someone is as beautiful on the inside as she is on the outside"—he glanced down at me before looking over at the bride—"but anyone who knows Blair will tell you she's living proof it can happen."

I smiled at Blair too.

"And even though Griffin was his usual stubborn self at first, even *he* realized that . . ." Cole paused for a second. "That when you have something precious in your hands, you need to hold on tight."

Chills swept across my back. I knew I'd heard the words somewhere, but at first I couldn't remember when. Then it came to me—my mother had said them to us, the night we shattered the wedding plate.

Cole lifted his champagne. "So let's raise a glass to Griffin and Blair, in celebration of their commitment to each other, this incredible evening, and holding on tight. Cheers!"

"Cheers!" The word echoed throughout the crowd, followed by the clinking of glasses all over the room. I swallowed some champagne, smiling through tears as the bubbles tickled my throat.

April came and took the mic from Cole, who sat down and wiped his forehead. "God, I'm glad that's over."

"You were great!" Moretti said. "Fucking fantastic."

"I can't believe you didn't have that written down," Mack commented. "I'd have forgotten everything."

"I forgot a lot of it," Cole admitted, stealing another glance at me. "And I started to panic. But something came to me at the end."

"It was perfect," I said softly, the lump refusing to leave my throat.

"Thanks." He spoke quietly then, only to me. "Think your mom will mind I quoted her?"

I had to laugh as I shook my head. "She might never let you forget it, but she'll be happy *someone* was listening."

"Cole Mitchell, you made me cry!" Blair exclaimed, getting out of her chair to come hug him. "How dare you!"

Griffin came over to shake his hand and give him a back-thumping embrace too, and by the time everyone was settled again, servers were placing dinner on the table. Cole reached for his napkin and spread it on his lap.

That's when I realized he wasn't wearing his ring.

I tried not to make too much of it, but it was difficult not to keep stealing glances at his hands throughout the meal. My appetite was almost nonexistent, even though the food was delicious. The wine was good too, but I was careful not to drink too much. I did *not* want a repeat of last night, and any time I got tipsy, I tended to shed my inhibitions where Cole was concerned.

I stayed quiet, if not silent, during the first three courses, and Cole didn't say much either. At one point, he got up to go check on Mariah, and Blair leaned over and whispered to me, "Everything okay? You guys both seem kind of down."

I forced a smile. "All good. Just enjoying dinner."

She glanced at my beef tenderloin and roasted potatoes. "What dinner? That one right there? The one that's still on your plate?"

Pressing my lips together, I reached for my water. "This dress is tight. I don't want to overeat."

"Cheyenne, you—"

"Shh," I admonished. "He's coming back."

"Bathroom break before cake?"

I nodded. "Fine."

Once our entrées were cleared, half of mine left uneaten, Blair and I grabbed our small clutches from beneath our chairs and headed for the ladies' room. I helped her use the bathroom—the ball gown style she'd chosen meant she needed some assistance—and freshened up as we waited a few minutes for the lounge to clear. When it was just the two of us, she turned to me, her expression worried.

"Talk to me. Are you really okay?"

I smiled and lied. "I'm really okay."

"Because the wedding party dance is coming up, and if you—"

"Blair." I held up my palms. "I'm fine. I can handle it."

The tension in her face eased. "Okay. Because we can always switch things up. Frannie can dance with Cole, and you can dance with Moretti."

"No need to change anything." I swallowed hard. "I'm used to this, remember? He was never mine, and he's never going to be mine, and dancing with someone else doesn't make that less true."

"But it might make it less painful," she said softly.

I shook my head, willing the sob in my chest to stay there. "Don't worry about me."

Two friends of my mother's entered the bathroom and immediately accosted Blair, telling her how beautiful everything was. After chatting with them for a moment, we headed back to the table, where cake had been served along with pitchers of coffee.

Cole was back at Mariah's table, but he looked over at me as I sat down. Averting my eyes, I poured myself some coffee, took a couple bites of cake without tasting them, and tried to keep breathing. He stayed at the kids' table, his cake left untouched.

"When's the wedding party dance?" I asked Blair.

"In about ten minutes," she said.

"Good. I'm just going to grab some air first if that's okay?"

She hesitated, and then nodded. "It's okay."

Without looking in Cole's direction, I went to the coat room and asked the attendant for my faux fur stole, which all the women in the wedding party had worn. Wrapping it around my shoulders, I slipped outside.

The snow had finally stopped falling, and the night was clear, a few stars visible in the sky. I tipped my face up and out of habit, wished on the first one I saw.

I wish Cole could be mine.

Then I shook my head, blinking away tears. I really needed to stop doing that—wishing on stars was for kids. I was fucking thirty, and that wish was never going to come true. Taking deep breaths of icy air, I shivered and pulled my stole tighter around me. But I didn't want to go in yet—I wanted to get so cold I felt numb.

"Cheyenne?"

At the sound of his voice, I turned. "Cole. Hey."

"What are you doing out here? You're going to freeze."

"Nah." I looked up at the sky again, at the traitorous stars. "I'm just getting some air."

"Blair said you were out here—I said I'd come get you. It's about time for the dance."

"Oh. Okay." Glancing at him, I tried a joke. "Ready to bust a move?"

He laughed a little. "I'm just hoping I don't bust your toes."

"Don't worry, I'll try to keep them out of your way." I moved for the door, but he reached for my arm.

"Cheyenne, wait. I was hoping we'd have a chance to talk."

"Maybe later, okay?" I said, gently shaking his hand off me. "We'd better get inside. I can hardly feel my feet, which won't help us on the dance floor."

Nodding, he pulled the door open for me without another word.

Inside, I dropped my stole in the coat room and made my way toward the edge of the dance floor, where I saw the rest of the wedding party waiting for the music to start.

Blair looked relieved when she saw me. "You're back."

"I'm back." I could feel it when Cole took his place beside me.

"So when the song begins, we're all just going to go out there," Blair said, addressing everyone. "No announcements or anything."

"Got it." I nodded, a shiver moving through me as Cole

placed a hand at the small of my back. I remembered being in his arms last night, the way his body had felt on mine, the way he'd kissed me. The song began, and he gently nudged me forward onto the floor.

I held my breath as he slipped one arm around me and took my hand in his. Placing my left palm on his broad shoulder, I made sure to keep my body several inches from his, so that our chests were not pressed together. We swayed a little awkwardly to the music, like middle schoolers at their first dance, afraid to get too close. My stomach jittered with nerves. Eventually I had to inhale, and when I did, the scent of him filled my head.

Oh God, how long was this song going to go on?

Over Cole's shoulder, I saw Griffin holding Blair tight, Beckett and Alexis laughing at something, and Frannie grinning as Moretti turned her beneath his arm. Everyone was having a better time than we were—was it obvious?

Glancing at the guests, I saw my mother dabbing at her eyes, Charlie Frankel smiling fondly, Mariah shifting her weight from side to side, impatient to have her turn on the dance floor. It gave me an idea.

"You should dance with Mariah," I said.

"Yeah, I promised her I would, at some point."

"No, I mean during this song. Like, trade me for her, so she can be part of this. After all, she's in the wedding party too."

Cole was silent a moment. And then, "I don't want to dance with Mariah right now. I want to dance with you."

"I really don't mind," I said, suddenly desperate to make an escape before I broke down. "In fact, I insist."

"Cheyenne."

"Let's move that way." I took the lead, maneuvering us over to the side where Mariah stood. "Hey sweetie," I said, smiling at her. "Want to dance with your dad?"

Her eyes lit up. "Can I?"

"Of course," I said, letting him go. "He's all yours."

"Yay!" She spread her arms, and Cole embraced her the way he'd held me, dancing her back out onto the floor without another glance in my direction.

I stood next to Mrs. Mitchell for a moment, a smile pasted on my face, laughing a little despite myself when Mariah tried executing a few fancy twirls. When the song was over, I applauded along with the rest of the guests, then watched as Griffin brought my mom onto the floor, and Blair asked Charlie Frankel to dance.

Cole and Mariah ended up on the other side of the room, but I felt his eyes on me. Careful not to meet them, I watched my brother dance with my mom and missed my dad with a ferocious ache in my heart. I wiped away tears when the song ended.

At that point, the DJ played an up-tempo oldie and invited everyone to the dance floor. I saw Mariah begging her dad to take her back out there, and Cole arguing before finally giving in. Feeling like I could use a drink, I made my way to the bar.

Glass of wine in my hand, I stood way over to one side, hoping to fade into the shadows. I hated myself for being such a party pooper at my brother's wedding—I was the maid of honor, for fuck's sake—but I felt like I just needed a little time-out before getting back on the dance floor. I decided I'd give myself ten minutes to breathe and finish my wine, then I'd set aside my feelings and act like a best friend and good sister should.

Even if I had to fake it.

It worked, to a point.

I drank more wine. I danced right out of my shoes. I smiled for pictures and laughed with friends and even went out onto the floor when Blair tossed the bouquet—which I missed, much to the dismay of my mother, who pointed out that I could have dived for it if I'd really cared.

But I discovered that faking a good time led to actually having a good time, even if beneath the surface, I was still heartbroken over Cole.

He danced a few times with Mariah, but other than that he mostly hung out with the guys near the bar. Our table was clearly my turf, and when I wasn't dancing, I sat there with Blair or Frannie or Mariah or my mom, sipping wine and trying not to look in his direction.

But I could feel his eyes on me.

Around eleven, the DJ announced the last song, an old Nat King Cole ballad my dad used to love. Misty-eyed, I pulled my heels back on and watched Griffin and Blair moving to the music. I was so emotional, I didn't see Cole approach.

"Cheyenne?" His voice was low in my ear. "Would you like to dance?"

I looked over my shoulder, my stomach flip-flopping. "Oh! Um, sure. Okay."

He offered his hand, and I took it, rising to my feet and walking on unsteady legs onto the dance floor. When he took me into his arms, he held me much closer than he had before. I was positive he could feel my heart pounding against his chest.

For a minute or so, we danced in silence, and I tried to let myself enjoy the fact that he'd actually *asked* me—this wasn't out of duty. He'd *crossed the room* to take my hand and hold me one more time. So why did it feel like the consolation prize?

"Did you have fun tonight?" he asked.

"Yes. Did you?"

"Yes. I think I danced more tonight than I have in thirty years."

I smiled. "I liked when Mariah stood on your feet."

He groaned. "As if dancing wasn't hard enough for me."

"I don't know. I think you move okay."

He said nothing, but pulled me even closer. Feelings bubbled perilously near the surface.

"My dad loved this song," I said, my throat tight. "It reminds me of him."

"He was a good guy."

I nodded. Took a deep breath. "We really missed him today." Then I remembered that I probably wasn't the only one struggling with grief. "Was today tough for you?"

"Yes."

Even though I'd suspected as much, his words still caused a sharp twinge in my chest.

"But not in the way you think."

I pulled back slightly to look at him. "What?"

"Today was mostly tough for me because I felt bad about last night."

I stiffened. "It's okay."

"No, it's not. The way it ended was all wrong."

"But it had to end that way, Cole. I know it's hard to understand, because I can't make you feel what I feel, but believe me when I say that we're better off today having stopped things last night." The song ended, so I let him go and stepped back just as Griffin and Blair approached.

"Hey, we're heading back over to the bar at the inn," my brother announced. "Coming, Cole?"

"Maybe," said Cole. "I need to make sure Mariah gets to bed."

"Chey?" Griffin looked at me.

"Actually, I'm a little tired, and my feet kind of hurt. I might just go back to my room."

Griffin frowned. "Don't be fucking lame. Go put some other shoes on and come down to the bar."

"If she's tired, she doesn't have to come." Blair caught my eye to let me know she understood.

"I'll think about it," I said, mostly to avoid an argument.

But when we finally made it back to the inn, I pulled Blair aside in the lobby. "Hey, will you be okay if I don't go to the bar?"

"Of course," she said, her eyes concerned. "Are you okay?"

"I'm fine. It was just a really long day." Out of the corner of my eye, I saw Cole saying goodnight to Mariah, giving her a hug and kiss before turning her over to his mom. "And I'm going to sneak off before Cole sees me go."

Her eyes widened. "Why?"

"Because he feels bad about last night, and I just can't listen to another apology. I want to forget what happened—or almost happened—and try to get back to normal. But that's not going to happen tonight."

"I understand." She hugged me. "You're amazing, and I love you, and someday we're going to do this all over again for your wedding."

I swallowed hard. "I hope so."

"Get some sleep. I'll see you in the morning."

"Okay." I let her go and headed immediately for the stairs before anyone could stop me.

In my room, I breathed a sigh of relief as the door shut behind me. Going over to the bed, I sank down and slipped off my shoes. From inside my evening bag, my phone buzzed, and reluctantly I took it out and looked at the screen.

Griffin: Get your ass down here.

Me: I love you but I'm too tired. Goodnight.

Griffin: Unacceptable.

Rather than fight him, I simply put my phone on Do Not Disturb and set it aside. There was no way I was going down to that bar. Griffin would get over it.

Flopping onto my back, I flung an arm across my eyes, blocking out the light from the bedside lamp. Waiting for tears. Surprised when they didn't come.

Was I simply too exhausted to let out all the feelings I'd held in all day? Was that possible? And what was I going to do about the future? I couldn't go on like this. Living next door to him was a special kind of torture. And even after he moved, he'd still be right there in town, at all family functions. We'd still bump into each other all the time.

Maybe it was time to think about moving away from Bellamy Creek. Applying for a teaching job somewhere else. Making a fresh start.

While I was pondering it, someone knocked on my door— three hard, staccato beats.

I groaned in annoyance. "Go away, Griffin. I'm not coming down."

Three more knocks.

Exasperated, I hauled my ass off the bed and shuffled to the door in my bare feet, my velvet gown dragging behind me. "Stop it, Griffin! You're going to wake the entire inn. And I'm not coming—" I opened the door.

Then I stopped talking.

It wasn't my brother.

Fifteen

Cole

PUSHING INSIDE HER ROOM WITHOUT BEING INVITED, I held the door open with my hand. "You don't have to come down, but goddammit, you need to listen to me."

She looked taken aback for a moment, then shook her head. "No."

"Why not?"

"Because we don't want the same thing, Cole. I mean, yes, tonight we probably want the same thing," she said, her eyes traveling over my shoulders and chest and down to my crotch before she quickly flicked them up again. "And there was a time in my life when I'd have done it in a heartbeat, just to be with you like that. But I'm—"

"Stop talking," I said, putting a finger over her perfect lips. The door slammed shut behind me. "Stop talking and listen. All night I've been trying to tell you you're wrong, and I can't fucking get the words out, because you keep cutting me off."

Her eyes flashed with fire as she pushed my hand away. "I'm protecting myself, Cole."

"You don't need protecting, Cheyenne. That's what I'm

trying to tell you." I took her head in my hands and looked her in the eye. "You're safe with me."

"But last night you said—"

"Last night, I was still confused. I couldn't think straight. I haven't been able to think straight for months where you're concerned. And then when you told me how you'd felt all that time, it was like being hit by a train. There were all these things I wanted to say to you but couldn't."

"Sorry," she said. "I know that was a lot—what I told you."

I shook my head. "Don't be sorry. I needed to hear it. I needed to be pushed into facing the truth."

"What's the truth?" Her voice was barely a whisper.

"That I have feelings for you. And they're not going to go away just because I ignore them."

Cheyenne's mouth had fallen open, and I traced her bottom lip with my thumb.

"Believe me, I've tried to ignore them. I've tried to talk myself out of them. I've denied them to anyone who asked."

She blinked. "People have asked?"

"Yes. Apparently I am not an expert at hiding the way I feel about you."

"You hid it from *me*."

"Well, I don't want to hide it anymore," I told her, loving the way it made her expression melt from surprise into bliss. "Not from you, not from myself, not from anyone. That's why today was tough—because I realized that even though I have no fucking idea what I'm doing, I don't want to lose you."

"You don't?"

"No." I kissed her lips, then whispered against them. "When you have something precious in your hands, you need to hold on tight."

She slid her hands up my chest and looped them around my neck, pulling me toward her. Slanting my mouth over hers, I moved my hands into her soft, thick hair the way I'd been dying to all night long. It fell in loose waves over her shoulders, pouring like champagne down her back. My fingers found the zipper at the back of her dress and pulled it down, the erotic sound sending a jolt of desire straight to my cock.

Her hands moved to my tie, loosened the knot, and pulled it free of my collar. I took my hands off her just long enough to shrug out of my suit jacket and toss it aside, then ran my palms down her velvet-covered rib cage and hips while she unbuckled my belt and yanked my shirt free of my pants.

Impatient to feel her skin against mine, I unbuttoned my shirt and threw it aside as she undid my pants. I groaned when she slipped her hand inside them, wrapping her fingers around my cock. For a moment, all I could do was stand there, reveling in the sensation of her touch. I'd been so hard for her so many times but had never felt her hand closing around me, or heard the sigh of desire on her lips, or the eager moan of anticipation as I thickened in her fist.

Recovering my senses, I whipped my T-shirt over my head and kicked off my shoes. Then I turned her to face the bed and slipped the off-the-shoulder sleeves of her dress down her arms. It fell to the floor, revealing a pair of lace underwear in a color that matched her skin tone. I gathered her hair in my hands and buried my face in it, inhaling deeply before sweeping it aside and putting my lips on her throat. She tilted her head and reached up with one arm, threading her fingers into my hair as I kissed my way down her neck, my cock pushing against her ass.

My mouth traveled down her shoulder blade, and I dropped to my knees behind her, pulling her underwear down her legs. She stepped out of them and the dress at the same time, and I turned her to face me. Looking up the length of her body, I felt a surge of arousal so powerful I nearly growled like an animal.

"You're so fucking beautiful," I managed to say instead, running my hands up the sides of her thighs, pausing to grip her hips.

Her lips curved into the kind of smile I hoped she'd never given to any other man. "Thank you."

Flattening my hands on her belly, I slid them up over her full, round breasts, her nipples tight and hard against the center of my palms. She moaned as I teased the stiff peaks with my fingers and traced a circle around her belly button with my tongue.

"Cole," she panted, reaching down as if to pull me to my feet. "I want you."

"You've got me." I stood up just long enough to tip her backward onto the bed, then I knelt at her feet again and pushed her knees apart. "So be patient. I've waited for this a long time."

"*You* have!" She sounded shocked as she propped herself up on her elbows.

But I wasn't interested in arguing who'd wanted each other first or more—all I cared about was now, and *now* was pretty fucking good because I was licking my way up one inner thigh and then the other, stopping just short of putting my mouth where I wanted it.

Above me, I heard her whimper and try to protest, but her frustrated sounds gave way to sweet little sighs of rapture when I finally stroked up her warm, wet center with my tongue, lingering at the top, teasing her clit with slow, sensual circles. Ravenous for her, I licked and sucked and buried my tongue inside her, my hands hooked beneath her legs, holding her to me as if she might try to escape.

She tasted as sweet as she looked—champagne and honey—and I groaned in agonized delight as I devoured her. When her sounds grew more frantic and her body writhed and bucked beneath my mouth, I slipped my fingers inside her, my jealous cock aching to ease into that soft, slick heat.

Beside her legs, her hands clawed at the sheets, and I could feel the muscles in her body go tense as she contracted around my fingers. I moved my tongue a little faster and harder, pushed my fingers a little deeper, and suddenly she was crying out in relief, her orgasm pulsing from her body into mine, like ripples on the water.

As soon as I felt her body relax slightly, I jumped to my feet, and ditched the rest of my clothes, pausing only to pull my wallet from my pants pocket. She lifted herself up onto her elbows and watched as I took out the condom and tore the wrapper open.

"Am I dreaming?" she asked breathlessly, scooting up toward the headboard.

"Want me to pinch you?" I rolled the condom on and stretched out above her.

"Yes, please." She opened her legs for me and put her hands on my chest. "I want you to do everything to me."

I braced myself over her and eased into her body slowly, even though my heart raced ahead and my instinct was to chase it. Below me, I watched Cheyenne's face change, her eyes closing as she took me in, heard her breathing become more labored as she struggled to relax and get used to my size.

"Are you okay?" I asked her.

"Yes," she whispered, her eyes opening again. She moved her hands over my shoulders and down my back. "I want to savor every single moment, even if it hurts."

"I don't want to hurt you," I said, my voice raw with need, my body tense with bound energy, a lion caged. "I want to make you feel good."

"Cole." She lifted her head and kissed my throat, my collarbone, my jaw. Her hands slid down over my ass and pulled me in deeper. "Give me everything. I've waited so long."

At her invitation, I began to move, slowly at first, deep, long strokes that made her arch and gasp and dig her fingernails into my skin. I wanted to be patient for her—I wanted to be gentle and tender and sweet—she'd waited for this, dreamed about this, and I wanted to be the man in her dreams who catered to her every whim, anticipated her every need, gave her everything she wanted. But instead I found myself struggling to hold onto control—she was so beautiful, so wet and warm and soft, and it felt so fucking good to be inside her, to give in to the temptation I'd fought for so damn long.

And she didn't help—she urged me on with her moans and sighs, with her hands that gripped and pulled, with her kisses that teased and tantalized, with her honey-and-champagne flavor still on my tongue. She met every thrust of mine with her own, our bodies moving rhythmically together as if they'd been made for each other, as if we'd been doing this all our lives.

"God, Cheyenne," I rasped, pausing with my cock buried deep inside her. "This feels too good. I'm too fucking close."

"Me too," she whispered, tilting her hips. "Don't stop."

Groaning, I began to move again, fucking her hard and deep. I remembered all the nights I'd fantasized about her, all the times I'd imagined being inside her this way—my hand had been a poor fucking substitute. This was a full-body experience, and every nerve ending was alive and on fire. Every sense was intensified—I could smell her, taste her, hear her crying out for me, for God, for release. Stars appeared behind my closed eyes as I reached the peak and clung to the edge, desperate to bring her with me, rocking into her again and again, until I felt the tension within her give way and her frustrated, pleading cries were eclipsed by one long sigh as her body clenched around me. I let go, and my body took over, exploding inside her, turning inside out, throbbing in hot, desperate, rippling waves of relief.

We lay there for a moment, tangled and clutching, our skin slick with sweat I hadn't even noticed before, our breath slowing down, our muscles gradually relaxing.

I buried my face in her hair and inhaled, my entire body humming with pleasure. She stroked my back, pressed her lips to my shoulder, wrapped her legs around me. For a few minutes, we said nothing and just held each other, the only two souls in the world. In the universe. In existence.

Eventually, I lifted my chest off her and looked down at her face, my heart beating hard. Those brown eyes threatened to undo me. "Hey."

She smiled. "Hey."

"You okay?"

The smile widened, and she nodded, eyes drifting shut. "Yes."

"Am I crushing you?"

"Yes. Never stop."

I laughed, shifting onto my side so that she wasn't bearing any of my weight, but taking her with me so we were face to face. "I just got here. Suffocating you is not part of my plan."

"I didn't know there was a plan."

"Actually, there isn't. Not beyond this anyway. My plan was to get you to listen to me, tell you how I felt, and then see if you'd let me take all your clothes off."

She giggled, her fingertips brushing against my chest. "It worked. Well done."

"But now I need a new plan."

"I'm good with more of the same," she said. "I liked every single part of the old one, even if you did cover my mouth to get me to shut up."

"I had to—you would not stop talking."

"I thought I was protecting myself."

"I know." I brushed her hair back from her face. "And you were right to stop things last night. It's not that I didn't feel this way then—because I did—but hearing you admit your feelings made it impossible to ignore mine any longer."

"Tell me again how you feel," she said shyly, her eyes on my chest.

I gathered her in close, tucking her head beneath my chin. For once, the words flowed easily. "I feel a lot of things. I feel like I want to hold you all night. I feel like all the oxygen goes out of the room when you enter it. I feel like I'm the only guy in the world when you look at me. I feel like there's nothing I wouldn't do to make you smile."

She snuggled closer, putting an arm and leg over me. "If this turns out to be a dream, I'm going to be so fucking mad."

I kissed the top of her head. "It's not."

"I wish I could go back in time and tell twelve-year-old me not to give up hope, that there's a reason she has all those feelings for you that won't ease up."

I chuckled. "Did you really have a crush on me all the way back then?"

"Yes," she said, laughing. "And it never ended."

"Get out, you've had plenty of boyfriends over the years. And I secretly hated every one of them."

"Did you?" She sounded surprised.

"Yes. I would tell myself it was just me being protective, but there was probably more to it. Especially that asshole you brought around at Christmas a few years ago. What was his name . . . Jake?"

She groaned. "Don't remind me. I only dated him because he was the total opposite of you. I was trying to distract myself."

"He pinched your ass at the tree lighting, and I wanted to fucking punch him in the face."

Pushing back from my chest, she propped herself up and looked down at me. "You saw him pinch my ass at the *outdoor tree lighting ceremony*? In that huge crowd?"

I rolled onto my back and put my hands behind my head. "Maybe."

"Were you *watching* me?"

"Maybe."

Her face lit up, and she slapped my chest. "You were!"

"Well, I could tell he was an asshole. I felt like I needed to keep an eye on you. You know, for your own safety."

She narrowed her eyes. "For my own safety?"

"Yes. Definitely not because *I* wanted to touch your ass."

"Of course not. Because you were always a perfect gentleman."

"Aren't I still?"

"Well, I don't know." She pretended to think about it, tapping a finger to her chin. "Now that I know what you were thinking, I might have to reconsider my assessment of you."

I reached out and grabbed her by the forearms, and she squealed as I flipped her beneath me. "Haven't you been reconsidering it since the moment in my bedroom when you insisted on seeing my belt?"

A sly grin took over her face. "Oh yeah. That."

"I warned you."

"You did." She wrapped her legs around me. "It was still a bit of a shock."

"I remember. You tried to leave through the closet door."

Her giggle warmed me all over. "God, that was embarrassing."

"Tell me about it."

"However, it took my fantasies to a whole new level. So thank you."

I grinned. "Like the one where I arrest you for being a bad girl?"

She nodded, catching her bottom lip between her teeth. "Uh huh."

"That text message fucking blew my mind." I leaned down and rubbed my lips against hers. "Will you do that again sometime?"

"Sure. I've got plenty of fantasies to choose from. There's this one where you bust into the bedroom on Prom night where Brody Nichols is pawing me and trying to talk me out of my virginity, and you kick his ass. Then you pop my cherry for yourself, of course."

My jaw was hanging open, anger shooting through my veins. "Wait a minute. Is any of that story true? Did that little shit Brody Nichols actually paw you?"

"Relax, it was years ago. I'm thirty, remember? And it was very minor pawing. Second base stuff."

"I will fucking tear him apart," I seethed. "I don't care how long it's been." I'd never liked Brody Nichols—he'd been a jackass as a teenager, and he was still a jackass as an adult. "He deserves an ass-kicking."

"He probably does, but it's not necessary on my account. I handled it."

"How?"

"I kneed him in the balls and told him to go fuck himself."

I laughed, shaking my head. "I cannot picture the sweet little Cheyenne Dempsey I knew doing that."

"You didn't know everything about me," she said coyly, bringing her hands to my chest. Her fingertips teased my nipples, making my blood rush faster.

"That's true." I lowered my mouth to hers, protectiveness and possessiveness igniting the fire in me again. "But from now on, the only hands that get near you are mine."

"Or mine," she whispered, "while I pretend they're yours."

"We're done pretending," I told her, rolling onto my back and bringing her on top of me. "From now on, we're the real thing."

Sixteen

Cheyenne

EVEN MY FANTASIES WEREN'T THIS GOOD—AND MY fantasies had been pretty fucking awesome.

But this—*this*—his hands in my hair and on my skin. His mouth open against mine, his tongue between my lips. His body, strong and muscular beneath me, sculpted with the kinds of curves and edges and lines I'd only imagined. His bare cock, thick and long and hard, hitting me so deep it stole my breath.

As I slid down onto it, slowly and carefully, my hands braced on his chest, I couldn't take my eyes off him. He watched me with a combination of lust and reverence in his blue eyes, his hands tight on my hips, his breathing ragged and heavy. Beneath my palms, his heart beat hard and fast—for me.

I couldn't believe it.

For *me*.

As if the threads to the past and all its hopelessness had been snipped, I raced ahead, unashamed and unafraid and unencumbered by worry and doubt. He wanted me, he wanted this, he wanted love.

"Cheyenne," he said, his jaw tight. "We need to stop so I can put a condom on."

"I'm okay with this if you are. I'm on the pill, and I haven't been with anybody else in over two years."

"I haven't either."

I smiled. "So we're good."

With that, I let go of my inhibitions and moved the way my body wanted to, riding him with reckless abandon, enjoying the way he groaned and gripped my hips to slow me down, or filled his hands with my breasts, or sat up and took them in his mouth, his tongue driving me crazy. When he got too close, he begged me to stop, but I didn't, intoxicated with the power I had over him in that moment—*finally*—the way *I* was in control. In fact, I moved my hips a little faster, rocked my body a little rougher, cried out a little louder, until I felt him stiffen and throb within me, which set off the billowing swells of my own orgasms—*yes, yes, yes*.

I was his, and he was mine, and we were finally, unbelievably, real.

"Can I ask you something?" Cole's tone was quiet and intimate, his hands gentle as they swept lazily up and down my back. Our bodies were still connected, and my cheek was pressed against his chest, where I'd collapsed.

"Sure."

"Why haven't you been with anyone else in so long?"

"It hasn't really been that long."

"You said over two years."

"True. But I guess that doesn't feel like that long. I haven't really missed it."

"No?"

"Uh huh. To be honest, sex never fulfilled me that much. There would be all this buildup, and then afterward I always ended up feeling disappointed in some way. It was never what I was looking for. At some point, I decided to stop sharing so much of myself with guys who didn't care enough."

"Good."

"What about you?" I asked, looking up at him.

He exhaled. "It took me years to even attempt being with someone after Trisha died. And even then, it never felt right."

"But there were . . . others?" I hated the jealousy that threatened to intrude on my happiness, but I was too curious not to ask.

"Only two. One random hookup at an out-of-town conference. And one woman I met at a coffee shop when Mariah was visiting her other grandparents in Indiana. She was newly single and lonely, and so was I. But like you said, it wasn't what I was looking for. Not at all."

I nodded slowly, the jealousy fading away. "What were you looking for?"

He cradled my face with his hands and kissed my forehead. "The girl next door."

Neither of us wanted the night to end, but eventually we wore ourselves out and fell asleep. When I woke up, I looked over at him, almost like I was afraid he wouldn't be there. But he was. My heart started to race as I took in his messy hair, his scruffy jawline, his bare chest. He was asleep on his back, one arm overhead, one hand at his waist. His armpit was hairy, and I stifled a laugh.

He opened his eyes. "What the hell? Are you laughing at me while I sleep? What kind of *good morning* is this?"

"I'm sorry," I said. "I just suddenly remembered the summer you and Griffin suddenly got hairy."

"Great."

"You got super tall, and then your voice changed, and I remember your *hands* suddenly seemed massive."

"That wasn't the only thing."

I laughed again, my belly swooshing. "I remember I could hardly look you in the eye because Mary Ellen Meyer and I had read about *nocturnal emissions*, and we were simultaneously fascinated and grossed out."

He shook his head. "Girls are so lucky. Everything is hidden away. And if it isn't, it's beautiful anyway. Boys can't hide anything."

"Don't even try to tell me that it's easier growing up as a girl. I will argue that."

"How about we agree that growing up is hard, period?"

"Deal."

"Good. Now come here."

I happily snuggled up against his warm side. He pulled the covers up to my shoulders and wrapped his arms around me. "Do we have to get out of bed already?"

"Maybe not quite yet. It's only eight."

"What time is breakfast?"

"Not until ten."

"Excellent. That is two hours I can keep you all to myself."

I giggled. "I do have to take a shower and clean up."

"Hm. I guess I need to do that too."

"We could conserve water," I suggested. "You know, for the environment."

"Oh yeah? Fight climate change? Save the turtles?"

"Well, I'm not sure we'll save any turtles by showering together, but I think it could be fun."

"Except that it would require me to get out of this nice warm bed, put my suit on, and go get clean clothes from my room. With my luck, I'll run into my mother."

"Or mine." I sat up. "Shit. I need to know how to handle this. Are we sort of a secret? You should probably talk to Mariah, right? Maybe you shouldn't shower here. I don't want her to—"

"Hey." He silenced me with a finger over my lips like he had last night. "Slow down. First, I'm a grown man. If I run into anyone's mother, I'll deal with it. Next, yes I need to talk to Mariah, but I don't need her permission to take a shower—alone or otherwise."

I circled his wrist with my hand and tugged it away from my mouth. "Will she be upset about . . . this?"

"I don't know. She adores you, no doubt about that, but she's terrified of losing me. I need to tread carefully."

"She knows how much you love her."

"I hope so, but she's learned that love doesn't protect you from loss."

Something about the way he said that sent a shiver of concern up my spine, but I brushed the worry away. "I understand. Let's not spring this on her right away. I can be patient."

"What if I can't?" His voice was gruff as he yanked on my arm, tucking me against his body again.

Grinning, I rubbed his chest. "You can sneak over to my house in the middle of the night."

"You live with your mom."

"So we'll be quiet."

"Like we were last night?"

"Ummm . . . good point."

"In the meantime . . ." His hands began to wander. "Can we still shower together?"

"Yes." I planted a kiss on his chest. "But why don't you go get your stuff now before we get carried away and lose track of time?"

He groaned. "Fine."

Laughing, I sat up and watched him drag himself out of bed and start to get dressed—pants, shirt, tie slung over his shoulders, jacket draped over his arms. Surprisingly, it was almost as intimate as watching him get undressed.

He sat down and tugged on his socks and shoes, then stood to kiss my forehead. "I'll be right back."

"Hey," I said as he headed for the door. "Take a key—there's one next to the television. I'll be waiting for you."

He pocketed the key, then turned around and grinned. "And I promise it will be worth the wait."

Once Cole was gone, I allowed myself a moment to scream happily into my pillow, kicking my feet and pounding my fists against the mattress. "Best! Night! Everrrrrr!" I yelled.

Then I sat up, breathless with excitement. I touched my hair, which had to be matted and tangled. Had I even taken my makeup off last night? My dress was still on the floor like a ruby-colored puddle. When I moved off the bed to hang it up, my muscles groaned—I was sore in all kinds of places.

But I couldn't keep the smile off my face as I slipped the velvet gown on a hanger and headed into the bathroom, where I took a few minutes to freshen up before turning on the hot water. With my face clean of makeup and my teeth brushed, I stepped beneath the spray.

I'd already shampooed my hair and had just rinsed out my conditioner when I heard the door to my room open and close. A minute later, Cole knocked on the bathroom door.

"Come in!" I called.

He entered and pulled the glass door open. "Room service," he said with a grin. He was completely naked.

I grinned too. "Just what I ordered. A hot breakfast."

"Hope you're hungry," he said, joining me.

"Ravenous." I stood aside and watched him get wet, my core muscles clenching and nipples tingling as I followed the rivulets of hot water streaming down his body. He wet his hair, and the movement of his arms over his head made his ab muscles do things that made me lick my lips. I wanted my mouth on him.

Dropping my gaze lower, I stared as his cock began to thicken and rise. It was mesmerizing.

"You know I'm dying to make some kind of sausage joke, right?" he asked, reaching for the soap and tearing off its paper wrapper.

I groaned. "Do you have to be an adolescent boy right now? I might have loved teenage Cole, but I don't necessarily need him in the shower with me."

"Come on," he said, running his soapy hands all over his body. "I'm funny."

Laughing, I reached for my shower gel, squirting some in my hand. "You're funny."

He rinsed off, watching me rub the gel over my skin. "Jesus Christ, that smells good. What is that?"

"Peach and honeysuckle."

He tipped his head back and moaned. "Can I lick it off you?"

"Sure, but I don't think it will taste as good as it smells."

"That is a risk I am willing to take." He pulled my gelled-up body toward him and kissed me as the water ran down our skin. His mouth was warm and firm and tasted like mint.

I looped my arms around his neck, pressing my chest against his, feeling his erection between us. His hands roamed across my back, down my spine, over my ass. He squeezed, pulling me against him, sending pulses of desire shooting from my core to the farthest reaches of my body, fingers and toes.

"I've thought about this," he whispered, his fingers slipping between my legs, teasing inside me.

"In the shower?" I wondered, because I had too.

"Yes. And in my bed."

"What did you do while you thought about it?"

"You know what I did."

Rising onto my tiptoes, I put my lips to his ear. "Do it now. Let me watch."

He went still. "You want to watch?"

I nodded and took his earlobe between my teeth, tugging gently, then kissed my way down his throat.

A groan rumbled in his chest and he squeezed my ass again. "There are so many things I want to do to you. And we have so little time."

"Please," I said breathlessly, pushing back from him. "Let me watch you. Even if it's just for a minute."

He stood still beneath the spray for a moment, arms at his sides, steam rising around him. I held my breath. With one hand, he reached up and placed a palm on the tiles. With the other, he fisted his cock.

My mouth fell open as I took it all in—his hot wet skin, the muscles in his arms and abs flexing, his midnight-blue eyes fixed on me, the hard set of his jaw, that massive dick sliding through his hand.

He went slower than I'd expected—nothing frantic or aggressive in his movement. He gripped himself hard but worked his arm and hand in sensual, fluid motions, fist up and down the length of his shaft, palm circling the crown, fingers gliding over the tip. I'd never in my life thought of a guy's erection as beautiful before, but Cole had a gorgeous cock—there was no other way to describe it.

His hand began to move faster, and his breathing changed. It grew louder, heavier, his stomach muscles were clenching tight. "Tell me what you want," he said, his voice low and raspy.

I dropped to my knees in front of him. Put my hands on his thighs. "I want to taste you."

He grimaced, almost like he was angry, but angled himself toward my mouth. Rubbed the tip of his cock on my lips. "You're making me crazy."

"Good." I swirled my tongue around his crown, and he moaned, moving his hands into my wet hair. Taking his shaft in both hands, I licked him with broad, decadent strokes, like I was determined to taste every last inch of him—and there were many. I slipped the first two in my mouth and sucked, making him curse. I moved my lips down a couple more, feeling his hands curl into fists, pulling my hair tight. I took him as deeply as I dared, letting him hit the back of my throat and lingering there for just a moment, angling my head this way and that.

"Fuck yes," he growled, hips flexing slightly, his body instinctively trying to go deeper.

I pulled back and took a breath, then took him to the back of my throat again, using my hands on what I couldn't work between my lips. By no means was I experienced at this, but all I wanted to do was please him, and every sound he made, every quick inhale of breath, every twitch of his cock in my mouth made me feel like a fucking blowjob queen. I could taste him—salty and sweet.

"Stop," he said suddenly, pulling back from me, taking himself from my mouth. "You have to stop."

"But I don't want to." I looked up at him pleadingly. "Let me finish."

"Some other time." He reached beneath my arms and pulled me to my feet. "Believe me, if we had all day and all night, I'd beg to come like that, with your mouth on my cock."

"Then let me—"

He silenced me with a hot, demanding kiss, his tongue slashing between my lips, his hands sliding over my hips. "Right now, there's something I want more."

"What?" I whispered.

He spun me to face the wall. Pressed me against it. Put his mouth at my ear. "I want to make you come with it." His hands skated around to my stomach, one moving up, one going down. The hot, solid length of his erection pushed against my lower back.

"But you did. Three times already."

"Shh. I'll never get enough. Now spread your legs."

I braced two hands on the tiles and did as he asked, panting as he worked his fingers between my thighs. His mouth traveled down my neck and shoulder, and his other hand covered one breast. His fingertips moved expertly over my clit, as if he'd learned exactly what I liked in the space of just one night. First slowly and lightly, then firmer and more insistent. He dipped inside me then licked his fingers, returning them to my swollen sweet spot and caressing me in a way that made it feel like his tongue.

In less than a minute, I was rocking against his hand, about to explode, desperate to feel his cock inside me. "Cole," I whispered. "Do it. Make me come again."

The low rumble from his throat—something between a laugh and a moan—twisted the tension in me even tighter. I leaned forward, pressing my cheek against the cool tiles, arching my back. He placed a palm between my shoulder blades and dragged it down my spine. "Your fucking body," he growled. "I want to do such bad things to it."

"Cole," I pleaded. "I'm so close."

A second later, he was pushing inside me, and I rested my forehead against the wall, my mouth open, my eyes shut tight against the twinge of pain. He was rougher than he'd been last night, thrusting into me with deep, hard strokes. I cried out at the peak of each one, but he didn't slow down or let up. It reminded me of the night he'd called me and talked me right into an orgasm—it was him, but it was a side of him he didn't show very often. Something private and intense.

He reached between my legs again and rubbed me like he had before, and the touch was like setting off fireworks inside me, my body erupting in glorious, pounding, bursts. Behind me, Cole grabbed my hips and held me still as my core muscles spasmed around him, and I could feel the throb of his cock as his orgasm moved through his body and into mine.

The first thing I became aware of was the sound of the water. Then the hard tile under my hands and beneath my forehead. Then my heavy breathing. Cole's arms came around me, and I opened my eyes.

"You okay?" he asked.

"I think so." I touched my forehead. "I might have grout lines etched in my skin."

He chuckled, dropping a kiss on my shoulder before gently pulling out of me. "Let me see."

I faced him, wrinkling my nose. "Well?"

Taking my face in his hands, he pretended to examine it. "You take my breath away. Just like always."

I smiled. "Good, because I'll need to distract people with my face this morning so they don't notice I'm walking funny and can hardly sit down."

He laughed. "Sorry."

I poked his chest. "Liar."

He took one of my hands in both of his and kissed my fingers. "Was I too rough?"

"No. I liked it—it's a different side of you." I looked at his hands and noticed again that he wasn't wearing his ring. The question was on the tip of my tongue, but I bit it back.

He saw me looking at his fingers and understood. "It's okay. You can ask."

I met his eyes. "Did you forget?"

He shook his head, a smile on his lips. "Nope. I put it on out of habit, and then I took it off on purpose. I've thought about no one but you for months, Cheyenne. I was thinking about you when I got dressed. And I knew I was going to go after you, try to make you understand. I didn't want to do that wearing the ring someone else put on my hand. I'm not married to her anymore." He wrapped his arms around me and held me close. "And I want to be with you."

I wound my arms around his waist and pressed my cheek to his chest. "That makes me happy. But if you feel like you should keep wearing the ring until you have a chance to talk through everything with Mariah, I'll understand. I know she likes you to wear it."

"You know, you're making it really easy to fall in love with you. Are you doing that on purpose?"

I laughed, blissfully happy. "Yes."

We decided it would be better to meet at breakfast than to walk in together, and ended up sitting at different tables. I sat with my mom, Griffin and Blair, and Cole was seated with Mariah, his mom, and Moretti. But we exchanged enough secretive glances that Blair pulled me aside while everyone was leaving the restaurant.

"Oh my God, what is happening?" she whispered frantically, her eyes darting over my shoulder. "Never mind, I know what's happening—or at least what happened. You slept with Cole!"

"Shhhh." Taking her arm, I tugged her into the lobby, away from where Cole and Mariah were chatting with Mr. and Mrs. Moretti. "Keep your voice down."

"Is it true?"

I faced her, unable to hide a smile. "Yes."

She gasped, then jumped up and down, squealing and fluttering her hands. "I can't believe it! And yet I can!"

"How did you know?"

"Number one, because it was inevitable. Two, because you guys were both conspicuously absent from the bar last night. And three, because you guys have been staring at each other the whole weekend, but this morning, instead of these longing, I-wish-we-could type looks, it's more like oh-yes-we-did-and-it-was-fucking-awesome."

"It was fucking awesome," I confirmed.

"I'm so happy for you guys," she gushed. "So how did it happen? Not the physical part, I get that, but did he *say* anything? Like, what made you change your mind from the night before?"

"He showed up at my door and demanded I let him in. He had to put his hand over my mouth to get me to stop talking so he could apologize, and then he told me he had feelings for me."

"Eeeep!" Blair clapped her hands. "So it wasn't just a one-time thing?"

"No," I said, shaking my head, still amazed. "He wants to be with me. He said it out loud."

Blair's face melted like she'd just seen a cute kitten, and she put a hand over her heart. "I'm so happy for you guys. So are you going to move into his new house with him?"

"What? No!" I laughed, shaking my head. "Jesus, give us a minute!"

"Sorry, I've got wedding brain. I'm in happily-ever-after mode right now."

"Well, you'll have to adjust your expectations for Cole and me, because we can't really even go public until he talks to Mariah."

Blair waved a hand in front of her face. "Easy peasy. Mariah is crazy about you."

"That's because I've never been a threat to her before. Kids take these things seriously, and Mariah is sensitive about Cole. He and I both agree we need to be gentle with her."

"I think you should get married next summer," Blair went on, as if I hadn't said anything. "Maybe outside at one of those old mansions on Center Avenue that's not a Bed & Breakfast. Or, oh! Oh! How about at the Beale's lavender farm?"

"Blair. Listen to me." I put my hands on her shoulders. "You need to calm down. I'm happy right now. The ever after can wait."

She sighed. "Fine." Then she took my arm as we started to walk back toward the restaurant, where Griffin was waiting for her. "But just in case, I think we should check the calendar at that lavender farm. I bet they book up early for the summer."

"Blair."

"I know, I know. I heard you. Ever after can wait."

"Thank you."

The truth was, of course, I was just as anxious as Blair to move forward with ever after. My God, I'd loved him all this time, and now that he'd said he wanted to be with me, it was as if every last dream I'd ever dreamed was coming true. But I'd meant what I said to Cole too—I could be patient. Reassuring Mariah that I wasn't a threat to her or even to her mother's memory was the most important thing we could do at this point.

And I was more than willing to play a role in that, but I knew it had to come from Cole first. I'd follow his lead. In the meantime, I'd enjoy the memories from this weekend and savor any stolen moments we could manage in the days to come.

Someday, I hoped we wouldn't have to steal them at all.

He texted me as I was about to leave my room and check out.

Cole: We're heading out. Please drive carefully and let me know when you get home.

Me: I will. You do the same, okay?

Cole: Okay.

I waited for a moment, hoping for something a little more intimate and personal, but no more messages arrived. I stuck my phone in my bag, grabbed my garment bag and roller suitcase, and took a last look at the room I'd always think of as *ours*.

"We'll come back sometime," I whispered, a promise to myself. "Together."

I took the elevator down to the lobby—the memory of Cole's kiss in there making my stomach cartwheel—and spotted my mother at the desk. As I was making my way over there, I heard Mariah calling my name.

"Miss Cheyenne!" she cried, running toward me and throwing her arms around my waist. She was all bundled up already. "Are you leaving now too?"

"Yes," I said, laughing as I nearly lost my balance.

"I don't want to go home. I love it here." She pouted, looking around the lobby.

"Me too," I said. "I was just thinking a minute ago that I already want to come back."

"Yes! And next time, let's come in the summer so we can ride the horses!"

"Sounds good to me," I told her.

Cole appeared over her shoulder, wearing his winter gear. He'd clearly been outside already, because his nose and cheeks were pink. "Hey."

"Hi," I said, knowing my cheeks were flushed with pink now too.

"Car's out front, Mariah. I already loaded it and we're taking up a spot, so let's get Grandma and hurry." Cole pulled off his gloves and hat. "She's over there by the door. Can you help her with her bags?"

"Okay." Mariah gave me one last squeeze. "Bye, Miss Cheyenne."

"Bye, honey." I patted her puffy jacket.

She took off running toward her grandmother, and I stood face to face with Cole. "Cold out there?"

"Yeah." He glanced outside and spoke quietly. "I wish I didn't know anyone in this lobby."

I smiled. "What would you do?"

He met my eyes. "I'd kiss you."

"I'd like that."

"Someday," he said, giving me that lopsided grin I loved. "Anyway, I better get a move on. Drive safe."

"I will."

He tugged his gloves on as he walked away, and my breath hitched.

The ring was back on his finger.

Seventeen

Cole

I WAS BEHIND THE WHEEL, MY EYES ON THE ROAD, MY mind lost in memories of Cheyenne, when my mother's voice suddenly registered.

"Huh?" I straightened up in the driver's seat and took another sip of my coffee.

"Cole Mitchell, have you heard a word I said?"

"Which word? You've said about a million of them since we left Cloverleigh Farms."

"Very funny. I was just saying how pretty the centerpieces were. Didn't you think so?"

"Sure." Truthfully, I couldn't even recall them.

"And the food was so good."

"Yeah." Had I eaten it? The only thing I remembered tasting last night had *not* been on the table.

"I think Mariah ate three pieces of cake." My mother laughed, glancing into the back seat, where Mariah had fallen asleep. "She was on a sugar high for hours after that. I wasn't sure I'd ever get her into bed!"

I sipped my coffee again, feeling a little guilty that my

mother had been left to deal with my daughter while I'd gone to Cheyenne's room for an all-night fuck fling. "Thanks for watching her."

"Oh, my pleasure." She sighed again. "Such a wonderful night. Did you enjoy yourself?"

"Yes."

"Cheyenne looked beautiful, didn't she?"

I swallowed more coffee. "Yes."

"Darlene said she's not seeing anyone."

She saw a hell of a lot of me last night, I thought. "No, I don't think she is."

"You two looked very sweet on the dance floor together."

"Mm."

"And I was thinking, maybe you might, you know, enjoy each other's company."

"Maybe." I hid my smile behind my cup. We had *definitely* enjoyed each other's company last night. In many positions.

"Look, I know it's none of my business and you don't like being told what to do, but I just want to say one thing."

"Okay."

"When I was pregnant with you, I was scared."

"Huh. That's not where I thought you were heading at all. Are you worried I'm pregnant?"

"Don't be a smartass. I was scared, because I worried I didn't have enough love for two kids. I worried about loving Greg less once you came along."

"Are you finally admitting I'm your favorite?"

"But then I learned something," she went on, ignoring me. "When you have a second child, you don't love the first any less. You make more room in your heart."

I snorted. "Did you read that on a fortune cookie?"

She exhaled sharply. "You're so exasperating. My point is that you might think falling in love again isn't possible, but it is. You've got a big heart, Cole. There's room."

I didn't say anything.

"Lightning can strike the same place twice, if you let it," she went on. "But you can't be afraid."

"Are you suggesting I run out on the golf course wielding a large metal object?"

"Yes. Figuratively speaking, I am."

I grinned and lifted my coffee cup again. "If it shuts you up, I'll consider it."

It worked—she remained quiet the rest of the way home— but I kept hearing her words in my head. Even though I knew she'd been half-joking, something she said had burrowed into my brain and taken root.

You can't be afraid.

Why was it bothering me?

I wasn't afraid. That wasn't it at all. I was only concerned for my daughter. It was Mariah's fears that needed calming, not my own. It was Mariah who associated love with loss, not me. It was Mariah who was terrified that something bad would happen. It was Mariah who needed protecting from it all.

It wasn't me.

After we got home, I unpacked, putting away toiletries, hanging up my suit, making a pile of things for the dry cleaner's, and tossing dirty laundry in my hamper. When my bag was empty, I shoved it to the back of my closet.

Then I stood in front of my mirror and removed the wedding band I'd worn almost every day for the last ten years. I'd put it back on this morning for two reasons—to avoid an uncomfortable conversation with Mariah in front of my mom if either of them noticed it was missing, and so that I wouldn't lose it. It didn't hold the emotional weight for me it once had, but it wasn't meaningless either.

In fact, placing it in a small cufflink box and tucking it at the back of a dresser drawer felt very meaningful—a conscious step out of the past and into the future.

It was time.

Hopefully, Mariah would see it that way too.

On Monday morning, I called Mariah's therapist and left a message requesting an appointment this week. She called me back later that afternoon, while I was catching up with some paperwork.

"Hello?"

"Hi, Cole, it's Jessalyn Wells returning your call."

"Hey, Jessalyn. Thanks for calling back."

"Sure thing. Your message said you're looking for an appointment later this week. So is this in addition to Mariah's usual Tuesday appointment or in place of it?"

"This would be in addition to Mariah's usual appointments, and actually . . ." I hesitated, wondering if this was weird. "She wouldn't even be there. It would only be me."

"Oh?"

"There's something I'd like to ask you about—something I need to approach Mariah with and I'd like to get your opinion on the best way to do it. I don't think it will take long."

"Oh. I see. Is it something we might discuss over the phone?"

"No, I think I'd better come in. This is a pretty big deal, and I really want to make sure I understand what the steps are."

"I understand," she said. A few clicks of her keyboard. "How's Thursday morning at ten?"

"Fine," I said, scribbling it down on a piece of paper. "I'll be there, thanks."

On my way home from work that evening, I called Cheyenne.

"Hello?"

My heart thumped harder at the sound of her voice. It had barely been twenty-four hours since I'd seen her, but it felt like longer. I wished I were driving home to her. "Hi, beautiful."

"Hi. How are you?"

"I'm good. Just on my way home. How are you?"

"Good. Tired. My kids wore me out today. I think they stored up all their energy over the weekend and unleashed it on me today in the classroom."

I laughed. "Aw, give 'em a break. Remember how tough those weeks were leading up to Christmas break? They can't concentrate."

"I still have to *teach* them."

"How many more school days until vacation?"

"Eleven." She sighed. "I'm not sure any of us will make it."

"I think you should play hooky this week. Take a day off and spend it with me."

She laughed. "Don't tempt me."

"I'm serious. I'm off Wednesday and Thursday."

"Lucky you. I wish I could, but I just took two days off last week. My principal would probably fire me if I took another so fast."

"Then I'd arrest him. Throw him in jail."

She giggled. "Her."

"Whatever."

"I'll think about it. What about this weekend? Any plans?"

"I told Mariah I'd take her skating at the park Friday evening."

"That sounds like fun."

"I'm thinking that's the night I'll tell her about us."

"Oh. That's—that's sooner than I thought." She hesitated. "Are you nervous?"

"Yes, which is why I made an appointment to talk to her therapist on Thursday morning. I'm going to ask her advice."

"That's great." Cheyenne sounded cheerful again. "I bet she'll have some really good insights."

"I hope so." I paused. "I miss you already. Is that weird?"

"Not to me. I miss you too."

"When can I see you?"

"Can you escape later?"

I thought for a moment. "What's tonight, Monday? No, I can't—it's my mother's bowling night. And tomorrow night I take Mariah to her therapist's appointment, and afterward I've got a pickup hockey game. Maybe Wednesday?"

"Sure. Oh wait—is that the second Wednesday of the month? I can't. That's my book club night. And I can't skip— I'm hosting."

"Oh." Aggravation was making my shoulders tense up.

"How about Thursday?" she suggested.

"That should work. I'll clear it with my mom and let you know for sure."

"Great. Maybe I'll take *you* to dinner this time. Or we could meet up with Griffin and Blair."

"That would be fun. Although what I really want is to get you alone. I guess it's too much to ask to have you all to myself somewhere I can take all your clothes off, huh?"

She laughed. "Not too much to ask. It's just the logistics that make it hard. It will be easier when you're in your new house."

I groaned. "You're saying I have to be *patient*?"

"Yes. But the inspection is this week, right?"

"Thursday."

"And how soon after can you close?"

"About a month, maybe less since no one has to move out. But there's a lot of bullshit with the mortgage lender, the escrow company, the title company, the appraiser . . . it's not fast." Unlike the pace at which I was falling for her.

"It's okay, Cole. I'm not going anywhere. We just have to be a little patient."

"You're too good to be true," I said.

"Not really." Then she laughed. "I just know that you're worth the wait."

On Thursday morning at ten a.m., I sat down on the couch in Jessalyn's office and told her why I was there.

"I think this is great. Really," Jessalyn said with a kind smile. "And even if it takes Mariah some time to accept or adapt to the idea of sharing you, it's going to be good for her."

I took out a small spiral notebook and pen. "So what tips do you have for making sure I do this the right way?"

Jessalyn, a young woman with dark skin and hazel eyes, looked impressed. "Wow. You're taking this really seriously."

"I have to," I said, feeling nervous and sweaty. "There's a reason I've never done this before. It's a big deal. And I can't afford to get it wrong."

"Relax, Cole." Jessalyn smiled at me again, getting up from her desk chair and coming over to an upholstered chair adjacent to the couch. She sat down and crossed her legs. "The fact that you're taking this seriously says that you understand this is a sensitive matter. It's going to take patience, love, and maybe some tough conversations and extra hugs, but I have faith in you."

"Thanks."

"So I want you to think about three things." She clasped her hands around her knee.

"Three things," I repeated, writing it down.

"First, and I know you're good at this already, you want to start by reassuring her that you love her and she'll always be your first priority, no matter what."

"Okay." That was an easy one.

"Mariah will want to hear that your relationship with this new person is not going to take you away from her."

"It won't," I said firmly.

"Next, tell her why you'd like to date this person—she's smart, she's kind, she makes you laugh—so that Mariah has a sense of what it is that's drawing you to her."

"Mariah already knows her pretty well," I said.

Jessalyn looked surprised and pleased. "Really? It's someone she knows?"

"Cheyenne lives next door to us. We grew up together—her older brother Griffin is my best friend. Actually, it was Cheyenne who gave me your name last year when I was looking for a therapist for Mariah."

"Oh, this is Cheyenne Dempsey we're talking about?" Jessalyn laughed. "I know her through the elementary school. And Mariah mentions her frequently."

"We do see her a lot—even more than usual this fall because of her brother's wedding. So it's not like I'd be introducing her to a stranger."

"No, and that could make it a bit easier," Jessalyn said. "But still best to be prepared for some resistance and fear."

"Of course." I glanced down at my notes. "So are we on number two or three?"

"Well, some of what I was going to say might be irrelevant now, since Mariah has already met her and they have a nice relationship. I was going to suggest the first few meetings be in neutral spaces, and not to introduce them at all until you were absolutely certain the relationship between the two of you was serious."

"It's—I'd say it's serious." I cleared my throat. "We've had feelings for each other for a while. It just took us some time to act on them. We wanted to be sure this was right."

Jessalyn nodded. "Sounds like you both have good, level heads on your shoulders. That said, I might avoid sleepovers until things are more settled."

"Well, considering that we both live with our mothers, those are pretty much out anyway," I said wryly. "I'm in the process of purchasing a new house, but I hear what you're saying, and I agree."

"Good. I'm not saying you *have* to be remarried for that to happen," she said gently, "but sometimes that is best."

I glanced down at my bare ring finger, my chest growing inexplicably tight. "I understand."

"Your situation is also a little unique in that there is no ex-spouse involved," Jessalyn went on. "But that doesn't mean that she'll jump at the opportunity to have a new mom. Every child is different, but many children don't like the thought of someone attempting to replace the parent they lost. You'll want to be sensitive to that, especially if Mariah isn't able to articulate what she's feeling exactly."

"Right."

"But remarriage is a wonderful thing." Jessalyn smiled and sat back. "It's another loving adult in her life, another reassuring presence. And a chance for you to demonstrate a healthy, intimate relationship. She needs that."

I nodded, clearing my throat. "Remarriage is kind of a scary topic."

"Oh?"

"Not necessarily for me personally," I said quickly, because I wasn't scared of anything. "But because of a promise I made to Mariah when she was five."

"What kind of promise?"

I told her about the time Mariah had come to me and asked if I ever planned to get married and leave her behind, and I'd vowed it would never happen. "A friend at school had been telling her that her father was getting remarried and moving away, and it was very upsetting to Mariah."

"Of course," said Jessalyn, nodding. "I can see how it would be. And sometimes we say things to our children to make them feel safe in the moment, and it's only later that we realize that the truth might have allowed for some needed emotional development."

"But it wasn't like I said something untrue," I argued. "I really never saw myself getting married again."

"It's wonderful that you met someone who made you change your mind, isn't it?" Jessalyn smiled knowingly at me.

"I guess. I mean yes—it is." But the topic of marriage was making me feel anxious, and I decided it was because I was worried my daughter would object. "What should I do if Mariah doesn't see it that way? If she sees it as a threat?"

"You tell her you love her. Give her a hug. And try again another day," Jessalyn said gently. "If you really care for Cheyenne, and you want her in your life, you want Mariah to feel good about it. Don't give her any reason to believe you're choosing someone else's happiness over hers."

I wrote frantically, copying down as many words as I could recall. "When do you think is the right time to do it?"

"That's up to you," she said. "But given the circumstances, I really don't see a reason to wait too long. If you're sure of your feelings for Cheyenne—"

"I'm sure of them."

"Then talk to her. Just remember, no matter how much she likes Cheyenne, she'll need time to get used to the idea of the two of you."

"Okay." I closed my notebook and stuck my pen inside the spiral. "Thanks a lot for talking to me. I really appreciate it."

"My pleasure. And no charge for the visit," she said, rising to her feet. "Just let me know how it goes."

Eighteen

Cole

THAT NIGHT, CHEYENNE AND I HAD DINNER OVER AT Griffin and Blair's.

They lived in what had previously been Griffin's bachelor pad, which was located on the second story of an old fire station that housed the Bellamy Creek Garage on the ground level. Griffin and Cheyenne's grandfather had started the business, their dad had run it for years before he died suddenly of a heart attack, and Griffin had run it for the past six years.

I was excited about spending the evening with her, but I was also distracted—going over Jessalyn's advice in my head constantly. On the drive over, I'd told Cheyenne all about it, and she was cautiously optimistic, just like Jessalyn was.

We entered the old firehouse through a glass door to the left of the lobby entrance, and as we went up the stairs to the apartment, the aroma of garlic and lemon and something roasting in the oven made my mouth water.

Blair, wearing an apron over her dress, greeted us with a hug, and Griffin handed me a beer and Cheyenne a glass of wine.

I made up my mind to stop fretting about things so much and just enjoy the time I had with Cheyenne and my friends. This was the first time in a *decade* I'd done something like this. I wanted to savor it.

Blair and Griffin had decided to delay their honeymoon until after the holidays and were planning a trip to Mexico just after the New Year. Over plates of lemony chicken piccata, smashed potatoes and sautéed spinach, Blair rapturously described the resort they'd chosen.

"I'm so jealous," Cheyenne said, taking a sip of her wine. "I wish I could get away to the beach this winter."

"Why don't you come with us?" Across the table, Blair flashed us an encouraging smile. "It would be fun!"

Next to her, Griffin frowned. "Did you just invite people on our honeymoon?"

"What, you and I are together all the time! I think it would be fun for the four of us to get away."

"That's a really sweet offer, Blair, but no." Cheyenne laughed as she set her glass down and picked up her fork. "I'm not going on my brother's honeymoon—or anyone's honeymoon."

"It would be impossible for me anyway," I added. "I couldn't leave Mariah for that long."

"You must be excited about the new house," Blair said. "Have you had the inspection yet?"

"Today," I confirmed.

"How'd it go?" Griffin asked.

"Great. No surprises. I should have a closing date by the end of the year."

"I can't wait to see it," Cheyenne bubbled. "Cole said he might even be able to show it to me next week."

"Really?" Blair looked at me in surprise.

I nodded. "No one is living there, and the agent said the current owners gave the okay for me to go in with a contractor and take measurements, get estimates on the work, and all that."

"Moretti doing the reno?" Griffin asked.

"Yeah." I grinned. "In between play dates with his girlfriend."

Everyone laughed, and Blair said, "You guys, I feel bad. We should meet her before we judge. What if Enzo really likes her? She could be the one."

"She's not the one," Griffin muttered.

Blair slapped his shoulder. "You don't know that for sure. He seems serious about her. I spoke with him at the wedding a little."

"I don't know, I gotta go with Griff on this one." I picked up my beer bottle and took a sip. "I think he's only dating her because he's feeling pressure from his parents to settle down. I don't get the feeling she's the one."

Blair sighed, like she was frustrated with both of us. "I don't know that I trust either one of you to recognize true love right off the bat."

"Did you hear that, Griff?" I teased. "Your wife doesn't think we know a good hit when we see one."

"I heard," Griffin said, pretending to be disgusted. "It's like she didn't see my in-the-park home run in the championship game this season."

"Or my triple that drove in the winning run." I shook my head. "Sad."

"Appalling." Griffin elbowed his wife.

Blair rolled her eyes. "I am not talking about old man baseball, and you know it!"

"Now she's trying to take back what she said about us." Griffin shook his head. "Good thing she's hot. That's what really matters in a relationship, am I right, Cole?"

"She's also a great cook, which is the second most

important thing." I ate another forkful of chicken piccata, which was delicious.

"True, true," Griffin agreed. "Or maybe the third. I won't mention the second at the table, but don't worry, she's good at that too."

Blair cleared her throat. "Cheyenne, remind me of this conversation next time I have the idea to get together for dinner."

"Will do, sister."

Griffin and I exchanged a grin, and something about the whole scene was both nostalgic—Griffin and I ganging up on some cute girls—and hopeful. I could imagine dinners like this in the future, with Moretti and Beckett and their wives, whoever they turned out to be, and maybe a bunch of kids running around too.

Beneath the table, I reached for Cheyenne's hand.

As we were finishing up tiramisu and coffee, I noticed Cheyenne checking her phone.

"Everything okay?" I asked.

"Everything's fine," she said. "I was just checking the time."

"What time is it?"

"Almost ten."

"Is it that late already?" Griffin asked, yawning and stretching.

Blair hit his arm. "Griffin, that's rude."

"What? I get up at six," he said. "And you get up even earlier."

"But you made it sound like you want them to leave."

"It's just my sister and Cole." Griffin gestured toward us. "If I really wanted them to leave, I'd say it right to their faces."

Blair clucked her tongue in disgust and looked at us across the table. "You do *not* have to go."

"Actually, we do," I said. "Cheyenne and I have to work

tomorrow, and I promised Mariah I'd poke my head in and kiss her goodnight."

"Won't she be asleep?" Blair asked.

"I hope so, but when I called her, she made me swear to do it anyway."

She smiled at me. "Such a good dad."

A couple minutes later, Cheyenne and I helped clear the table, said goodnight, and headed out. We'd just left their building and started walking down the street toward my car when Cheyenne stopped.

"What's wrong? Did you forget something?" I asked.

"No. I just don't want to go home yet." She turned to face me. "I wish we could be alone."

"Me too," I said, feeling like an asshole that I had nowhere to take her. What kind of cretinous basement-dweller still lived with his mother at age thirty-three?

"I was thinking . . ."

"What?"

She turned around and looked back at the building. "I have a key to the garage."

"You do?"

She laughed and shrugged. "Better than nothing, right?"

I grabbed her arm and started running back up the street.

"But we need to be quiet," she said breathlessly, unlocking the door. "I don't want them to hear us. And we should be quick too."

"No fucking problem." I was already getting hard just thinking about it.

As soon as the door was shut behind us, I turned the lock and took her hand, leading her out of the lobby area and into the service bay. I'd been in the garage enough times to know my way around, even in the pitch-dark.

At least, I thought I did.

"Oh, shit!" I said after knocking over something that clanged noisily as it hit the cement floor.

Cheyenne started laughing uncontrollably, and to shut her up, I spun her against the wall and kissed her. Unbuttoned her coat. Shrugged mine off my shoulders.

"Hurry," she panted.

"I'm trying," I said, reaching beneath her skirt. "Fucking winter clothes. What are you wearing?"

"Tights," she said. "Hold on. I'll get them off." She ditched her boots and whipped off her tights—at least, that's what I assumed she was doing. It was so dark I couldn't see shit.

"Okay," she said, putting her arms around me.

"You're still wearing a giant sweater," I complained, desperate to get closer to her.

"I can't take that off, Cole! We have to hurry!"

"Okay, okay," I told her, reaching beneath her skirt once more, this time finding her bare skin. "But I haven't been able to think about anything but this all week, so you have to give me a minute here." I stroked her patiently, working my tongue between her lips and my fingers over her clit.

"Cole, now," she begged in a heated whisper, rubbing me through my jeans. "I want you right *now*."

I unzipped my jeans and shoved them down just enough to work my cock free and pushed up her skirt. She jumped up, wrapping her legs around me, holding herself aloft while I positioned myself—then groaned loudly as she slid down my shaft.

"Shhhhh!" she scolded. "Quiet!"

But it was fucking impossible to be quiet. I wanted her too much, it had been too long, and I had no idea when we'd get this chance again. I had zero control.

I fucked her savagely, her back against the wall. Against a metal cabinet. Against a tool bench, which was unfortunately on wheels and made a giant rattling noise when I shoved it against some kind of shelving unit—or maybe it was a rack of tires— and then spilled a bunch of its contents on the floor.

Both of us were loud—between my caveman grunting and

Cheyenne's high-pitched cries, you could hardly hear all the racket made by the tools and equipment we were knocking around.

But the kicker was that I set her against the side of someone's SUV right before we both came, and our spontaneous orgasm was so violent we set off the car's alarm.

Cheyenne screamed and I cursed, setting her on her feet. "Fuck!"

"Oh my God!" she shrieked. "Make it stop!"

"Give me a second," I said, zipping my pants and frantically wondering if someone was calling the cops right now and a couple of my colleagues were about to show up here and laugh their asses off.

"We don't have a second! And I can't find my tights!"

Five seconds later, the lights came on and Griffin came barreling into the service bay. "What the fuck, you guys?"

I stood next to Cheyenne while he grabbed the SUV's key fob from a rack on the wall, pressed a button, and stopped the noise. Then he turned to face us, and he was not amused.

He kind of looked like Darlene after the broken plate incident.

"What. The fuck," he repeated. But it wasn't really a question.

"Sorry," I said. My heart was still hammering, and the car alarm still rang in my ears.

"Sorry," echoed Cheyenne. She wore her skirt but no tights, and covered one bare foot with the other. About ten feet away, closer to the door, I could see where her black tights had been abandoned.

"Um, I can explain," I said.

"No, don't." Griffin held up his hand and started heading for the door. "Really. Just don't."

"I'll lock up," Cheyenne called, like she was trying to be helpful.

Griffin said nothing and disappeared, leaving Cheyenne and I alone again. We looked at each other.

"Oops," I said, unable to hide a grin. "Sorry. That was a bit loud. And rough."

"I liked it."

"Your brother didn't."

"No," she said, laughing as she went and scooped up her tights. "He really didn't. Come on, let's get out of here."

I pulled into her driveway and put my car in park. "I guess Griffin knows about us for sure now, huh?"

Cheyenne giggled. "The whole block might know about us for sure now."

I grimaced. "I was afraid the police would show up when that alarm went off."

"Oh my God, can you imagine? I would have died. *Died.*"

"You and me both." I exhaled, stroking the back of her hand with my thumb, wishing I didn't have to say goodbye to her, even for the night. "I'll be glad when things are different and we don't have to sneak around."

"Me too."

"Once I'm in the new house, things will get easier." But then I frowned, remembering what Jessalyn had said about sleepovers. How long would we have to wait?

"I'm nervous about tomorrow night," Cheyenne said quietly, "about how Mariah will react. I'm trying not to be, but I am."

"I understand," I said, putting my arm around her and holding her as closely as I could. "But remember that Jessalyn said resistance would only be natural, even though she loves you."

"I know. I just really, really want it to go well."

"Me too." I kissed the top of her head. "But even if she's upset tomorrow night, it doesn't mean she won't come around eventually."

"You're right. I'm sorry—I'm sure you're nervous too. I don't want to make it harder on you."

"You're not. Now you better get inside, before I lose my mind and try to get your clothes off in the back seat."

She laughed, pressing her hand to my cheek and her lips to mine. "Call me tomorrow. And good luck."

After making sure she got in safely, I went home and put my car in the garage. As I was walking to the back door, I couldn't help admitting I *was* nervous about tomorrow night. There was a very real possibility that Mariah would not be comfortable with our relationship.

And what would I do then? Give Cheyenne up? Go back to secretly longing for her? Spend all my nights alone, missing her?

No. It was out of the question. I'd just have to work harder to make Mariah understand that I had enough room in my heart for both of them.

I was willing to fight for her.

Upstairs, I snuck into Mariah's room, and looked down at her sweet, sleeping angel face, then bent to place a kiss on her forehead. *It's going to be okay, baby,* I promised her silently. *You don't have to be afraid. You're never going to lose me.*

But that night, after slipping beneath the covers, I did something I hadn't done in years—closed my eyes and said a prayer.

It wasn't that I didn't believe in God, but our relationship had been a bit strained after losing Trisha. I'd never understood how a God who was supposed to be good and just had allowed something like that to happen. It was an unsettling feeling, to have your faith stolen. To wake up one morning believing in something, and by nightfall, discover that belief has been destroyed. It made it hard to trust your instincts. Hard to plan for the future. Hard to believe that you can protect those you love—or protect yourself. Nothing was promised. Nothing was certain. And prayers went unanswered all the time.

But tonight, I found myself willing to try again.

Nineteen

Cole

THE FOLLOWING EVENING, MARIAH AND I LEFT FOR the ice rink as soon as I got home from work.

It was crowded, but we had fun circling the ice together hand in hand, and she showed off some of her moves from her figure skating class. She recognized a few classmates, and I was more than happy to stand to the side with the other parents while they darted around the rink, playing games and judging one another's attempts at fancy twirls and jumps.

When we were done skating, we put our boots back on, tossed our skates in the car, and walked down to our favorite pizzeria. The owner greeted me with a handshake and made a big deal about how tall Mariah was getting before seating us in a red vinyl booth along the wall.

We ordered soft drinks and pizza, and I gave Mariah some quarters to go play video games while we waited for the food to arrive. I told myself I wasn't putting off the conversation, I was just ensuring she was in the best possible mood before broaching a difficult topic. No sense in trying to talk seriously to her while she was hungry, or grumpy that I wouldn't give her any game time like I usually did.

While she was gone, I looked at a TV screen that hung in the corner, barely registering the hockey game that was on. I sipped a Coke, wishing it was a beer, but knowing I needed to stay clear-headed. I texted Cheyenne that I was at the pizzeria and promised to call her when I got home.

And I twisted my wedding band around my finger. I'd dug it out of the drawer and put it on at the last minute, although I wasn't even sure exactly why. Maybe I thought it would soften the blow of my announcement. Maybe I wanted to reassure her that I took my promises seriously. Maybe I hoped it would show her that she could still trust me to protect her from her fears.

Eventually she returned and the pizza was placed on a tall stand in the middle of our table. After sending her to the bathroom to wash her hands, I served her a piece and took one for myself, although my stomach was too knotted up to eat.

"So I wanted to talk to you about something," I said as she picked all the pepperoni off her slice.

"What?"

"Well, first I want you to know that you are the most important person in the world to me, and your feelings matter more than anything."

"'Kay," she said, licking her fingers.

"And you know how much I love you, right? How much I will always love you?"

She gave me a weird look. "Yeah."

"Good." I was tempted to pull the folded-up piece of notebook paper from my jeans pocket, but I didn't. "Okay. Good."

"Are you going away somewhere?" Her voice shook slightly.

"No," I said firmly. "Nope, I'm not going anywhere."

"Okay, good." She picked up her slice of pizza and took a bite.

"I will never leave you. You understand that? It's you and me forever, kiddo."

She nodded and smiled, her mouth full. "In our new house."

"In our new house." I cleared my throat. "But sometimes moms and dads who don't have a husband or wife anymore like to spend time with someone their own age. Sometimes they get a little lonely being on their own without a partner, and they meet someone they like spending time with, and they . . . they want to date that person."

"You mean you met someone you want to date?"

"Yes."

Mariah's face fell. "Oh."

"Does that make you sad?"

She set her pizza down. "Kind of."

My chest tightened, and I reached across the table for her hand. "Is it that you feel scared I won't want to spend time with *you* anymore? Because that would never happen."

She shook her head. "It's not that. It's just . . . I was hoping you would date Miss Cheyenne. Not some new person."

My jaw fell open. "You were hoping I'd date Miss Cheyenne?"

"Well, yes." She shrugged. "I love Miss Cheyenne. And she comes over a lot. And she needs a boyfriend, so I thought maybe it could be you."

I laughed, letting go of her hand. "She needs a boyfriend?"

"Yes. Well, she didn't say it like that, but I'm pretty sure she wants one."

I shook my head, amazed. "Mariah, I *do* want to date Cheyenne. That's who I'm talking about."

She perked right up. "Really?"

"Yes."

"Yay!" She picked up her pizza again and took another bite.

I waited for her to say something else—put up some semblance of resistance—but she didn't.

There was *no fucking way* this could be that easy.

I scratched my head. "Do you—do you want to ask me anything?"

Mariah chomped on her pizza for a moment. "Are you guys going to get married?"

"I haven't thought that far ahead yet."

"I think you should. Then she can live with us."

My head was spinning. "Well . . . I'll think about that."

"But Daddy, if you're going to ask her to marry you, you should definitely take off that other wedding ring you wear. It might make her feel bad."

My jaw hung open. "It won't—it wouldn't—bother you if I took it off? You once asked me to wear it every day."

"Did I?" She looked surprised and amused, as if she were hearing a cute story about something she'd done as a toddler.

"Yes. When you were afraid I'd get remarried and move away."

"Oh," she said, nodding in understanding. "Yeah, I remember that. It was, like, in kindergarten."

"Right."

"I don't think that anymore. I know you wouldn't leave me."

"That's true," I said seriously. "I would never leave you."

"If you did get married to Miss Cheyenne, would you have kids?"

I was beginning to feel like I was being pranked. "I haven't thought about that either."

"I really want a little sister," she said. "But not a little brother, so don't have any boy babies."

"Okay," I said, laughing nervously. "Well, I'm not sure it works like that, but I'm glad to know you're open to the idea of being a big sister."

She grinned. "I am. I think I'd be a really good big sister."

"I think so too." I stared at the pizza on my plate like it was a foreign object, then looked up at Mariah again, hardly recognizing her. "You're sure you're okay with this? You're not worried at all?"

"No. Should I be?"

"No," I said quickly. "Not at all. I just . . . want to be sure I'm addressing all your concerns. I know sometimes you worry about me."

"But you said I shouldn't worry." Her face grew uneasy, and I told myself to stop digging around for a problem where there clearly wasn't one.

"That's right—you shouldn't. Nothing is going to change just because Cheyenne and I like being together."

"Good. So are you like . . . in *love*?"

I rolled my eyes, trying to relax. "Now you're just being silly."

"It's not silly. I want to know," she said, setting her slice of pizza down again. "Because it has to be the kind of love that's real, not the kind that wears the fancy costume. Because that kind fades away, and she doesn't want that."

"I have no idea what you're talking about. I feel like I'm on another planet right now."

Mariah sighed, like she was the parent trying to explain something, and I was the kid refusing to get it. "Never mind. Just make sure you love her the right way."

"I'll try. Is that all?"

"That's all. Can we eat now?"

"Yes." I picked up my pizza and took a bite without tasting it.

Was this for real? Just like that, there was nothing standing in the way of Cheyenne and I being together? No resistance? No tears? No *fight*?

I couldn't help feeling like I'd just been handed the keys to the castle, but the place had been unlocked to begin with.

Where was the moat? Where was the drawbridge?

Where was the goddamn dragon?

Twenty

Cheyenne

I WAS ON PINS AND NEEDLES ALL NIGHT.

My mother had gone out with friends, and Blair had asked if I wanted to come over and hang out with her and Griffin, but I'd said no. I knew I wouldn't be good company.

Instead I spent the evening alone, baking sugar cookies, nibbling the dough, and watching stop-motion animated Christmas specials.

Around nine-thirty, my phone rang. It was Cole.

"Hello?" I answered breathlessly, as if I'd been running a marathon and not buried beneath blankets on the couch.

"Hey."

I sat up straight. "How did it go? Did you talk to her?"

"I did, and it went fine."

"Oh my God, Cole, really? She was okay?" I clutched my heart in relief.

"She *seems* okay."

"I'm so glad! Aren't you?"

"Yeah," he said. "I am." There was something odd in his voice, as if a *but* was coming, but he didn't go on.

"So you're home now?" I asked.

"Yes. Just put her to bed and snuck into my room to call you. How was your night?"

"Good. I have the house to myself. My mom is out." I changed up my tone to sound more suggestive. "She'll be gone at least another couple hours . . ."

"Oh yeah?" His tone changed too.

"Yes. Can you come over?"

"I'm on my way."

Frantic and excited, I ran upstairs, tore off my socks and sweatpants, took down my hair, and brushed my teeth. Two minutes later, he was knocking on my front door.

I pulled it open wearing nothing but a short white T-shirt. "Evening, Officer Mitchell. Can I help you?"

"I don't think so," he said, taking in my bare legs. He came in and shut the door behind him. "You see, I'm here to arrest you."

"Arrest me—oh dear," I said, backing up the stairs, a hand on my chest. "There must be some mistake. What's my crime?"

He followed, pursuing me as he unbuckled his belt and slipped it from the loops. "Indecent exposure. Disturbing the peace. Making me want you so fucking badly I can't see straight."

I backed into my bedroom. "Oh my, that does sound like terribly deviant behavior. I think you'd better proceed with that arrest."

Moving fast, he shut my bedroom door and turned me roughly against it. Yanking my arms behind my back, he had my wrists in place and secured them with his belt.

I struggled just for fun. "Really, Officer. Is this necessary? Can't we work something out?"

He leaned up against me and whispered in my ear. "You have the right to remain silent—but I like it better when you're loud."

"Are you going to give me a reason to scream?"

"Yeah." He pushed his cock against my ass. "A fucking big one."

Afterward, we got dressed quickly in case my mother came home.

"Do you have to leave right away?" I asked.

He zipped up his jeans, hesitating. "I guess I could stay a little longer."

I smiled and hopped onto my bed. "Good. Come lie with me."

We stretched out on top of the covers, Cole on his back and me tucked against his side. Outside, the wind whipped at my bedroom windows, and I shuddered at the thought of his having to go out there. "So cold tonight. I wish you didn't have to leave."

"Me too." He kissed the top of my head. "If your mom comes home, do I have to go out the window?"

I laughed. "No, silly. You can use the door. We are grown adults, and besides, I'm pretty sure she would let you spend the night."

"Oh yeah?"

"Yes. She'll be thrilled about this—when you're ready to tell people."

"You can tell her. My mom knows."

"She does?" I picked up my head, surprised.

"I'm pretty sure. I went flying through the living room on my way out, and I think I yelled something like, *'Going to Cheyenne's for a quick fuck, don't wait up!'* And I may have already been taking my pants off."

Giggling, I slapped his chest before lowering my head again. "You did not say that. Although, it's like seventeen degrees outside and you were not wearing a coat when you got here, so that might have tipped her off that you were excited to see me."

"Probably. She suggested on the way home from the wedding that we might enjoy each other's company. I could barely keep a straight face."

"*My* mother kept going on and on about how handsome you looked, and how eloquently you spoke, and did I hear the part where you quoted her?" I laughed, slipping my hand beneath his sweater and T-shirt, resting it on his warm, bare skin. "It was nothing but Cole, Cole, Cole on the drive home."

"Sorry." He squeezed me.

"You know I didn't mind." I stroked his chest beneath his clothing.

"And I'm sorry we have to sneak around and rush all the time. I hate it."

"It's only temporary." I snuggled closer. "Tell me more about your talk with Mariah."

"There's not much more to tell. She seemed genuinely happy and excited. It was actually kind of . . . weird."

"What do you mean, *weird*?"

"It just seemed too easy. Like shooting fish in a barrel." He paused. "In all honesty, I can't shake this feeling that something was off about it."

"Like you think maybe she told you what she thought you wanted to hear?"

"Maybe. I can't put my finger on it. But I'm not convinced she's as okay with it as she acted today."

I sat up again and looked down at him. "You really think she was acting?"

"I don't know." He thought for a moment. "I was prepared for resistance, you know? Tears. A meltdown or something. I had notes in my pocket that I never even had to consult."

"Cole, this is a *good* thing."

"I know," he said. "But I feel like I was prepared to slay a dragon for you, and the dragon didn't even show."

I laughed. "You were going to fight for me and you didn't get to, huh? Is that where all tonight's aggression came from?"

"Maybe." He tugged me down again. "And I don't mean to

say that I'm not happy about her reaction. It *is* a good thing. It's just . . . good things can be deceiving, you know?"

Something in his voice set off the faintest alarm bell in my head. "How so?"

"Well, it's important never to take for granted that everything is fine. You can't be too complacent."

I was completely still, letting his words sink in, trying to make sense of them. "Or else what?"

"Or else life will bite you in the ass when you're least expecting it." Then he said, quieter, "I suppose, now that I'm really happy for the first time in years, I'm just . . . a little bit afraid."

"Of what?"

He hesitated. "Of something I can't see coming."

I curled up tighter against him, throwing my leg over his thighs and wrapping my arm around his torso, as if I could protect him from whatever it was he was scared of. I spoke fiercely. "Nothing bad is coming, Cole."

He chuckled. "You sound so sure of that."

"I am sure."

"How?"

I picked up my head and looked at him. "Because I have been waiting for this moment my entire life, and the universe knows it."

His lips curved into a smile. "This moment right here?"

"Mmhm."

"What's so special about it?"

"You're here next to me."

"That's it? No, no, no. Let's make it more special than that." He rolled over so that I lay beneath him and looked down at me. "I love you, Cheyenne. And I'm so happy you never gave up on me. I hope you know that."

My heart threatened to explode. "I love you too."

He pressed his lips to mine. "Say it again."

"I love you, Cole," I whispered. "And everything is going to be okay. The best is yet to come."

Twenty-One

Cole

THAT NIGHT, I COULDN'T SLEEP.

I lay awake in the dark, anxious and sweaty, aware of every creak of the house, every click and whoosh of the furnace, every gust of wind whistling against my bedroom window.

There *was* a fucking dragon. I was sure of it. I could sense it. I could hear it creeping up on me. I just couldn't see it.

It was waiting for me to drop my guard, that was all. It was waiting for the exact moment I was alone and unprotected. The moment I thought I had it all. Then it was going to attack. I felt it in every blood cell, every nerve ending, every bone in my body.

The next morning, I called Jessalyn. I knew she had Saturday morning office hours, and even though I was technically on shift, I felt like I *had* to talk to her.

"I need to see you," I said. "It's an emergency."

"Cole, is everything okay?"

"I don't know."

"I'm fully booked this morning, but I could see you on my lunch hour."

"Fine."

"Be here at noon," she said.

At eleven-forty-five, I told the dispatcher I was going out of service and headed to Jessalyn's office, which was on the second floor of a small office building downtown.

Too restless to sit—probably due to the six cups of coffee I'd had this morning—I paced the floor in the waiting room, ignoring the stares of a kid about Mariah's age and his mother, as well as the receptionist.

"What's wrong with that policeman?" I heard the kid ask, pushing his glasses up his nose.

"Nothing. And don't stare," she whispered back, although she peered over the top of her magazine at me suspiciously before taking her own advice.

A few minutes before noon, they were called into the office of another therapist in the practice, and I was left alone. Too agitated to sit still and tired of pacing, I started stacking all the magazines into a pile on the coffee table.

A minute later, Jessalyn's door opened, and a teenage girl with a nose ring and pink hair came out. She gave me an odd look before hurrying into the hallway.

"Cole?" Jessalyn said, appearing in the doorway to her office. "Come on in."

I tossed the magazine in my hands aside and strode into her office.

She shut the door behind me. "Please take a seat."

I did, perching stiffly on the very edge of the couch.

She sat in her desk chair. "So what's—"

"You were wrong," I blurted, jumping to my feet.

"I'm sorry, what?"

"You got everything all wrong." I paced back and forth in front of the couch. "I did everything you said, and it didn't go like you said it would."

"Do you mean telling Mariah about Cheyenne?"

"Yes," I snapped.

"She didn't handle the news well?"

"She handled it great," I said. "Which is why you got every-thing all wrong."

She shook her head. "Cole, I'm confused."

"*You* said there would be resistance." I pointed at her accusingly.

"I said there *might* be resistance."

"You said it would be a tough conversation, and I might have to give her extra hugs."

"Okay," she said patiently.

"You said I'd have to explain why I want to date Cheyenne, and—and be sensitive to Mariah's fears, and make sure she knows that my relationship with Cheyenne is not going to take me away from her." I listed everything out, using my fingers like tick marks.

"Right."

"I didn't have to do any of that!" I exploded. "She just accepted it! With hardly any explanation and certainly no resistance."

Jessalyn sat back and crossed her legs. Folded her arms. "I see."

"You said we shouldn't have any sleepovers because it would scare her. You said she'd worry that I was trying to replace the parent she lost. You said I would have to be careful not to give her any reason to believe I'm choosing my happiness over hers."

"And you didn't have to do any of those things?"

"No! None of them!"

"Cole, can you please lower your voice? I can see that you're very emotional right now, but we do need to be respectful of the other therapists and their clients."

"Sorry," I muttered, continuing to pace. "It just really threw me off. There was no dragon." I whirled to face her. "Where's the *dragon*, Jessalyn?"

She blinked at me. "The what now?"

"The dragon." Part of me knew how insane I sounded, but I couldn't stop. I was going on too little sleep and too much caffeine. "The thing that's waiting for me to breathe easy before it destroys my life right in front of me."

She regarded me silently for a moment. "Cole, you're not my client, but I would like to ask you about something."

"Go ahead."

"Will you sit down?"

Reluctantly, I lowered myself onto the couch. Ran a hand through my hair.

"This is the first time you've dated anyone seriously since losing your wife, correct?"

"Yes."

"Can I ask why you've waited so long?"

"Because of Mariah."

Jessalyn nodded. "Because of that promise you made when she was five?"

"Yes." I thought for a second. "Also because I didn't like it when other people told me I should. I don't like being told what to do. I don't like being told I'm unhappy or stuck or that Trisha wouldn't have wanted me to stay single."

"Fair enough. But Mariah is older now, Cole. And she understands that dating Cheyenne doesn't mean she's going to lose you."

"You don't understand," I said, jumping to my feet again. "She's afraid. She's very, very afraid. She just won't admit it."

"I think *you're* afraid, Cole," Jessalyn said gently. "And you were looking for Mariah to give you a reason to retreat from your feelings for Cheyenne."

"What? That's ridiculous! The only thing I'm looking for is the dragon!"

She sighed. "The dragon is *you*. It's your refusal to believe that happiness can last. Your fear of loss. Your anxiety about being vulnerable again."

"*I* do not have any *anxiety* about being *vulnerable*," I informed her in a huff. "Because I'm *not* vulnerable. I'm a guy. I'm tough. I'm a cop." I puffed up my chest and stood taller.

Jessalyn arched a brow. "I can see that."

"So that's not what this is about. I'm not worried for *myself,*

I'm worried for the people I love. I want to protect them. I'm a *very protective person.*" I thumped a fist against my sternum on the last three words.

"Of course you are," she said. "But in this instance, I think—subconsciously—the person you're most worried about protecting is yourself. I think you're in love with Cheyenne, and it's making you feel threatened and exposed because of the way you lost your first wife. You suffered a deep wound, Cole. It's only natural to harbor some fear it could happen again."

"You're wrong," I informed her, moving her name to the list of people who thought they knew how I felt or what was best for me. My upper lip twitched. "I am fine. F-I-N-E fine."

"Have you considered therapy, Cole?"

"I don't need therapy." At my sides, my hands began to tremble, and I crossed my arms, shoving them in my armpits.

"I don't see adults, but I'd be happy to—"

"I *said*, I don't need therapy. And I've taken up enough of your time," I announced abruptly, heading for the door. "Sorry for yelling that way."

"Cole, please. Let me help you."

But I didn't want her help. I didn't need her help.

What the hell was the matter with me, barging into her office like that?

I was fine.

In fact, I was more than fine. I was crazy in love with a beautiful, sweet, sexy woman I'd known almost all my life. My daughter loved her. My mother loved her. Her mother loved me. Her brother was my best friend.

Everything was perfect.

And just because there was nothing standing in the way of me being completely happy for the rest of my life didn't mean something terrible was sneaking up behind me.

That shadow was nothing.

I could ignore it.

Twenty-Two

Cheyenne

O N MONDAY MORNING MARIAH POPPED HER HEAD into my classroom before school while I was restocking the pencil trays on each kindergarten table.

"Hi, Miss Cheyenne!"

"Good morning, Mariah! How was your weekend?" Since Cole had worked Saturday and Sunday, we hadn't gotten a chance to hang out, although we'd talked on the phone both nights for hours. Going to sleep after hearing him say I love you had brought the sweetest dreams I'd ever had.

"It was good," she said enthusiastically. "My dad took me skating on Friday and he told me about you guys."

I nodded, perching on the edge of a table. "That's what he said."

"I told him about the kind of love you were looking for." She sighed and shook her head. "Hopefully, he was listening."

"I'm sure he was," I said, hiding a smile. "Thank you."

"I hope you guys get married," she went on, her eyes lighting up. "And then you can have a baby. I told him I wanted a little sister, not a little brother, but I guess I'd be okay with a little brother too."

"Oh—oh my." I put a hand over my stomach. "Well, we haven't really talked about that yet."

"I know." She grinned. "I'm just really excited."

Two more girls entered my classroom—I recognized them as former students, now fourth graders like Mariah. I stood up and smiled. "Good morning, girls."

"Good morning, Miss Dempsey," they recited together.

"You coming, Mariah?" one of them asked.

"Yes," she said. Then she threw her arms around me. "Have a good day, Miss Cheyenne."

I patted her shoulder. "You too, sweetie."

Then she rushed out, saying to her friends, "She's my dad's girlfriend now. They're probably gonna get married."

"Lucky!" one of them replied.

I laughed, but it was easy for me to see how Cole might have suffered a bit from whiplash if he'd been expecting any objections from her. She clearly had none.

While I was eating lunch at my desk, I got a text from him.

Cole: Run away with me.

Me: Right now?

Cole: Yes. To the new house. I have the key for a few hours.

Me: I can't get there until four at the soonest.

Cole: But Moretti will be here by then, and you'll want to have your clothes back on.

Me: That is a definite yes. But I'd still love to come by after school.

Cole: Do it.

He gave me the address and I told him I'd be there by four o'clock. Then I asked him if he wanted me to bring Mariah along.

My phone vibrated with a call from him, and I answered it.

"Hey," I said. "I just have a few minutes before the kids come in from recess."

"No fair, they get you all day."

I laughed. "So should I bring Mariah with me to the house?"

"I'm sure she'd love that. I'll let my mom know she won't be on the bus and call the school as well. They'll get a note to her to go to your classroom after the bell. Does that work?"

"That's perfect. We'll see you at four."

"Can't wait. I love you."

I smiled, knowing I would *never* get tired of hearing him say those words, or saying them back. "I love you too."

After school, Mariah came to my room and we headed over to the new house. She babbled nonstop on the drive about how excited she was to move in, what color she might paint her room, and the bunk beds her dad had let her pick out online.

"They won't be delivered until January, but Daddy says that's okay because we probably won't be able to move in much before that anyway. There's lots of work that needs to be done."

I parked in front of the house behind a white pickup and Enzo's SUV. As Mariah and I made our way up the walk toward the old brick house with a white wraparound porch, I couldn't help smiling. It was gorgeous all covered with snow, but I could imagine it in the spring with tulips and daffodils in the beds by the porch and green leaves on the towering weeping willow to one side. Cole came out the front door and waved.

Mariah ran the rest of the way, racing up the steps to stand next to him so she could welcome me. "This is the porch," she said as I approached.

"The porch that needs a new coat of paint," Cole added.

"I love it," I said.

"Daddy says we can get some rocking chairs and maybe even a swing." She looked at him. "Right?"

"Right."

"That sounds heavenly. I love reading a book on the porch in summertime." I climbed the steps, and Cole kissed my cheek.

"How was your day?" he asked, opening the front door.

"Good. Yours?"

He shrugged. "The estimate for the renovation is getting a little scary, but Moretti seems to think we can keep it down by using some repurposed materials and doing some labor ourselves."

"That's good," I said, entering the front hall with a gasp. "Oh, Cole." Wide-eyed, I looked around at the high ceilings, wood floors, and natural light pouring in the windows surrounding the door. I put a hand over my heart. "This is beautiful."

He shut the door behind us. "Not yet, but it will be. Come in, and we'll show you around."

Mariah led the way into the living room, where I was charmed by the fireplace, the tall windows, and what I could see of the parquet floor, revealed where someone had pulled back the musty old carpet. In the dining room, I admired the bay window and antique chandelier, which Cole hated but Mariah thought was fancy. In the kitchen, I said hello to Enzo and smiled at another guy, who was kneeling on the floor with a tape measure extended across the room.

"Cheyenne, this is Kevin Dodson. He's going to be doing most of the kitchen remodel. Kevin, this is my girlfriend, Cheyenne Dempsey."

Already on my way to shake Kevin's hand, I nearly fell to the floor in a dead faint when I heard the word *girlfriend*.

I was Cole Mitchell's girlfriend! How was that even possible?

I practically floated upstairs, where Mariah flitted from room to room, chirping about which one was hers, which one was her dad's, and which room could be the baby's.

"Baby?" Enzo's eyebrows shot up and he looked from me to Cole to my stomach. "Is there something I don't know?"

Cole rolled his eyes. "Yes. My daughter is crazy."

"There's no baby," I said, laughing.

But later, when Enzo and Mariah were heading back downstairs, Cole tugged my hand and pulled me back into his bedroom for a kiss.

It was a deep, long, passionate kiss that made my heart race, my toes tingle, and my stomach muscles tighten. His hands traveled over my back and down to my ass.

"Cole, stop." Breathless, I looked over my shoulder at the doorway. "What if she comes back up?"

"I don't care. This is my room."

"But she might—"

He reached behind me and slammed the door. "There. Feel better?"

I started to laugh, but then his mouth was on mine once more, and I couldn't think about anything but his kiss. Pretty soon, his breathing grew heavier and he backed me up against the door. I could feel his erection against my belly as he moved against me. Even though I knew it was a bad idea, I reached between us and rubbed it through his jeans, making him groan.

Giggling, I took my hand off him. "Sorry. I couldn't help it. Should we go downstairs?"

"I need a minute." He pushed himself back from me, his arms braced on either side of my head. "I wish we had more time."

"Soon." I smiled. "Tell me what you'll do with this room. New paint? A rug? A big new bed?"

"I'm open to suggestions. Tell me what will entice you to come over a lot."

"Hmmm." I ducked beneath his arms and studied the room. "Are there wood floors beneath this carpet?"

"Yes."

"I'd rip out all the carpet and polish up the floors. Get a great big bed with a fluffy down comforter, and put a cozy rug beneath it. Over by the fireplace, I'd put another rug and maybe a couple chairs. And over there . . ." I pointed to the big window overlooking the yard. "I'd put in a window seat with lots of pillows."

"A window seat, huh?"

"Yes. And that's where I will sit with my mug of tea and a romance novel, wrapped in a fuzzy blanket with a scented candle lit beside me."

He wrapped his arms around me from behind. "You expect me to build a window seat so you can come here and read a book? That's not what I had in mind."

I laughed, placing my hands on his forearms. "I didn't say a window seat would be more enticing than you by the fireplace or you in that great big bed. But one of my dreams is to have a quiet place to read where I'm surrounded by books and natural light."

"Oh." He exhaled. "Then I guess I have to build it for you."

Turning in his embrace to face him, I slipped my arms around his waist and smiled up at him. "You don't have to build anything for me. You're the best dream I've ever had, and you're already right here."

"But I like doing things for you. And I feel like I wasted so much time trying not to fall for you, I want to make up for it."

"We're not in a rush, Cole. This is the real thing, remember? It's not going anywhere. And no one can take it from us."

For a fleeting second, a shadow crossed his face.

"What's wrong?" I asked.

"Nothing." He pulled me close, tucking my head beneath his chin, and we stayed that way for a moment. And then from below, we heard Mariah shrieking with laughter.

"Moretti always makes her laugh," said Cole. "She loves him."

"What female doesn't?" I joked.

"Actually, believe it or not, I recently met a woman from his past who seems to be immune to his charms."

"Seriously?"

"Yes. She's an interior designer. Bianca DeRossi."

Gasping, I tipped my head back and looked up at him. "I know her! She's in my book club. So she's the one woman who can resist him, huh?"

"She's the one."

"I'll have to ask her why sometime." Then I sighed. "I guess we better go back downstairs, huh?"

"I guess."

Hand in hand, we left the master bedroom. When we passed the other bedrooms on our way to the steps, Cole pointed to one and said, "Should we check on the baby?"

I laughed. "Is it a boy or a girl?"

"A sister, of course. No brothers allowed."

"Do you think she'll like pancakes for dinner?"

"I mean, who wouldn't?"

At the bottom of the stairs, he turned to face me. Everyone else was in the kitchen, but he still spoke quietly. "You know, a year ago—hell, a month ago—if anyone had asked me if I saw myself having more kids, I'd have said no fucking way."

I held my breath. "And now?"

He hesitated, almost like he wasn't quite sure how to put it. "Now there's you."

My throat tightened. "Now there's *us*."

"Yes. Now there's us."

I shook my head. "I can't even believe we're having this conversation. It's like suddenly finding yourself at the all-you-can-eat buffet of your wildest dreams."

Laughing, he squeezed my hand. "I want to make all your dreams come true. If I can."

My eyes misted over. "You know what? Today was a pretty good start."

Twenty-Three

Cole

THE DAY AFTER I TOOK CHEYENNE THROUGH THE house, I called Moretti and asked if he had Bianca DeRossi's contact information.

"Why do you need it?"

"Because she's an interior designer and I have some questions about the interior of the house."

"Ask *me*. I have good taste."

I rolled my eyes. "Just give me her number please."

"I don't have it." Heavy sigh. "But I could probably get it."

"Thanks."

"Or you could just try 1-800-HELLCAT. I bet she'd answer."

"Could you just get the number please?"

"Fine," he muttered. "Are you off work again today? What are you up to?"

"Yeah. I'm just getting shit done, ordering some furniture. I want to hit the paint store for some samples later—"

"Don't buy anything yet. I get a discount."

"Want to meet me there?"

"What time?"

I checked my watch. "Can you go now? I have to be over at the school before three-thirty."

"Why? Doesn't Mariah take the bus home?"

"It's not for Mariah. It's for Cheyenne. It's been snowing all day and I want to scrape off her car. She mentioned yesterday how much she hates doing that in her work clothes."

Moretti started to laugh.

"What's so funny?"

"Dude," he said. "You're a mess."

"Fuck off."

"Hey, I'm kidding. So things are going well, huh?"

"Yeah," I said, ignoring that icy little sliver of doubt that kept trying to get under my skin. "They're going great."

"Told you there was nothing to worry about."

I had to laugh. "Are you serious? That's not what you said at all."

"What did I say?"

"You said I could totally fuck it up and things could always go wrong."

"Oh, yeah."

"Which did not exactly inspire confidence. Thankfully, I ignored you."

"Then my advice is to keep on ignoring me. Somehow, I'm helping. I'm sure of it."

After I took care of Cheyenne's car, I got out of there quickly so she wouldn't catch me.

She called me around four o'clock. I was sitting at the kitchen table, waiting for Mariah to get home.

"Hello?"

"Cole Mitchell! Did you do this?"

"What?" I couldn't keep a grin off my face.

"My car! I was so grumpy, expecting to come out and find it all covered with snow, but it was totally cleaned off!"

"You must have a secret admirer," I told her.

"Well, it was the best thing ever. Please tell him he's the perfect man."

"Come on, nobody's perfect."

"You don't know him like I do," she insisted. "I'm telling you. He's perfect."

I grinned. "Go on."

"He's gorgeous and sweet and generous. He makes me laugh, he's the best dad ever, and everyone who knows him says what a great guy he is."

"Yeah?"

"Plus," she went on, lowering her voice, "he's an incredible kisser, he's good with his hands, and as an added bonus, he has a huge dick and knows how to use it."

I felt like thumping my chest. "Good for him."

"I'm madly in love with him," she said. "I always have been, always will be."

"Frankly, I'm not sure he deserves you," I told her. "What makes you think he can make you happy?"

She laughed. "Some things, you just know."

The following day, Wednesday, Moretti shared Bianca DeRossi's contact information with me. At least, I assumed it was Bianca's. He had her first and last name as Witchy Vixen. After shooting him a quick thanks, I saved her info—under the correct name—and gave her a call after work.

"Hello?"

"Hi, Bianca?"

"This is she."

"Hey, this is Cole Mitchell. I'm a friend of Enzo Moretti's and we met—"

"Of course! How are you, Cole?"

"Good. How are you?"

"Doing great, thanks. How's the house coming along?"

"That's actually what I'd like to talk to you about. I wondered if you might be able to give me some advice on the master bedroom. Specifically, I'd like to put in a window seat. Maybe some bookshelves."

"Ooh, how nice. Are you a reader?"

"It's actually for my girlfriend."

"Even better."

I smiled. "I think you might know her—Cheyenne Dempsey."

"Of course I do! She's in my book club. I love Cheyenne."

"Me too. This is a secret project, though. I don't want her to know I'm doing it."

"My lips are sealed. This is so sweet, Cole. I didn't realize you two were a couple."

"Well, it's still kind of new," I said. "But it's serious. We've known each other forever."

She sighed. "So romantic. And I promise, we will design you a book nook that will make Cheyenne lose her mind. She'll never want to leave your new house."

I laughed. "Good."

"This isn't a Christmas present, is it? Because I don't think we'll be able to get it done in time."

"No, I don't close until the twenty-ninth, and I won't move in until after the first. I don't even own any furniture yet. We've been living with my mother since Mariah's mom died, so . . ."

"I understand. And I'm sorry for your loss."

"Thank you." I tried to lighten the mood. "It's been nine years. You'd think I'd have at least a couch by now."

She laughed politely. "We'll fix you right up. I'm not that busy in January, and I'd love to help you out. I have a lot of good contacts in Chicago and around here too—why don't you let me help you?"

"I'd love that, but I'm not sure I can afford you."

"I'll consider it a favor. How's that?"

"Really? I don't mean you'll have to work for nothing, just that I—"

"I'm positive we can work it out. Who knows? I might need your help with something in the future."

"Just say the word," I told her. "I'd be glad to return the favor."

"Perfect. Let's look at the calendar and set up a time to look at your new house."

My new house. I loved the sound of that.

And it wasn't just a new house to me—it was the start of a new life.

Maybe it wasn't the life that I'd originally planned, but it was a good life, a beautiful life, one that I would give my all to build, to cherish, to protect.

I breathed deeply, my body relaxed, my heart full. Maybe Cheyenne was right and I didn't need to worry so much. Maybe there was no dragon. Maybe that shadow behind me was gone. Maybe the best really was yet to come, all I had to do was keep moving toward it.

But it was hard not to look back.

Twenty-Four

Cheyenne

"FINALLY!" BLAIR TURNED THE SIGN IN HER BAKERY window to CLOSED and locked the door. "I thought those people would never leave, and I'm dying to talk to you. How's everything going?"

"Great." I was sitting at one of the little round café tables along one wall with a cup of tea and an uneaten pastry. "Everything is great."

It was late Friday afternoon—a week had gone by since the night Cole had told Mariah about us and said he loved me.

Blair poured herself a cup of coffee and came and sat down across from me. "Things are great? How come I don't entirely believe you?"

"I don't know." I took a sip of tea.

"Out with it," she demanded. "I know that look on your face."

"What are you talking about? I swear, I could not be happier."

"But you're not eating that scone and I happen to know that blueberry-lemon-thyme is your favorite."

I laughed. "I told you I wasn't that hungry. And I'm meeting Cole and Mariah for dinner soon. We're going to do some shopping and then go for tacos."

"Nice. Have you gotten him something for Christmas yet?"

I nodded. "A sweater and a scarf. Do you think that's too boring?"

"Not at all."

"I got Mariah a giant furry blanket, plus some lip gloss and nail polish."

"She'll love it. Do you have any idea what Cole is getting you?"

"No. He might not even get me anything."

Blair rolled her eyes. "Because he might forget the woman he loves at Christmas?"

I blushed. As soon as Cole had left my house last Friday night, I'd texted her HE JUST TOLD ME HE LOVES ME!!! in giant shouty caps. "I don't know. Maybe he hasn't had time to shop yet. He's been busy with the house."

"Give me a break." She took another sip of coffee. "How are things going with the house?"

I sat up taller and smiled. "Good. I saw it on Monday, and it's incredible. I mean, it needs a ton of work, but it's a beautiful old brick house with a wraparound porch and a huge yard."

"When does he move in?"

"Closing is the twenty-ninth, but I don't think he's moving in until after the first."

"When do *you* move in?" She smiled deviously.

"Blair!" I rolled my eyes. "I'm not moving in. Good grief, it's only been a few weeks."

"It's only been a few weeks since you guys did something about your feelings," she clarified. "But the feelings have been there a lot longer than that. And it sounds like everything is perfect, so *what* on earth is bothering you?"

Sighing, I took one more sip of tea and set the cup down.

"Okay, I'll tell you, but this is going to sound totally stupid, and you're probably going to tell me I'm nuts."

"I'd like nothing more."

I rolled my eyes and sat up taller. "So everything is going really well. We see each other every day, even if it's just for a little bit. We talk for hours on the phone each night. And the way he looks at me—it's the cutest thing, almost like he's afraid I'm going to disappear."

"Awww." She sipped her coffee, holding the cup in two hands.

"We don't get enough alone time, of course, but when we do, the sex is like rattle-the-ceiling good."

"Yes, I know—because you rattled my kitchen floor when you were going at it downstairs in the garage."

My cheeks got hot, and I laughed. "Sorry about that. We were trying to be fast. And quiet, I swear."

"*Fail*," she said. "But I'm still not hearing any cause for concern here, Chey."

"I'm getting to it. A week ago, the night he told me he loved me, in fact, he mentioned something about being afraid."

Blair's eyes widened. "What did he say he was afraid of?"

"Something he can't see coming." I let it sink in for a moment. "And ever since then, I cannot shake the feeling that he's, like, looking over his shoulder, waiting for disaster to strike."

"Hmm. Are you sure you're not imagining it?"

"I'm sure. He seems happy, but he goes silent a lot too. And when I ask if he's okay, he says he's just thinking about the house or something at work, or he gives me the dreaded '*I'm fine*.'"

She nodded. "It kind of makes sense, you know? The whole 'waiting for disaster' thing? Looking at you like he's worried you'll disappear? He's probably nervous about feeling so happy. Like, he's looking around for the anvil about to drop on his head because that's what happened when he loved someone before."

"You might be right." I thought for a moment, chewing

my lip. "He said something else once, and I never forgot it. He was talking about Mariah, and he said, 'She's learned that love doesn't protect you from loss.' Like it was a fact."

"Well . . ." Blair's shoulders rose. "It kind of is."

"But that doesn't mean you shouldn't love people," I said, frustrated that she agreed with him.

"No, and he wasn't saying that. He was saying that love isn't some kind of magic shield you can wear that will prevent you from getting hurt. In fact, love makes you *more* vulnerable to pain."

"Blaaaaair," I moaned. "You're not helping. You were supposed to tell me I'm being paranoid."

"Sorry. But I don't think you are." She set her cup down and reached for my hand. "Listen. You're in love with a man who suffered a horrible loss, out of the blue, on the happiest day of his life. He wouldn't be human if he wasn't a little scared of falling in love again."

"But he's not *saying* that."

She gave me a look. "Are you kidding? What *man* is going to volunteer to talk about his emotional baggage when you ask if they're okay? Remember that episode of Friends where Ross finds out Rachel and Joey are a couple and he's all 'I'm fine' over and over again, but it's obvious he isn't?"

Despite everything, I smiled. "Oh yeah."

"Cole is kind of like Ross here. He's just working through it. Take a breath, okay?"

I did what she said, inhaling deeply and exhaling slowly. "Sorry. Maybe you're right. I guess I'm still learning things about him. I get nervous when he goes quiet. And it's still hard for me to believe that after all this time, he's really mine."

"Get him talking about old man baseball. That'll perk him right up."

I burst out laughing. "I bet you're right." Then I picked up the scone and took a bite. "Thanks. I feel better."

Cole and Mariah met me at the bakery, and we strolled up and down the streets of downtown Bellamy Creek, which were all decked out for the holidays. Strands of lights stretched across Main Street. Boughs of evergreens adorned every streetlamp. Wreaths hung on every door. Christmas carols played in every shop.

As we walked along, Cole held my hand, and some of the unease I'd felt earlier dissipated. When people we knew stopped on the street to say hello, he didn't let go. When we went into a store to look around, he'd show me something that he knew would make me laugh, or drop an arm over my shoulder, and once he even kissed my forehead.

I decided Blair was right, and I was being paranoid. So what if he occasionally seemed a little broody? So what if he didn't tell me *everything* that was on his mind? So what if he needed some time to realize that there was no dragon waiting to snatch his happiness away?

What mattered was that *I* was the one he'd been willing to fight for. That we were together now. That when he looked into his future, he saw me. Us. A family.

I would continue to show him patience, love, and understanding.

I wanted him to feel safe with me.

Twenty-Five

Cole

"MARIAH, COME ON," I COMPLAINED SATURDAY night. "You've been sitting between us all day."

I'd had the day off, and we'd taken Mariah over to a neighboring farm, which offered horse-drawn sleigh rides. She'd wanted to sit between us in the sled, and we'd said of course, the three of us cuddling up beneath a thick wool blanket. Afterward, we'd returned to town for an early supper, and Mariah had requested to sit at the counter of the Bellamy Creek Diner. We'd laughed when she insisted on the counter stool in between us. Back at our house, we were going to watch The Grinch, and once again, she was claiming the couch real estate between us.

"So what?" she asked.

"So *I* get to sit next to Cheyenne now." I got her in a gentle headlock and pretended to strangle her.

Mariah squirmed and giggled, tugging at my arms. "No!"

"How about if I paint your nails while we watch, Mariah?" Cheyenne suggested.

"Okay," she said. "I'll go get the polish."

I dropped my arms, and Mariah darted upstairs. "You know," I said, getting Cheyenne in a headlock this time, "that didn't solve the problem."

"What problem?" she asked, laughing as I squeezed her.

"That I want to be next to you for once. She's hogging you." I loosened my grip, and she turned to face me, twining her arms around my waist.

"It's cute. I don't mind."

"I do," I said gruffly.

"Listen. I feel really lucky that she's happy about us. I want her to feel included. If it means letting her sit between us, I'm okay with it. It won't be forever. Soon she'll be a teenager and she won't want anything to do with us."

Groaning, I kissed her temple. "I can't think about that. I'm going to throw some popcorn in the microwave and grab a beer. Want something to drink?"

"No thanks."

I went into the kitchen, got the popcorn going, and uncapped a beer. While I waited for the microwave to go off, I listened to Mariah and Cheyenne chatter in the next room. My mom was visiting her sister in Gaylord this weekend, so it was just the three of us.

This is how it would be at the new house if she lived with us, I thought. The three of us home on a snowy Saturday night, Christmas just days away, a perfect winter afternoon behind us. A brand new year ahead of us. It was comfortable, easy, intimate.

So why couldn't I shake the uneasy feeling that it couldn't last?

Stop it, I told myself, lifting my beer to my lips. I was determined not to let negative thoughts distract me tonight. More than once Cheyenne had caught me brooding silently over the last week, and I always said it was nothing. I didn't want her to worry, and sooner or later this stupid nagging fear would loosen its grip on me, wouldn't it? I just had to tough it out.

"So which color?" I heard Mariah ask from the next room.

"Hmm. I like the darker one," Cheyenne replied. "More dramatic for Christmas Eve. Think you can make it last until Thursday night?"

"I'll try," Mariah said.

Then I heard clicking noises, as if Cheyenne were shaking the polish. "Are you excited for Santa to come?"

"Yes," Mariah said. "I'm still hoping for a puppy. Daddy says he doesn't bring animals, but Avery Frankel in my class said that's a lie because she got a rabbit from Santa last year."

Cheyenne laughed. "Well . . . good luck."

"What did *you* ask him for?"

"A winning lottery ticket."

"Why?"

"So that I can move out of my mother's house and get a place of my own," Cheyenne said, her voice determined. "And rescue a dog."

"You could move in with us," Mariah suggested. "Then we could share the dog!"

Cheyenne laughed. "Thanks for the offer, but I think you and your dad should make that house all your own."

"But it's big enough for you too," Mariah insisted. "You could even have your own room."

That made me smile—as if I'd let her sleep anywhere but next to me.

"You're sweet," Cheyenne told her. "And I promise to come visit you a lot, how's that?"

A loud sigh from my daughter. "I guess that's good." Then her tone brightened. "Hey, maybe you could buy the house next door!"

Cheyenne burst out laughing. "We'll see, sweetie. Right now, I couldn't even afford that doghouse in the yard. Come on, let's get some paper towels so we don't make a mess."

A moment later, they appeared in the kitchen, and I have

no idea why my heart chose that moment to fall through the floor but it did. I took one look at Cheyenne in that giant sweater with the floppy arms, and the fuzzy socks and the hat hair and the mascara that had run earlier because she'd laughed so hard she'd cried and was now smudged beneath her eyes— and I knew I loved her so much I never wanted to be without her. This was it for me. She was the one.

My chest grew tight. My breathing was shallow.

I wanted her to live with us. I wanted to put up our own Christmas tree. I wanted to play Santa with her after our kids went to bed and then take her to our own bedroom, undress her, and wrap myself up in her warm, soft body and stay there all night, until our kids came flying into the room in the morning again to wake us up, squealing that Santa had come. I wanted to wash the wedding china with her after Christmas dinner. I wanted the *wedding*.

I wanted it all. More than that—I could see it all.

The bed that was *ours*, in a home that we shared, in a life that we'd started together.

The promise of a new forever was unfolding right in front of me.

But promises could be broken.

I started to sweat. My hands tingled, and I had to set my beer bottle on the counter because I was afraid I would drop it.

"We need paper towels," Mariah announced, going over to the roll to rip some off.

"Hey. You okay?" Cheyenne asked, eyeing me with concern.

No, I wasn't okay. Not only was I in love with her, I was in love with the future I'd imagined for us—and it could all be destroyed in an instant.

"I'm fine," I said, clearing my throat. "Sure you don't want a beer? Let me just get you one." I turned toward the fridge.

"Okay." She came over and rubbed my back as I popped

the cap off for her, hoping she wouldn't see my hands tremble. "Sure you're alright?"

I nodded.

But I wasn't sure at all.

I was a zombie the rest of the night.

Distracted. Anxious. Two seconds away from a panic attack at all times. The effort to keep it from happening exhausted me.

I couldn't relax during the movie. I couldn't keep my hands still. I couldn't stop my leg from twitching.

Cheyenne knew something was off, but didn't ask again. And since Mariah was between us, she couldn't touch me either. But maybe it was better that way. Maybe I shouldn't depend on her touch to soothe me.

After the movie, I sent Mariah up to bed and told her I'd be back after I walked Cheyenne home.

"But I want Cheyenne to say goodnight too," she whined.

"No."

"But it's not even that late."

"Not tonight," I said sharply.

"But Daddy, she always—"

"Enough!" I yelled. "You can't always get what you want. Now go up and get ready for bed!"

Cheyenne spoke up gently. "Cole, I really don't mind—"

"I mind." I cut her off.

Hurt, Mariah hugged Cheyenne and then plodded up the stairs, sniffling. I felt horrible—I rarely raised my voice to her. But it was for her own good. I didn't want her to get too used to Cheyenne being there to say goodnight to her all the time.

"Ready to go?" I asked her stiffly.

"Yes. Let me just get my coat."

"I'll get it." I grabbed her coat from the closet and held it out so she could slip her arms in. When she was all zipped up, she pulled her hat and gloves from her pocket and tugged them on.

"I'm ready." She was looking at me kind of like she didn't know me, and it made me feel like shit.

I opened the front door for her.

"Don't you want a coat?" she asked.

"Nah. I'm coming right back." But fuck, it was freezing outside. I shoved my hands in my jeans pockets as we walked.

Cheyenne said nothing until we were on her doorstep. "Well, thanks for everything today. I had a great time."

"Me too." I faced her. "And I'm sorry I lost my temper with Mariah back there. I'm just in a weird mood."

"I can tell. It sort of came out of nowhere."

"Sorry," I said again, frustrated and angry with myself. Why should I panic about wanting to be with the woman I loved?

She bit her lip. "I don't want to keep asking if you're okay, so I won't. I'll just . . ." Looping her arms around my neck, she hugged me tight, pressing her body to mine.

I wrapped my arms around her, inhaling her scent, and felt the tension in me ease up. "You always know what I need."

"I love you," she told me.

"I love you too," I said, squeezing her tight. "So much. And I'm tired of walking you home at night."

"Cole, you never have to—"

"I want you to spend nights with me."

A pause. "What?"

"You heard me. I want you to spend nights with me. I want to say goodnight to you in a warm bed, not freezing my ass off on this porch. I want to wake up next to you. I want to make you coffee in the morning and scrape the ice off your car windows and let you pick out all my party outfits."

She laughed. "Cole, I would love that. But I don't think it's possible."

"It is if you move in with me."

She pulled back and looked up at me with wide, shocked eyes. "*What*?"

"Move in with me. With us. To the new house." I grinned. "You can try to have your own room, but I won't let you."

She laughed nervously. "You heard that conversation, huh?"

"Yes. And it made me laugh too, especially when she said you could buy the house next door." I kissed her lips. "I don't want you next door anymore, Cheyenne. You belong with me. You belong with us."

Her eyes teared up. "But Cole, I'm not quite out of debt yet. And I can't afford to pay you—"

"Jesus Christ, Chey." I shook her gently. "I'm not asking you to be my roommate. I don't want your money. I just want to be with you as much as possible."

"I want that too, but . . . it's only been a month, Cole. Aren't you worried we're moving too fast?"

"No. I'm thirty-three years old, and I know what I feel. I don't want to play games or put things off. Life is short. Don't you agree?"

"Yes," she said quickly, laughing again. "I know how I feel too. I just want you to be sure."

"I'm sure." I kissed her again. "And we know how Mariah feels about this, so there's nothing to hold us back. You're already family to me, Cheyenne. Let me take care of you. It will make me happy."

The smile blossomed on her lips and took over her whole face, making it glow. "Okay."

After she went into the house, I stood there for a second on the porch, scratching my head.

Holy shit—I'd asked Cheyenne to move in with me.

And it had felt *good*. Fucking great.

Take that, Jessalyn, I thought as I strutted back home. *Fuck you, panic attacks. Sayonara, dragon.*

I'd done it—I'd looked over the edge of the cliff and taken the leap. I was safely on the other side, and I was fucking *fine*.

As soon as I got home, I went up to Mariah's room.

"Hey," I said, sitting on the edge of her bed.

She was facing the other way. Giving me the silent treatment.

"You mad at me?"

"I don't know."

I put a hand on her back. "I'm sorry."

She didn't answer.

"I try my hardest to do things right, but I mess up sometimes."

Still nothing.

"I was angry at myself and I yelled at you instead. You didn't do anything wrong."

Mariah rolled over and looked at me. "I just like it when she tucks me in. We talk."

"Yeah? About what?"

"Girl stuff."

That made me smile. "You can't talk to *me* about girl stuff?"

She rolled her eyes. "No, Daddy."

I sighed heavily. "I guess I can understand that."

"I invited her to live with us."

"I heard."

"But she said no."

"I think she was thinking about getting her own place."

"But don't you think it would be fun if our place was also her place?"

"As a matter of fact, I do. That's why *I* asked her if she'd like to live with us."

Mariah's eyes went wide. "What did she say?"

"She said yes."

A gasp. "She did?"

"Yep."

Then a pout. "How come she said no to me but yes to you?"

I chuckled, tapping her nose. "I think she needed both of us to ask her. If I'd asked her first, she probably would have said no too."

She squeezed the stuffed dog in her arms. "I'm so glad she said yes!"

"Me too, peanut."

"Are you guys going to get married?"

"One thing at a time, okay?"

"Okay, but do you really love her?"

"Yes. I do."

Mariah smiled. "I love her too. I know she isn't my real mom, but this will be like having a bonus mom."

My throat grew tight. "I think that's a great way to look at it."

Mariah glanced at the photo of Trisha on her dresser. "Cheyenne says that Mommy was nice to everyone."

"She was."

"I try to be nice to everyone too. I want to be like her."

Leaning over, I kissed her forehead. "I'm the luckiest dad in the whole world. I love you, peanut."

She looped her arms around my neck and hugged me. "I love you too."

I went to bed feeling pretty damn pleased with myself.

That night, I had horrible nightmares.

I was trapped in the dark with an evil thing I couldn't see except for two toxic green eyes.

I could hear it breathing. I could feel its heat. I could smell its rot. It watched me, moving closer, then retreating, but always ready to dig in its claws and tear me to shreds.

I heard Mariah's voice. "Daddy?"

I fucking panicked—she was there somewhere in that stinking dark, and I had to protect her. But where was she? Where was she? I started to scream for her.

"Daddy!"

I woke up in a pool of sweat, my heart pounding, adrenaline pumping.

Mariah was standing at the foot of my bed. "Daddy, you're scaring me."

"Oh, honey. I'm sorry." I rubbed my face. "I had a bad dream. I'm okay."

"I heard you yelling. It woke me up."

"I'm sorry, baby." I checked the clock—not even two. "I'll take you back to bed," I said, swinging my legs over the side of the mattress.

"Okay."

In her room, I tucked her in and kissed her forehead. She gave me a hug, but recoiled a second later. "Ew. You're sweaty."

"Sorry."

She lay back. "Was it a really bad dream?"

"Yeah."

"Was I in it?"

I hesitated. I didn't want to scare her. "There was a monster."

"Did he want to eat you?"

"I think maybe he did."

"You told me monsters aren't real."

"They're not."

"But just in case, you gave me Prewitt to protect me."

"Prewitt?"

"Yes." She leaned over the side of her bed where several stuffed animals had fallen to the floor. "Here he is. He's a platypus. You said monsters were only scared of one thing—platypuses."

I had to smile. "That's right."

She handed me the stuffed animal. "Here. You can sleep with Prewitt tonight. He'll protect you."

"Thanks." I kissed her forehead. "Go to sleep. I'll see you in the morning."

I took Prewitt back into my bedroom and tossed him onto the bed. Then I stripped off my sweat-soaked T-shirt and yanked on a new one before climbing under the covers again.

Fuck. What the hell? I hadn't had a nightmare like that

in years. As a kid, I'd had bad dreams about the usual stuff—a monster under the bed, a bogeyman in the closet, a shark in the lake. But I'd learned to combat the fear of something bad happening to me by always telling the truth, always doing the right thing, always standing up for people. And eventually, the nightmares had stopped.

Of course, later I learned that nothing you did could prevent bad things from happening. You could never be one hundred percent safe.

My pulse began to race again, my chest growing painfully tight. I was hot and sweaty, but chills racked my body. My breathing was quick and shallow.

I wanted to reach for my phone and call Cheyenne, ask her to come over and hold me. Let me hold her. Beg her to sleep right next to me so that I would know she was safe.

But that wouldn't be the reason she wanted to hear. She'd probably be upset if I said that. She'd tell me I was being paranoid. She'd probably suggest I needed therapy, just like Jessalyn had.

But I wasn't going to fucking therapy. Spilling my guts to some stranger wasn't going to help. I would conquer this bullshit on my own, one way or another, because I wasn't a six-year-old boy, I was a grown-ass man.

I fought it off alone, like a man should.

Twenty-Six

Cheyenne

SUNDAY MORNING, I WOKE UP EARLY, FULL OF ENERGY and spark. I jumped out of bed, put on some workout clothes, and practically skipped down to the kitchen.

My mother was drinking coffee at the table in her robe, reading her newspaper just like always.

"Morning, Mom!" I sang.

"Morning, dear. You're up early."

"I'm too excited to sleep." I poured some coffee, smiling like an idiot as I recalled the way Cole had said he wanted to make it for me in the morning.

"Why?"

Turning around, I leaned back against the counter and took a breath. "Cole asked me to move in with him last night."

"He what?" My mother's jaw dropped, and she set her mug down.

"You heard me." For once, I wore the smug face as I sipped my coffee.

"Well. My goodness." Her expression was something between shock and happiness. "That was fast."

"I said the same thing, and I asked him if he was sure, and he said yes. He said he's too old for games and he knows what he wants."

My mother sat up even straighter. "Really? Good for him."

"But Mom, I don't want you to freak out about this. He didn't propose."

"But he will, don't you think?" She cocked her head. "I mean, if you're going to have kids, you'll want to—"

"Oh my God, Mom! I'm not pregnant! We're just going to live together."

"For now." She took the smug back as she picked up her coffee cup again.

"Okay, whatever. I just came down to grab a quick sip of coffee before I work out."

"You work out?"

I rolled my eyes. "Yes, Mom, I work out. What do you think I bought all those yoga classes for?"

"Beats me. You only went a couple times."

"Okay, fine, I didn't love yoga. But I'm going to find an online workout video and maybe get on a new program. I'd like to eat healthier too. Not so much sugar and junk."

"You picked a tough time to start that, since Christmas is on Friday," my mother said.

"Good point." I thought for a moment. "It'll be my New Year's resolution, how about that? I'm going to treat my body better. But I'm still going to work out now. I'm filled with energy!"

My mother laughed. "Glad to hear it."

After I worked out, I took a shower and got dressed. While I was blow drying my hair, I got a text from Cole.

Cole: Good morning, beautiful. Pretty soon I'll be able to say that instead of type it.

Me: I am still pinching myself.

Cole: So is Mariah.

I was so excited to hear about her reaction, I decided to call him.

"Hello?"

"You told her already?" I squealed.

"Yes. Last night."

"And she was happy?"

"Ecstatic." He yawned. "Sorry. Didn't sleep much last night."

I smiled. "I'm surprised I slept at all."

He laughed a little. "Hey, is the rescue shelter open on Sundays? I was going to ask you if you'd like to go over there with me and see if there are any rescue dogs that might be a good fit for Mariah. Then maybe I can give her a picture on Christmas morning or something."

"That's an adorable idea, and I'd love to help! What time are you thinking? I'm pretty sure the Sunday hours are noon to five."

"I have to wait for my mom to get back, which I think will be around three. Does that work?"

"Perfect," I said. "I'm meeting Blair for lunch at one."

"Just text me when you get back."

"Okay. Hey, is it okay to tell her?"

He laughed. "Yes. Go ahead. Tell everyone."

Blair's jaw dropped just like my mom's had. "He *what*?"

"Asked me to move in with him." Seated across from her in a booth at the Bellamy Creek Diner, I grinned.

She grinned back. "I told you!"

I laughed. "Yes, you did."

"And I was sort of kidding. Wow." She blinked and shook her head. "So I guess he worked through his baggage quick, huh?"

"I guess," I said, ignoring the tiny tremor in my belly.

The server came by to take our orders, and Blair raised an eyebrow when I ordered just a garden salad.

"I'm trying to watch what I eat," I explained.

"Oh. Well, while I watch you eat a salad, I'm going to eat a grilled cheese and tomato sandwich with fries."

My mouth watered at the thought of hot, gooey provolone. Thick, crispy fries. "Okay."

When the server had gone, Blair said, "Okay, tell me everything. Leave nothing out."

Taking a deep breath, I told her everything about the previous twenty-four hours—how we'd enjoyed the day together, how Mariah kept wanting to sit between us, how he'd walked me home after the movie and asked me to live with him right there on my front porch.

"It's so perfect," she gushed. "How did you even sleep last night?"

"I don't know," I admitted, fiddling with my napkin in my lap. "There was *one* thing that had me kind of worried, though."

"What?"

"Just this weird mood shift at one point. The entire day had been so great, and then back at his house, I suddenly felt like he was on the verge of a breakdown or something. He was anxious and silent. Fidgety and sweaty and hardly able to sit still. I was listening to him breathe during the movie and I totally thought he was about to have a heart attack."

Blair's eyes went wide. "Seriously?"

"Yes. Then after the movie he lost his temper with Mariah, which I've never seen before. In fact, I don't think I've seen Cole lose his temper, *ever*. Not in twenty-five years."

"Really? God, Griffin loses his temper daily at something or other."

"But Griffin has always been a hothead. Cole's always been the cool hand, the level head."

"Hm." Blair sipped her iced tea. "Those symptoms you described almost sound like a panic attack. Does he ever have those?"

"I don't know. Not that he's told me." I thought for a moment. "He kind of prides himself on his control, you know? On keeping calm in a crisis. Maybe it's his police training."

"Makes sense." She thought for a moment. "So maybe the occasional broody silence or temper tantrum is just part of his personality that he hides from everyone else, especially on the job. Maybe showing it to you means he feels close to you. It could be a good thing."

"Maybe. And anyway, once he walked me home, everything was fine. Better than fine."

"Sounds like it."

The server returned with our lunches, and I eyeballed Blair's sandwich and fries with envy. Not that there was anything wrong with my salad, but . . .

"Would you like half my sandwich?" she asked.

"No." Sitting up taller, I picked up my fork. "The salad is fine. I really do want to eat better."

"Good for you."

"And I'm feeling really strong today. Really good about myself."

"I *love* that."

"I mean, it's still hard for me to believe I'm the one he wants, but—"

"Stop." Blair pinned me with a look. "He wants you."

"He wants me." I couldn't help smiling.

"So let's have a toast." Blair picked up a French fry and raised it.

Plucking one from her plate, I lifted it to hers. "To happily ever after."

"Yes," she said. "*Amor vincit omnia.*"

"What does that mean?"

She smiled. "Love conquers all."

Twenty-Seven

Cole

DURING MONDAY'S SHIFT, I RESPONDED TO THE kind of call that every police officer dreads.

An infant, just a few weeks old, had stopped breathing.

When I pulled up to the house, a woman I assumed was the mother came running out with the baby in her arms.

"She's not breathing! She's not breathing!" she screamed over and over again. "Help me!"

Nothing is worse than a situation where a child is in danger, but my training kicked in and I remained calm, even as my own heart was firing like a machine gun.

"Okay, let me have the baby. Let me have her." I took the infant from the hysterical mother and assessed her quickly. The baby's color was okay, and she was blinking at me. Her huge eyes were dark and trusting.

But she wasn't breathing.

While continuing to soothe the frantic mother by speaking calmly, I checked the baby's mouth and airway but saw nothing obstructing it. Then I rotated her to face down on my forearm and delivered three blows to the upper middle portion of her back. A few seconds later, she started to cry.

Part of me wanted to fall to my knees in relief, but I remained upright and stoic, holding the baby against my chest as I radioed back that the baby was breathing and crying, and the EMT had arrived.

Afterward, I wrapped up the call like it was any other, accepting hugs from the grateful mother, handshakes from neighbors who'd come out to see what the trouble was, and claps on the back from colleagues at the station. I finished my shift as if nothing was amiss.

Then I went home and had a full-on panic attack, alone in my room.

What if I hadn't gotten there in time? Or worse, what if I'd been unable to save the baby? What if I'd been too late, or so panicked I'd forgotten my training, or simply hadn't been able to clear the obstruction? That innocent little life would have been gone on my watch.

My watch.

It was the perfect example of why you couldn't trust the universe or God or anyone else to protect you. You were on your own. Anything and anyone could be taken from you inside a minute.

An accident. A mistake. A lightning strike. An error in judgment. A split second. A wrong choice.

There were so many ways fate could turn on you, no matter how smart or careful or good you tried to be.

After pulling myself together, I changed out of my uniform and went downstairs.

The episode with the baby had made the evening news, and footage from my cruiser's dash cam had been released to the media. By the time I made it downstairs for supper, the phone had started ringing—townspeople calling to praise and congratulate me.

My mother was beside herself, beaming with pride, scolding me for not saying anything sooner. "Cole Mitchell! You walked right by me at the stove and went upstairs to change without telling me what you did!"

"Sorry, Mom," I muttered. "I needed a minute."

My daughter was impressed too, hugging me hard, playing the video online again and again. "Wow, Daddy! Can I bring you in for Show and Tell?"

"Uh, no."

Cheyenne came rushing in the back door, practically knocking me off my feet the way she hurtled herself at me. "Why didn't you say anything, you big jerk?" she cried. "You're a hero!"

"I'm not. I was just doing my job," I told her as she sobbed on my shoulder.

That night, the soundtrack of my nightmare included the sound of a child gasping for air.

I yelled so loud, I woke my mother.

The following day, baskets of fruit and plates of cookies showed up at the police department, and I fielded phone calls from reporters who wanted to interview me. My boss had to essentially give me the day off just to keep up, but he said he was glad to do it.

Burying all my emotions, I calmly relayed the events the way they'd occurred, saying only that I was grateful for my training and happy the baby was okay. It was all in a day's work of keeping Bellamy Creek safe. The baby's family came to the station, and we took a photo together, me holding the baby and the child's parents standing beside me. By the time I got home, my mother had printed it and taped it to the refrigerator.

Local Hero Saves Baby, read the headline.

I looked at the picture. Beneath my bloodshot eyes were dark circles. My smile looked forced. My chest seemed artificially inflated.

My legs trembled as I went upstairs to change out of my uniform.

I didn't feel like a hero. I felt like I was faking it.

That evening, I took Mariah to her therapy appointment.

While she was in the office with Jessalyn, I sat in the waiting room, staring at a dog-eared parenting magazine and sipping a cup of coffee. I was exhausted and on edge, hoping it wouldn't show. I was also hoping Mariah told her therapist that I'd asked Cheyenne to move in with us—that would prove to her she'd been wrong about me, wouldn't it?

When the hour was up, Jessalyn and Mariah came out. I rose to my feet.

"Hello, Cole." Jessalyn smiled at me. "I heard the news."

"About Cheyenne?"

"About the baby." Her grin widened, and she shook her head. "Quite a story. Thank goodness you're so good at what you do."

"Thank you." I looked at my daughter. "How did it go tonight?"

"Great!" She beamed. "We made a—oh!" She flicked worried eyes to Jessalyn. "I left my perfect-day collage on the table so the glue would dry. Can I get it?"

"Sure." Jessalyn stood aside, and Mariah scooted past her.

"So did she tell you about Cheyenne moving in?" I asked the second we were alone.

"She did."

"Told you I was fine," I blurted.

She was silent a moment. Then she cocked her head. "Are you?"

"Of course I am. Why else do you think I asked Cheyenne to live with us?"

"Is that why you asked her? To prove you're fine?"

I opened my mouth and shut it. It seemed like a trick question.

Mariah came bustling out again, carefully carrying a sheet of paper with pictures cut out from magazines posted on it. "Look, Daddy! I made a perfect day collage."

I took it from her and carefully held it by the edges. There was a picture of a dog, a snowman, a pizza, someone ice skating, an old-fashioned horse-drawn sleigh, a house strung with Christmas lights, and several photos of families that included a mom, a dad, and children. There was also a picture of a girl about Mariah's age cradling a baby.

It was the baby that threatened to undo me—the room spun, and my breathing was labored all of a sudden.

But I fended off the panic.

"Wow, Mariah. This looks great."

She pointed at the photo of the girl holding the infant. "That's me with my little sister. Penelope."

"Penelope, huh?" I hoped Jessalyn didn't notice the way I'd begun to sweat.

"Yes. Penelope Mitchell. Doesn't that sound good?"

I swiped my forehead. "We should get going, Mariah. I'm sure Jessalyn wants to get home. Zip up your coat."

"Okay."

I looked at the therapist. "See you in two weeks?"

She nodded. "Yes. Off next week for break."

"Enjoy the holidays," I told her.

"Same to you." Just for a second, I thought I saw something like sympathy on her face.

But I hustled Mariah out the door before I could be sure.

Wednesday night, the guys and I got together at the pub—all except Griffin, who was on a plane to Nashville. He and Blair were going down to spend Christmas with her family, since they'd been unable to make the wedding. Mariah was with Cheyenne at her house—they were baking cookies and wrapping gifts.

We sat at a table near the back of the pub, ordered some beers and bar food, and caught up a little. It was the first time we'd seen each other since the wedding.

After they made a big deal about the incident with the baby and gave me a bunch of shit about being a hero—people kept coming over to shake my hand or hug me—Moretti took over the conversation, bemoaning his unsuccessful attempt to convince his parents to give him some more time to find the right bride.

"What happened to Reina?" I asked, happy to discuss something other than myself.

He shrugged. "Reina's fine. But I just don't think she's the right fit," he said, like he was talking about ceiling joists and not marriage. "Hey Beckett, how's your old man? He seemed okay at the wedding, although he did think I was my dad all night."

Beckett frowned. "Yeah, the signs of dementia are all getting worse. He wandered away from the house again yesterday, and a neighbor saw him walking down the highway without a coat. Luckily she recognized him and drove him home."

"Shit. Is it that bad?" I asked.

"Yeah," he said. "I keep trying to lock him in, but it doesn't work. And I can't be inside with him all day. I'm running a fucking cattle ranch by myself at this point."

Beckett's parents had divorced when he was young, and his mom had been out of the picture for years. He'd been raised by his dad and two older siblings. The best student of all of us— also the biggest and brawniest thanks to all the manual labor he did growing up on a farm—he'd left Bellamy Creek right after high school on a college scholarship and hit Wall Street after that. But city life hadn't been for him, so a few years ago, he'd left it behind and never looked back.

Even now, his cowboy hat was resting on the couch between

us next to him—brim side up, and don't fucking get him started on why you can't set a cowboy hat down any other way. We sometimes teased him that he was more Texas than Michigan, despite having been born and raised right up the road.

"What about your sisters?" Moretti asked. "Can they help?"

"They've got jobs and kids, and Amy lives an hour away. They can't really do much." Beckett pinched the bridge of his nose. "I'll probably have to hire someone eventually. There's no way he'll move to a facility, and I can't babysit him all day."

"That's a good idea," Moretti said. "I once dated a girl who did that—home care for an elderly guy. She'd help him get dressed and all that."

"Dated her for how long?" Beckett gave him the side eye.

"At least an hour," Moretti quipped, tipping up his beer. "Long enough for her to *un*dress me. I dressed myself."

We laughed, and I felt more like my old self. It was good to be around the guys, even though I was so tired I couldn't stop yawning.

"What's going on with you?" Moretti asked me. "You look a little rough. Cheyenne keeping you up nights?"

"Ha. Right. At my mom's house?"

"You'll be in your new place soon enough."

"Yeah," I said, grabbing my beer bottle off the table.

"That's cool about you and Cheyenne," Beckett said. "So is it serious?"

"Um, yeah, you know." I took a sip of beer. "I guess it's serious. I asked her to move in with me. To the new house."

"Shit, did you really?" Moretti looked surprised.

"Yeah." I shifted in my chair.

"That *is* serious," said Beckett.

"And Mariah's doing okay with it?" Moretti asked.

I shrugged. "She says she is."

"You don't believe her?" Beckett paused with his beer half-way to his mouth.

"I do, it's just kind of hard to believe she doesn't have any issue whatsoever with me being in a serious relationship. She's always been so scared of losing me. At one point she made me promise I'd never get remarried."

"But this is Cheyenne," Beckett pointed out. "It's not some stranger. She's known Cheyenne her entire life."

"Right, but that's exactly why she might not feel like she can be entirely honest about how she feels. She doesn't want to hurt Cheyenne's feelings." It was total bullshit and I knew it, but for some reason, I couldn't stop talking.

"And wasn't she really tiny when she made you promise that?" Moretti asked. "I remember it, but it seems like it was a long time ago."

"Yes, she was only five, but that doesn't mean the fear isn't still there—in fact, I worry that it's moved from her conscious mind into her subconscious and she doesn't even recognize it. But is it going to blow up later?" My lip was starting to twitch, and I covered it with my beer bottle.

"I don't know, man." Moretti frowned and shook his head. "You and Mariah have such a great relationship. I feel like she'd be up front about her feelings with you. And she seemed fine that day at the house."

"You don't know her as well as I do," I shot back, sitting up taller in my chair. "There was this period of time last year where she was writing these letters to me and hiding them in her room. They were full of questions she was too afraid to ask me."

"Oh." Moretti's face was grim. "I didn't know that."

"And she's been having these nightmares." The words were out of my mouth before I could stop them. My hands started to shake, and I set my beer bottle down and crossed my arms over my chest, hiding them in my armpits.

"What kind of nightmares?" Beckett asked.

"She's, um, alone in the dark. Trapped. And there's a monster or something that's going to attack her and she can't escape. So she's just like *waiting* in there to be attacked."

"That sucks. You know what my sister did when my nephew was having monster nightmares?" Moretti said. "She had this spray bottle and she put a label on it that said Anti-Monster Spray, and every night she'd spray his room. Worked like a charm."

I couldn't even smile. "Yeah, I don't think that's going to work in this case."

"Does she see a therapist?" Beckett asked. "If not, you might consider it."

"She does."

"What does the therapist say about the nightmares?"

"Um, I don't know. Mariah never tells me what they discuss." I swiped my beer off the table and took another drink in the attempt to disguise my trembling lip. But my hand shook so much I knocked the lip of the bottle against my tooth. I set it down again. "I just need to talk to Cheyenne."

"That's a good idea," Moretti said. "Maybe Cheyenne can help her. She's good with kids."

I squirmed in my chair. "No, I mean I need to talk to Cheyenne about *us*. Maybe we're moving too fast."

Beckett and Moretti exchanged a look that pissed me off.

"Didn't you just say things were going great?" Beckett asked.

"They are," I said, knowing I was making no sense and getting aggravated about it. "Maybe they're going too great."

"Cole, what the hell are you talking about?" Moretti looked totally confused.

"I'm talking about the fact that I'm in love with her, okay?" I snapped. "*I'm* in love with her, and *Mariah's* in love with her, and everything is so perfect, there has to be something wrong."

"Are you listening to yourself?" Beckett shook his head. "There's nothing wrong, Cole."

"Except that you don't trust good things," Moretti said.

"Why should I?" I demanded, taking another big swallow from my beer. "Huh? Why should I?"

"Because they're real, Cole."

"You know what else is real? Bad luck. Tragedy." I locked my jaw. "Look at what just happened Monday. One second that baby was fine, the next, she couldn't breathe."

"But you were there, Cole," Beckett reminded me. "You saved her. That was a good thing."

"It could have easily gone the other way." I was not going to be talked out of this.

Moretti leaned on the table. "We're not saying bad things don't happen to good people, because they do—we know it. But you can't live in fear of them. And you don't have to go looking for them."

"I'm not *looking* for them," I said defensively. "I'm just not choosing to be blind to them."

Moretti sighed, lifting his beer. "Look, I've never been in love, so I don't know what it feels like. It sounds scary as fuck."

"It is," I confirmed.

"But I do know you. And I think you'll regret it if you walk away."

"I do too," Beckett added.

"I'm not walking away," I said irritably. "Nothing I've said is about walking away."

"Then what's it about?" Moretti demanded.

"It's about being smart. Strong. Tough. It's about protecting the people you love. It's about making decisions based on what you know is true, not about how you feel in the moment. You have to—you have to put aside what you feel in the moment and go with what you *know*." My body was sweaty beneath my clothes, and my heart was pumping fast inside my ribs. "Maybe I just need to take a step back and make sure I'm doing the right thing."

"Okay." Moretti held up both hands, as if offering a truce. "Didn't mean to upset you."

"I'm not upset." I pulled out my wallet and threw down some cash. "But I better go pick up Mariah now. It's getting late."

❄

In the car on the way home, I went over the uncomfortable conversation again and again, hating myself for lying to my friends but also irritated that they thought they knew better than I did how to handle the situation. It was easy for them to trust in good things. They weren't me. They hadn't been through what I had.

I had to take a few minutes and calm down before I walked over to Cheyenne's.

She greeted me at the front door with a hug and a smile, flour dusted all over her clothes. "Come on in! We're just waiting for the second batch to come out of the oven."

I went inside, inhaling the homey scent of fresh-baked cookies mingling with the Balsam fir Christmas tree, trying desperately to relax. Cheyenne was good at reading my face, and I didn't want her to ask me what was wrong tonight. I was too exhausted to be convincing.

"Daddy!" Mariah yelled when I entered the kitchen. She wore a red apron that was way too big for her, which she'd obviously wiped her hands on many times. "Want to help us decorate?"

I yawned. "How about I just watch?"

"Tired?" Cheyenne asked.

"A little."

"Want a cup of coffee?"

"That sounds great."

"Hello, dear," Darlene called from the sink, where she was washing out a mixing bowl.

"Hi, Mrs. Dempsey."

I sat at the dining room table with a cup of coffee and watched Mariah and Cheyenne frost and sprinkle their cookies. They laughed and teased each other, trading funny looks and making inside jokes that should have made me trust in good things.

But I couldn't. I just couldn't.

Over Cheyenne's shoulder, there was a clock on the wall. I could hear it ticking.

Twenty-Eight

Cheyenne

CHRISTMAS EVE, I WAS GETTING READY TO HEAD OVER to the Mitchells' house when my mother popped her head into my room. "Got a minute?"

"Sure," I said, holding up two different earrings and checking the mirror to see which one I liked better with the high-necked black lace top I had on. "Which one do you think?"

My mother sat on the bed behind me and looked at my reflection. "Hmmm, I like the smaller ones."

"Okay." I set the dangly one down and put on the little hoops. "What's up?"

"I just wondered if you'd noticed anything unusual about Cole last night."

"What do you mean?"

"I mean, he just seemed off to me. Not his usual self."

"How so?" I asked, even though I knew.

"Quiet. Distracted. Even anxious."

"He said he was tired. And he had a really eventful week." I felt the need to defend him, even though I was worried too. "I get the feeling he hasn't been sleeping well lately."

"That could be it." She hesitated. "So he's mentioned the nightmares to you?"

"Nightmares?" I finished fastening the second hoop and turned to face her. "No. What nightmares?"

"Oh, dear. Well, maybe I shouldn't have said anything, but his mother mentioned to me that he's been having nightmares so bad he wakes up yelling in the middle of the night."

A chill swept up my spine. "What? Since when?"

"She didn't say exactly when it started, but I had lunch with her yesterday and she seemed so tense about something—it took me a while to get it out of her, but then she confessed. She said it happened at least twice this week."

"Wow." My heart ached that Cole hadn't felt he could confide in me about it. "That's . . . that's awful."

"I knew he used to have them when he was younger," my mother went on, "and for the longest time he couldn't sleep over with Griffin. But he grew out of them. Odd that they're back all of a sudden."

"Yes, it is," I said, a strange mix of dread and sadness in my belly. "Maybe it was the episode with the baby?"

"Maybe." My mother sighed. "But it makes sense now why he's seeing a therapist."

"A therapist?"

"Yes. Deb Culpepper saw him in the waiting room of her son's therapist a couple weeks ago, and said he was acting very strange."

"Is she sure it was him?"

"He was wearing his uniform," my mother said with a shrug.

"Oh." My brow furrowed and then relaxed. "Oh! I bet it was *Mariah's* therapist whose office he was at. He spoke with her recently about us, in fact."

"Oh. Well, that's good. Anyway, I'm sure it's all fine, but I just wondered if things were okay with the two of you."

"Yes," I said, turning back to the mirror and picking up a lipstick. "They are."

"Any news on the move?"

"He's moving after the first, I told you." I carefully applied the poppy-red color to my lips.

"I meant *your* move—when do you move in?"

"Trying to get rid of me?" I rubbed my lips together and puckered up before capping the tube.

"Of course not, dear. You know I love having you here. I was only curious." Suddenly she rose to her feet. "Anyway, I'm glad to hear things are going so well. Are you ready to go?"

"One minute," I said. "I'll meet you downstairs, okay?"

"Sure."

As soon as she was out the door, I grabbed my phone and called Blair.

"Hello?"

"It's me," I said quietly. "I'm so sorry to bug you on Christmas Eve, but I have to ask your advice about something."

"Of course. Go ahead. We're not at the table yet. It's still cocktail hour down here." She laughed. "The Beauforts do not skimp on their cocktail hour."

"How's it going down there?" I asked, feeling guilty I hadn't led with that.

"Great! My folks adore Griffin, my grandmother is completely smitten, and he's been talking classic cars with my uncle all night."

"That's awesome."

"Okay, I'm hiding in the bathroom now. Tell me what's up."

Quickly, I ran through the conversation I'd just had with my mom. "So now I don't know what to do! Do I ask him about the nightmares? Wait for him to tell me? I don't want to make things weird for him and his mom. But why hasn't he told me?"

"Hmm, this is a tough one." Blair was silent for a moment.

From downstairs, I heard my mother calling me. "Shit," I whispered. "I have to go. Tell me what to do, fast."

"I'd ask him," she said. "If it were me, I'd ask him."

"What if he denies it?"

"Then I'd come clean about the conversation with your mom." She paused. "But maybe not on Christmas Eve. I'd wait."

"Okay." I felt slightly better. "Thanks. I know you think I'm nuts for worrying all the time, but this isn't just me being paranoid."

"No, it isn't," she said. "I think you have to ask. If you guys can't be honest with each other about these kinds of deeply personal things, it's not going to work."

"Cheyenne Dempsey!" my mother howled. "Do not make me climb these stairs again! I'm leaving without you!"

"Coming!" I yelled. To Blair I said, "Okay, gotta go. Thanks again. Merry Christmas. Give my brother a hug for me."

"I will. Merry Christmas," she said. "Love you, let me know how it goes."

With one more glance in the mirror—I tried to replace my tense expression with a more party-appropriate one—I grabbed my purse and hurried out of my room.

The Mitchells' Christmas Eve Open House was a tradition in our neighborhood. It started early, and almost every family stopped in before heading to their family dinners and parties. The house was already full of revelers when my mother and I arrived.

After placing the gifts I'd brought beneath the tree, I found Cole pouring drinks at the makeshift bar in the dining room. The moment I saw him, my stomach flipped like a pancake. He was so handsome in his French blue shirt with the sleeves cuffed up, his charcoal gray dress pants, and shiny dress shoes. His scruff was trimmed back, his hair was neatly combed, and he smelled like he had our first night together.

"Hey there," I said, approaching the bar with a grin. "Don't tell my boyfriend, but you're the cutest bartender I've ever seen."

"Oh yeah? Well, you see what's right above our heads?"

I looked up. "Mistletoe. How convenient."

"I know. Come here." He leaned forward over the bar and I did too, our lips meeting in the middle.

"Eww," said a high-pitched voice. "That's gross."

We looked to see Mariah standing to one side of the bar with a few neighborhood friends. "I know, and they do it all the time," Mariah said, rolling her eyes.

"Beat it," Cole said, jerking his thumb. "No kids allowed in my bar."

The kids scampered off, and I turned back to Cole, studying him more closely. "How are you?"

"Good." He smiled, but I could see the dark circles under his eyes, the pallor beneath his normally golden complexion. "How are you?"

"Good. Want to pour me some wine?"

"Of course. Red or white?"

"Red, please."

He opened a bottle and poured me a glass, handing it over the bar. "There you go."

"Thanks." I took a sip as a few dads from the neighborhood approached the bar, wanting to clap Cole on the back for the rescue earlier in the week and open a bottle of good whiskey one of them had brought.

A discussion ensued about the merits of Irish versus Japanese versus Tennessee whiskey, and I excused myself, saying I was going to offer my help to his mom in the kitchen. He gave me a look that said he was sorry, and I reassured him with a smile.

In the kitchen, I found a harried Mrs. Mitchell trying to keep the trays of appetizers full, make room on the table for dishes neighbors had brought, and keep up with the empty plate and glass collection. When I offered to help, she called me an angel and asked me if I'd stir the meatballs, then dump them into the serving bowl on the counter.

I stayed busy in the kitchen for the next hour, during which Cole brought me a second glass of wine and kissed my cheek before disappearing again. When the second glass was gone, I had to use the bathroom, and since someone was in the one on the first floor, I went upstairs to the second. The door was closed, but I decided to wait rather than go back downstairs.

I couldn't resist peeking into Cole's room, pushing the door all the way open and snapping on the light. I hadn't been in here since the night I'd helped choose his outfit for Griffin's party over a month ago. It made me smile, thinking how much things had changed.

But one thing hadn't—the wedding photo was still on his dresser. Unable to help myself, I picked it up and looked closer. Surprisingly, I didn't feel a punch of jealousy because he'd loved her. I understood she was part of his story the way Mariah was too. And even though I knew he'd always have a place in his heart for her, it didn't bother me. I knew there was room for me too.

I just wanted to be part of his story—even if I hadn't been the beginning, I could be the happily ever after.

If he'd let me.

"Cheyenne?"

I turned and discovered Mariah in the doorway. "Oh! Hey, honey. I was just . . ." I set the photo down and decided to change the subject. "Are you having a good time?"

"I was, but my friends had to leave." She shrugged. "Now I'll be bored the rest of the night. What are you doing up here?"

"Um, I came up to use the bathroom, but someone was in there."

"I was. Sorry." She looked guilty.

"That's okay." I smiled at her. "Then I just wandered in here. Your dad is a very neat person, isn't he?"

"We have to be. Grandma gets mad if we don't make our beds first thing when we get up."

"Well, it's not a bad habit to form." I turned and looked at

Cole's bed, surprised to see a stuffed animal there. Laughing, I pointed at it. "What is that?"

"Oh, that's Prewitt." Giggling, she went over and retrieved it. "He's a platypus. My dad gave it to me once because I was scared there were monsters under my bed. He first tried to tell me there was no such thing as monsters, but I didn't believe him, so he got me Prewitt, because monsters are only afraid of one thing, and that's platypuses."

I laughed, taking the stuffed animal from her. "Your dad is smart. What's it doing in here?"

"Oh, I gave it to him for a while because of his bad dreams."

My heart skipped a few beats. "Bad dreams?"

"Yes. He said there's a monster in them."

I nodded slowly. "Oh."

"He woke me up one night last week because he was yelling so loud, so I offered to let him sleep with Prewitt." She made a face. "Then he hugged me, but he was all sweaty so it was gross."

I tried to smile, but I'm not sure I did. "What—what night was that? When he woke you?"

"Hmm, let me think." She squinted. "It was the night my grandma was gone. The night we watched The Grinch." Her face lit up. "Hey, I bet that's why Daddy had a nightmare about a monster!"

I swallowed, but the lump in my throat remained. "You could be right. But we better put Prewitt back so your daddy doesn't miss him."

"Okay." She took the stuffed platypus from my hands and replaced it on Cole's bed. "Daddy said you'll share his room at the new house. So maybe he won't need Prewitt."

"And is that okay with you? If I share his room?"

"Sure. I can't wait for you to live with us." She hesitated, like she wasn't sure she should say what was on her mind.

"It's okay," I said. "You can tell me anything."

"He says he loves you the right way—the way that will last," she said in one breathless rush. "I asked him, because I wanted to make sure it wasn't the wrong kind that wears the costume."

I smiled, even as the lump in my throat got bigger. "Thanks for looking out for me."

"You're welcome." She looked proud of herself. "Should we go downstairs and open gifts? I have one for you."

"I have something for you too," I told her. "Come on, let's go downstairs. I'll use the bathroom down there."

With one last glance at Cole's bed, I turned off the light and shut the door.

That fucking platypus was making me want to cry.

The rest of the evening passed in a blur. I could hardly look Cole in the eye because I was constantly on the verge of tears, but I held myself together. On the inside, though, I was a mess. If Cole was having such bad nightmares, why hadn't he said anything to me about them? Did he think it was something he needed to hide? That it would make him less attractive? Or was it possible his bad dreams had something to do with our relationship? What about the timing? Was it coincidence he'd just started having them within the last week? That he'd had one the night he'd asked me to move in with him?

Stop it, I told myself. *Stop being paranoid. This probably has nothing to do with you at all. You just have to talk to him, but NOT on Christmas Eve.*

Mariah and I exchanged gifts—she went crazy over her blanket, nail polish, and lip gloss from me, and I squealed with delight at the giant black hoodie she'd gotten me that said RYDELL HIGH on the front above a big varsity letter R and Miss Dempsey on the back. "Mariah, it's perfect! Thank you so much."

My mother and I stayed late, helping to gather and distribute coats, wish departing guests Merry Christmas, and clean up.

Mariah, exhausted but positive she'd be unable to sleep because she was so excited for Santa to come, eventually went up to bed, and Cole and I said goodnight to her together.

"It's okay if I wake up early, right?" she asked him.

"Sure." He yawned. "I have to be at work at seven, so I'll be up early too. That way I can see you open some gifts if Santa comes tonight."

"He will," she said confidently. "The Santa tracker app said he's over North America now."

"Oh, good," Cole said. "Then you better get to sleep."

When we went downstairs, Mrs. Mitchell said goodnight as well.

"Night, Mom," said Cole, dropping onto the couch.

"Let me know if you need help bringing up all the Santa gifts from the basement," she whispered.

"I'm good," he said, fighting off another yawn.

"I can help you," I said, sitting next to him.

Mrs. Mitchell disappeared up the stairs, and it was just Cole and me.

"Want to open your present from me?" I asked.

"Sure."

I grabbed the package I'd placed beneath their tree and set it in his lap. "Here. It's not very exciting."

He gave me a look, tore off the paper, and opened the box. "I love it," he said, holding up the sweater. "Thank you."

"You know how I love you in blue," I said.

"You know I love it when you pick my clothing. Okay, now your turn," he said, reaching under the tree and handing me an envelope the size of a greeting card that said *Cheyenne* on it in his handwriting.

Smiling, I opened the envelope and pulled out a post-card sized gift certificate from Cloverleigh Farms for a Romantic Weekend for Two. Gasping, I held it to my chest. "Oh my gosh, did you really?"

"Did I really what? Buy you a Christmas present that was also a gift for myself? Yes."

I laughed. "I meant, did you do this when we were there?"

"Yes. Right before we left." He shrugged. "I knew it would always be a special place for us. I thought maybe we could go back every year."

"Oh, Cole, I love that idea." I leaned toward him, still clutching the gift certificate, melting into his chest. His arms enveloped me, and he kissed my head. Closing my eyes, I took a deep breath. Everything was going to be okay. "Maybe we can use this weekend away over my winter break. I don't have to go back until the fourth."

"Maybe." He hesitated. "But I'll be pretty busy with the house."

"Oh, that's true." I took a breath. "So we haven't really talked about this yet, but when do you want me to move in?"

"I was thinking of waiting a little bit on that."

Something about the way he said it made me stiffen up. "Waiting a little bit?"

"Yes. Just maybe a couple months or so. You know."

I sat up and looked at him. "A couple *months*?"

"Well, yeah." He shrugged and met my eyes only briefly. "I thought it might be best to give Mariah some time to adjust to the new place. On our own."

"Oh." Hurt had taken root in my chest. "And that will take months?"

"Hard to say."

A tear slipped down my cheek. I couldn't help it.

"Hey, I don't want you to worry, okay?" He took my hand. "I love you. You know I do. I want to be with you."

"So why don't you want us to live together?"

"I do want that. I'm just making sure we're not rushing it." His eyes dropped to our hands. "I'm—I'm worried about Mariah. See, she's been having nightmares."

A chill moved up my spine. Something was way, way off. "*Mariah* has been having nightmares?"

"Yes." Letting go of my hand, he crossed his arms over his chest.

"What kind of nightmares?"

"She says . . . she says they're about a monster in the dark. She's terrified of it, even though it's just there in the dark with her. Because she knows at any minute, it might attack."

"Something she can't see coming," I said.

"Right," he said, oblivious that I'd just used his own words. "She's obviously frightened by something that feels unsafe or— or unpredictable to her. She senses danger and doesn't know how to protect herself. So I think we'd better just give her some more time to feel, you know, safe."

"More time . . . so Mariah feels safe." It was all making sense to me now. Blair had been right—Cole did have some things to work through. But he wasn't working through them, he was burying them even deeper.

And he was lying to me about it.

"Yes. I love you, Cheyenne. And I want to be with you all the time. But my first priority has to be my daughter. You understand, right?"

I closed my eyes as more tears fell, and swallowed hard. "Yes. I understand."

"Good." He reached for me but I stood up. "This isn't going to work for me, Cole."

"Huh?"

"You're not being honest."

He looked indignant. "Yes, I am."

I shook my head. "You're not. You're scared of what's happening between us. You're afraid that what we have can't last."

"That's not it at all!" Cole jumped up from the couch and glanced toward the stairs. We had to keep our voices down, but it was hard, because we were both worked up. "I'm only concerned about—"

I held up one hand. "Don't say Mariah, Cole, because I know the truth."

"What truth?"

"Mariah isn't the one having the nightmares, you are. Mariah isn't the one frightened about something she can't see coming, you are. Mariah isn't the one lying to me about how she feels, you are." I started to cry for real. "She told me, Cole. Tonight, we were talking earlier, and she told me about your bad dreams and how she gave you a stuffed animal to scare the monster away. And even if she hadn't, your mother mentioned them to my mother."

"Jesus Christ," he snapped, his chest inflating with anger. "This is why I need my own house."

"And that's fine." I put up my hands. "That's fine, Cole. Move into your own house. I'll be staying in mine."

"Cheyenne, please." His expression was furious, his tone heated. "I told you from the beginning that this wasn't going to be easy for me."

"I never expected it to be easy. But I did expect you to let me in."

"I did let you in! I let you get closer to me than anyone!" he whispered frantically. "*You're* the one saying it's not enough."

"Because it isn't, Cole." Tears continued to fall, and I slashed at them angrily. "Yes, you let me get close to you. But now you're pushing me away. And I have this feeling that you're going to keep pushing."

"That's ridiculous." He crossed his arms again.

"Is it? I can deal with you wanting more time until we move in together. But that's not what this is about."

"Huh?"

"This is about you saying you're fine and you're not. This is about you looking for reasons to keep yourself from being happy, so that it can't be stolen from you. This is about you wanting to *cause* the bad thing, so that the bad thing can't take you by surprise."

He set his jaw. "You're wrong."

"I'm not, Cole." I had to wipe my eyes again. "Look, I've loved you for so many years—what would another couple months be until we could live together? In the grand scheme of things, it's no time at all."

"Then why can't you just agree to it?" he begged, his tone softer. "That's all I need."

"No, it isn't. This is not about time, Cole. It's not about time, it's not about Mariah, and it's not even about Trisha anymore—it's about you." I choked back a sob. "Anyone would have wounds after going through what you did. And in order to survive and be there for Mariah, you had to ignore them. But the scars are still there, and you have to *look* at them now if you want to move on and be happy. You have to talk about them. Share them with me."

"You sound like Jessalyn," he said angrily. "And maybe women and children need to talk about all their issues in order to get past them, but men don't."

"Says who?"

"Says me." He thumped his chest.

I shook my head. It would have been funny if it weren't so sad. "You're wrong, Cole. It's going to break my heart to walk out of here tonight, but if you won't let me love you, scars and all, that's what I have to do." With tears streaming down my face, I turned to leave.

"Cheyenne, wait. Don't go." He grabbed my arm and forced me to look at him. "I love you," he said, his eyes shining in the dark.

"All of me? Even the scars? Even that girl who still can't believe Cole Mitchell would ever choose her? Because she's in there too."

He swallowed. "Of course."

"Then prove it." I took a deep breath and shook off his arm. "You said you wanted to fight for me, Cole. Here's your chance."

Summoning all the strength I had, I held back the tears and walked out.

Twenty-Nine

Cheyenne

THREE DAYS AFTER THE WORST CHRISTMAS EVER, I went over to Griffin and Blair's apartment for coffee.

I hadn't told Blair anything about the Christmas Eve breakup because I didn't want to interrupt her time with her family or cause her to spend time worrying about me on her trip. But they'd flown in last night, and I couldn't hold it in any longer. I'd spent the last seventy-two hours crying in my bedroom, ignoring my mom's attempts to talk, and wondering if I'd made the biggest mistake of my life.

"Good morning," Blair said with a smile, answering my knock in ivory flannel pajamas that were embroidered with Mrs. Dempsey on the top's pocket. Then she saw my face, and her smile faded. "What's wrong? Are you okay?"

"No," I said, tearing up. "I need caffeine and talk therapy and maybe some kind of muffin or pastry with either like some icing on it or some crumble topping."

She brought me inside and gave me a hug. "You've come to the right place."

I ditched my snow boots, followed her up the stairs and

plunked myself on a stool at their kitchen island. "Where's Griff?"

"He ran over to the gym this morning." She poured me a cup of coffee and set an oversized muffin on a plate in front of me. "There. Now you have caffeine and crumble topping. So let's get to the therapy. What happened?"

"Cole and I broke up," I said, tears leaking from my eyes.

"What? Oh no!" She grabbed a box of tissues and placed it in front of me before coming around the island to sit on the stool next to mine. Rubbing my arm, she waited for me to mop my cheeks. "Tell me what happened. Did you ask him about the nightmares?"

I shook my head. "I didn't even get a chance."

"So what was it?"

Taking a shuddering breath, I told her the whole story. By the end of it, she was dabbing her eyes with a tissue too. "Oh, no. Oh Cole, what are you *doing*?"

"He thinks he's being a man, but he's just being a coward," I said irritably. "I get why, but it still sucks."

"It does," she agreed. "You sort of can't fault him, but you want to."

"I don't fault him for being scared and not knowing how to handle it—I just wish he'd admit it, you know? He's so damn determined to just tough it out."

"Men," Blair muttered. "They're such fixers. And he's looking to paint the front door when the wood is rotten."

"Exactly." I sniffed again. Took a sip of coffee. "I think even Mariah's therapist knew something was up, because he mentioned her name during our argument. I wonder if she suggested he talk to someone professional."

"Maybe," Blair said. "It certainly sounds like he needs it."

I exhaled, closing my eyes. "I was kind of afraid you were going to tell me I was being too demanding. That I shouldn't have walked out when all he asked for was more time before we move in together."

"Not at all! You're only demanding one thing—honesty. Okay two things—honesty and a willingness to conquer those demons."

"I thought love conquered all," I said, tears welling again. "But it doesn't."

"Oh, honey." She slid off her stool and wrapped her arms around me. "I'm so sorry."

"I really thought this was it," I sobbed. "I thought for once I didn't pick the unavailable person. I thought I wouldn't end up disappointed. I thought finally my feelings for Cole made sense. I thought he'd chosen me."

"He did, sweetie. He really did." She rubbed my back. "And I know that he loves you and he's going to be sorry."

From the bottom of the stairwell, we heard the door open and close.

"Don't tell him," I whispered.

"Okay, but he's going to know something is up," she whispered back.

Quickly, I dried my eyes and took another sip of coffee.

A moment later, Griffin appeared at the top of the steps, looking sweaty and disheveled in sweatpants and a hoodie. "Hey."

"Morning," I said without meeting his eyes.

"Cole here?" he asked, going over to the fridge.

"No."

Griffin took the orange juice out, turned around, and leaned back against the counter. "What's wrong?"

I decided there was no point in lying. My brother wasn't an idiot. "Cole and I broke up."

His eyebrows peaked. "Seriously?"

"Yes. On Christmas Eve."

"Damn." He took a drink right from the carton. "What happened?"

"Griffin!" Blair took a glass from the cupboard and handed it to him. "What have I told you about that? It grosses me out."

"Why? You don't even drink O.J."

"Because we are not Neanderthals without proper drinkware. Use the glass, please."

Griffin rolled his eyes but poured juice from the carton into the glass. "So what happened with Cole? I thought everything was good."

"It was . . . but it also wasn't, and he never told me."

"Huh?"

I took a deep breath. "I think Cole is scared of being happy with me because of what happened to him before. He doesn't believe happiness can last."

Griffin took a drink and nodded thoughtfully. "I could see that about him."

"And I think after he asked me to move in with him, it hit him really hard. But even before that—as soon as he realized how happy Mariah was about the whole situation—he was kind of freaking out internally, but wouldn't admit it. I could tell something was off with him, but he just kept saying he was fine."

"Sounds like Cole."

It struck me that Griffin was Cole's best friend. He knew him better than anyone. "Has Cole ever mentioned anything to you about, like, panic attacks?"

"No. But I do know that he had pretty bad nightmares as a kid."

Blair and I exchanged a look. "He's having them again," I said. "Only he refused to admit it. And then in a weird twist, he tried to tell me *Mariah* was having nightmares." I told him about my conversations with my mother and Mariah, and then my argument with Cole.

Griffin's mouth was set in a grim line. "Jesus. You gotta feel bad for him."

"I do," I said helplessly, my eyes tearing up again. "But I can't help him if he won't even talk to me."

"Has Cole ever seen a therapist?" Blair asked Griffin. "Like maybe after Trisha died?"

"I don't remember," he said. "I just remember him being really focused on Mariah. From that point on, all he cared about was her. I think he swept a lot of shit under the rug."

I nodded. "I think so too. But it was always there, and now that it's uncovered, he needs to deal with it. Except he won't."

"He won't talk to a therapist?" Griffin asked.

"Nope. He said therapy is for women and kids."

Blair made a disgusted noise and rolled her eyes. "Why do men think they have to be so tough all the time? It's okay to show your emotions."

"He *did* show them," I said, grabbing another tissue. "And he *talked* about them. He *told* me he loved me. Was he lying?"

"No," Griffin said firmly. "That I know for sure. I've never seen him so crazy about someone. And he doesn't bullshit people like that. He never has. If he told you he loved you, he meant it."

"Really?" I asked, hope rising in my heart.

He nodded. "Yeah. Like at Thanksgiving, and at the wedding, and at dinner here that night . . . it was obvious the guy was *messed up*."

"To be clear, that's supposed to be a compliment," Blair said, rolling her eyes.

"I asked him about you on Thanksgiving, and he tried to deny something was going on, but Cole is a really shitty liar." Griffin shook his head. "His upper lip does, like, this weird, twitchy thing, and his eyes dart all over the place. And he sweats."

"Yes!" I exclaimed. "I've seen it!"

"Sometimes his hands twitch too, so he folds his arms and sticks his hands in his armpits. It's fucking ridiculous. He's such a Boy Scout."

"Oh my God, he totally did that during our argument."

Blair laughed sympathetically. "Poor Cole."

I looked at Griffin, needing to hear it again. "Do you really think he was happy with me?"

Griffin shrugged. "Yeah. I mean, dudes don't go around saying shit like '*I can't believe how happy I am*'"—he spoke in a high-pitched voice with an exaggerated version of Blair's Tennessee lilt—"but if I had to be the judge, I'd say he was, and right now he's probably miserable."

"Could you maybe check on him?" I asked, clasping my hands together. "I can't stop worrying about him."

"Why don't *you* reach out to him? Maybe he's changed his mind."

"I can't, Griffin." My eyes filled again. "It will hurt too much. Every time I see him or Mariah outside with the new dog, I melt down."

My brother exhaled heavily. "Okay. I'll give him a call later."

"Thank you."

Griffin put his glass in the sink and disappeared down the hall to their bedroom.

"Now how about eating a little something?" Blair pushed my plate closer to me.

Giving in, I took a bite of the muffin. "Thanks. It's really good. Way better than a garden salad."

She laughed. "No one wants raw vegetables during an emotional crisis."

I shook my head. "Nope."

"Finish your muffin, and then we'll go do something fun. Get our nails done or something. Go shopping. Buy something cute for New Year's Eve."

"Ugh, don't even talk about it. For once, I was going to get to kiss the man of my dreams at midnight. Instead I'll be home with my mother, wearing sweatpants, watching the ball drop while eating raw cookie dough and drinking wine out of a box."

"No way, sister. Griffin and I decided we're going to have a few people over here, and you'll be here in a sequin miniskirt with a glass of bubbly in your hand at midnight. Guys will be knocking each other over to be the one you kiss at midnight."

"A sequin miniskirt?" I looked at her sideways. "You're crazy."

"I know." She tipped her head onto my shoulder. "But at least I made you laugh."

Thirty

Cole

AT THE CLOSING, I GOT THE KEYS TO MY NEW HOUSE, but I didn't feel like celebrating.

I'd imagined the day so much differently—I'd pick up Mariah and Cheyenne and go straight to the house, and we'd walk through it together, knowing it was finally ours.

Instead, it was just like every other day had been since Cheyenne walked out—agony.

I couldn't sleep. Had no appetite. Didn't feel like working out. I was ignoring calls and texts from friends, evading my mother's questions, and getting through work on autopilot.

Mariah was still so upset, she was hardly talking to me. I hadn't told her much—just that it had been Cheyenne's decision to end the relationship, and I asked her to please respect Cheyenne's privacy and not go running over there to ask her questions or beg her to come back. I hadn't wanted to ruin Mariah's Christmas morning by telling her right away, but she was desperate to tell Cheyenne about all her new presents—and show her the photo of Buddy, a nine-year-old Terrier mix who'd been abandoned and was always passed over at the shelter because people wanted younger dogs. I'd felt for the animal, who must have thought all his best days were behind him. Mariah had taken one look at the photograph and burst into tears, grabbing onto me and refusing to let go, even though I was already going to be late for work.

"Is he really mine?" she sobbed.

"Yes, if you want him. We can pick him up tomorrow."

"I want him," she said. "Can I call Cheyenne and tell her?"

I hesitated. "You can, but there's something I need to tell you first."

I'd delivered the news, and she'd run up to her room and slammed the door.

My mother, who'd heard the exchange, gave me a sympathetic look. "Oh, Cole," she whispered. "I'm sorry."

I struggled to keep my face impassive. "It's fine."

"Do you want to talk about it?"

"No. I'm late already." But I glanced up the stairs—I felt horrible leaving with Mariah so upset, but how was I going to comfort her? I felt the same way she did.

"Go to work," my mother said, heading up the steps. "I'll deal with her. We can talk later."

"Thanks."

During my shift, I went over the argument with Cheyenne again and again. My chest ached every time I thought about her tears, but my jaw clenched up in stubborn refusal whenever I thought about what she was asking me to do.

If she loved me the way she said she did, shouldn't she respect my decision to deal with *my* baggage *my* way?

After work, I sat down to a late supper at the kitchen table, and my mother sat across from me. Mariah, who'd already eaten, was up in her room.

"So it was Cheyenne's decision?" my mother asked.

"Yes." I poked at the food on my plate, unable to eat. My stomach had been in knots all day.

"Maybe she just needs some space."

"I don't think so."

"Well, what was it specifically that made her want to break things off?" my mother pressed. "You two seemed so happy together."

"Leave it, Mom. I don't want to talk about it. She's gone, and it was her choice."

She lifted a cup of tea to her lips. "Was it a choice you forced her to make?"

I glared at her across the table. "I said leave it."

A heavy sigh. "Mariah is very upset. You'll need to talk to her. She thinks she did something wrong."

Closing my eyes, I set down my fork and rubbed my face. "I'll talk to her."

But Mariah wouldn't talk to me. No matter how much I coaxed and begged her to open her door, she said she didn't want to talk, and I didn't have it in me to fight.

After work the next night, I asked her if she wanted to go pick up Buddy with me, and she said yes. But in the car on the way to the shelter, she remained silent and sullen.

"Mariah," I said, pulling into a parking spot. "What happened between Cheyenne and me isn't your fault. Sometimes grown-ups just decide they want different things."

"But she wanted the *same* things we did. She wanted us to be a family. I know it. So either you did something wrong, or I did."

"It wasn't you," I said firmly. "*I* said something that made her upset."

She finally looked at me. "What did you say?"

I stared out the windshield. "I told her a lie."

"About what?"

I turned off the engine and sat for a moment in silence. "I told her that you'd been having nightmares, not me."

"Why? Were you embarrassed?"

"Yes," I answered, figuring that was the easiest way to explain it to a nine-year-old. "I was embarrassed."

"You shouldn't be," Mariah said fiercely. "Cheyenne loves you. She would never make fun of you for having bad dreams."

"I know she wouldn't."

"You told me a lie too."

I met her eyes. "What do you mean?"

"You said you loved her the real way."

"I do love her the real way," I insisted.

She crossed her arms, pinning me with an accusing stare. "Then you wouldn't have let her go."

Mariah cheered up when she met Buddy, and we brought him home. While my mother wasn't ecstatic about having an animal in the house, she was happy to see Mariah smiling again. With Buddy came a tentative peace and a fun distraction, and I was grateful to the dog for providing both.

But as the days crawled by, I continued to miss Cheyenne with an intensity that refused to let up. Not only that, but I mourned the life I'd imagined for us—and holding the keys to a house we were going to share brought only sadness and regret.

I picked up Mariah and Buddy, and we drove over to our new address, where my daughter and I watched our new dog run around the snow-covered yard and check out his own little abode.

"You think he likes it?" Mariah asked as he sniffed around the old doghouse.

"I think so. Look at his tail wagging."

She laughed. "He's so cute. I wish Cheyenne could see him."

At the mention of her name, my chest caved in. It was unfathomable to me that I'd never hold her again, kiss her again, make her smile, make her laugh, hear her whisper my name while I moved inside her.

Was this really all my fault? Was Mariah right? Had I not loved her the right way? Had I not loved her *enough*? Had I not tried hard enough to show it?

I had no idea anymore. All I knew was that I was back at the bottom of the rut with no light above me and no way out, sinking in the muck. And it felt like I'd thrown myself there.

When Griffin texted and asked me to go out for a beer that night, I almost turned him down. I was exhausted, I was behind on packing for the move, and I didn't necessarily want to hear a lecture. No doubt Cheyenne had told her family about the breakup. Was he going to be angry with me for hurting her? He understood that it had been *her* choice, right?

In the end, I decided to meet him, if only to get out of my bedroom. The walls were closing in on me.

We met at the pub and sat at the bar. McIntyre came over and poured us a couple beers. For a few minutes, we nursed them in silence. Since I'd sort of felt like a kid sitting in the principal's office waiting to get in trouble, I was a little surprised that he wasn't talking.

"How was your trip to Nashville?" I asked.

"It was good. Blair's family is . . . something else."

"You got along with them?"

"I did, but four days of Beaufort will last me a while."

I almost laughed.

"So what's going on with you?" he asked, casually sipping his beer. It was obvious he knew.

"I take it you've talked to Cheyenne."

"Yes."

"Is she . . . okay?"

"No, Cole. She isn't."

I felt like he'd punched me in the gut. "Fuck."

"What happened?"

"I don't even know." I straightened up in my seat. "One minute things were fine, and the next she was crying." I felt my lip begin to twitch.

"Really?"

I slumped over again. Elbows on the bar, head in my hands. "No."

We sat in silence for a minute. Griffin nursed his beer. "Look, I don't want you to be mad at this, but I also talked to Beckett and Moretti."

"About me?" Sitting back, I glared at him. "What the fuck for?"

"Because we're worried about you, Cole. You're not okay."

I stared at the surface of the bar, scuffed and nicked and beat-up from years of abuse. "No. I'm not."

"So I'm going to ask you about some stuff, and don't bother lying. You're the fucking worst liar in the world, and we both know it."

I grimaced. "Fine."

"Who's having the nightmares? You or Mariah?"

"Me," I said through clenched teeth.

"Did you lie about that to my sister because you don't trust her?"

I shook my head. "I lied because I was ashamed."

"Okay. So far, so good. But this next one might be tough." He fortified himself with another sip of his beer first. "Did you fuck shit up with Cheyenne so that you wouldn't have to deal with your glass-half-empty attitude?"

I glared at him again. "It's more than that and you know it."

"You're right. It's more than that, which is why you need to be talking to someone who isn't a mechanic right now. I can fix anything under the hood, because I can see it." He reached over and rapped on my skull with his knuckles. "But whatever's wrong under there needs somebody else."

"I'm not fucking broken," I said defensively, pushing his hand away. "Maybe this is just the way I am, and people around me need to deal with it."

"Maybe," he agreed with a shrug.

"See? This is why I was better off alone. I don't know why no one believed me."

He held up his hands. "Totally fine. If you wanted to be alone for the rest of your life, Cole, that would be A-OK with me. I'll still be your friend. But that's not what you want."

I scowled, because he was right.

"Last question. Are you in love with her?"

"Yes." That one was easy.

"Then I lied. I have another question. Do you remember what you said to me when I was being a dipshit about Blair? When I broke up with her and told her to leave because I never wanted to need someone?"

I tried to recall my exact words but couldn't. "No."

"Well, I do. You said losing someone you love hurts like hell. But there wasn't one day with Trisha you'd take back, even knowing how it ended."

"Oh." I swallowed. "Now I remember."

"You still feel that way?"

"Yes," I admitted.

"So then why are you throwing away all the days you could have with Cheyenne, even if you knew exactly when the world was going to end?"

"But if I *knew*, I'd be prepared," I snapped, angry that he was poking so close to the bone. "That's the point."

Griffin exhaled. "Okay. Last thing for real, and it's not even a question. During that same conversation we had back then, you said that given how long we'd been friends, you'd expect me to tell you if you were fucking something up in a big way."

I grimaced, knowing what was coming.

"And so, Cole, I say to you, as you did to me, you're fucking something up in a big way. You also told me I was being a real asshole about it, but I'm going to be the bigger man and not call you names."

"Thanks," I said flatly.

At that point, we were interrupted by a few people who'd seen the news story about the baby, and I had to shake some hands and pose for a picture. When we were alone again, Griffin chuckled. "Guess this town really needed a hero."

"I'm not a fucking hero," I said for what felt like the hundredth time. "I was doing my *job*."

"You saved a life either way, jackass. And maybe that little girl is going to grow up and cure cancer. Or be President. Or save the whales. You never know what good things can happen, Cole. But you have to believe they can."

I frowned, although I fucking loved the idea of that tiny baby growing up to do great things. Nothing made me happier than imagining the good Mariah was going to do. I loved being a father. Watching my daughter grow up was the greatest gift that life had ever given me.

Suddenly I pictured her perfect-day collage, which was still hanging on my mother's refrigerator. It was obvious from the photos she'd chosen what mattered to her—family, tradition, love. Those things mattered to her because I'd raised her that way—they mattered to me too.

I thought about *my* perfect day—it was summertime, and I was on the pitcher's mound at the ball field, and Griff was over on first base, Moretti was at second, and Beckett was behind the plate. The Mavs were down, and I had a no-hitter going. I looked over to my right, and there was Mariah, playing by the fence with her friends, and in the stands, there was Cheyenne. She was holding a baby on her hip and pointing at me with a smile on her face, and I knew she was saying, *That's your daddy right there.*

It was so real I could feel the sun on my skin, smell the dirt and the sweat, feel the love in my heart.

I wanted it—and it wasn't going to happen at the bottom of this rut.

Could I claw my way out? But how?

Cheyenne had said I had to fight—but when the enemy was something buried deep within you, how could you face it down?

"You think she would talk to me?" I asked Griffin.

"*Now* I'm going to call you an asshole. Of course she would. She loves you." He pointed at me. "And even though I told you jerks never to touch my sister, I'm going to let this go."

Finally, I managed to laugh. "Sorry about that."

"You should be." He finished his beer. "I will say this, though. Do not mess with her. She's always been a pain-in-the-ass little punk sister, but she's *my* pain-in-the-ass little punk sister. And no matter what she says, she still needs her big brother to look out for her."

I nodded. "I hear you."

"Good." He clapped me on the back. "She'll be at our place for New Year's Eve. Show your face. Say nice things. Don't be a dick."

As if it were that simple.

But I would try.

Thirty-One

Cheyenne

I CHECKED MY PHONE FOR THE HUNDREDTH TIME, agonized to see it had only been ten minutes since I'd last looked.

"Will you stop?" Blair said, taking a tray of spring rolls from the oven. "It's not even nine yet, and already I can tell you want to go home. You've got hours until midnight."

"I can't believe you talked me into this."

"Into what?" she asked, grabbing her kitchen tongs to transfer the rolls to a platter. "Leaving your house? Putting on lipstick? Trading your I-give-up sweatpants for a gold sequin miniskirt?"

"All of it." I looked down at my outfit. "But especially the miniskirt."

She laughed. "You look fucking hot, and every guy in here is trying to work up the nerve to approach you. You need to stop hiding out in the kitchen."

"Give me a break. Most of the guys in here I've known since I was born. They're all Griffin's friends."

"Not true," she argued. "I specifically invited some new

people tonight to make the party more interesting. See that guy talking to Beckett by the window?"

I looked over and saw who she meant. "Yeah."

"Well, he's been staring at you since he got here."

Self-conscious, I touched my hair. "Who is he?"

"His name is Zachary Simon. He's a lawyer, new in town. Just moved from Mason City."

"How'd you meet him?"

"He's a regular at the bakery every morning. He said he had no plans tonight because he doesn't know many people in town, so I invited him. You should go introduce yourself."

"Blair! He could be a serial killer or something. You don't even know this guy."

"I'm not saying you should go out to the alley with him, I'm just trying to get you out of my way here." She moved around me to grab her oven mitt. "And it wouldn't kill you to have a conversation with someone new."

"It's no use," I said with a sigh. "I'm not over Cole. I don't know if I ever will be."

Blair gave me a sympathetic look. "I'm sorry."

"Still no word on whether he'll show up tonight?"

She shook her head. "Griffin didn't say much about their conversation. Just that Cole said he still loves you and he's trying to work through some stuff. He might come tonight, he might not."

"Yeah. That's what Griffin told me too." A lump jumped into my throat, and I tried to wash it away with champagne.

"He was annoyingly tight-lipped about it all. But I guess you can't fault him—Cole's been his bestie for what, almost thirty years? They're loyal to each other."

"I know."

Blair finally stopped bustling around and faced me. "Look. You're here, you've got a nice glass of champagne, you look like a million bucks, just go say hi to the new guy, okay? For me. Do it now. Beckett just walked away from him, and he's all alone. I feel bad."

I sighed again. "Fine. For you. But I'm warning you now, I don't think I'm going to make it to midnight. I miss my couch and my sweatpants already, and if Cole shows up, I might embarrass myself by crying in my bubbly."

She gave me a shove in the direction of the window. "Go."

Pressing my lips together, I walked casually over toward the new guy, who gave me a friendly smile as I approached. He was really very handsome, with wavy dark hair, warm brown eyes, and an athletic build. But I didn't care. In a way, it would have been much easier if my pulse had started to race when I got close to him, but it didn't. In fact, he wore too much cologne, and the first instinct I had was to sneeze.

Thankfully, I held it off.

"Hi," I said, holding out my hand. "I'm Cheyenne."

"Zachary," he said, closing his hand around mine. "You're Blair's friend. She told me about you."

"She talks a lot," I said, shooting Blair a murderous look over my shoulder. "I hear you're new in town."

"Yes. Only been here about a month. But I like it."

"What brought you to Bellamy Creek?"

"My job. I'm an attorney for . . ."

But I completely lost track of what he was saying because suddenly I saw Cole appear at the top of the stairs. I might have gasped, because Zachary broke off mid-sentence and looked at me a little funny. "Are you okay?"

"I'm fine," I said, anything but. "Sorry. What were you saying?"

He started up again about whatever it was he did, but I didn't hear a word of it because Cole and I had locked eyes, and he was headed my way. The look on his face told me he was *not* happy to see me talking to some other guy.

Well, *tough*!

He hadn't so much as called me in a week! I'd thought seeing him would make me cry, but seeing him like *this*—jealous and possessive, all fists clenched and chest puffed out—just made me mad.

Even if it was kind of hot.

I moved a little closer to Zachary and laughed as if he'd said something funny, which totally confused him.

Cole reached us, his jaw tight. "Cheyenne."

"Cole." My heart was banging hard against my ribs.

"Can I talk to you for a moment?"

"I'm already talking to someone." I glanced at Zachary, who looked annoyed and baffled in equal measure, not that I blamed him.

"I can see that."

Zachary held out his hand. "Zachary Simon."

Cole hesitated before taking it. "We've met before. I'm Cole Mitchell. I pitch for the Bulldogs."

"Ah." After a very brief handshake, Zachary nodded.

"You two know each other?" I asked.

"He plays for the Mavs," Cole said, his icy blue eyes trained on Zachary.

Oh, Jesus. Fucking old man baseball.

"Not anymore," Zachary said with a laugh. "I moved to Bellamy Creek, so I'm hoping there might be a spot on the Bulldog roster next season."

"We'll see." Cole looked at me. "Cheyenne, please. Can we talk?"

"Go ahead," Zachary said graciously, moving toward the couches. "Nice meeting you both."

I faced Cole. "What do you want?"

"Lots of things." His eyes, softer now, traveled over me from head to foot. "But you're so beautiful, I can't think straight."

My walls crumbled a little, but I was determined to stand tall, just like he was. "Thank you."

He struggled for words. "I miss you. Mariah misses you."

At the mention of his daughter, I softened further. "I miss her too. How is she? Does she love her new dog?"

"Yes. But she's been pretty miserable without seeing you. And so have I."

"Guess that's the theme this Christmas," I said, taking a sip of champagne. The glass trembled in my fingers.

"I know, and it's my fault." Then he glanced around. "And I have a lot of things I want to say to you, but this doesn't feel like the right place."

Hope was rising in my heart, but I refused to let it come to the surface. I'd missed him too, but missing each other wasn't enough. "What's the right place?"

"Will you leave with me?"

"Now?"

He nodded, taking my hand. "Please."

"It's New Year's Eve, Cole. I'm at a party," I said, as if I gave a shit about any of it.

"I know, and I'm sorry. This wasn't the plan. I just"—he glanced toward Zachary Simon—"saw you talking to that guy and fucking hated it."

I pulled my hand back. "No. That's not good enough."

"Huh?"

"Missing me isn't enough. Getting jealous isn't enough."

His expression turned angry. "What will be enough? I'm fucking trying here, Cheyenne. Why won't you listen?"

"I *am* listening, Cole. But what I'm hearing is nothing new, nothing that reassures me you're ready to deal with your issues."

"And what *will* prove that?"

"I don't know," I said, the tears finally spilling over. "But not this."

Without another word, I left him standing there, set my glass on the kitchen counter and went to grab my coat from the bedroom. When I came back out, he was waiting for me in the hallway.

"Please don't go," he said, his expression tortured. "Let me try again."

"Don't make this difficult, Cole." I buttoned up my coat, my eyes blurry with tears. "It will embarrass us both."

"Everything okay?" Blair appeared behind him.

"Everything is fine," I said. "I'm just getting my coat on. I'm taking off."

Cole took me by the shoulders and spoke quietly but ferociously. "Listen to me. I *love* you. I want a life with you, and I'm willing to do whatever it takes to have it. Somehow I'll find a way to prove it to you."

At that moment, I desperately wanted to melt into his arms and tell him it would be okay, but I knew that wasn't the answer. If I did, nothing would ever change. "I hope so, Cole."

He took his arms off me, and I shouldered past him, heading for the door, already digging my keys from my coat pocket. Blair trailed me all the way down the steps to the door.

"Cheyenne, wait!"

I turned to face her. "I'm leaving, Blair, I have to."

"I know." She threw her arms around me and held me tight. "It's going to be okay."

Crying openly, I hugged her back.

"Blair?" Griffin called from the top of the steps. "The oven timer is going off."

She released me. "I better go. I'm sorry if any of this is my fault. Maybe I shouldn't have made you come over."

"It's not your fault. I'll talk to you tomorrow." Then I pushed the door open and slipped into the icy night air, the tears freezing on my cheeks.

I hurried down the street, jumped into my car, and drove home. Thankful my mother was out with friends, I went straight upstairs, put my pajamas on, and got into bed, wondering for the *millionth* time why I couldn't just give up on Cole Mitchell.

But then I pictured those blue eyes, and felt his arms around me, and remembered his words tonight.

I love you. I want a life with you, and I'm willing to do whatever it takes to have it. Somehow I'll find a way to prove it to you.

I crossed my fingers and hugged my pillow close, desperately hoping he wouldn't give up.

I wouldn't either.

Thirty-Two

Cole

IT HAD TAKEN MONUMENTAL FORTITUDE TO LET HER walk past me, but I knew using physical strength to force her to remain there until I somehow found the right words to win her back was not a good plan.

After she'd gone, I stood there alone in the hallway, wondering how I'd managed to fuck up so colossally in five minutes.

I'd just fucking gotten here! I was still wearing my goddamn coat!

"Hey. You okay?"

I turned around to see Griffin standing there. "Hey. No."

"I saw Cheyenne go flying for the door. What happened?"

"Fuck if I know, exactly. I walked in prepared to calmly ask her for another chance and promise to do better, then I saw her talking to that asshole from the Mavs. What the hell is he doing here anyway?" I asked angrily, like it was his fault I'd messed up with Cheyenne.

Griffin rolled his eyes. "Blair invited him. He's a regular at the bakery. New in town."

"Oh." I rubbed a hand over my jaw. "Anyway, when I saw them together, I fucking forgot everything I was supposed to say and got all territorial."

Griffin shrugged. "It happens."

"Did she leave?"

"I think so."

"Fuck." I leaned back against the wall. "I need to figure this out. What does she need to hear?"

Before Griffin could answer, the oven timer went off. "I need to get that," he said. "Are you going to be okay?"

"Yeah, I'm fine."

He left me alone in the hallway again, and I stayed there for a minute, trying to decide if I wanted to stay or go. After making up my mind to take off, I went to say goodbye to Blair in the kitchen.

"Hey," she said, glancing at my coat. "Are you leaving too?"

"Yeah. I'm not in the mood for a crowd. I'm really sorry if I ruined anything. I didn't mean to upset her."

"I know you didn't." She shook her head, her expression sympathetic. "What are we going to do with you?"

"Tell me what to do, Blair. Tell me what to say."

"I can't, Cole. I wish I could. But it has to come authentically from you or she'll know it's not real. Cheyenne can read you like a book, my friend."

I nodded. "Right."

"Hey. Come here." She opened her arms and gave me a quick hug. "You're going to figure this out."

"Thanks. I just hope I figure it out before some other guy comes along and gets it right with her from the start."

She shook her head. "Cole Mitchell, you know damn well you've been the only boy for her since she laid eyes on you. Now go convince her she's the only girl for you."

❄

I went home and watched the ball drop with my mom and Mariah, but my mind was somewhere else. Something Blair said had stuck with me.

Cheyenne can read you like a book.

She was right. There was no use trying to hide things from Cheyenne. She could tell when something was bothering me just from looking at my face or listening to my body language. And I didn't *want* to hide things from her. Even if it wasn't in my nature to show people my scars, I'd learn to do it for her.

I'd do anything for her.

The next day, I made two phone calls.

The first was to Bianca DeRossi. "Hey, Bianca. Sorry to call you on a holiday, but I was wondering if we might get moving on that window seat we talked about. If you're not busy this weekend, I'm off the next three days, and I'll be moving some things over to the house. Let me know, thanks."

Next, I left a message for Jessalyn Wells, asking her for the name and number of the therapist she'd tried to recommend for me.

Bianca called me back later that day, thrilled to get moving on the project for Cheyenne as well as walk through the house with me now that I owned it.

"How's tomorrow at ten a.m.?" she asked.

"That's great for me. You sure it won't disrupt your Saturday plans?"

"Not at all," she said. "I'll see you tomorrow."

The following morning, I was waiting for her at the new house when Jessalyn returned my call.

"Hello?"

"Hi, Cole. This is Jessalyn Wells."

"Hi, Jessalyn. Thanks for getting back to me so quickly."

"Of course. So you've decided to speak with a therapist?"

I took a breath. "Yes. I'm at least going to give it a try."

"I think that's great, Cole. Really great." She gave me the name and number of someone in her office that counseled adults and had done a lot of work with group grief therapy. "Not that you have to do that," she said quickly, as if she knew I'd been about to protest at the idea of talking in front of a group. "I just wanted you to know she has experience working with people who have lost loved ones."

"Thank you. I appreciate it."

"Well, I'll let you go. Happy new year."

"Happy new year," I said.

We hung up, and I looked at the name and number I'd written down. Before I lost my nerve, I called it and left a message requesting an appointment. I wanted to have at least one session under my belt the next time I asked Cheyenne to give me another chance.

And by having the window seat built in the master bedroom, I wanted to show her that this would be our house—that her dreams and mine were intertwined now, that our future was here, together.

Bianca was one hundred percent on board. "You know what?" she said, eyeballing the space that morning. "We could knock this project out in a few days."

"Really?"

"Sure. With some help." She glanced at me. "You think you could get Enzo over here with some wood and a hammer?" Then she laughed and flashed her palms at me. "No pun intended."

I laughed too. "I bet I could."

"Excellent. Why don't you give him a call? He's much more likely to say yes to you than me."

"Agreed," I said, digging my cell from my pocket. "Calling him now."

Moretti was in.

But he said if we were really going to do it right within only a few days, we'd need a couple more pairs of hands, so we enlisted Griffin and Beckett too.

We worked the entire weekend, and Moretti came back Monday to help me finish up. Bianca was fantastic as well. While the guys yanked up the carpeting, refinished the wood floors, and constructed not only a window seat but built-in bookshelves on either side of it, she rolled up her sleeves and painted the walls a soft gray.

She also shopped like her life depended on it.

By Tuesday evening, I had a king-sized bed with an upholstered headboard, made up with brand new sheets Bianca insisted Cheyenne would appreciate for their high thread count, a fluffy white quilt, and more pillows than two adults could possibly need. At the foot of the bed was a cozy throw blanket in a soft pink that reminded me of something Cheyenne would wear. Next to the bed on either side were two matching antique tables for nightstands with twin lamps sitting on top of them. Beneath the bed was a gray and white patterned rug. Over by the fireplace, which Beckett helped me get in working order, were two easy chairs and a small table in between, upon which Bianca had set a little tray with a bottle of wine and two glasses.

Standing in the doorway of the bedroom after work, I could hardly believe it. "Wow," I said to Bianca on the phone as I drove home. "I don't know how to thank you. Everything is perfect. Please send me the bill for everything."

She laughed. "We'll get to that. When are you going to show it to her?"

"Soon, I hope. Maybe this weekend."

"And you're moving in for real the following week?"

"Yes."

"Nice." Then she paused. "This might be a personal question, but is Cheyenne going to live at the new house with you?"

"I hope so."

She laughed. "Well, if anything can convince her, that master bedroom will do the trick. Let me know how she likes it—although I already know she's going to love it."

"I will. Thanks again, Bianca."

Later that night, I went in to say goodnight to Mariah. She was speaking to me again, but our relationship had been strained since Christmas.

I sat on her bed. "A week from tonight, you'll be sleeping in your new bunk beds in the new house."

"Yeah."

"You're not excited about it?"

"I am. I just wish Cheyenne was moving in with us too, like she was supposed to. I miss her." She looked up at me. "Don't you?"

"I do," I said. "In fact, I wanted to talk to you about that."

She propped herself up on her elbows. "Are you going to try to get her back?"

I smiled. "I'm going to try to get her back."

Mariah fell back on her pillow, a relieved smile on her face. "*Yesss.*" But then she frowned. "Wait, what are you going to do?"

"I'm going to bring her over to the new house and show her something I've been working on."

"What is it?"

"It's a window seat, the kind she said she'd like to curl up on and read a book."

Mariah nodded. "That's a good idea."

"I'm also going to apologize for lying to her about the bad dreams. And tell her that I'm going to talk to a therapist about them."

Her eyes widened. "You are?"

"Yes. I have my first appointment on Thursday."

"Are you nervous?"

"A little," I admitted with a smile. "But I'm still going to go."

"Don't worry. It's not that bad."

"That's because you're so brave." I brushed the hair back from her forehead. "And I'm going to remember how brave you are if I get worried."

She smiled. "Good."

"Any other ideas for when I talk to Cheyenne?"

"Hmmm." Her brow furrowed. "Definitely tell her about the dog. She likes dogs."

"I will definitely tell her."

"And maybe sing her a song. That's what Danny did for Sandy in *Grease*. And she wore tight shiny pants for him."

"I will not be singing her a song or wearing any kind of shiny pants."

She sighed. "How about candles? In movies when someone tries to be romantic, there are always candles."

"Now you're talking. I can do candles."

"Okay. When are you going to talk to her?"

"Well, if she agrees, I'm hoping Friday evening."

Mariah frowned again. "What if she doesn't agree? She's really mad at you, isn't she? I mean, maybe I should ask her."

I was about to argue with her, but I decided she might be right—and besides, Mariah deserved to play a role in bringing us back together. "You know what? I'd love your help winning her back."

She grinned at me. "You got it."

Thirty-Three

Cheyenne

FRIDAY AFTER WORK, I CAME HOME AND FLOPPED FACE down on the couch. I was trying to decide between a workout and a nap when my phone rang. Blair Dempsey calling.

The name on the screen almost made me smile. I flopped onto my back. "Hello."

"Hey. How's it going?"

"Same."

"Still no word from Cole, huh?"

"Nope. And it's been a week since New Year's Eve. A week and a *day*."

She sighed. "I'm sorry. I really thought he was going to get himself together. And Griffin isn't saying *anything*, even though he was over at the new house all weekend!"

"I don't want him caught in the middle anyway."

"Want to come over tonight?" she asked brightly. "Watch a movie or something?"

"Thanks, but I'm too tired. I haven't slept well this week."

"Okay. Hang in there. Let me know if you need anything."

"I will." We'd just hung up when I heard a knock on the front door. Curious, I sat up, tightened my ponytail, and went to answer it. It was Mariah.

"Hi there," I said, smiling at her. "It's good to see you."

"Hi." She looked serious. "I'm sorry to bother you, but I need help with something. Could you come over?"

"You never bother me. What do you need help with?"

"Homework."

I raised my eyebrows. "Homework? On a Friday afternoon?"

"Yes. It's, um, a really hard math problem. And Grandma doesn't remember how to do it."

"Okay. Just let me grab my coat and get my boots back on."

A minute later, we were heading up her driveway. "I didn't see you much this week," I said. "Did you have a nice break?"

"It was okay. Sorry I didn't come to see you. I wanted to, but my dad said it was better if I didn't."

Annoyed, I shoved my hands in my pockets. "You can come say hello at school any time."

We stepped onto her back porch and stamped the snow off our boots. She put a hand on the door handle and looked at me. "Okay, don't be mad."

"About what?"

"I lied about the math problem."

"Why?" But I understood a second later when Cole pulled open the back door.

"Hi," he said.

"Hi." My heart was pounding. What was this?

"Will you come in?" he asked.

I hesitated, and Mariah grabbed my hand. "Please? I really do need your help with something."

"Okay," I said, letting her pull me into the kitchen. Right away, the dog came trotting over to say hello, and I knelt down to give him some attention. Then I stood up and looked from daughter to father. "So what's going on here?"

Cole wore the sweater I'd given him for Christmas. His brilliant blue eyes, as always, put my heart in a vise. "I have things I want to say to you," he said, "but I promised Mariah I would let her talk first."

"I'm sorry I lied about the math problem," Mariah began solemnly. "I'll never do it again. But I was scared he was going to mess this up."

"Mess what up?" I asked, bewildered.

"Winning you back," she said. "And I really want him to get it right, because I miss you so much."

My eyes filled. "I miss you too."

"So will you give him another chance? He wants to take you somewhere."

"Where?" I asked, dabbing at my eyes before I looked at Cole.

"Home." He reached for my hand. "Let me take you home."

"What home? Whose?"

He and Mariah exchanged a smile, then he looked at me again. "Ours."

Neither of us spoke on the drive, but he held my hand the entire time. Mariah had stayed home with her grandmother, and without her chatter, the ride seemed even more tense and silent.

I was too scared to speak, worried I'd break the spell. There was something different about him tonight—something had changed—but I'd gotten my hopes up one too many times before.

He pulled up in front of the house, along the street. To my surprise, there was another car in front of the house—I didn't recognize it at first, but when we got close enough, Cole's headlights lit up the license plate, which read BDR.

"Give me one second," he said, pulling out his phone. After sending a quick text, the car in front of us pulled away from the curb.

Totally confused, I let him come around and open the passenger door. He took my hand once more and helped me onto the sidewalk. It was cold and dark, but all the lights were on in the house, making it look warm and cozy, like a scene from a snow globe.

He stood behind me and wrapped me in his arms. "The night I walked you home for the first time, I remember how you said it was something you used to dream about when we were kids."

"It was."

"And maybe I was just too dumb to see it back then, or maybe it just wasn't our time, but I see it now—you and me, we belong together."

I put my hands over his forearms, holding them tight to my chest.

He pressed his mouth to my hair. "Nothing is right without you, Chey. I'm sorry I hid the truth from you. You were right—I let you in, but not all the way. I didn't fight for you the way I should have. But I want to, and I will. Please give me another chance."

I turned to face him. "I want to, Cole. But I'm scared."

"I know you are. But let me tell you this. My life has taken some unexpected twists and turns, but I know a few things for sure. I know I was meant to be Mariah's father. I know I was meant to live in this house. And I *know* I was meant to spend the rest of my life with you." He cradled my face in his hands. "You're home to me, Cheyenne. You're family to me. The way you love me makes me want to be a better man."

Tears filled my eyes. "You're the best man I know, Cole Mitchell. You always have been."

"But I can be better." He paused to take a breath. "I had my first appointment with a therapist yesterday."

Gasping, I tipped my head back to look at him. My heart beat even faster. "Really? You did?"

"Yes. And I survived." His shoulders rose. "My scars aren't pretty, but if you want to see them, I'll show them all to you."

"Cole, that means everything to me," I whispered, rising up on my toes to kiss his lips. "Everything."

"Good. Now come inside. There's one more thing I want to show you."

He took my hand and led me up the walk, through the front door, and up the stairs.

When we reached the closed door to the master bedroom, he paused and turned to me. "Close your eyes."

I did as he asked. A moment later, he took both my hands and I felt myself being pulled forward into the room. It was warm, and smelled delicious—like Blair's bakery in the morning.

"Okay. You can open them."

I opened them and gasped. My hands flew to my cheeks. I turned in a slow circle, looking at the bedroom of my dreams, lit by dozens of candles. My eyes traveled over the elegant bedding, the soft colors, the plush fabrics, the shining floors.

And the window seat—he'd built a window seat. With a cushioned bench upon which half a dozen pillows rested, along with a soft throw blanket. Not only that, but it was bookended by floor-to-ceiling shelves, freshly painted white and waiting to be filled.

"Cole," I choked out over a sob. "Did you do all this?"

"I had help," he confessed, looking happy about my reaction. "The guys were here all last weekend. Moretti was a godsend. And Bianca DeRossi—no matter what he thinks—is an angel. That was her in the car out front. She lit the candles for me and waited to make sure it was safe."

BDR—Bianca DeRossi. Now it made sense. And yet it was still beyond belief.

"I'm stunned." I shook my head, wiping my eyes again. "It's so beautiful. Everything is perfect. Better than I dreamed it could be."

He came over and wrapped his arms around me. "That's what I want for you. Something better than a dream."

Our mouths came together, open and hungry, our hands working to remove coats and sweaters and jeans and boots and what seemed like an endless amount of layers of winter clothing. Finally, we scrambled beneath the covers of the bed, naked and desperate to lie skin to skin, to make up for lost time, to express with our bodies what words could not.

"God, I swore to myself I was going to take my time with you," he whispered, moving inside me hard and deep. "And now we're here and I can't slow down."

"Don't," I begged, pulling him tighter to me, rocking my hips beneath his. "Don't slow down. For once, I won't say there's no rush. There's a rush. There's definitely a rush."

He laughed, pausing only to bring his lips to mine. "I love you so much."

"I love you too."

And then we were lost to each other, and just like he promised, it was something better than a dream.

Afterward, we lay on our sides, facing each other, covers pulled up to our waists.

"I'm sorry I made you wait so long before getting this right," he said, propping his head up in one hand. "I was dying to call you every day last week, but I felt like I couldn't, not unless I had something real to offer you."

"All I've ever wanted was this." I placed one hand over his heart.

"It's all yours."

"*Finally.*"

"Now you tell that girl inside you that I chose her, and I fuck-ing meant it." He poked a finger playfully against my sternum.

I laughed. "She heard you."

"Does she believe me?"

"Yes."

He grabbed me and rolled me on top of him. "Well, just in case she needs more convincing, let her know I've got all night."

"All night?" Surprised, I looked down at him. "We have all night?"

"We have all night." He kissed me, brushing my messy hair back from my face. "Our first night in *our* bed in *our* house. That is, if you'll agree to live here with me."

"Can we have pancakes for dinner?"

He grinned. "All the time."

"Yes," I said, a shiver moving through me. "I'll live here with you."

He kissed me once more. "This is the real New Year's Eve," he whispered. "This is the real beginning."

"Mmm," I murmured against his lips. "Finally, I get to kiss Cole Mitchell at midnight."

Suddenly he flipped me beneath him, pinning my wrists to the bed, staring down at me with narrowed eyes. "You weren't really going to kiss that fucking Mavs player on New Year's, were you?"

I rolled my eyes. "What do you think?"

His crooked grin appeared, slow and sexy. "No way."

"So you get it now, huh?" I took his face in my hands. "It was always you, Cole."

"I get it now." He kissed me softly. "I get *you* now. And I'll never let go."

Epilogue

Cole

"**IS THAT WHAT YOU'RE GOING TO WEAR?**" MARIAH assessed me from my bedroom doorway, her nose wrinkled.

I studied my reflection in the mirror above my dresser. "Yeah. What's wrong with it?"

"It's boring. You can't wear a boring outfit to propose to Cheyenne."

"Shhh!" I scolded, rushing to check the hallway to make sure Cheyenne wasn't right there."

"Don't worry. She's downstairs on the phone with Aunt Blair."

"Still." I yanked her into the room and shut the door. "Keep your voice down. And I'm not wearing this to propose. I'm going to change before dinner." I zipped up the weekend bag I'd just packed.

"Into what?" she asked suspiciously.

"A suit. What do *you* want me to wear, tight shiny pants?"

She giggled. "No. You'd look terrible in tight shiny pants."

I gave her a dirty look. "Are you and Buddy ready to go to Grandma's?"

"Yes." Then she sighed. "I wish I could come with you."

"We've been over this, honey. We love you very much, but—"

"I know, I know." She flipped her hand in the air. "Some things are better in private."

"Right. Plus she'd be suspicious if you were there. I don't want her to know what's coming."

Mariah pouted. "But call right afterward, okay?"

"I will."

"And I get to help plan the wedding," she whispered.

"Of course. You and Cheyenne can plan it all."

"And be in it too."

"Other than the bride, you will be the most important girl there."

She beamed at me. "Got the ring?"

"Got it." I'd picked it up from the jeweler that morning, and the box was tucked inside my bag.

"And you're going to do it tonight at dinner?"

"That's the plan." I'd enlisted April Sawyer's help in booking what she called the most romantic booth in the restaurant at Cloverleigh Farms for nine o'clock tonight. "But we better stop talking about it now."

"Right." Mariah mimed zipping her lips, which had been our secret signal over the last month, ever since I'd told her that I wanted to ask Cheyenne to marry me.

Finally, she'd said.

We'd gone to the jewelry store together and she'd helped me pick out a ring, for which I then sought Blair's approval, just in case a nine-year-old girl and thirty-three-year-old man did not have good taste in diamond rings. But Blair had taken one look and said it was absolutely perfect. I was worried she was going to let the cat out of the bag, since she and Cheyenne were so close and talked almost every day, but somehow she'd managed to keep the secret.

The jeweler had said he could have it ready for me by Valentine's Day with no problem at all, "our" room at the Cloverleigh Farms inn was booked for the entire weekend (again, thanks to a little assistance from April Sawyer), and my mother—who knew but had been sworn to secrecy on pain of letting Buddy track mud on her new white living room rug—had happily agreed to watch Mariah and the dog at her house while Cheyenne and I were away. Last night I'd told Griffin, Moretti, and Beckett about my weekend proposal plans over beers at the pub, and they were happy for me—for both of us.

The only other person who knew was Liza, my therapist. We'd discussed it a lot, in fact, and I felt good that she'd been supportive of the idea. Not because I was "cured" or anything, but because I was openly talking about how taking such a big step might affect me and what I could do to cope with the panic attacks that still occasionally snuck up on me. I can't say that I enjoyed putting all my emotions out on display and dissecting them the way she liked to at our sessions, but I could see how it helped to stop pretending they didn't exist and take steps to anticipate and mitigate the negative stuff. I liked having a process for dealing with it, and best of all, Cheyenne could see that I was willing to do the work on myself in order to be a better partner to her. I could even see how it made me a better father—more patient, empathetic, and understanding.

Everything was in place.

All I needed was the love of my life.

Cheyenne

I gasped. "You got our same room!"

"Of course I did," Cole said, opening the door for me. "After you."

I moved past him into the beautiful, familiar room, my heart thumping happily. On the table by the window was a champagne bottle in an ice bucket and two glasses. The drapes were pulled open to reveal a winter wonderland—a pasture and red barn, the rolling hills of the vineyard, the rows of bare trees in the orchard—all blanketed with snow. Removing my coat, I laid it over the back of a chair and stood in front of the glass, taking it all in.

"God, this reminds me so much of Blair and Griffin's wedding day. Remember that blizzard?"

Cole came up behind, wrapping his arms around me. He kissed my temple. "I remember everything about that day. And that night."

Smiling, I placed my arms over his. "Seems like yesterday, doesn't it? And yet it seems like we've been together for a hundred years."

"I agree. I don't know what I did without you. Were you really right there next door all that time?"

"Pretty much."

"God, I was stupid."

"Don't feel bad." I patted his hand. "Most men are."

He switched his grip to a headlock and growled in my ear. "Careful, little girl. I've got you all alone in the woods now."

Giggling, I pretended to fight him off. "Oh no! Whatever are you going to do to me?"

He swept me off my feet and carried me over to the bed, tossing me onto it and stretching out above me. "Well, I was going to pour you some champagne, run a bubble bath for you, maybe book you a massage before our dinner reservation . . . but now I've changed my mind."

"Oh yeah?" I wrapped my arms and legs around him.

"Yeah." He buried his face in my neck and kissed my throat, his hand stealing beneath my sweater. "Now I just want you right here in this bed."

"Mmm. Works for me."

"And I want you naked."

I laughed. "Even better."

He picked his head up and whispered against my lips. "And I want to make you scream as loud as you did that first night in this room."

Smiling, I rubbed my lips back and forth against his. We always had to be so quiet at home, so that we wouldn't wake Mariah. "Well, then. You better get busy."

The first time was frantic, fast, rough, and—yes—loud. So loud that I felt bad for any guests staying in the surrounding rooms at the inn.

"Don't feel bad," Cole said, running his fingertips up and down my spine. "I hope everyone heard. Then they'll know what a man I am."

"Oh, Lordy." His stomach growled noisily. I picked up my head and grinned at him. "I think you worked up an appetite."

"You might be right."

"Should we go down to dinner?"

"Does that mean we'd have to put clothes on?"

"Um, yes."

He frowned. "Maybe I'll switch my vote to room service."

"But I brought pretty clothes to wear. And I think you'll like my outfit for tonight."

"More than I like your naked body?"

"Well, maybe not *that* much." I laughed. "But you'll still like it."

"Okay, fine. We can get dressed and go eat."

I gave him a quick kiss. "I promise, we will get naked again right after dinner. What time is our reservation?"

"Nine."

I checked the clock on the nightstand. "Ooh! I barely have

forty-five minutes to get ready!" Rolling off him, I scrambled from the bed to the bathroom and switched on the shower. I didn't have time to wash my hair, so I just threw it up so it wouldn't get wet.

Being in the shower reminded me of the morning after Griffin and Blair's wedding. It made me smile, remembering the way he'd said, *You're making it really easy to fall in love with you.*

I got out of the shower and dried off, and while I was getting dressed, Cole slipped in. He left the bathroom door open, and as I was pulling the sweater dress I'd worn at Thanksgiving over my head, I heard him say, "I've got some fond memories in this shower. Is it too late to ask you to get back in?"

I smiled. "Yes!"

"Dammit."

By the time he got out five minutes later, I'd already tugged on the thigh-high burgundy boots and I was fussing with my hair.

Holding a towel around his waist, he stood behind me in the mirror and shook his head. "Fucking hell. Not the boots."

Grinning mischievously, I added another pin to my loose, messy bun. "The boots."

"But I won't make it through dinner."

"You won't even see them during dinner."

"Doesn't matter. I'll know they're there." He came up right behind me and kissed the back of my neck. "Let's stay in."

"Cole, you're getting me all wet," I said, laughing. "Now go put some clothes on before I lose my mind. You look too good in a towel."

He tossed it aside. "How about without the towel?"

Groaning, I spun around and faced him, looking him over head to foot. The messy wet hair, those gorgeous eyes, the five o'clock shadow, the broad shoulders and chest, the sculpted arms and abs, the massive cock between his muscular thighs, stirring again. I forced my eyes up to his. Placed my hands on his chest. "Without the towel, you look even better. I still can't believe you're mine."

"Believe it." He kissed me softly. "I guess we can have dinner before I ravage you again. The torture will be bittersweet."

I laughed. "I'll be ready in five."

He disappeared into the bedroom area while I finished getting ready at the mirror. When my hair was neat enough and my makeup complete, I turned off the light.

"Well?" I said, presenting myself to Cole, who was dressed in a charcoal suit with a light blue dress shirt. His hair was combed, his shoes were shined, and the room smelled like his cologne. As always, he set off butterflies in my stomach. "How do I look?" I asked.

He looked up from adjusting a cufflink. "Hmm."

"Hmm?" I stuck my hands on my hips and pouted. "That's not the right answer."

"I know, but . . ." He studied me as he came closer.

"What?" I looked down at the chunky, off-the-shoulder sweater dress. "I thought you'd like this outfit. It's the same one I wore on—"

"I know. I do like it." He circled me like I was a bride trying on a wedding gown and he was the dude from *Say Yes to the Dress*. "It's just missing something."

"It is?" I touched my earlobes. "Oh, I forgot my earrings!"

"No. That's not what's missing." He moved around to the front of me again, reached into his pocket and took out a small box. Then he opened it. "This is."

I couldn't breathe. Twinkling against the black velvet cushion inside the box was a gorgeous diamond solitaire on a delicate silver band.

Cole got down on one knee. "This was supposed to happen at dinner," he said. "But I just can't wait another minute."

I covered my mouth with both hands and squeaked.

"Cheyenne Dempsey, I've known you almost my entire life.

And even though our paths took us in different directions for a while, I know in my heart that right now, I'm exactly where I'm supposed to be. I'm with the woman I want to spend the rest of my life with. And when I think about our future together, I'm happier than I ever imagined was possible."

I started to cry and had to wipe tears from beneath my eyes.

He smiled, although his eyes shone too. "Now I don't come alone," he said. "Mariah and I are sort of a package deal."

Laughing, I sniffed and nodded.

"But she and I agree that you make our family complete— for now, at least. Hopefully we'll continue to grow it in the years to come." He plucked the solitaire from the box and took my left hand, slipping it onto my ring finger. "I love you more than I could ever say." His smile turned boyish and a little crooked. "And as someone once told me, when you have something precious in your hands, you need to hold on tight. Tonight, I'm asking to hold onto you forever. Will you marry me?"

"Yes," I bawled, tears spilling down my face. "Yes, yes, yes!"

He rose to his feet and kissed me quickly before embracing me, lifting me right off my feet. I wrapped my arms around his neck and held on tight, just like he said.

After I'd blubbered into his shoulder for a minute or two, he set me on my feet and I finally looked at the ring on my finger. "I can't believe it!" I said, laughing and crying at the same time. "Is it real?"

"It's real."

I whirled around, expecting people to jump out of the closet. "Where's Mariah? Are Griffin and Blair here? Our mothers?"

"No," he said. "I thought about it, but decided this was something I wanted to do without an audience."

"I get it." I couldn't take my eyes off my ring—*my engagement ring!* "But do they know?"

"They know," he admitted. "And I promised Mariah we'd call her as soon as it happened."

"Oh, let's call her really quick!" I grabbed my phone. "I know it's almost nine, but I need to show this ring off or I'm going to burst!"

He laughed. "Okay, I also need to change my shirt."

I winced, looking at the wet splotch, which also had black mascara smudges. "Sorry."

"It's okay. I have another."

"I bet my face looks like that too, huh?"

He didn't bother lying. "A bit."

I took thirty seconds to repair my mascara and eyeliner and then sat on the bed to FaceTime Cole's mom.

She and Mariah appeared on the screen. "Hello?" His mother said.

"Did he do it?" Mariah shrieked.

I held up my left hand. "He did it!"

"Yay!" They both cheered, and Mrs. Mitchell wiped her eyes. "I'm so happy," she said.

"Me too," chirped Mariah. "Daddy said I can be in the wedding!"

"Well, of course you can," I said. "You have to be my maid of honor!"

"Really?" Her eyes widened. "But what about Aunt Blair? Won't she want to be maid of honor?"

"I'll just have two," I said. "It's my wedding, so I make the rules."

She laughed. "Where's Daddy?"

"He's changing his shirt," I said, glancing over to where he stood tucking it into his pants. "I sort of cried all over the first one."

They both smiled. "So when will the wedding be?" his mother asked.

"Mom, what did I say about that?" Cole, a white shirt beneath his charcoal jacket now, came to sit beside me. "We've only been engaged for five minutes. No pressuring us yet."

She held up one palm. "Okay, okay. I'm just excited is all."

"I am too," I said. "Maybe this spring or summer?"

"I think that would be perfect," Mrs. Mitchell said, beaming. Mariah looked overjoyed too.

"We should head down to dinner," I said. "We're late for our reservation. But I was so excited, I couldn't wait until afterward to tell you!"

They laughed again. "Congratulations, darlings." Misty-eyed, Mrs. Mitchell blew us a kiss and Mariah waved happily. "We'll see you when you get home."

We waved goodbye and ended the call. "I'll call my mom from the table," I said, rising to my feet. "Let's head out."

He took my hand and we left the room. "Were you serious about getting married this spring or summer?" he asked as we walked down the hall.

"Yes. Why, you think it's too quick?"

"Not at all. I'd marry you tomorrow if you said you would."

I laughed as we headed down the grand staircase into the lobby. "Tomorrow might be a little bit soon, but I don't really want to wait very long."

"Good. I don't either." We reached the bottom of the steps and headed for the restaurant.

"I waited long enough for you," I teased as we approached the hostess stand.

"Are you always going to give me hell for that?"

I laughed. "Probably."

"Your name?" asked the hostess.

"Mitchell," Cole answered.

She smiled at us. "Right this way, Mr. and Mrs. Mitchell."

Cole looked at me and squeezed my hand, his mouth curving into that smile I'd loved for so long.

I smiled back and walked with him, hand in hand.

He held on tight.

THE END

Want a peek into Cole and Cheyenne's future? Subscribe to my mailing list and you'll get access to an exclusive MAKE ME YOURS bonus scene!

Pancakes for dinner

Ingredients
2 cups buttermilk
2 eggs
1/4 cup olive oil
1 cup all-purpose flour
3/4 cup almond four
2 tsp. baking powder
1 tsp baking soda
2 Tbsp. sugar
1/4 tsp. salt

1) Mix dry ingredients in large bowl

2) Add wet ingredients and mix just until combined. Let sit for 5 minutes before cooking.

3) Heat large nonstick griddle or skillet to medium low. Once it is heated, spray with cooking spray. Ladle about 1/3-1/2 cup of batter into the skillet. Wait for bubbles to rise to the surface and the bottom of the pancake is a deep golden brown before flipping. The pancake will be almost all the way cooked through at this point. This will prevent The batter from going all over the place when you flip! Once the other side is golden, remove from pan and place in warm oven until read to serve.

Crispy Asian Brussels Sprouts

Ingredients
1 lb. Brussels sprouts, cut in half lengthwise
2 Tbsp. extra virgin olive oil
1/4 tsp. kosher salt
1/4 tsp. freshly ground black pepper

Sauce:
2 Tbsp. soy sauce
2 Tbsp. honey
1 1/2 tsp. sesame oil
1 tsp. sriracha
2 cloves garlic, minced
1 tsp. finely grated fresh ginger
2 Tbsp. lemon juice

1) Preheat oven to 400 degrees.

2) In a large bowl, toss the Brussel sprouts with olive oil, salt and pepper. Spread onto baking sheet and bake for 30-35 minutes or until browned.

3) Meanwhile, place all sauce ingredients into a small saucepan and simmer for 2-3 minutes or until slightly thickened.

4) Once Brussel sprouts come out of oven, immediately pour the sauce over the sprouts and toss until coated.

Mashed potatoes with roasted garlic and leek

Ingredients
2.5 lbs. potatoes, peeled and cut into 1" cubes
1 head garlic
2 leeks
1.5 oz butter
1/3 cup sour cream
1/2 cup milk
1 tsp. salt
Salt
Ground pepper

Start by roasting the garlic and leek.

1) Preheat oven to 400 degrees

2) Slice off top of the head of garlic and drizzle with oil. Season with a pinch of salt and pepper. Wrap in foil and place on pan. Roast for around 40 minutes, or until golden and very soft. Let cool.

3) Trim off the leeks' dark green leaves and rinse thoroughly with water to remove any dirt. Pat dry. Slice the leeks lengthwise, whites and pale green, and cut into 4" chunks.

4) Place leeks close together cut side down on a pan lined with foil or silicone mat. Drizzle with olive oil and rub the oil onto the leeks to coat both sides. Season with salt and pepper. Cover leeks loosely with aluminum foil. Bake for 20 minutes, and remove foil. Bake for another 15-20 minutes or until soft and golden brown.

5) Meanwhile, cook the potatoes. Peel potatoes and cut into 1" cubes. Place in large pot with 1 tsp of salt and enough water to cover the potatoes by 2". Cook potatoes until soft and easily broken apart with a fork (about 15-20 minutes). Drain well.

6) Add milk, butter, sour cream, 1 tsp. salt and plenty of ground black pepper to hot potatoes and mash with potato masher until smooth.

7) Place roasted leek and garlic into food processor and pulse 10-15 times until a paste starts to form. Mix the paste into the mashed potatoes. Season with salt and pepper as needed.

Sweet Potato Mash with Chimichurri

Ingredients

2 lbs. sweet potatoes, unpeeled, cut in half lengthwise
1 Tbsp. olive oil
Kosher Salt and Black pepper
1/2 cup roughly chopped parsley
1/2 cup roughly chopped cilantro
2 tsp. dried oregano
1 Fresno pepper, roughly chopped
3 garlic cloves, chopped
1 tsp. salt
1/2 tsp. black pepper
1/4 cup red wine vinegar
1/4 cup water
3/4-1 cup extra virgin olive oil

1) Preheat oven to 450 degrees

2) Rub potatoes with olive oil and season with a pinch of salt. Place potatoes cut-side down on a baking sheet lined with parchment, aluminum foil or silicone mat. Roast for about 25-35 minutes, until very soft.

3) While the potatoes are roasting, make the chimichurri. Place parsley, cilantro, Fresno pepper, garlic, oregano, red wine vinegar, water, salt and pepper in food processor and blend until very finely chopped (almost a paste). Remove from blender and place in medium bowl. Stir in olive oil. If the mixture is too thick, you can stir in more olive oil a tablespoon at a time until a pourable consistency. You can also add more salt to taste.

4) Once the potatoes are cooled slightly, remove the skins and mash the flesh together with 1/4 tsp kosher salt and black pepper to taste. Transfer mash to platter and spoon chimichurri evenly over the potatoes.

Carrot Cupcakes with Brown Butter Cream Cheese Icing

Ingredients

1 1/4 cup all-purpose flour

1 tsp. baking soda

1/4 tsp. fine salt

1 tsp. ground cinnamon

1/2 tsp. ground ginger

1/2 tsp. cardamom

1/2 tsp. ground nutmeg

Pinch of ground black pepper

3/4 cup firmly packed light brown sugar

1/4 cup coconut oil

2 large eggs

1 1/2 cups finely shredded carrots (about 2 medium carrots, peeled)

1/2 cup applesauce

1/2 teaspoon vanilla extract

Icing:

- 8 ounces cream cheese, soft
- 6 ounces unsalted butter, cut into small pieces
- 1/4 teaspoon salt
- 3 and 1/2 cups confectioners' sugar, sifted

1) Preheat the oven to 350 F. Line 12 standard muffin cups with paper cupcake liners.

2) Mix together the flour, baking soda, salt, and spices in medium bowl. In a large stand mixer with the paddle attachment, combine the brown sugar, oil and eggs until well combined. Add the carrots, applesauce and vanilla. Add the dry ingredients and mix just until combined.

3) Divide the batter among the muffin cups. Bake until a toothpick comes out clean, about 20 minutes. Transfer to a wire rack to cool completely.

4) In a small saucepan, melt butter and stir on medium heat until it turns golden brown and smells nutty, around 5-8 minutes. Let cool and solidify before making icing.

5) Once cooled, beat cream cheese, browned butter and salt until light and fluffy, about 2 minutes. Add sugar and beat until light and fluffy, another 3-4 minutes.

6) Once the cupcakes are cooled, ice cupcake using a piping bag or spatula. Top with toasted pecans or dust with cinnamon!

Be a Harlot!

Want new release alerts, access to bonus materials and exclusive giveaways, and all my announcements first? Subscribe to my twice monthly newsletter!
www.melanieharlow.com/subscribe

Want to stay up to date on all things Harlow day to day, get exclusive access to ARCs and giveaways, and be part of a fun, positive, sexy and drama-free zone? Become a Harlot!
www.facebook.com/groups/351191341756563

Want a chance to become a Top Fan and win exclusive prizes? Check out my Facebook page!
www.facebook.com/AuthorMelanieHarlow

Want to be notified about freebies and sales? Try Bookbub!
www.bookbub.com/authors/melanie-harlow

Interested in excerpts and little bites of my romances so you can read more before buying or borrowing? Try Book + Main!
bookandmainbites.com/melanieharlow/bites

Also by Melanie Harlow

The Frenched Series

Frenched

Yanked

Forked

Floored

The Happy Crazy Love Series

Some Sort of Happy

Some Sort of Crazy

Some Sort of Love

The After We Fall Series

Man Candy

After We Fall

If You Were Mine

From This Moment

The One and Only Series

Only You

Only Him

Only Love

The Cloverleigh Farms Series

Irresistible

Undeniable

Insatiable

Unbreakable

Unforgettable

Want a reading order?

www.melanieharlow.com/reading-order

Acknowledgments

Once again, I need to thank Dina Cimarusti for all the delicious recipes in this book. I hope you enjoy making them as much as I do!

As always, my appreciation and gratitude go to the following people for their talent, support, wisdom, friendship, and encouragement . . .

Melissa Gaston, Brandi Zelenka, Jenn Watson, Hang Le, Devyn Jensen, Kayti McGee, Laurelin Paige, Corinne Michaels, the entire Social Butterfly team, Anthony Colletti, Rebecca Friedman, Flavia Viotti & Meire Dias at Bookcase Literary, Nancy Smay at Evident Ink, Julia Griffis at The Romance Bibliophile, proofreaders Michele Ficht, Shannon Mummey, and Alison Evans Maxwell, Stacey Blake at Champagne Book Design, Katie Robinson at Lyric Audiobooks, narrators Aiden Snow and Anti Arndt, the Shop Talkers, the Sisterhood, the Harlots and the Harlot ARC Team, bloggers and event organizers, my Queens, my betas, my proofers, my readers all over the world . . .

And once again, to my family, with all my love, especially my sweet Violet, who introduced me to the song that inspired this book.

About the Author

Melanie Harlow likes her heels high, her martini dry, and her history with the naughty bits left in. She's the author of the Cloverleigh Farms Series, the One & Only series, the After We Fall Series, the Happy Crazy Love Series, and the Frenched Series.

She writes from her home outside of Detroit, where she lives with her husband and two daughters. When she's not writing, she's probably got a cocktail in hand. And sometimes when she is.

Find her at www.melanieharlow.com.

11457563R20215